Last Call at the Nightingale

Also by Katharine Schellman

The Lily Adler Mysteries
The Body in the Garden
Silence in the Library

Last
Call at the
Nightingale

KATHARINE SCHELLMAN

MINOTAUR BOOKS
NEW YORK

First published in the United States by Minotaur Books, an imprint of St. Martin's Publishing Group

LAST CALL AT THE NIGHTINGALE. Copyright © 2022 by Katharine Schellman Paljug. All rights reserved. Printed in the United States of America. For information, address St. Martin's Publishing Group, 120 Broadway, New York, NY 10271.

www.minotaurbooks.com

Designed by Gabriel Guma

Library of Congress Cataloging-in-Publication Data

Names: Schellman, Katharine, author.
Title: Last Call at the Nightingale / Katharine Schellman.
Description: First edition. | New York: Minotaur Books, 2022.
Identifiers: LCCN 2022002308 | ISBN 9781250831828 (hardcover) | ISBN 9781250831835 (ebook)
Subjects: LCGFT: Thrillers (Fiction) | Novels.
Classification: LCC PS3619.C3482 L37 2022 | DDC 813/.6—dc23/eng/20220128
LC record available at https://lccn.loc.gov/2022002308

Our books may be purchased in bulk for promotional, educational, or business use. Please contact your local bookseller or the Macmillan Corporate and Premium Sales Department at 1-800-221-7945, extension 5442, or by email at MacmillanSpecialMarkets@macmillan.com.

First Edition: 2022

10 9 8 7 6 5 4 3 2 1

For Neena, who walked all over NYC with me to research
these characters and their world.
And for Brian, even though he thought Jazz & Murder
was a good title.

Last Call at the Nightingale

ONE

New York City, 1924

The long, drawn-out wail of a trumpet could hide almost anything.

The breathless conversation in the middle of a dance, when one partner's lips were so close to the other's ear, just long enough for a whispered invitation, *Meet me in the alley,* greeted with either a slap or a smile that meant *Yes.*

The girl who slipped up to the bar, who didn't have any money, not with the wages they paid at the factory, but who looked like she needed that little bit of living the Nightingale could provide, so the bartender poured a drink anyway and winked as he slid it over.

The stammered invitation, *Would you like to dance?*, of a new boy, still unfailingly polite, before he learned to grin sideways and place a hand on his heart, pleading, *Dust off your shoes, doll, no one can catch a quickstep like you!*

When the trumpet wailed, all that mattered was whether you could keep time for the foxtrot, move fast enough for the quickstep, feel the reckless joy of the Charleston.

It hid the way Vivian swallowed her champagne too quickly, bubbles burning her throat and making her feel brave. It hid the ugly shoes that were all she could afford, the secondhand spangles sewn onto the hem of her dress, the way she didn't seem to belong anywhere else but here, alive and breathless and something like happy, even if it was only for a few hours.

The long, drawn-out wail of a trumpet could hide almost anything. Even the sound of murder.

TWO

Y ou don't have to sit with me the whole time."

The comment broke into Vivian's thoughts, which had been swaying out on the floor in time to the slow waltz the band was crooning. She jumped and glanced at her friend, feeling guilty. "You only get twenty minutes of break, Bea. Of course I'm sitting with you."

Bea took a long drink of water—the waitresses were the only ones who ever asked for water at the Nightingale—and settled back in her chair, one eyebrow lifting toward where her curly hair had been wrestled into a careful wave across her forehead. She had worked at the Nightingale so long that she always looked perfectly at home there, whether she was serving, resting, drinking, or dancing. Vivian envied her that.

"That's sweet of you, but it's too loud to talk anyway. So why don't I rest these poor little puppies"—Bea stretched out one foot, rotating the ankle slowly—"while you catch Mr. Lawrence's eye over there and see if he'll take the hint."

Vivian didn't have time to object. Mr. Lawrence had already seen Bea looking and, giving the gray wings of his hair a delicate touch, strolled over. "Evening, Miss Vivian," he said, polite as always. Ms. Huxley, the Nightingale's owner—no miss for her, as she made clear to anyone who got it wrong—insisted on manners in her club. "Enjoying your break, Beatrice?"

"Soaking it up, sir," Bea agreed with an earnest smile. "But poor Viv here can't keep her feet still, even with this sad stuff playing. You'll take her for a twirl, won't you, Mr. Lawrence?"

If they had been out on the street, Vivian knew that Bea would have never spoken to the distinguished white man at all, and he would never have glanced at the Black waitress or her Irish friend, no matter how pretty they were or polite he was. But the rules could be different behind back-alley doors with no addresses—the ones that opened only when you knocked the right number of times, where the steps swept down to the dance floor and the gin made its way from Chicago. Mr. Lawrence smiled and held out his hand. "Miss Vivian. I haven't had the pleasure this evening."

She could have declined. But Bea was nodding encouragement, and the band was drawing out the melody with a perfect flair. So Vivian swallowed the rest of her champagne and let him lead her into the line of couples slowly revolving around the dance floor. He glanced down at her hands as they settled into the rhythm.

"Factory work?" he asked. A waltz left plenty of breath for talking if you wanted to.

"Sewing," Vivian said, wiggling fingertips that were reddened from years of needle pricks.

"Must be a nice escape for you, then, coming here," he said.

"As long as someone else is buying my drinks," she agreed, and they both laughed.

"Well, I'm always good for a round, especially for a girl who dances as prettily as you." There was something delightfully old-fashioned about his politeness, especially in the middle of an underground dance hall.

"And what are you escaping from?" she asked. "I doubt you spend your days working in a factory."

"No, I am very fortunate," he said gravely, which made Vivian like him even more. "But we all have responsibilities we want to forget about from time to time." He smiled, and the serious mood lightened as he added, "Besides, Ms. Huxley stocks her bar like a lush's dream." It was true. The Nightingale was a smaller club, but the bar held its own with the best.

They had danced before only a couple of times, but their bodies moved together easily with the sway of the waltz. The freedom to stand so close to someone who was nearly a stranger, but whose secrets she was trusted to keep and who was trusted to keep hers, made Vivian feel even giddier than the champagne. She would never tire of it.

The band leader knew just how to get his musicians to draw out the last note, sweet and melancholy, overlapping the polite applause before the trumpet swung into the first notes of "Charleston Charlie." There was a mad rush to grab a partner and get back on the dance floor.

A stylish girl, her curly brunette bob glittering with spangles, made a beeline for Mr. Lawrence, calling, "Laurie promised me this one, you'll just have to wait!" to the grumpy-looking young man who watched her with his arms crossed. Vivian smiled, waving away Mr. Lawrence's apologetic look as she ducked out of the brunette's way. It was almost painful to miss a Charleston—if she had known it was coming up, she would never have let Bea persuade her onto the floor for a waltz—but it was also her only chance to spend time with her friend that evening.

Bea had moved to the bar, where the smirking bartender was just sliding a drink toward her. There were always two bartenders serving, and in the months that Vivian had been coming to the Nightingale, the second one had changed half a dozen times, a rotating cast of dark blond hair and forgettable faces.

But Danny Chin was always there, working every patron with an experienced patter and a charming smile. He was the club's unofficial second-in-command, Honor Huxley's loyal right hand who could spot a plainclothes cop from the top of the stairs and danced like a dream on the rare occasions when he slipped out from behind the bar. All the girls who made their way to the Nightingale were half in love with him, at least when he was smiling right at them.

Even though Vivian was too smart to think it meant anything, she still blushed when he turned that grin on her as she slid in next to her friend. "One for you too, kitten?"

Vivian sighed. "Wish I could, Danny, but I'm short of change tonight."

"I'm sure you can spot her one on the house, can't you?" Bea said. "Nightingale needs girls on the dance floor, and Lord knows they don't come prettier than Viv. Or better dancers."

Danny glanced at something over their heads, and his grin grew wider. "Looks like you're drinking on Mr. Lawrence's tab tonight. Must have charmed him during that waltz."

"Wish I could've charmed him during the Charleston, instead," Vivian said with a grimace. "What's Bea drinking?"

"French Seventy-Five," said Danny proudly. "One of my specialties, if I can brag a little."

"You always do," Bea said, rolling her eyes, though she sighed with appreciation as she sipped her drink. "Golly, this song sounds dull without a singer. Why hasn't Honor hired one yet?" There was a look of longing in her eyes as she glanced toward the bandstand, singing quietly under her breath.

"I will never understand the point of mixing champagne with anything else." Vivian eyed Bea's drink and shook her head. "It's perfect on its own. Your best, then, if Mr. Lawrence is paying. I have a feeling he can afford it."

"He can," Danny laughed, pouring her a coupe of dancing bubbles. "Sorry you missed your favorite dance."

"I'd be happy to partner you for the Charleston, Vivian."

The low voice, honey-smooth and smoky, made Vivian jump, champagne spilling over her fingers.

"Hux, don't startle her into wasting the good stuff," Danny complained as Bea snorted with amusement and handed over a napkin.

Vivian felt her cheeks burning as she met the eyes of the woman who was now leaning one elbow on the bar and watching her.

No one who met Honor Huxley was surprised to find out that she ran a place like the Nightingale. Someone like Honor seemed made for the underground world, for back alleys and illegal booze, for dimly lit dance floors and strangers holding each other close.

She was tall for a woman and looked taller still because of the sharply tailored lines of her black trousers. Her crisp white shirt was open at the neck, framed by the stark lines of black suspenders. Her hair and makeup, by contrast, were almost defiantly feminine, her curly blond hair worn unfashionably long and pinned around her head, her full lips painted deep red. Those lips were curved in amusement as she eyed Vivian. "In the mood for a dance, pet?"

Vivian ignored Danny and Bea's twin smirks as she shook her head, hoping she didn't look as flustered as she felt. She had spent months hoping the Nightingale's glamorous owner would remember her name. Now that she knew Honor did remember, more than remember, Vivian wasn't quite sure what she wanted to do about that.

"Thanks for the offer, but Bea's only got ten more minutes on her break, and that's all the time we get together." Vivian took a gulp of her champagne and added recklessly, "Maybe later tonight?"

Honor raised an eyebrow, as if Vivian had surprised her, and her smile grew. "Maybe later," she agreed before turning to Danny, her expression growing more serious. "Where is she?"

"Missed the waltz—probably in the ladies', but it's not like I can follow her there. She just got back in time to snag a partner for this one. Looks like a classy gent," he replied. "Seems to be holding her own all right."

Honor nodded. "I'll be around. Get my attention if you notice anything. Beatrice—" She smiled. "Take an extra ten on your break. You're lucky to have such a sweet friend." Her eyes rested on Vivian a moment before something else caught her attention and she disappeared back into the crowd.

"I do have a sweet friend," Bea agreed, leaning over to bump her shoulder against Vivian's. "Pour me another, Danny, I get an extra ten. Who's she having you watch tonight?"

"You still shouldn't get smoked when you're working," he pointed out, but he was already pulling out gin and the last of a bottle of champagne. He nodded at the dance floor, chin tipping toward the corner where a mousy-looking girl in cheap shoes was dancing. "New girl."

Bea laughed. "Lord above, she looks as terrified as you did your first night here, Viv."

Vivian frowned. "Why are you watching her?"

Danny shrugged. "Because Hux told me to, and I do what Hux says."

Vivian rolled her eyes. "Sure, but *why* did she tell you to?" She lowered her voice, though there wasn't much need. The band and the crowd were both loud enough that anyone who wanted to eavesdrop would have to sit practically in her lap to overhear. "Does she always tell you to keep an eye on people?"

"Most nights. Honor likes to know what's going on in her joint," Bea said carelessly, then raised a brow at Danny's suddenly pointed look. "Oh come on, who's she gonna tell?"

"Sometimes it's a fella who looks likely to cause trouble," Danny said, relenting. "Or someone who might try to duck out instead of paying. Tonight it's a first-timer." He glanced back at the girl he had indicated before, and Vivian couldn't help following his lead, though Bea didn't look away from her drink. "I'd say it's her first time out at all, not just here. Though she can dance decent enough, I'll give her that."

Vivian frowned. "Why watch a girl who's not making trouble?"

"To make sure she doesn't find any." Bea took a long swallow of the second drink that Danny handed her and sighed with pleasure. "Lord love you for treating the staff to the good stuff too, honey. Honor doesn't like it when men bother women in her place. So we keep an

8

eye on them. Same reason she had Danny watch out for you when you first started dancing here."

"She had you watch me?" Vivian could feel her cheeks getting hot again. "For how long?"

"Only one night, kitten. Bea told her you were made of tough stuff, and after that we left you to fend for yourself. I guess Hux just keeps her own eye on you now," he added with a wink.

Vivian rolled her eyes at his teasing, though she could feel her blush spreading. "You still got my purse back there, Danny?" When he handed the tiny beaded bag over—stashing her things behind the bar was a perk that Bea always arranged for her—Vivian slid off her stool. "Gonna go powder my nose. Bea, don't drink all my champagne while I'm gone."

"You barely left enough for me to swipe anyway!"

Vivian grinned at her friend's grumpy protest as she made her way through the crowd. The doorway at the end of the bar led to a long corridor, ending in one staircase up and one door. The door led to the alley, where cases of booze were delivered at dusk and sweaty couples went to neck in the shadows. At the top of the staircase, according to Bea, were the rooms that the club owner sometimes lived in. Halfway up, another door, always locked, led to Honor Huxley's office. Only select patrons were ever invited up there—or ones who caused the kind of trouble that was dealt with out of earshot of the rest of the club.

Vivian ducked into the ladies' powder room, the first door after the dance hall. The noise level barely decreased as the door swung shut behind her.

Inside, women reapplied lipstick in a cloud of smoke and Shalimar, stretched out aching feet, and chatted about their partners of the night and the husbands and fathers that waited—knowingly or unknowingly— at home. Vivian smiled at the girls she knew as she ducked into the adjoining room and waited her turn, eventually making her way back to the powder room to check her paint. The space in front of the mirror was crowded, though. Just as she found a corner where she could catch her own reflection, someone jostled her elbow. She dropped her lipstick, half the tube's contents smearing into the carpet.

"Damn," Vivian muttered, bending down to retrieve it.

"Oh golly, I'm sorry." The nervous girl who'd bumped her peered at the damage, and Vivian recognized the new girl Danny had pointed out on the dance floor. "Any hope for it?"

"Probably not," Vivian said, forcing a smile. It was hard to do—makeup was an indulgence, as both the weeks of saving and her sister's disapproving sighs reminded her—but the girl looked so flustered that Vivian didn't have it in her to get upset. "Honest, don't worry about it. It's nothing."

"I really am sorry," the girl said again, glancing around as if looking for something helpful to do, before she was jostled out of the way by the press of sweaty, glitzy bodies. Vivian eyed the ruined stick of color warily, trying to decide whether it could be saved.

"I wouldn't recommend putting that anywhere near your mouth after it's been on this floor," someone said. It was the stylish brunette who had claimed Mr. Lawrence for the Charleston. She gave Vivian a friendly nudge with her elbow. "It's a jungle, isn't it? Here." She fished in her purse and handed her own lipstick over to Vivian. "Use mine, doll."

"Thanks." Vivian slid the color over her lips with a practiced flick. "It's Margaret, isn't it? I've seen you here before."

"Mags, I beg you. Only Mother and Dad call me Margaret." The brunette made a pouting grimace in the mirror, then laughed. "Sorry I stole Laurie from you out there. He's such a sweet old thing, isn't he? How did you get so chummy with the bartender? He won't give me the time of day, cruel man."

"My friend's one of the waitresses here," Vivian said. She tried to hand the lipstick back, but Mags gestured her away with a careless wave.

"Keep it, honey, it looks swell on you."

Vivian glanced down at the lipstick in her hand. The tiny silver tube had a red stone on the cap—the sort that was part of a set, that you could take to a makeup counter and have refilled with your personal shade when you used it up. It probably cost more than the shoes she was wearing. She closed her hand around it enviously, then hesitated. "You sure?"

Mags didn't even glance down. "Of course. If you need to pay me back, you can introduce me to your bartender friend sometime."

"I'll do that."

"Lovely. If you see my fella out there, tell him I'll be another minute, will you?"

"The grumpy-looking one from the dance floor?"

"That's the one," Mags agreed, seeming not at all bothered by the unflattering description. "Roy's a peach when you get him dancing, but Lord, can he be a stick-in-the-mud!" She waved over her shoulder as she headed toward the back room. "See you out there."

The bright notes of a quickstep pattered down the hallway as Vivian emerged from the powder room, but for the moment it was empty. There was a brief, welcome draft of cool night air as someone opened the door to the alley, and she shivered as it hit her flushed skin. She glanced over, expecting to see a giggling couple finding their way back inside, but it was a single man, tucking a carton of cigarettes inside his jacket as he let the door slam behind him. In the hallway's dim light, it took her a moment to recognize Mags's date. His former surly look was smoothed into a pleased smile, and Vivian couldn't help enjoying the view. He was decidedly good-looking, with the sort of square-jawed, tanned face, framed by thick wavy hair, that smiled out of ads for Barbasol and Coca-Cola. No wonder the pretty brunette kept him around.

He caught sight of her as the door closed, and for a brief moment his smile faltered. "You looking for me, sweetheart?"

"Not especially," Vivian said. "Roy, right? Your girl said to tell you she'd be a minute more."

"She's always a minute more," he said, his brows drawing down into a scowl once again. "Well, thanks," he added, brushing past her without bothering to meet her eyes. "Suppose I have time for another drink."

Roy drew up sharply at the door back into the dance hall, nearly running into Bea as she came through. For a moment they both eyed each other in surprise before Bea pulled back to let him pass, eyes fastened on the ground and head ducked protectively down as he looked her over. Vivian couldn't hear what he muttered, but she saw Bea flinch and pull even further into herself as Roy pushed past and disappeared into the crowded room.

Bea didn't move, her back still pressed against the wall, even after he was gone, and Vivian hurried over. "Bea? You okay?"

"Fine." Bea shook her head, sliding into the hall so she was out of sight from the other room. "Just got careless, is all. Can't do that anywhere. Not even here."

Vivian nodded, still keeping a little bit of distance between them, though she reached out to squeeze her friend's hand. Bea wasn't the sort of girl who liked to be cuddled or hugged, even when she was upset, but after a moment she squeezed back.

"Mama would bawl me out if she knew the way I talked to white folks here, you know."

"She hears how you talk to me all the time," Vivian said, attempting a joke, though it fell flat, even to her own ears. Bea shot her a withering look. "Sorry. I know, I'm sorry."

Bea rolled her eyes. "Yeah, you're poor Irish trash, girl. You don't count."

"Poor *orphan* Irish trash, even better." Vivian glanced at the doorway where Roy had disappeared. "Any time left on your break? We could go outside for some air if you don't want to go back in there yet."

"I've got a few minutes still." Bea hesitated, then nodded firmly. "I'd like that."

"And while we're breathing that healthy New York air"—Vivian smiled as Bea snorted—"I can tell you about the fancy new lipstick I just got treated to."

"Never tell me you're taking gifts from gentlemen!" Bea said, feigning horror. "Why, Vivian, don't you know what sort of things men expect when they give a girl presents?"

"Well, lucky me then, this was from another girl . . ."

The light spilling from the door threw the brick walls of the alley into sharp relief as they tumbled into the night. Even though the air was heavy with the dirt and smoke of the city, it was still fresh compared to the sweaty, boozy heat of the Nightingale.

Vivian took a deep breath. Somewhere nearby a man and a woman argued, and the screech of a cat was nearly drowned out by a church bell—one in the morning already, she realized with surprise, wondering if she would be late enough to avoid a disapproving lecture when she finally slunk home for a few hours of sleep. The alley was a mass of shadows and dim patches of light from the windows of other buildings, but Bea snagged a loose brick with her foot. When she slid it into place before the door closed, a bright streak of electric light from the club stuttered its way over the piles of empty crates and trash bins.

"Anyone out here getting frisky?" she called as she finished propping the door open. There was a muffled gasp from one end of the alley and the sound of frantic feet. "Don't mind us if you are, just getting a breath of air."

"Lord, Bea, leave them in peace," Vivian laughed. "I don't suppose you snagged a bottle of anything before you came out? I'm parched."

"No, Danny wasn't there when I left—had to go deal with some business or other for Honor. And the new bartender is damned stingy about letting the staff wander off with hooch," Bea said, twitching up her skirt to pull a packet of cigarettes and a lighter out of her garter. "Smoke?"

"In a minute. Can you swing the door open wider?" Vivian squinted across the alley, in the opposite direction of whoever was necking, her eye caught by something peeking out from behind a precarious pile of trash. "I think there's a fella passed out in the corner there."

"When will men learn to hold their liquor?" Bea blew out a delicate stream of smoke. "Hey, mister, you all right?"

There was no answer. It was definitely a pair of men's shoes sticking out, Vivian saw as Bea nudged the brick to prop the door open wider.

One pant leg was hiked up high enough to show a red garter at the top of his socks, and the other was plastered wetly to a leg, as if the fellow had gotten so drunk he pissed himself before passing out. Vivian grimaced in secondhand embarrassment.

"Mister?" Vivian ignored Bea's quiet hiss to mind her own business as she walked over. "You need some help?"

For a moment, as she peered around the stack of rubble, she saw exactly what she expected. The well-dressed man was slumped awkwardly against the wall, as if he had slid slowly down it before finally reaching the stability of the ground, his pomaded hair undisturbed even as his head tilted toward his chest. He was sitting in a puddle of something dark, and Vivian took a quick step back, not wanting to get her only dancing shoes stained with city filth. It took a long moment for her mind to catch up to what her eyes were seeing.

The man wasn't moving at all, not even to breathe, and the air around him was heavy with the reek of a butcher shop. The puddle beneath him glinted red-brown, and where his jacket fell open, she could see a dark stain had spread across his otherwise pristine shirt.

Vivian stumbled back. "Oh God, Bea," she gasped, her voice hoarse. "I . . . I think he's dead."

THREE

W hat the hell do you mean?"

"I mean he's got a goddamn hole in his chest and—" Vivian broke off, swallowing rapidly, over and over, as her mouth filled with a sour taste.

She wanted to look away, but her gaze was fixed on the dead man's hands. They hung limply open, pale fingers trailing in the puddle of blood beneath him. A single lit cigarette still smoldered in his lap where it had fallen. One end was bitten off; the other burned a weak hole in his trousers. Those were custom-made, she noticed, her mind fixing on any details that could distract her. She knew quality stitching when she saw it. Not off the rack. A man who could afford stitching like that had money to burn.

"Vivian? Viv?"

Vivian glanced over just in time to see the raised hand that Bea quickly tucked behind her back. "Were you about to slap me?"

"If I had to." Bea glanced at the dead man, then shuddered. She took a long drag from her cigarette before turning away. "Come on."

"What?"

"We have to get back inside."

"Bea, he's dead!"

"So let's get out of here. Unless you want to be found with a body?"

Vivian didn't try to shake off the hands that were urging her back toward the door. "Don't we need to tell someone?"

Bea blew out a long, frustrated breath, then glanced back toward the body again. She looked like she was about to be sick, and the hand clutching her cigarette trembled. "We'll tell Honor," she said at last. "I bet she knows exactly what to do with a dead body—or she'll know someone who does."

"The people over there—" Vivian turned suddenly, starting toward the opposite end of the alley before Bea caught her arm.

"They're gone. Probably ran for it as soon as they heard you say someone was dead. Not our problem."

"But what if it was one of them—"

"Vivian." Bea pulled her firmly away. "Do you want to get mixed up in this?"

"No, but—"

"We're going to tell my boss, and then it's not our business anymore." She pushed Vivian toward the door. "Come on."

"Wait." Vivian glanced inside uneasily. "We can't just leave. Someone else might find him. It might not be our business, but I guess your boss wouldn't like it if more customers found a dead body sitting behind her club."

"Damn." Bea tossed her cigarette down and ground it angrily with the toe of her shoe. "All right, I'll have an easier time finding her. Are you going to be okay waiting here on your own? You can stay inside, just keep anyone else from coming out."

"I'll be fine." Vivian glanced over her shoulder and shuddered. "Just hurry, will you?"

The spangles on Bea's dress sent a scattering of reflected light across the bricks as she vanished inside. Vivian followed the dancing lights with her eyes, her gaze landing once more on the corner where the dead man's shoes were still visible. She shuddered. But a morbid, uncomfortable curiosity was creeping over her. She glanced over her shoulder at the door once more, hesitated, then stepped across the alley before she could talk herself out of it.

There was something fascinating about the dead man's stillness, something vulnerable and unreal, that made it hard to look away. Vivian felt as if he were no longer human, or perhaps so human that it was almost unbearable. She wanted to reach out, settle his neck and shoulders in a more comfortable position, move the cigarette that was slowly burning a hole in his pants, as if there were some way that she could help him. As if there were anything that could still help him.

But she couldn't do something like that. She didn't have much to do with police—no one in their right mind would. But she had been to the cinema enough to know that they never wanted anyone to touch things before they had a chance to look around.

Vivian snorted. There wouldn't be any police. No matter how much protection money Honor Huxley paid, there was no way she would report a dead man slumped in an alley behind her club. And if someone did come to collect the body, the odds of them carefully looking around for evidence of who committed the crime were practically zero. No, this wasn't going to the police in any official capacity.

And it also wasn't her problem, as Bea had pointed out. Vivian turned to go back toward the door, and as she did, her eye was caught by something glinting on the ground. It was a silver cigarette case, its edge just catching the light from the door, open on the pavement with a handful of cigarettes scattered around it.

There was only one cigarette missing from the case, the rest of them still tucked into place in spite of their fall. And the ones on the ground were cheap, less carefully rolled than the pristine white stub that glowed in the dead man's lap.

Looking at that smoldering hole made her feel sick again, and she took a quick step back from the body, her foot catching the edge of a crate. Stumbling forward, she clapped one hand over her mouth and nose as the overwhelming smell of death and filth filled her head.

The boxes that hid the body were more of a pile than a stack, many of them knocked over and broken, then shoved hastily back into place. Vivian glanced down to make sure she didn't trip again and caught sight of the man's hat lying on the ground a few feet away.

Vivian let out a low whistle. The hat was expertly made and matched the man's suit to perfection—which meant he probably had one to match every single suit he owned. Glancing back toward the door, Vivian scooped up the hat and checked inside. *Howard's on Seventh Avenue* was stitched neatly on the band. Vivian nodded as she let it fall back to the ground. Howard's was even pricier than the dress store where she and her sister worked. Whoever the dead man was, clearly he had money.

For a moment, Vivian was tempted to check his pockets to see if there was anything valuable in them, in spite of the smell. But the last thing she wanted was for someone to come out and find her stealing from a corpse, or to risk getting blood on her clothes.

"See anything interesting?"

The voice cut sharply through her thoughts, leaving her flustered as she turned to find Honor Huxley just coming out of the Nightingale's back door, two bruisers in dark suits following her. Vivian recognized them from their usual position looking over guests at the door or escorting problem customers out of the club. She could guess that there were other, less public jobs that they did for their employer. By the stoic set of their faces as they came into the alley, taking up positions on either side of the door, Vivian could imagine they were very skilled at those jobs.

She stepped quickly away from the dead man. "Nothing interesting, no."

The other woman glanced at her set face, and one eyebrow rose. "You've seen a dead body before, then?"

Vivian swallowed, then shrugged, trying to look as casual as the other woman sounded, wanting to sound cool and put together and impressive. "I grew up in an orphanage. I live in a tenement. People die faster there than on Park Avenue."

"People can die pretty quick on Park Avenue, too," Ms. Huxley said, an odd note in her voice as she stepped carefully around the puddle of blood to examine the body from another angle. "Do you know him?"

"No, do you?"

"I know a lot of people," Ms. Huxley replied cryptically as she lifted the dead man's hat with the tip of her shoe. Letting it fall again, she pursed her lips together for a moment as she eyed the scene, then sighed loudly and gestured for Vivian to step back. "Now, what did you see when you came out here?"

"Didn't Bea tell you——"

"She did. But I want to hear what you saw, too."

Vivian narrowed her eyes. Ms. Huxley wasn't looking at her, and she wondered whether that was for her own sake or the club owner's. She suspected the second—anyone who ran a dance hall had plenty of secrets to keep, and Ms. Huxley wasn't known for showing delicacy about the feelings of others.

For a moment, Vivian was tempted to refuse to answer, just to show that she couldn't be pushed around. But there was no point in that, really. Bea had likely already told her boss everything she saw. And it wasn't as if Vivian cared one way or another how Ms. Huxley ran her business, so long as the Nightingale was able to keep its doors open to the men and women who wouldn't find a welcome elsewhere.

So she sighed and answered. "There wasn't much to see when we first came out. Bea propped the door open a little, and we heard someone over there." She gestured toward the opposite end of the alley from where they stood. "Figured it was someone out for a bit of petting, so we didn't pay any attention. But that's when I noticed . . ." She glanced at the dead man, swallowed, and filled in the rest of the story.

Ms. Huxley nodded along, glancing once or twice at the bruisers waiting by the door. She didn't say anything until Vivian trailed off. "And you didn't see anyone else out here?"

"No." Vivian hesitated. She had seen Roy come inside only a few minutes before she and Bea stepped out. He certainly hadn't acted like a man who'd just committed murder. But then, what did she know about how people acted after shooting someone? With the door closed, he'd certainly had the opportunity. And she couldn't resist the urge to show that she knew a thing or two. "There's a fella named Roy, handsome when he's not in a bad mood, goes around with a brunette named Margaret?" Ms. Huxley looked up sharply, meeting Vivian's eyes at last. "I saw him coming inside a few minutes before Bea and I came out here."

"Know how long he'd been out here for?"

"No idea. Looked like he'd just been out for a smoke." Seeing Ms. Huxley glance at her bruisers, Vivian immediately tried to take it back. She didn't want to be the reason someone got roughed up by those two pairs of fists. "I'm not pointing fingers, you know—it's dark enough out here, Bea and I almost didn't notice anything either. But I did see him, so . . ."

"Got it." Ms. Huxley glanced down at the body once more, then shrugged, herding Vivian back toward the door as she gestured to the still-silent men. "This sorry fella looks like he's been dead more than a few minutes, so unless Roy was out here for a while . . ." She shrugged again. "But he might have been." She stepped close enough to lay one finger lightly on Vivian's cheek, her lips lifting in a slow smile. "Thanks for letting me know."

Vivian could feel heat spreading across her face from the touch. It was a struggle to look away from those curving lips, but she managed to meet Ms. Huxley's eyes. In the dim light of the alley, it was hard to tell what color they were, but the amusement in them was easy to see. Vivian swallowed, but she didn't step back as she answered. "I hope that thanks at least comes with a free drink."

Ms. Huxley's smile grew. "Get back inside, pet. We'll handle it from here. And Vivian—" Ms. Huxley caught her arm as she was about to turn away. "You're a smart girl. I don't need to tell you not to spend your time worrying over what you saw tonight."

"Clearly you think you do," Vivian said. The words didn't have quite the bravado she meant them to, but she managed to meet the other woman's eyes, at least.

But Ms. Huxley only grinned. "Tell Danny your next drink is on the house, then, smart girl, and forget you saw anything out here. I'll see you around."

Vivian squared her shoulders to walk past those silent, suited men and down the long hallway, and she kept her chin lifted as she paused at the door to the main room, letting the music from the bandstand wrap around her senses, familiar and reassuring. They were playing a foxtrot, the dance that almost anyone could be halfway decent at, and the floor was crowded with couples. That meant the bar was emptier than usual, so Vivian made a beeline for Danny. The sideways look he gave her while he finished up with another customer told her immediately that he knew something had happened, even if he didn't yet know what.

"What's the word from Hux?" he asked as soon as the other patrons were far enough away.

"That my next drink is on the house," Vivian said, forcing a playful smile as his eyebrows shot up, though it took more effort than she wanted to admit.

"You're learning to play it pretty cool, kitten," he said, his eyes lingering on her for a moment before he turned back to the rows of bottles and glasses.

Vivian shivered as soon as he looked away. "Did you see where Bea ended up?"

Danny's hands were busy pouring, but he gestured with his chin. "Back at work."

Vivian's bravado lasted until she met her friend's eyes across the crowded dance floor. And then it slowly began to crumble as she remembered the animal smell of the alley, the blood on the dead man's shirt, the cigarette burning a hole through those stupidly expensive pants of his. Vivian hadn't been lying when she said she had seen dead people before. But tonight was the first time she had been face-to-face with one who had been murdered.

For a moment she felt like she was going to be sick, and she quickly gulped down half of the drink Danny handed her. Even from a distance, she could see the warning shake of Bea's head. She didn't want to have anything more to do with whatever had happened in that alley, and Vivian knew she should be putting it behind her too.

Forget you saw anything out here, Honor Huxley had said, her cold smile unreadable.

Vivian held back another shiver. Whatever had happened, it was nothing to do with her.

"Danny, find a girl a partner, will you?" Vivian looked over her shoulder to give him a smile. "I need a dance something awful."

"Feeling jittery, kitten?"

She was, her whole body tingling with nerves, but she would never admit it. "Just like this song, is all."

Danny knew all the regulars, and they knew him; a moment later, a stylish young man with tidy brown hair and a forgettably handsome face was beaming at her as the band slid seamlessly into a quickstep. "Up for a spin, doll?" he asked, holding out his hand.

Vivian tossed back the rest of her drink, unconsciously imitating Honor Huxley's slow smile as she put her hand in his. "I hope you can keep up."

Forget you saw anything out here.

Whatever had happened, it was nothing to do with her.

FOUR

New York was a city of streetlights now, puddles of gold breaking through the shadows, leaving the spaces in between even darker than they used to feel. Factories sent clouds of smoke sweeping across the sky, even at night when they were shut for a few hours. Soon their workers would stumble, yawning, in to work.

Maybe there were parts of the city that fell quiet at night, but there was never silence in the New York that Vivian and Bea walked through. Music drifted out from restaurants and clubs, from the speakeasies that were written up in society columns instead of tucked into alleys. The wealthier the patrons the louder the laughter, because folks that rich didn't need to time their lives around the factory bell and could afford to drink and eat and dance late into the night. The streets were filled with people, even as the moon rose and sank and the stars tried to push through the grimy sky. There were always people singing and laughing, people calling for cabs in slurred voices, people crying for help from the shadows.

Their steps took them straight home, to the crowded, teetering buildings wedged too close together, west and south of Central Park, where Vivian and her sister could just afford two rooms and there was sometimes a little hot water in the shared hallway washroom. The noise changed here, to the sound of too many people with too many troubles living too close together.

Vivian knew what it sounded like when Mr. Mulligan across the way had too much to drink, knew the pitch of his sobs when he hadn't had enough. She could tell the difference between the cry of Mrs. Thomas's youngest baby and Mrs. Gonzales's oldest. She knew the sounds of arguments and lovemaking and shady deals and desperate pleas for more time, more money, more kindness, more everything. They were the sounds of home.

"Night, Viv," Bea said. She had two more blocks to walk until she reached home; the girls blew goodnight kisses as they went their separate ways. Bea's brothers and sister would be asleep, all tucked into one bed where they shared covers and dreams, only hours to go before they needed to be up for what school they could manage to squeeze into their lives. Mrs. Henry would be waiting for her oldest daughter, unable to sleep until all her children were safe at home.

As Vivian climbed the stairs of her own building, she knew where the steps rattled and creaked, the spots to skip over if she didn't want Mr. Brown's mangy dog to wake up and start yapping his head off. She knew the sound of stylish Will Freeman's snores, and smiled to herself as she tried to imagine what jaunty new outfit he would have managed to cobble together for himself that week.

And she knew what her own home would sound like if her sister were asleep, peaceful and oblivious and uncritical.

Vivian paused with her hand on the knob, listening. A deep sigh, the creak of a chair, the snip of scissors.

She scowled at the ugly wood of the door. Florence was awake.

FIVE

Florence only glanced up briefly as the door swung open before looking back down, her fingers still busy with needle and thread as she attached glass beads to the hem of a dress with nearly invisible stitches. In front of her, three trays of beads in different shapes and colors were laid out. Their single lamp was drawn close, illuminating her work and leaving the rest of the room in shadow. "Do you know what time it is?"

"Yes." Vivian eased the door shut behind her so it wouldn't wake any of their neighbors and locked it, proud of how calm her voice sounded. The last thing she wanted tonight was an argument with her sister. "Couldn't that wait until we're at the shop tomorrow? You'll ruin your eyes sewing in this light."

"Beads are as much by feel as by sight, you know that. And it needs to be finished before opening tomorrow. Mrs. Parker's coming to pick it up first thing."

"It wasn't supposed to be finished until next week!"

"The Parkers changed their plans. They're leaving town tomorrow, and Mrs. Parker wants the new dress to take with her."

"And is Miss Ethel paying you extra to finish it at home?"

"You know she's not," Florence said, her voice unruffled as she stitched another circle of beads into place. "It doesn't matter. At least it gives me something to do while I wait for you to stumble in."

"I don't stumble, Flo, and it does matter," Vivian said, kicking off her shoes and tossing her purse down on the table where Florence was sewing. "It's flat wrong for her to make you do extra work without pay, and you know it. God, I want to just march down there and—"

"And what?" Florence asked sharply, looking up again. "Get both of us fired? Take a job at the Palmolive factory instead? You'd hate that even more. The one good thing they taught us at the home was how to sew, and—"

"And dressmaking is respectable, and we need all the respectability we can manage," Vivian finished for her, slumping into the chair across from her sister. "But it isn't fooling anyone, you know. Anyway, why are we arguing about Miss Ethel?"

"Because you'd rather do that than argue about how late it is and what you've been doing all night," Florence said, setting down her needle as she looked her sister up and down. Her forehead creased in concern. "What happened tonight?"

Vivian handed Florence the scissors before she needed to ask. "I went out dancing, of course."

"I know that. I mean what happened that upset you?"

Vivian scowled, a pang that was equal parts gratitude and anger thumping through her chest. Somehow, Florence could always tell when something was wrong with her little sister. When they were children at the orphan home, Florence knew when Vivian had a night full of bad dreams, even if she didn't say anything in the morning, or if Vivian had been in trouble with one of the nuns, even if Florence hadn't seen it happen. It made Vivian furious that she was somehow so transparent. And it soothed the places that had been rubbed raw by a childhood where no one ever quite wanted them. "Nothing upset me."

"Some man got fresh with you?"

"I like it when they get a little fresh, Flo," Vivian said, trying to make her sister blush and feeling spitefully glad when she succeeded. "And if I don't like it, I know how to make them stop just fine."

"All right then, don't tell me." Florence leaned back, setting down the scissors and rolling out her neck as she yawned. The lamplight gleamed across the long braid of dark hair that hung over her shoulder. In the morning she would unbraid it and pin the wavy coils ruthlessly back. Florence hadn't said anything the day Vivian had come home with her own hair, true black and stick straight, bobbed like a Hollywood starlet. She hadn't said anything about it in the two years since, either, and her stubborn, disapproving silence made Vivian want to scream. "You should get to bed."

Vivian sighed. "I'm wide awake. You sleep, I'll finish this up," she said gently, reaching out to slide the pile of fabric from her sister's grasp.

"It's almost done," Florence protested, though she didn't try to hold on to the dress.

"Good, then I won't mess it up too badly. Call it my penance for all the booze I drank tonight."

"I don't like it when you talk that way."

"I know. That's why I do it." Vivian turned a cheeky smile on her sister as Florence rolled her eyes and stood, stretching and rubbing the small of her back. She waited until Florence had opened the door to their bedroom—the only other room they had, even more sparsely furnished than the main room—before adding, "I love you."

Florence's sigh was so quiet it barely traveled across the space between them. "I love you too, Vivian."

Vivian waited for the click of the door, then pulled the lamp closer and bent over her work. There was no reason to tell her sister about the dead man at the club. Florence's disapproval was already a headache without a body to justify it. And Honor Huxley was clearly a woman who could handle things on her own.

Vivian's stockinged feet tapped out a quiet Charleston beat against the floor. There was no need to tell Florence anything at all.

The clatter of the stove jolted Vivian out of sleep. She lifted her head off her arms with a groan, rubbing her eyes as the room came into slow focus. "What time is it?"

Florence glanced over from where she was making coffee. "Six thirty. Did you mean to sleep out here?"

"Of course not," Vivian muttered, running her fingers through her hair. "I fell asleep after I finished the dress, is all." Vivian gestured at the neatly folded bundle, yawning so widely that her jaw popped. "Mrs. Parker had better be thrilled with that thing. I don't even want to think how many beads are on there." She watched as Florence unfolded a corner of the dress, rubbing the silk between two fingers.

For a moment there was an unmistakable look of longing on Florence's face, but when she saw Vivian watching she dropped the cloth abruptly and turned back to her task. "You did a good job with the beading. Go wash, and for God's sake put on something decent. I can't believe you let strangers touch you when you're wearing that."

Vivian bit the inside of her cheek to keep from saying anything. She had found her dress in a secondhand shop and made it over herself to match the newest fashion. But it wasn't worth arguing.

"Coffee will be ready when you're respectable. I'm heading out to the market."

"We have to be at the shop at eight."

"I won't take long."

Florence had already brought in a bucket of water from the building's common washroom and left it in the bedroom. Vivian poured a basin full of water, then stripped out of her dress, brassiere, and drawers, rolling her stockings down carefully to avoid snagging them, since she wouldn't be able to afford a new pair for a couple of months. The water was frigid, and she scrubbed with a flannel until her skin was pink and tingling.

Her clothing from the night before was stiff with perspiration and

smelled of smoke, so she wrapped up in Florence's dressing gown—
her own had finally finished falling apart a few months ago and been
turned into a curtain in the main room—and washed her dress and
stockings in what was left of the water before hanging them over the
creaky metal footboard of her bed. She took her time with the washing, careful of the spangles on her dress, but that meant she had to dress
quickly or risk Florence returning and finding her still not ready for
work.

Hemlines had been creeping up for two years. It was a style that Vivian loved and her sister detested, but working at a dressmaker's shop
meant they both had to be fashionable at work, though not too fashionable or customers would think they were getting above themselves.
Miss Ethel, the shop's owner, preferred her seamstresses and shopgirls
to look a little conservative—to counteract what she clearly believed
were the loose morals of any girl without a family supporting her in
the city—so Vivian pulled a simple cotton skirt and sailor sweater over
her underthings. There was no makeup or jewelry permitted at work,
so all that was left was to run a brush over her bob until each sleek black
hair fell into place.

By the time Florence returned, clad in a skirt and pretty blouse, the
felt hat that she had trimmed herself perched on her tidy head, Vivian
was seated at the table once more, sipping black coffee and wishing they
could afford sugar.

"You look pretty today, Flo," Vivian said. "That shade of pink always
looks nice on you."

Florence paused in the middle of unpacking the groceries and
glanced over. "You look nice too." She glanced back at the groceries
and grimaced. "I hate to ask, but—"

"Are some of those for Mrs. Thomas?"

Florence nodded. "I don't mind buying things for her," she said,
a defensive note creeping into her voice. "Really, I don't. She has an
unreasonable number of children to provide for. And I'm grateful for
everything she did for us."

"We're both grateful. But she's also mean as a cat and doesn't know when to keep her mouth shut." Vivian finished her coffee and stood. "I'd rather you not talk to her, anyway. You'll be upset for the rest of the day if you do."

"I don't know how you deal with her," Florence said, sighing as she handed over the basket of Mrs. Thomas's groceries.

"I ignore her. That's what you have to do with about three-quarters of the people in this world."

"Well, my skin's not as thick as yours."

"I know." Vivian stood beside her for a moment, then leaned over to press her shoulder against her sister's. Neither of them were particularly affectionate with the other—the nuns at the home had frowned on too much touching or hugging—but that much at least she knew Florence wouldn't flinch at. "Will you pack sandwiches? I'll meet you downstairs."

Vivian slipped on her shoes and tucked her purse into the basket, which she needed two hands to carry to Mrs. Thomas and her unreasonable number of children, ranging in age from five to twenty-five. Most of the older children would be out at work, though the oldest two had five children between them now and lived next door to their mother. Mrs. Thomas had married a second time ten years ago, and the second round of children that resulted had left her even sharper and more sullen than she had been when she'd had no husband around at all. Vivian had to steel herself before she knocked on the door.

"Whoever it is, you can let yourself in if you ain't too proud, I've got my hands full in here!"

Vivian poked her head around the door. "Only me, Mrs. Thomas. Florence picked up some groceries for you and asked me to bring them by."

Mrs. Thomas was ladling out oatmeal to six children, four of them her grandchildren, who were crowded around her table. Regular thumping and clattering tumbled out from the other rooms, punctuated by shouts for someone to get more wash water, as the other members of the family tried to get ready for the day without tripping over each other.

"Well, put them by the stove, then," Mrs. Thomas snapped. "I hope there's milk in there, the babies have been asking for it since yesterday."

"Two bottles, bought fresh not even an hour ago," Vivian said, forcefully cheerful as she unpacked the groceries. "And some apples too, do you want me to cut those up?"

"What, do you think we're so poor we can't afford teeth? They can eat them whole."

Vivian passed out apples to the six children, who were quarreling among themselves, while Mrs. Thomas continued to complain.

"And don't think I don't know why you're the one coming by, instead of that sister of yours. Looks down on me, she does. Thinks she's better than me, in that fancy shop of hers with those fine clothes she makes, and me trying to keep food on the table for my children and my children's children while she resents buying a few groceries . . ."

"The fancy shop doesn't belong to Florence any more than the clothes do," Vivian said dryly as, without being asked, she began to make a new batch of coffee. "We both work there, as you know. And neither of us mind the groceries."

"And why should you, I'd like to know, after all I've done for you," said Mrs. Thomas without missing a beat, sinking into a rocking chair by the stove with a groan. "Who knows where you two would have ended up after your mother died, pale little nothing that she was. How she survived birthing two babies beats me. What would have happened to you if I hadn't stepped in? Your father, whoever he was, sure as hell wasn't coming back . . ."

"You know we're very grateful to you, Mrs. Thomas," Vivian said, holding in a sigh. The comments about her parents were nothing new. She knew from long, bitter experience that trying to cut off the flow of bile would only make things worse. And she *was* grateful. Nasty though Mrs. Thomas could be, she had kept Vivian and Florence together, feeding them from her own table until they were taken to the orphan home, even visiting once a year to make sure they were treated well enough. She had earned groceries and a few minutes of conversation.

"As you should be. You wouldn't have ended up together, that's damn sure. And I made sure you ended up with them papists, too, because I knew that's what your mother would want, and that they called you by your real names. How would you have liked to spend your life called Honesty or Charity or some nonsense like that?"

"Catholics name babies after saints, Mrs. Thomas, not virtues."

Mrs. Thomas ignored the correction, instead turning to eye the children at the table, who were gnawing on their apple cores. "Are you done yet?" she snapped. "Get out, then, and let me have five minutes of peace. Sarah!" she yelled, and a ten-year-old head peeked in from the bedroom. "Get the babies dressed, will you?" She turned the same narrow-eyed glare on Vivian. "Taking long enough with that coffee?"

Vivian silently handed over a cup, then poured one out for herself as the children scampered from the room. She didn't have long before she needed to meet Florence, but Mrs. Thomas would be angry if she vanished too quickly.

"Thanks," the older woman said, settling back in her chair with a sigh. "Oh, my back is killing me today. I'm that ready to be done with hauling babies up and down those stairs. Never have children past forty, girl, even if your man wants them. He's not the one who has to break his body over them." She sighed noisily. "Though if your taste is anything like your mother's, you'll end up alone before you're thirty. No family, even, not that wanted her or you. She always said they cut her off after she married your father, though Lord knows why, it's not like you can go lower than Irish, and May Kelly was already that."

"If his name was Kelly, he'd have been Irish too, wouldn't he?" Vivian asked carefully. She always held out hope that Mrs. Thomas would let fall some new information about her parents, something that would help her discover who they were. Florence had given up long ago, but Vivian couldn't bring herself to stop.

Mrs. Thomas snorted. "If that was his name. If she was married

32

at all. Lord knows she kept quiet enough about him from the day she moved next door."

Vivian turned to the basin to wash out her coffee cup, not wanting her neighbor to see how startled she was. "Do you think she wasn't married to my father?"

"You know I'd never say anything ill about a dead woman, Vivian," Mrs. Thomas snapped, as shocked as if she hadn't suggested it first. "And you shouldn't say such things about your own mother. Lord knows she deserves your respect, raising two little babies all by herself. And you're lucky you look like her, you and your snooty sister both, she was a pretty little thing, aside from that orange hair. Shame she had such godawful taste in men."

"How do you know he left?" Vivian demanded, drying her cup more vigorously than was necessary. "Maybe he died too."

"That's what she always said." Mrs. Thomas sighed. "Don't you have a job to get to? I can't sit here and listen to your yattering all day, you know. Tell your sister to come next time. At least she lets a body get a word in edgewise."

Vivian played through at least three sharp replies in her head, but out loud she only said, "Let us know if you need anything else, Mrs. Thomas," before picking up the basket and heading out to meet her sister.

Florence was waiting at the bottom of the rickety stairs, holding a bag of sandwiches for their lunch and the dress for Mrs. Parker, carefully wrapped in brown paper and string. She took one look at her sister's face and silently slipped the parcel into the basket, taking it out of Vivian's hands. "Come on, we'll be late." She turned away, the heels of her sensible shoes sharp on the pavement as she headed to another day of work.

Vivian sighed and followed.

SIX

"Y ou can finish it tomorrow."

Vivian stretched her neck as Florence's voice pulled her back to reality, her eyes still swimming with the pattern of the lace she had been tacking onto a tea dress. Glancing at the clock, she was startled to realize it was already six o'clock. The sun was vanishing behind the buildings, and Miss Ethel didn't like paying for the lights to stay on after dark, even if it meant her seamstresses could work longer hours. The other girls in the shop were packing up, chatting with each other about who had dates that night or whose parents were trying to convince her to leave the city and return to the family farm. Miss Ethel watched over them all with an eagle eye, lips pursed in disapproval, to make sure nothing valuable left the shop.

Florence was waiting by Vivian's table, holding both their hats and bags, as well as the empty lunch basket. "Do you want to stop by the automat for dinner on the way home?" she asked as Vivian tucked her supplies back into her sewing box and hung the half-finished gown on a dress form.

"Sure, I wouldn't mind a cup of coffee that's actually drinkable," Vivian said as they waved their good-byes to the other seamstresses and stepped out of the shop.

"And maybe some food?" Florence suggested. They fell into step with each other, turning to cut through the narrower side streets—their usual route home—without either of them needing to say anything.

"Well, sure, that too," Vivian agreed, yawning. "But mostly the coffee. I'm beat. And it's the cheapest thing they've got."

"Oh, don't, now you've got me—" Florence broke off on a yawn of her own, covering her mouth. She glanced around, embarrassed, to make sure that no one on the street had seen.

"Looks like you could use a cup too," Vivian teased, taking the basket out of her sister's hands. When Florence scowled, Vivian rolled her eyes. "Lighten up, Flo, no one saw, and it's not a big deal if they did. Everyone going home from work at the end of the day is tired."

"Yes, but it's not polite for ladies to—"

"Well, we're not ladies," Vivian broke in. "As we're constantly reminded. Now, I've got twenty-five cents with me, how much do you have?"

"Twenty," Florence said, then grimaced. "Guess we won't be eating like queens tonight."

"We'll make do," Vivian said quickly, glancing at the worried lines that had appeared around her sister's mouth. If she stuck with baked beans and coffee, there would be plenty for Florence's dinner—though she would have to be careful to keep her sister from noticing what she was doing. "I'm honestly not feeling very—Well, look who it is!"

A familiar figure was waiting for them, leaning against a lamppost with a large market bag at her feet. Vivian waved, and even Florence left off worrying long enough to smile.

"Figured I'd just wait here for you instead of risking the wrath of that dragon you work for. Good thing you two walk the same way every time," Bea said, stretching out her arms briefly as she eyed her bag. "Lord, lugging that thing around is work."

"You're not exactly dressed for heavy lifting," Vivian laughed. Bea was wearing a smart day dress and matching light coat, her hat perched just far enough back on her head to show off the careful wave of her bob.

"You look real nice, Beatrice," Florence added, only a slight edge of wistfulness creeping into the words.

"You too, Kellys," Bea said. She hoisted the bag. "Picked up a chicken for dinner. Mama told me to ask if you girls want to join us?"

"Sounds swell," Vivian said before Florence could reply. "Right, Flo?"

She didn't need to worry. Florence's pride rarely let her accept help from anyone, but saying no to Mrs. Henry's kindness was impossible even for her.

"Sure does," Florence said. She smiled at Bea. "But let's still swing by the automat. The least we can do to say thanks is bring the little ones a slice or two of pie."

"Better buy the whole thing," Bea advised as they set off. "Odds are Mama invited half the neighbors too."

———·———

It wasn't until after dinner that Vivian learned what was really on her friend's mind.

As Bea predicted, Mrs. Henry's generosity had extended to new neighbors, a young Black family recently arrived in the city and still finding their feet. The two adults eyed the Irish girls in their midst with understandable wariness, but their daughter was happy to help devour the apple pie that Florence had bought. After the neighbors left, Bea and Vivian took over in the kitchen. Bea washed the dishes, cheerfully singing "Five Foot Two, Eyes of Blue" in her rich, smoky voice, while Vivian hummed along and dried.

When Florence and Mrs. Henry went into the next room to put the children to bed, though, Bea broke off abruptly. "Gonna come out with me tonight?"

"To the Nightingale?"

"Of course to the Nightingale, where else would I go?"

"I didn't know you were working tonight."

"I'm not." Bea dropped her voice. "I want to find out if there's any gossip about the fella who was shot last night."

"I thought you didn't want to have anything to do with that," Vivian said, pausing with a dish dripping into the sink. "Ms. Huxley warned me off getting involved, didn't she say the same to you?"

"I don't want to get involved," said Bea, rolling her eyes. "I just want to find out what people are saying. I'm sure word's got 'round by now. Seeing as we were the ones who found the body, it doesn't seem fair that we miss out on all the gab about it. You in?"

There really wasn't any question, and the expectant smile on Bea's face said she knew it. Vivian found herself agreeing, though she added sternly, "Not a word to anyone that we found him though, right? Last thing we want is anyone thinking we're mixed up in it somehow."

"Of course not." Bea dropped her voice as her mother and Florence returned to the room. "Meet you outside your building at nine?"

"I'll have my dancing shoes on," Vivian promised, a tingle of excitement chasing its way down her spine.

———

The excitement lasted until she and her sister were back in their own home. The moment the door shut behind them, Florence blocked her way, arms crossed and a worried expression on her face. "You can't go out tonight, Vivian."

Vivian bristled. "Who says?"

"I say," Florence snapped. "I won't allow it."

"Since when do you get to tell me where I can and can't go?"

"I'm your older sister, aren't I?"

"Yes. My sister. Not my mother." Vivian pushed past and headed toward the bedroom. "I know you don't like dancing and drinking, Flo, but there's no real harm in it. Even poor girls are allowed to have fun sometimes, you know."

"It's not safe," Florence insisted, following close behind her.

"It's perfectly safe," Vivian said, pulling off her sweater and skirt and dragging a clean slip over her head. "Folks there know me, and the owner looks out for the regulars. I'm probably safer there than I am here. God knows there's enough sad drunks wandering this part of town looking for whatever rat poison they can get their hands on."

"And what about people getting shot in alleys?" Florence demanded, throwing her words down like a challenge.

Vivian paused. "What do you mean?"

"For heaven's sake, I heard you and Beatrice talking. And you said you found—How can you act as if—" She broke off and took a deep breath. Her voice was back under control when she spoke again. "I won't have you getting mixed up in that."

"I'm not mixed up in anything, I promise," Vivian said, shimmying into her second dancing dress. It wasn't as fashionable as the one she had worn the night before—she'd been meaning to take the hem up a few inches—but she refused to wear the same dress two nights in a row. "We're just going to see some friends and listen to some gossip."

"And what if people find out you had something to do with this, this dead man?" Florence looked as if just saying the words made her feel ill. "It's not safe. You know what bootleggers are like—"

"In the first place, who said he was a bootlegger? If I have no idea who he was, I don't see how you could know," Vivian pointed out, eyeing herself in the mirror as she slid a feathered headband over her bob. "And in the second, I think I know a sight more about bootleggers than you do, considering where I spend my nights."

"Where you spend your—! Well, you won't spend them there anymore, because I forbid you to go to that dance hall ever again," Florence said.

The desperation in her voice made Vivian pause in the middle of tying her shoes. She knew Florence was the timid one, the one afraid of causing trouble or attracting notice. She was probably safer that way.

But safety had never been what Vivian wanted, not at that price. She needed to feel like she belonged somewhere, to feel there was something in her life that actually belonged to her. She couldn't bring herself to give that up, not even to make Florence happy.

She shook her head. "You don't get to do that," she said. "You don't get to take the Nightingale away from me. And anyway, Bea's expecting me, I can't keep her waiting."

"Vivian—"

"Nothing's going to happen, so just quit it, will you?" Vivian was already pushing past her, heading toward the front door. She felt a sting of guilt as she caught a glimpse of Florence's face, lit with angry patches of red on each pale cheek, but it wasn't enough to make her stop. "No need to wait up tonight, I know how much you hate it," she said over her shoulder before yanking the door shut behind her.

SEVEN

"Come on, Danny," Bea cajoled, leaning her elbows on the edge of the bar. "I know you know more than you're letting on."

The Nightingale was as crowded and noisy as ever that night, the band in top form as they swung their way through one fast beat after another, barely pausing to let the dancers take a breath before launching into the next song. The club's patrons had caught the same energy, and even though the night was young, more than one fellow had already stripped off his jacket. Women stumbled off the dance floor, laughing and complaining of their aching feet as they called for something to drink, and every table was littered with empty glasses.

But to Vivian's surprise, no one was talking about the dead man in the alley. A few people had mentioned "some trouble last night" when she and Bea said hello, but no one seemed to have any details about who or what was involved. Whatever Ms. Huxley had done, she had done it quietly.

Vivian scanned the faces in the room, many familiar, none worried. There were gang killings in New York what seemed like every week, ever since Prohibition had become law, and people always seemed to find out eventually. Maybe word just hadn't spread yet.

"Hux doesn't want anyone talking about it," Danny said quietly. Vivian looked back in time to see him glance down the bar, toward where the other bartender was mixing drinks for a laughing group, before dropping his voice even lower. "And that means you too, Bea. You should know better than to ask questions like that."

"I'm not planning to tell anyone," Bea protested. "I just like to know what's going on."

"Yeah, well, you should like to keep your job, too."

They continued sniping at each other as the band finally took pity on the dancers, slowing the tempo of the music down and sliding into the sultry opening bars of a tango. A collective murmur went around the room, mixed with breathless laughter. A new style of tango had been making the rounds in New York's underground dance halls, and it was considered shocking even in places like the Nightingale. But that didn't stop couples from slinking onto the floor.

Vivian closed her eyes, drinking in the music with a small smile on her face, until a quiet voice spoke next to her ear.

"You look like you'd love to be on that dance floor."

Her eyes snapped open.

The man who had appeared next to her grinned at her surprise. "Sorry to startle you, but there wasn't a good way for you to see me coming." He held out his hand. "Care to tango?"

Vivian gave him a quick look up and down. He was dressed well, his suit sharply cut over broad shoulders, the fabric an unremarkable black. He still held his hat, which meant he either hadn't been there long or he hadn't had a dance yet. Dark hair waved over his forehead, and one side of his smile lifted up even higher as he saw her looking him over. "I promise I'm a gentleman."

"If you were a gentleman you wouldn't be here," she retorted, but that didn't stop her from sliding her hand into his. "Bea, put my purse behind the bar, will you?" she said over her shoulder as she slid off the barstool. "I'll be back in a minute."

The stranger's hand was large and cool around hers, and his lead was strong but not pushy, easy to follow without trying to do anything too flashy. Vivian relaxed, and he must have felt it, because his smile returned. "Were you worried I couldn't tango?"

"I was worried you were one of those fellas who'd use it as an excuse to get all handsy instead of actually dancing," Vivian said.

He laughed. "Do you have a name you use here?"

"I have a name I use everywhere. What about you?"

"Leo." He slowed them into a languorous break as he said it, pausing with the music so that for a moment they were frozen, bodies pressed together.

Vivian drew in a shivery breath in time with the break, and together they slid back into the movement. "Nicely done, Leo."

"You too."

He didn't pause at the end or draw it out into a question, and that undemanding politeness made her relent. "Vivian," she said.

"Vivian," he repeated.

"You like dancing just for the sake of dancing, don't you?" she asked, feeling a little breathless. Warmth fizzed up her spine from the place where his hand rested, and he hadn't taken his eyes away from hers yet.

"You do, too."

"Yes."

For the next minute they danced without speaking, until he noticed her exchanging smiles with a few of the other dancers. "You're a regular here?" he asked.

"When I can be," she admitted. "If I could be here every night I would. But I don't think I could afford all the shoes I'd go through," she added, flattered when he laughed at the joke.

"Well, you're clearly here enough if you're on chatting terms with the bartender," he said, his voice teasing. "You probably know everyone in the joint."

"A few of them. But I don't think I've seen you here before."

"That's because I haven't been in New York for a few years," he admitted. "Just came back to the city a few weeks ago."

"Where were you before that?"

"Chicago."

Vivian stiffened. The way he said it, so deliberately casual, as if Chicago were just a small town that no one could ever find on a map, gave her an instant idea about what he'd been doing there. Prohibition had made Chicago even more dangerous than New York, if the newspapers were to be believed. And from what Danny had let fall about the business of running liquor, the Chicago boys in that line of work weren't the sort you wanted to get to know too well. Florence's sharp words about bootleggers flashed through Vivian's mind before she could stop them.

Leo seemed to feel her hesitation, and the smoothness of their movement faltered. Rather than dragging her back into the dance, he lowered his arms, easing them both toward the edge of the floor. "Are you done dancing with me?" he asked quietly.

The genuine regret in his voice made her pause. "Should I be?" she asked, sounding more vulnerable than she liked.

He started to reply, but before he could say anything, something over her shoulder caught his eye. "Oh hell," he whispered.

Vivian glanced where he was looking. Whatever she had expected to see—a jealous wife? One of the Nightingale's bruisers?—it was not what met her eye.

She was looking at an unremarkable man in a suit, sitting quietly at a table by himself, a glass of something amber-colored a few inches from his fingertips as he checked his watch. Vivian frowned, about to turn back to Leo and ask what was wrong, when she realized that the glass next to the man hadn't been touched. Her eyes widened in alarm as she saw his lips moving. He was counting down.

She spun back to Leo. "Is he—"

"Go, quick—" he said at the same moment.

But neither of them had a chance to move before the sound of whistles filled the air. The dancers froze in confusion that quickly turned to panic as men in uniforms streamed through the front door and people rushed for the exits.

The Nightingale was being raided.

EIGHT

T he air crackled with the sound of shattering glass as people dropped their drinks and bolted. Everyone was trying to get out, yelling and swearing and shouting. Officers swarmed the dance floor, their whistles slicing through the confusion. The press of bodies carried Vivian along until someone knocked her off balance, and she stumbled to the floor, catching herself with her hands. Pain shot through her left palm. She gasped in shock, then, as the pain hit more fully, whimpered, cradling one hand against her chest as she curled into a ball to avoid the rushing crowd.

As suddenly as it had begun, the panic was over. The people who had gotten out were long gone. The rest were settling down as they discovered officers at every door, calmly herding them back into the main room. There was a disorienting mix of reactions: some people looked genuinely scared at the prospect of being rounded up, others seemed amused or annoyed.

Danny and Bea were nowhere to be seen, and as Vivian looked around, she saw only white faces remaining. Someone had hustled the other patrons and employees out, and Vivian wondered if Honor Huxley had a plan in place for exactly that. The club owner herself wasn't around, but Vivian watched in disbelief as Mags, looking collected and cheerful as ever, asked a blushing young policeman if he had an extra cigarette for her.

"Miss, can you stand?"

Vivian realized with a start that she was still on the ground, her hand clutched in a tight, pained ball. A middle-aged policeman was reaching down to grab her elbow, and she stumbled a little as he hauled her to her feet. "Let me see it," he ordered briskly, uncurling her hand to examine the cut.

"There was glass on the floor," she replied, feeling like her mind wasn't working at its normal speed. The slice across her palm wasn't deep, but it looked nasty. "Someone knocked me down."

"Well, that's a risk you take when you hang out in a place like this," he said. There was nothing about his voice that was kind or sympathetic, but he pulled out his own handkerchief and wrapped it around her hand to serve as a bandage. "They'll fix that up better for you at the station. No one wants a girl bleeding all over the place."

"The station?" Vivian repeated, feeling a cold lump settle in her stomach.

The policeman raised his eyebrows. "You're under arrest for imbibing. Just like everyone here."

"I don't think you can prove that you saw me drink anything," she said, wondering if it was the pain in her hand that made her so reckless and hoping she wasn't going to get slapped around because of it.

But he just laughed at her. "And you're free to go in front of a judge and say exactly that. If you're anything like the rest of your friends here, though, I'm guessing you'll pay your bail and disappear again."

"How much is bail?"

"For folks in the drunk tank?" He shrugged. "Twenty-five dollars a head. You'll have a chance to call home and ask them to come pay your fine."

The cold lump grew heavier. Even if Florence, by some miracle, had twenty-five dollars tucked away in the cash box, there was no way to reach her. No one in their building, or anyone she knew in the neighborhood, had a telephone. "What if I don't have anyone to call?" she asked. The question came out as a whisper.

This time, there was an edge of sympathy in the look he gave her. "I guess you better make a friend real quick, then." He gave her a push toward the side of the room where the women had been rounded up. "You behave and don't make any trouble when we take you in, and they won't set it no higher."

Vivian nodded, trying to swallow down fear as she clutched her hand against her chest and did as she was told.

———— •———

The men and women were herded into two lines when they arrived at the nearest police station. The officers there were less grim than the ones who had conducted the raid, and some of the panic must have worn off because people in line were chatting almost as casually as they would in line at a shop counter. Only a few, like Vivian, stayed quiet; one of them she recognized as the girl Honor Huxley had ordered Danny to watch the night before. Vivian wondered if the girl was also trying to figure out how to come up with twenty-five dollars, but she was too far away in line to ask.

"I believe there's been a mistake."

The confident voice carried across the station lobby, leaving a hush in its wake. Vivian spotted Mr. Lawrence, her sometime dancing partner, at the front of the men's line. "I suggest you summon your captain."

The sergeant looked like he was going to argue, then changed his mind and shrugged instead. "Your funeral, mister."

The rest of the station watched with a mix of curiosity and trepidation as Mr. Lawrence was escorted back to the captain's office.

And there was a collective murmur of shock as he emerged less than five minutes later, with the captain in the middle of a profuse apology.

"Sly old bastard," Mags muttered. When the women around her turned in surprise, she shrugged. "His brother's an alderman."

"How do you know that?" someone demanded.

Mags shrugged again. "Dad's had them to dinner before."

"I'm sure you understand that my friends and I were just having a little get-together," Mr. Lawrence was saying, clapping the captain on the back. "So of course there's no need to take anyone—"

But the captain shook his head. "No, sir. I have orders about that place," he said firmly. "But I believe you were out with a . . . friend? Perhaps a brother? Or a niece?"

Mr. Lawrence shrugged. "Well, if it's the best you can do. My niece Margaret," he agreed, raising his voice slightly and glancing over at the line of women.

Mags straightened when she heard her name and stepped out of line to take Mr. Lawrence's arm, smiling. "Dad would be furious if I needed bail money again. You're a peach, Laurie."

Vivian watched, too numb to be angry, as they were escorted out of the station. The woman ahead of her in line was called; Vivian heard her refuse to give her name, though she didn't hesitate to provide a phone number for the sergeant to call. And then it was Vivian's turn, and a burly officer was nudging her out of line and nodding toward the sergeant's desk.

"Your name, miss?" he asked with the disinterested efficiency of someone going through a script that he had already recited a dozen times.

Vivian swallowed. There was no way she was giving her real name. "Jane?"

The man behind the desk snorted. "Any chance that would be Jane Doe?"

She let out a shaky breath. "That sounds right," she agreed.

"You're our tenth Jane Doe of the night," the officer sighed, making a note in his log book. "One call. You tell me the number, I dial it."

Vivian shivered. She felt cold and exposed in her spangled, sleeveless dancing dress, though the precinct was a sweltering mass of sweaty bodies crowded together. "I don't have anyone to call."

He shrugged, clearly unsurprised. "Hope you made some friends in this lot, then. We'll come back to you in a few hours and see if you've changed your mind. What happened to your hand, Jane Doe?"

"Got cut during the raid."

"You gonna faint or anything?"

"No, but it hurts something awful."

He shrugged again. "If you're still here in the morning, someone will probably take a look. Keep the bandage on, we don't need you bleeding all over the cell." The sergeant jerked his chin toward a seat in the corner where two other women waited. "Women's matron will be along in a moment. Don't make any trouble."

Vivian started to say that of course she wouldn't, but the officer was already turning to the next person in line, clearly finished with her. So she just nodded and went to sit down.

One of the women waiting was complaining that she had lost her headband in the raid—"And it was the first time I wore it, too! That's the last time I go to such a seedy little place. I think I'll stick with the Swan from now on"—and the other one nodded along, looking bored and occasionally wondering aloud when her gentleman friend would arrive with her bail money.

Listening to them, Vivian realized that most of the people in the precinct, including the officers running the drunk tank, were treating the whole thing as more of an inconvenience than anything else. And why wouldn't they, she wondered, feeling dazed. New York had barely made a pretense at Prohibition before the booze started flowing once more. For the police, arrests for imbibing were a nightly occurrence. Most of the people they had picked up at the Nightingale seemed confident that, sooner or later, someone would be along to pay their fine and pick them up. They would never set foot in front of a judge or have a record attached to their name.

Looking around the room, she saw the man she had been dancing with, Leo, had just reached the head of the men's line. He had been watching her, she realized, and when he caught her eye at last, he gave her a wide smile and mouthed, *You okay?* Vivian nodded, momentarily lulled into a false sense of calm. If no one else seemed to think it was anything more than a bother, why was she so worried?

That feeling lasted until Leo stepped up to speak to the officer at the desk and a moment later was handed a telephone receiver. Vivian felt sick all over again. Being arrested was nothing more than a bother if you had someone to call, and if that someone on the other end of the phone had money. But when poor girls with no family were caught dancing and drinking, they ended up in workhouses and reformatories.

Especially if someone wanted to make an example. *I have orders about that place,* the captain had said to Mr. Lawrence. Most raids were just to make arrests, an example that would end up in the papers and show some politician cracking down on immorality. But—Vivian shivered— were his orders this time about the Nightingale itself?

"Jane Doe?"

The brisk voice made her jump, and Vivian looked up to find a tall woman standing in front of her, still wrapped in her overcoat, with dark hair pinned severely back under a plain hat of gray felt. Though she wasn't in any kind of uniform, she looked exactly like the sort of person who would be a women's matron for the police.

"Jane Doe?" the matron repeated, impatient. "Number ten, I believe?"

Vivian realized she had been staring and nodded quickly. "Yes, ma'am."

"Up you get. Either of you stuck here tonight?" the matron demanded, turning on the other two women sitting there as Vivian stood up.

Her stern tone made them both sit up straighter. "No, matron," they said, nearly in unison, and Vivian felt as though she were in the orphan home being called up in front of the nuns once more.

"Well, come along then," the matron said, ignoring the other two women as she gestured to Vivian. "Back to women's holding. You'd think they'd have a matron on duty when they know there will be raids. Pack of idiots. Do they think only men go out drinking in this city?"

She didn't seem to expect an answer, so Vivian didn't give one, just silently followed her out of the front room of the precinct and back into the holding cell known as the drunk tank. Once there, they stopped, and the matron gestured for her to raise her arms. Confused, Vivian complied, and found herself on the receiving end of a brisk, impersonal pat-down.

"Have to check for weapons or contraband," the matron explained, stepping back. "You'd be surprised what a girl can stash in a garter." Vivian thought that she wouldn't be surprised at all but decided against saying anything. "How old are you?"

"Twenty-three."

The policewoman laughed sharply as she unlocked the holding cell. "You're probably lying, but keep telling them that, unless you want them to take you up as a wayward minor. What happened to your hand?"

Involuntarily, Vivian moved to clutch it behind her back. "It's nothing, ma'am."

"I asked you what happened to it." The matron's voice was firm, reminding Vivian once more of the nuns, but her hands were careful as she stripped the makeshift bandage away when Vivian held it out. "That doesn't look like nothing."

"Someone knocked me down during the raid," Vivian explained, uncomfortably aware of the other women in the holding cell watching them. "I landed on a glass that broke."

"And I don't suppose any of the men out there suggested doing anything about it?"

"No, ma'am."

"Of course not. Because you getting ill under our watch and having to be transferred to a hospital is exactly the paperwork they want to deal with after a night of raids." The matron rolled her eyes. "All right, get in there. I'll be back once I've handled the other girls."

"Thank you, ma'am." Vivian stepped into the cell, trying to ignore the sound of it clanging shut and locking behind her. Once there was no way for her to leave, the cell felt a hundred times smaller than it had looked from the outside.

"Don't thank me. If I had my way, you'd end up in a reformatory tomorrow, no matter how old you are, and hope they beat some sense in you."

With that uncomforting remark, the matron left, shoes clicking on the polished floor in a way that reminded Vivian of her sister. The thought made her flinch—would Florence come looking for her when she didn't come home? And would that be better or worse than the situation she was currently in?

Vivian found a corner seat where she could press her back against the wall, hoping she didn't look as scared as she felt. The matron came back three other times with women who had no one to pay their bail yet, then returned with a fresh bandage. Gesturing impatiently for Vivian to stick her hand through the bars, she removed the blood-stiffened handkerchief and rewrapped it with clean linen. Vivian thanked her again because good manners seemed like a smart idea when she was stuck in jail.

As she pulled her hand back into the cell, Vivian was struck with a sudden thought. "Matron . . ." She regretted it as soon as she opened her mouth, but the policewoman had already turned back impatiently, so she barreled on. "Why was the club raided tonight?"

The matron's eyebrows climbed toward her severe hairline. "Are you somehow unaware that drinking alcohol is illegal in this country?"

"No. I mean, yes, ma'am, of course I know. I meant, why was that particular club raided? I heard the captain saying he had his orders. Is there a reason that they went there tonight?"

The policewoman sighed. "Shocking though it may be, the captain of this precinct receives his orders from the commissioner, not from me. My job is to save young women from the wretched life of vice that you seem desperate to throw yourself into. So I suggest you worry more about how to come up with your bail than what's going on in the captain's office."

"Yes, ma'am." Vivian ducked her head, not wanting to push the woman's goodwill any further. "Thank you for the bandage."

The policewoman snorted as she strode off. Vivian settled back on the bench, watching through the cell's single barred window as the sky faded to gray and began to lighten. Women were brought in and taken out, and she listened to their chatter without trying to join in. If she thought too long about the bail money, her chest tightened with panic, so instead she focused on the other question in front of her: Why would someone want the Nightingale raided?

Her mind instantly jumped to the dead man in the alley. But why would the commissioner of police need to send a message to a club that already paid hefty protection money, over nothing more than a dead bootlegger? It made no sense, unless . . .

Vivian frowned, remembering the man's perfectly tailored suit and expensive hat. *People can die pretty quick on Park Avenue, too,* Honor Huxley had said, as if she knew or suspected something about the dead man.

But if he wasn't a bootlegger, then what was he doing in the alley behind a nightclub on the Lower West Side?

"Jane Doe."

The sharp voice of the women's matron interrupted her thoughts, and Vivian started out of her half doze. The edge of dawn was creeping through the window now, and there were only two other women left in the cell. Vivian stumbled to her feet. "Yes, ma'am?"

"There's someone here for you."

NINE

V ivian stared in shock. "Here for me?"

The matron stood at the cell door, scowling. "She didn't ask for you by name—not that you told us what it is—but the description sounds like you." She unlocked the door and motioned Vivian to step out. "Though why you would want help from a girl like her . . ."

Vivian barely caught the muttered words as she followed the matron back to the front room, but they told her exactly who had come to bail her out. So she was anxious, but not surprised, when she found Bea waiting in front of the sergeant's desk, shifting nervously from foot to foot, her overcoat hanging open over the dancing dress she wore to work at the Nightingale.

"Look, we don't have any of you girls here," the sergeant was saying.

Bea shook her head, chin ducked down while she glanced up at the man's face. "No, sir. She's an Irish girl. I've checked everywhere else. If you would please just send someone back to look—"

"I'm here," Vivian interrupted, impulsively stepping forward only to be stopped by the policewoman's strong arm, which shot out like a bar in front of her.

"You don't go any further toward that door unless your bail is paid," the matron snapped.

Bea's sigh of relief was audible from across the room. "That's her, sir. I'd like to pay her bail. How much is it?"

The sergeant's eyes narrowed as he looked Bea up and down, and an unpleasant smile stretched out the corners of his mouth. "Bail is thirty-five—"

"Twenty-five dollars a person for imbibing," the matron said sharply. The sergeant scowled at her, but since he had to look up at the tall policewoman to do it, the effect wasn't as intimidating as it could have been. "I'm sure that's what you were about to say, Mr. Morris."

The sergeant seemed ready to argue, then apparently thought better of it. Instead, he jerked his head toward the door in the corner of the room where two men were just emerging. "Twenty-five dollars. You pay over there."

"I'll take you over, girl," the matron said briskly. "You—" She pointed to Vivian, then to the bench by the wall. "Sit there until we're back."

Vivian obeyed, though she didn't take her eyes from her friend as the policewoman escorted Bea to the office. She was watching so intently that she didn't recognize the men until one of them stopped directly in the path of the two women.

"Fancy seeing you here, miss."

Vivian started, recognizing Danny's voice before she saw his face. Bea's anxious posture relaxed a touch, and Vivian saw her flash a smile over her shoulder as the matron nudged her forward. "Familiar face waiting for you in the lobby," Bea told him. "Be back in a jiff."

Vivian started to rise, then thought better of it, not wanting to get on the matron's bad side if the woman came back and saw that her instructions hadn't been precisely obeyed.

Danny took the seat next to her, grinning widely. "Spent your whole night in the lockup?"

"Were you in, too?" Vivian asked, surprised. "I didn't see you when they rounded us up."

"Not me." Danny jerked his thumb toward his companion, who was still standing. "Just finished bailing out my pal here."

Vivian lifted her eyes. "Leo."

He smiled at her. "Glad to see you made it out in one piece."

"More or less." Vivian glanced between them. "I didn't realize you knew each other."

"Grew up only a few blocks apart," Danny said cheerfully. "Opposite sides of Bowery. I didn't know he was back in the city until he said hello at the bar last night." He gave Leo a playful punch on the shoulder. "Forgot to tell me you were coming back, but you remembered my number when you needed bail, hm?"

"I'll pay you back," Leo said easily, not taking his eyes from Vivian.

"Damn right you will." Danny glanced at the office, his smile fading into concern. "You think she's all right in there?"

His question was answered as Bea and the police matron emerged, the latter nodding stiffly as she pointed at Vivian. "She's free to go." She eyed the men and sniffed, then shook her head. "Go home to your parents, girls, or you'll end up right back here again."

"Yes, matron," Bea said earnestly. "I promise, I'm going home to my mother this very day."

It wasn't until they were outside on the street, the door to the precinct shut behind them, that Vivian pointed out, "You go home to your mother every day of the week, Bea."

Bea smiled, lifting her chin as she gave the bottom edge of her hair a careful fluff. "I never lie if I can help it." She shivered as she wrapped her coat more tightly around her. "One of you boys want to lend Viv your jacket? She'll freeze in that skimpy thing this early in the morning. And we've got somewhere to be."

Vivian glanced down, almost surprised to see she still wore her evening dress and nothing else. There was an edge of hysterical relief to her laughter. It already felt like a week ago that she had asked Bea to stash her purse while she danced with the handsome stranger who was now standing next to her, asking Danny for a cigarette. "I'm too jittery to be cold. I didn't know how I was going to get out of there. Thanks, Bea. Really. Thanks a million."

"You'll feel it in a minute," Leo said, shrugging off his jacket and laying it over her shoulders. It smelled like sandalwood and smoke and whiskey, and Vivian tamped down an embarrassing urge to bury her nose in the collar and breathe deeply.

"Where in God's name did you find twenty-five dollars?" she asked instead.

"Borrowed it," Bea said. "Can we not stand around in front of the police station? They'll start looking for a reason to give us trouble soon."

"What happened to you last night?" Danny asked at last, glancing at Vivian as they walked.

"Me?" Vivian snorted. The panic of her night in jail was distant enough now that she could force herself to look back on it dismissively, though she knew the fear was still there. "I spent the night convinced I'd end up in a reformatory. What happened to you? Seemed like the folks who worked there disappeared pretty quick."

"Trapdoor behind the bar," Danny said, shrugging. "And a tunnel in the back. Helpful in our line of work. Hux doesn't want her staff getting picked up. And we get out whoever we can."

"Smart thinking," Leo said, nodding approvingly. He rolled his shoulders and neck to stretch them out, but other than that he looked wide awake and perfectly at ease.

Vivian narrowed her eyes. "You don't look too upset from your night in jail, Mr. . . . I didn't catch your last name?"

He laughed. "It's Green. I don't mind you knowing. But you should keep calling me Leo," he said, winking. "And it wasn't my first night in the lockup. They get easier to handle after a while."

"For you, maybe," Danny said mildly, but there was an hint of warning to his smile. "No one's sending you to a reformatory. Lot riskier for Viv to get picked up. Or for me and Bea to step into that station."

Leo's expression sobered. "Thanks for coming to bail me out anyway."

"Anytime." Danny punched him in the shoulder again. "That's what friends do, even if they haven't set eyes on each other in . . . has it really been five years?"

"Almost six. You were just a kid when I left," Leo said, rubbing his shoulder. "Knew how to throw a punch even back then, though. I see you still do."

Danny grinned. "Things Chinese boys learn in this great city. How to throw a punch. How to help their mothers wash the dishes. How to avoid the cops when they come knocking at work."

"But why was the Nightingale raided at all?" Vivian asked, frowning. "I thought you had things sorted out with the police."

"We do," Bea said quietly. "That shouldn't have happened."

"Sounds like your boss forgot the milk money this month," Leo said, his smile sympathetic as he reached out to settle his coat more snugly around Vivian's shoulders.

"Hux never forgets," Danny insisted, shaking his head.

"And the Nightingale wasn't the only place raided last night," Bea said, earning stares from the others. "I overheard Honor talking. Three other places in the neighborhood got a surprise visit last night."

Danny let out a low whistle. "Four in one night? Did she think it was some kind of threat?"

"Or a warning. Because, get this." Bea lowered her voice even further. "All four of them were places where the dead fella was seen before he ended up in our alley."

Vivian stopped again, surprised into stillness. "The captain back there at the precinct said he had orders about raiding the Nightingale, and from what I got out of the matron, those orders would've come direct from the commissioner." She hesitated, remembering Honor Huxley's warning once more. *Forget you saw anything.* But she couldn't help thinking it through. "That means either the raids were about something else. Or whoever the dead fella was . . ."

"He was somebody important," Bea finished. "Or he meant something to somebody important, someone the commissioner needs to stay in good with. God, what a mess. Glad no one knows we're the ones who found him."

"Bea, can it," Vivian said quickly, glancing at Leo.

Luckily, he didn't seem to have heard. He had already gone a few steps further when she stopped and was busy looking up and down the street. "Anywhere nearby that we can get some breakfast?" he asked. "What's around that's open this early?"

"Early isn't the issue." There was a quiet edge to Bea's voice. "And who are you?"

"Leo," he said. "You're a waitress at the Nightingale, right?"

"Bea is one of our best," Danny said. "And she happens to be right. We're not going to find a place nearby where she and I are welcome."

Vivian was glad to see that Leo looked embarrassed. "Oh," he said quietly. "Right. Wasn't thinking."

"A complication of going out in daylight hours," Danny said, his voice somewhere between resigned and mocking.

"And like I said, Viv and I have somewhere to be. So no breakfast for us." Bea gestured to Vivian to start walking again. "Come on, we need to hustle."

"You girls gonna be okay getting home?" Leo asked, a worried frown drawing deep lines between his brows. "Plenty of drunks wandering around this early."

"We don't have far to go. Danny, she wants to see you too, I think."

Bea's words made Vivian, who had been following along with dazed, sleepy footsteps, frown in confusion. She had assumed Bea meant they needed to get home—home to Florence, who had been waiting up all night with no idea where her little sister had gone or how to find her. But Danny didn't even know Florence, much less need to see her.

"Where are we going, Bea?" she asked.

"To the Nightingale, of course. Honor paid your bail, and now she wants to see you."

"What?" Vivian stopped so suddenly that Danny bumped into her.

"I thought you'd have borrowed it from your neighbors, or maybe some of mine."

"Tried to." Bea pulled a beaded evening bag out of the pocket of her coat and tossed it to Vivian. "Been holding on to that for you. I went all over my building trying to find someone with money to lend who wouldn't ask too many questions, but it was too damn late. Or early, however you want to look at it. So I ended up having to go back to the Nightingale."

"Honor Huxley bailed me out? Why?"

"That's the owner of the place, right? She didn't get picked up in the raid?" Leo asked. He nudged Vivian's arm to get her moving again.

"But why'd she bail me out? I don't pay for my own drinks most of the time, so she can't know whether I'll pay her back. And I certainly don't know anyone worth knowing in the city."

"Pretty girls who dance well are good to keep around," Danny pointed out.

"Maybe she felt bad you were in a jam. Maybe it's just because . . ." Bea grinned. "Because she thinks you're sweet. Why does it matter?"

"Because when people like her do favors, they expect something in return."

"And wouldn't you rather owe her than be back in jail and waiting your turn at the Women's Court?" Bea asked, exasperated. "Would you rather I hadn't gone to her?"

"No, of course not." Vivian shivered at the thought and pulled her borrowed jacket closer around her. "You're the best of friends to get me out of there, really. I don't know what I'd have done without you."

"Damn right I am," Bea said, but her tone was playful.

"I'd just like to know what the favor is," Vivian said. "She makes me nervous."

"Well, you're probably about to find out. Come on, she's waiting for us. Danny, you coming?"

The bartender shook his head. "I was there before I went to spring Leo. We've said what we need to, for a few hours at least. I'll be there once I finish my shift in my parents' kitchen."

"Will she shut down now?" Vivian asked, not bothering to hide her worry.

Danny slung an arm around her shoulders. "Hux would never let a little thing like a police raid shut her down. We'll be back up and swinging by tonight. Cheer up, kitten," he added, giving her a quick squeeze. "Hux'll never ask you for something you can't do. And she doesn't bite, unless you like that sort of thing."

"Gee, thanks," Vivian said dryly, uncomforted by his teasing.

He only laughed as he dropped his arm. "See you later, Bea?"

"Count on it."

They moved off in different directions, Danny jerking his chin toward Leo to motion him to follow. "Come on. We can snag breakfast at my parents' restaurant. It's not open this early, of course, but Ma and Pop will already be in the kitchen prepping breakfast. Where I'll be soon enough, but they won't mind feeding us first. Will their jaws hit the floor when they see you again . . ."

"One sec," Leo said, hanging back, his eyes still on Vivian.

She had been about to follow Bea, but she stopped in surprise as he took her hand. She noticed that he checked carefully to make sure it was the uninjured one before he did, and she felt a glow of pleasure at his concern.

"You sure you're all right?" he asked. For the moment, their friends were far enough away that they could speak almost privately, but she could see them watching—Danny looking unsurprised, Bea scowling. "First night in the lockup's a scary thing."

"Right now I'm tired more than anything," Vivian said. "I just want to go home and not think about it."

He frowned, and for a moment he looked like he was going to say something else. Vivian prepared herself to tell him to mind his own business, that she was perfectly able to take care of herself. But then he surprised her again.

"So, was Bea right about her boss?" Leo asked quietly, still not letting go of her hand.

"Which part?"

"The part where she thinks you're sweet."

Vivian's cheeks heated. She knew what he was really asking, and it wasn't just an awkward question to answer. In the wrong company, it could be a dangerous one. "I don't know," she said, settling for as unrevealing a truth as she could manage.

Leo brushed his thumb across the back of her hand so lightly she almost thought she imagined it. "And what do you think of her?"

Vivian felt her blush grow hotter. "I don't know her too well."

Leo's thumb stilled as he thought that over, and his grip on her hand loosened. His expression was carefully neutral as he asked, "Do you think I'm sweet?"

Vivian laughed. "I don't know you too well, either. And if I did, I doubt sweet would be the word I'd choose to describe you." But she didn't pull her hand away as she said it.

Judging by his grin, he noticed. "Aren't you going to ask what I think of you?"

"No." Vivian smirked. "I think I can tell the answer to that one."

He shook his head ruefully, running a hand through his hair. "You're a pretty observant girl, Miss Vivian."

"Right now, I'm a pretty tired girl," she said, pulling her hand away at last. "And I've got a day of work still ahead after whatever Honor puts me through. But maybe I'll see you around."

He was smiling as she turned to catch up with Bea. "Count on it," he said. She glanced over her shoulder, and he grinned before he lifted his hat and went to join Danny once more.

"They've moved to Baxter Street now, by the way," she heard Danny say as they disappeared around the corner. "The old place you called is my uncle's now—"

"Come on, Viv," Bea said, a touch of impatience in her voice. "I'm beat, and I bet you are too. The sooner we talk to Honor, the sooner we can get home and get to sleep."

"Home." A slug of guilt hit Vivian in the stomach. "I can't go to the

Nightingale yet, Bea, Florence has been waiting up all night. I have to go tell her I'm okay—"

"Cool it, okay? She already knows." At Vivian's suddenly horrified look, Bea rolled her eyes. "Not that you were in jail, of course. I left her a note that you were fine and would be back in the morning."

"Oh." Vivian sagged with relief. "I'm still gonna have a lot of explaining to do when I get back."

"You and me both, girl." Bea gave Vivian a sympathetic look as she took her arm and pulled her gently but relentlessly along. "So let's get this done quick and not make it any worse than it has to be."

TEN

The bouncer who opened the door in response to Bea's knock gave her a nod of recognition and stepped aside, but he blocked Vivian's way without a hint of emotion. "Wrong place, sweetheart," he grunted.

"I'll dance 'til last call," Vivian said, wedging her foot against the door when he tried to close it. It was the normal password to get past the Nightingale's back-alley door.

"Ms. Huxley's expecting her," Bea said, pulling Vivian in the building. "Let's not keep the door open, okay?"

He grunted again and stepped out of their way. After he shut the door and locked it, he gave a tiny jerk of his chin that was all the indication they had to follow him.

The silent doorman led them straight across the dance floor and toward the back hall. He was clearly the kind of person who didn't bother with small talk, and Bea didn't seem bothered by his silence. Vivian didn't mind. She was too busy looking around the club to chat.

There were no windows, and the furnishings were stark under the glare of electric lights that were never all turned on at once during business hours. Empty of people, with no musicians on the bandstand or bartenders slinging drinks, the whole space felt as if it were waiting to come to life.

"Don't try to swipe anything," the doorman said as they passed the bar, glancing over his shoulder at her. The suddenness of the gruff statement made her jump in a way that she hoped didn't make her look guilty. "Mr. Chin does inventory every day."

"Of course," Vivian said, mostly because she felt like she was expected to say something. Bea snickered quietly. The doorman grunted and kept walking, but she felt like he was still watching her, even though he was facing forward again.

Vivian wondered how many people had seen the Nightingale after hours. Likely only the ones Honor invited. The thought made her smile, as if the Nightingale suddenly belonged to her, and she to it, in a way that it didn't to most of the men and women who came there to dance and drink and escape their daylight lives.

The lights were all turned on in the back hall, too, and Vivian glanced at the door to the alley. In spite of the warm glow, she shivered, remembering the dead man there, the puddle of blood slowly spreading beneath him, her night in jail that somehow was because of him. That place, at least, still felt dangerous, still felt mysterious.

She didn't have time to dwell on the thought as the doorman led them to the stairs. Pausing at the bottom, he gave one curt gesture upward. "Ms. Huxley's waiting in her rooms. The door on the landing is unlocked."

"If you knew we were coming, why all that fuss at the door, Silence?" Bea said, exasperated.

He shrugged, the ghost of a smile on his face, as he went back to his post.

"His name is Silence?" Vivian asked, once they were alone again.

"Silas, if you want to be accurate about it. But he barely talks, so the nickname sticks to him." As she spoke, Bea led the way up the stairs.

"Glad it wasn't just that he didn't like me," Vivian muttered.

"I'm sure he didn't, but don't take it too hard. It's his job not to like much of anyone." At the first landing, there were two doors. Bea went to the one on the right, which was unlocked, just as the bouncer had said. Vivian assumed the other one was Honor's office.

The staircase that stretched beyond the door was narrow and turned sharply after the landing. Vivian followed her friend up, surprised to find that it looked more like someone's home. There were prints on the wall, seascapes that had been carefully framed and hung, and at the top stood a basket of folded clothes that looked like it had been recently delivered from the laundromat. She caught Bea watching her and looking amused, and she blushed at being caught peeking around.

"You knew Honor lives up here most of the time, right?" Bea asked.

"Well, sure. I just somehow never pictured her with laundry." A thought occurred to her. "Isn't it dangerous for her to live above the club? If there are raids, or someone tries to, I don't know, shake her down for something?"

"That's why it's only most of the time," Bea said. She rapped against one door in a quick, staccato rhythm, then called out, "Vivian's here to see you, boss."

The Honor Huxley who opened the door was someone Vivian could only have imagined. Her curly yellow hair was still pinned back, and her makeup was done for the day, or maybe still left from the night before. But instead of her usual sharply tailored suit, she wore a stunning silk wrapper with draped sleeves, patterned with birds and flowers in bright colors. She was in the middle of tying the robe's sash, and she wasn't wearing shoes. Vivian felt her skin heat at the unexpected sight of the other woman's bare toes. She glanced back up quickly.

"Thank you, Beatrice," Honor said, her eyes on Vivian. "Is Danny here?"

"We just left him heading to breakfast with a pal."

"Ah." Honor's expression turned thoughtful, then she shook her head. "Are you going home or waiting downstairs?"

Bea glanced sideways at Vivian. "I'll wait, if that's all right, and have a chat with Silence until you're done with Viv."

Honor laughed. "Well, we won't be long. If Mr. Smith comes, tell him we're set to open on time tonight, and I want the band playing at its best. And if Danny does show up, remind him we're checking inventory at five."

"Yes, ma'am." Bea gave a small salute. "You gonna shake Vivian down while I'm waiting?"

The way they laughed together did little to calm Vivian's nerves. Honor smiled. "She'll still be in one piece when I'm done. But thanks for coming to me last night, Beatrice." She glanced at Vivian, her smile warming even further. "I'd have hated for one of you girls to be in a jam and not help out."

"You're the best, Ms. Huxley," Bea said, reaching out to give Vivian's arm a comforting squeeze. "I'll see you down there soon, okay, Viv?"

"Swell," Vivian agreed, trying to sound casual in spite of her dry throat and rapidly beating heart.

As Bea disappeared down the stairs once more, Honor opened the door a little wider. "Come in please, Vivian."

Vivian glanced around, curious and uneasy, as the door closed behind her. The room was furnished half like an office and half like a sitting room. To her surprise, Honor gestured her toward the sitting room side, where a plate of toast and a coffeepot sat on the table between two stylish, masculine chairs.

"I'm sorry to interrupt your breakfast, Ms. Huxley."

"I was the one who asked you to come."

"It didn't seem like a request," Vivian pointed out. "The way Bea put it, sounded like I didn't have much of a choice."

"People always have a choice," Honor said, taking a seat in one of the chic leather chairs and gesturing for Vivian to do the same.

"Not if I want to come back here, Ms. Huxley."

"You should really call me Honor, since I have no intention of calling you Miss Kelly." The club owner leaned back, bare knees flashing briefly into sight as she crossed her legs and resettled her robe. "So, you had an exciting night."

"And I hear I have you to thank for bailing me out."

Honor's expression grew serious. "It's not smart to go out the way you do without someone to call."

Vivian rolled her eyes. "It's not smart to go out the way I do at all. Can't seem to stop myself, though."

"Well, I hope there won't be a next time, but it pays to have a plan, just in case."

She wasn't sure what made her so daring—maybe the sight of those bare knees behind the flutter of bright silk—but Vivian found herself asking, "What if I want to call you?"

Judging by the lift of her eyebrows, the question caught Honor off guard. But she smiled as she stood. "You should always feel free to call me," she said, crossing to the desk to retrieve a business card. She held it out to Vivian, but didn't let go right away, and her smile grew deeper as their fingertips brushed against each other. "But I think you know that I'm not the sort of person who does favors for free."

Vivian swallowed, but she tugged the card deliberately from the other woman's hand, glancing down at the number on it before looking back up to meet Honor's eyes. "And what is last night's favor going to cost me?"

"A favor in return." Honor went back to the desk, bending down to open one of the lower drawers. A moment later she stood, an unmarked bottle full of maple-colored liquor in one hand and two glasses in the other. Her toes were pointed as delicately as a dancer's as she nudged the drawer closed with her foot. "Since the favor I did you last night was rather substantial, I'm going to ask you to do something important, though I hope it won't be too dangerous. But I think you're in a position to do it."

"You hope it won't be too . . ." Vivian trailed off, her eyes narrowing as Honor sat back down. If the conversation needed to be lubricated with something stronger than coffee, that had to mean . . . "It's something to do with that dead man, then?"

Honor looked surprised by how blunt the question was, as though she had expected to dance around the heart of the matter for a while longer. "I knew you were a smart girl."

"Why me? I'm sure you've got better resources available, given your line of work."

"That's true," Honor said, not taking her eyes off Vivian as she set down the bottle. "But those resources weren't the ones who discovered the body. And they don't know the people who come to this club the way you do." She smiled. "You like to know people, Vivian. It's part of your charm."

"It's the best way to get a free drink," Vivian said, shrugging.

"I'm not asking you to solve the whole fiasco. I just need you to keep your ears open around the club and let me know what you hear. And . . . you can start by getting to know a particular person. He'll be here tonight. See what you can find out about him, then tell me what you learn."

Vivian snorted. "You expect me to believe that twenty-five dollars in bail money meant that much to you?"

Honor poured an inch of glowing liquid into both glasses. "No, twenty-five dollars didn't mean that much to me. But it meant a hell of a lot to you, especially last night."

There was no arguing with that. "I'll pay you back, Ms. Huxley."

The other woman took one glass for herself, then slid the second one across the table. "Honor."

"I'll pay you back, Honor." Just saying the name made Vivian blush, and she quickly took a drink to cover it. The amber liquid burned as it slid down her throat—it was real whiskey, not the dyed moonshine that passed for whiskey in most of the city, and even some nights downstairs—and it made her eyes water as she swallowed a cough.

Honor took a slow sip of her own drink. "How? Do you actually plan to show up in court?"

"I have a job."

"It'll take you a long time to save twenty-five dollars on what you make from Miss Ethel."

Vivian couldn't hide her surprise. "You know where I work?" She narrowed her eyes. "Did Bea tell you?"

"Indirectly." Honor leaned one elbow on the arm of her chair, resting her cheek against her fist. One of her feet made slow circles in the air, but her expression was sharp and focused. "I like to know a thing or two about the regulars in my club. It's a good way to stay in business."

It was on the tip of Vivian's tongue to ask what else the club owner knew about her, but she hesitated. Sparring with Honor didn't seem safe, especially with what the woman was asking her to do. "And did you agree to pay my bail so that you could trap me into doing what you wanted?"

"Of course not." Honor set down her glass abruptly, her smile gone, replaced by a look that was more sincere than any she had yet shown. One of her hands settled over Vivian's own. "I gave Beatrice the money because I wanted to help you." Her stare was disconcertingly direct. "I hated the thought of you in jail."

Vivian swallowed, aware of every inch of that hand pressed against hers. "But you'll still ask me to pay you back."

"That's how this world works," Honor said, shrugging. "And if you're going to play down here with us, pet, then you're going to end up owing a little favor from time to time."

In spite of herself, Vivian laughed. "Why do I get the feeling there are a lot of people who find themselves in the position of owing you a little favor?"

Honor's slow smile returned. "I think you'll be very good at this. You might even enjoy it."

"You said you wanted me to listen around and tell you what I hear, but also to get to know one fella in particular. Who is that?"

Honor leaned forward. "A man named Leo Green."

For a moment, Vivian was sure she had heard wrong. "Leo Green?"

"And luckily, I think you've already met him."

"I have," Vivian said warily. "He seemed . . ." She frowned. "He seemed like a nice enough fella. And he's friends with Danny, so what makes you think he has anything to do with this?"

"They were friends," Honor corrected her. "Mr. Green spent the last five years living in Chicago, and he has . . . well, let's just say a bit of a reputation has followed him here."

Vivian swallowed, thinking of her dance with Leo just before the raid, his flirting when they went their separate ways that morning. She had liked him. He'd been fun and charming. Was Honor saying . . . "You think he's a killer?"

"Not necessarily. But that fella ends up shot behind my club, and then Mr. Green starts showing up?" Honor shook her head. "I don't like coincidences. No one does, if they want to survive in this business. I'm saying his timing makes me curious, especially since there's no word yet who he's working for here in New York."

"What makes you think he's working for anyone?"

"He might not be," Honor admitted, leaning back in her chair. "That's what I want you to find out. Spend some time with him. Find out what he's doing in the city. Find out if he knows anything that I should know. Would that really be such a hardship?" Honor smiled. "I was watching you last night. It looked like the two of you were getting along pretty well already."

They *had* been getting along pretty well. And the fact that Honor knew it and didn't seem bothered by it—even though she had deliberately set out to fluster Vivian throughout their meeting, even though she admitted she'd been watching Vivian last night—pricked Vivian's pride. "And if there's nothing odd about him at all?" she demanded, hoping she didn't sound defensive. "If it turns out he's just some Chicago bootlegger who moved back home to be close to his old dad or something?"

"Then you've just spent a little extra time with a new friend. But if you find out anything more interesting than that, you let me know. If you hear anything around the club, or learn anything about the dead man, you let me know. And hopefully one way or another, I end up with enough to satisfy the people who are threatening to shut the Nightingale down if they don't get answers. What do you say, pet? Sound fair?"

"That depends."

Honor lifted a puzzled eyebrow. "On what?" she murmured as she leaned forward again, her deep red lips curving up.

Vivian leaned forward in response, her eyes never leaving the other woman's as she smiled. "On what you say next," she said, matching her tone to Honor's. "Because you still haven't told me the dead fella's name." As Honor blinked in surprise, Vivian leaned back, not bothering to sound sultry this time. "I saw your face that night. You recognized him. And unless you tell me, you aren't serious about having me find anything out. If that's the case, I'll say thanks for the bail money and walk out that door."

Honor pursed her lips, then sighed. "You're a suspicious girl, Vivian. Yes, I'd seen him around before. His name was Willard Wilson."

Vivian made a face. "Did his parents hate him?"

"Someone did," Honor said dryly. "He got shot, after all. So what do you think?"

"I think you had a good reason to tell me to forget about it, and that I should listen to what you said then, not what you're saying now. I don't think I'm the girl for the job."

Honor raised her eyebrows. "I think you are."

"And you're never wrong?"

"Everyone's wrong sometimes. But I'm rarely wrong about people." She leaned forward again, her hand brushing against Vivian's once more. "And neither, I think, are you."

Vivian pulled her hand deliberately away and took a deep breath. Honor's flirting might throw her off balance, might make her blush, but it didn't make her stop thinking.

"Maybe you're right," she said. "I get to know a lot of people around the Nightingale. People like to talk to me, and they can say some pretty revealing things when a friendly girl looks at them with big eyes or laughs with them in the powder room. So sure, I could probably find out a thing or two that would help you." Her heart was beating fast, and she didn't take her eyes off Honor. "But what I think right now is that you're not sure how to get me to say yes, so you're trying your best to distract me into agreeing. I think you could've easily been dressed and ready when I got here, but you decided not to be. And I think that if I do say yes, you're not planning to tell me the whole truth about what you already know, which makes me wonder why you want me to bother in the first place."

Vivian looked away at last, draining the rest of her whiskey and setting the glass down with a sharp motion. "And no, I'm rarely wrong about people. But go ahead and tell me if I am this time."

Honor's eyes had grown wider with each word, and by the time Vivian finished speaking, the club's owner was speechless for a full ten seconds. "Well," she said at last, a wry expression creeping across her face as she shook her head. "Not this time, no."

Vivian stood up. "Thanks for the bail money then, Ms. Huxley. If you need some other favor, you can always ask. But I think you know my answer to this one."

Her heart was hammering as she turned to leave, waiting for Honor to make her stop, to tell her she wasn't welcome at the Nightingale anymore—anything. But she made it all the way to the door before the other woman spoke.

"I don't usually take no for an answer, Vivian."

Vivian, her hand on the doorknob, paused but didn't turn around. She swallowed, then lifted her chin, even though Honor couldn't see her face. "First time for everything," she said, as flippantly as possible.

She heard Honor's short, surprised laugh as she pulled the door closed. Her heart was still beating fast by the time she made it down to the first floor.

ELEVEN

Bea was waiting for her downstairs, sitting at the bar with one foot tapping anxiously. The bartender whose name Vivian could never remember was sweeping up in one corner, but other than that, the room was empty. Bea sprang to her feet when Vivian appeared at the door.

"Everything okay?"

Vivian hesitated. She and Bea told each other everything. And she desperately wanted to talk things over with her friend, hoping for reassurance that she had made the right call—the safe call—for once in her life.

But she didn't know what would happen now that she'd turned down Honor's favor. And she didn't want to force Bea to get any more mixed up in things than she already was. They had been the ones to find the dead man. But as long as no one knew that . . . *Forget you saw anything.*

"Just fine," Vivian said, her voice as sunny as she could make it. "She just wanted to make sure I was okay after last night. Favor's coming later, it seems." She shrugged. "Guess I'll have to wait to find out what it is, but right now, I'm beat. Ready to head home?"

"Absolutely."

"Wait up, girls."

They both turned, startled to find the bartender had put down his broom and followed them to the door. "I'm not supposed to let you go home alone this morning. Honor's orders."

"Why?" Vivian demanded.

"Chivalry ain't all the way dead. And she's paying, so no need to fuss," he said cheerfully before turning to the hulking doorman. "Silence, can you call us a cab?"

"She doesn't like her staff coming and going on foot after a raid," Bea explained quietly as they followed the men up to the street level. "Didn't know if that would apply this morning. But it's safer if you can't be followed as easy."

It made sense, though Vivian wondered if Honor would have been so generous if she had known Vivian would refuse to play her games. But she didn't say anything. A free cab ride was nothing to turn up her nose at. And the sooner she got home to Florence, the better.

The cabdriver who eventually pulled over in response to Silence's wave eyed them with quickly concealed surprise. "Where to, boss?" he asked pleasantly, hiding a quick yawn. He was a young Black man, dark circles of exhaustion bruising the skin beneath his eyes. Vivian wondered if he'd been taking fares all night.

"Well, that's a good question," the bartender said as the driver got out to open the door for them. "Where to, girls?"

"Not far," Bea said, opening the door on her side. She paused as the driver, returning to his own door, put a hand on her arm and asked her something in a low voice.

Vivian paused, eyeing them warily to make sure Bea was okay. But Bea only smiled and reached out to pat the driver's cheek. "Right as rain," she said, without a trace of her normal laughter. "They're friends. But you're a sweet fella to check."

As Bea slid into the seat and closed the door, Vivian leaned over. "Do you know him?"

Bea shook her head. "We're an odd-looking group to be climbing into a cab together," she pointed out, her voice quiet. "He wanted to make sure I was okay, is all." She raised her voice to address the driver. "Ninth below Thirty-Fourth, please."

Vivian was quiet as they drove, watching the early-morning bustle out the window. The bartender's presence put a damper on any urge she might have had to admit what had actually happened upstairs, and the nervous energy that had kept her going after Bea bailed her out was fading, leaving her drained and exhausted in its wake. But more than that, she couldn't stop wondering who exactly had ended up in the Nightingale's alley. If the person behind the raids was trying to flush out his killer . . . what did that mean for the Nightingale?

Forget you saw anything.

It had nothing to do with her. There were only a few people who knew she and Bea had been the ones to find him. And now, more than ever, she was determined to keep it that way.

She was yawning by the time the cab slid to a halt in front of her building. Bea, by contrast, looked energetic as ever as she thanked the driver and slid out on her side of the car. Vivian eyed her friend's perky steps grumpily as she nudged the bartender's shoulder. "Hop up, will you? You're blocking the door."

He looked surprised to see them both getting out. "You can live in the same building?" He opened the door, then remembered the driver. "I'm not getting out here, so I'll pay for all of us at my stop," he said as he climbed out.

Vivian covered another yawn as she slid across the seat and stumbled out of the cab. "Different buildings. It's a mixed little corner of the city."

"At least for now. Neighborhood's changing pretty quick these days," Bea added, overhearing the last comment. She bent down to grin through the driver's window. "Take care of yourself."

"Maybe I'll see you around," the driver said as she straightened.

Vivian couldn't see his face from where she stood, but she shook her head at the hopeful sound of his voice and, catching Bea's eye over the roof of the cab, raised her eyebrows meaningfully.

Bea laughed. "You never know," she said in response to the driver. Waving to the bartender, she added, "Thanks for the ride. My little puppies are always barking after that walk."

"Do you want me to walk home with you?" Vivian asked, trying not to glance at the fifth-floor window where she knew Florence would be waiting for her.

"Nah." Bea shook her head. "Get yourself home before that sister of yours calls the cops." She laughed again at the face Vivian made. "I know, I know. Even Florence wouldn't take that risk. See you soon."

As she climbed the stairs, Vivian thanked whatever luck meant that she didn't encounter any of her neighbors. There was no way any of them would have let her early-morning, scantily dressed arrival slide without half a dozen questions that she didn't want to answer. Taking a deep breath, she opened her own door.

Florence was waiting at the table, fully dressed, a cup of coffee in front of her next to a small, limp pile of cash. Her face was expressionless, pale except for two spots of bright red color high on her cheekbones. Florence was furious.

But when she saw Vivian, she sagged with relief. "You're back," she said quietly. "Guess I won't need to start searching jails, then."

"Didn't you get Bea's note?" Vivian swallowed, hating that somehow, Florence could always guess exactly what kind of trouble her little sister was in. "You thought I was in jail?"

"I got Bea's note. But you never stay out this late. I knew you were in trouble. I didn't want to think what other kind it might be." There was a bite to Florence's words. But then she sighed, and when she spoke again, the heat was gone from her voice. She rubbed her back as she stood. "I didn't have a plan to find you, though. Just walk from jail to jail, I guess. Glad I didn't need to."

As Florence went to put the money back in their cash box, Vivian could see that it wouldn't have been enough. She shivered, her hands clenching into tight fists before a sharp burst of pain made her remember her injury and relax them again. She didn't want to think about her night in jail, didn't want to think what would have happened if Florence had searched all over the city to bail her out, only to come up still short.

Instead, she took refuge in the carelessness that she knew would push her sister away again. "Yeah, that wouldn't have been any fun," she said, letting her borrowed coat fall to the floor in an untidy pile. Kicking off her heels and leaving them by the door, she tossed her purse on the table and shrugged. "Sorry to make you fuss."

Florence had stiffened, and her jaw clenched as she turned around to face Vivian again. "Me too. Were you?"

"Was I what?"

"In jail," Florence said quietly. "Or were you with a man?"

Vivian made the mistake of meeting her sister's eyes. She was tired, and her hand ached, and it was too hard to pretend to be thoughtless when Florence was staring at her like that. "Jail," she admitted, her voice barely above a whisper.

She waited for the storm of anger, but Florence just shook her head. "And I suppose some man got you out."

"No." At her sister's skeptical look, Vivian grew indignant. "I'm telling the truth. Bea spent all night scrounging up bail money for me."

"Well, thank God for Bea, then." Florence shook her head. "The things we owe that family."

"I know." It was one of the few things they always agreed on.

Vivian waited for her sister to ask why Bea hadn't come to her for help if she needed cash for Vivian's bail. But Florence just sighed again. "What happened to your hand?"

Vivian glanced down. The bandage had gotten dirty, and it was starting to come untied. "Got cut. I should probably clean it up."

"I'll do it. Sit down," Florence said.

Vivian didn't argue. As she sat, she unwrapped the cloth with her good hand while Florence retrieved a basket of fresh bandages from their place in a kitchen cabinet, along with an unmarked amber bottle. There was still water in the kettle from the day before; she poured that into a bowl, then grabbed a fresh towel. Bringing them to the table, she pulled Vivian's hand toward her and examined the ugly cut, her forehead creasing in worry. Then she sighed, spread the towel underneath, and picked up the amber bottle.

"Keep still." Florence held her sister's hand in a surprisingly strong grip as she poured a thin stream of liquid over the cut.

Vivian yelped in surprise and pain. "God*damn,* that hurts."

"Vivian!" Florence's voice was sharp, but her hands were gentle as she sponged clean water over the cut to rinse away the clots of blood that had loosened. "You know better than to take the Lord's name in vain."

"Not when something stings that bad, I don't," Vivian countered, gritting her teeth. "What the hell was it?"

Florence's mouth tightened. For a moment Vivian thought she was still annoyed by the cursing. Then she realized Florence was blushing. "Some of Mr. Brown's homebrew. I bought a bottle last month for emergencies."

"You keep a stash of moonshine in our kitchen? How did I not know that?"

"It's a bottle of antiseptic," Florence countered. "Drinking it would be like drinking gasoline."

Vivian tried to pull her hand away as Florence pulled out a clean bandage. "I can do that."

"Not with one hand you can't," her sister said, a note of exasperation in her voice. "Please, just hold still, will you?"

Vivian relented, sighing as she watched. "You don't have to act like my mother, you know."

Florence's hands stilled for a moment before she continued wrapping the bandage. "Well, I don't have much chance of mothering anyone else. You should be used to it by now."

An uncomfortable weight settled in Vivian's chest at her sister's words. "Flo," she said hesitantly. "Do you want to have children?"

Florence finished tucking in the ends of the bandage. "Don't you?"

"Never really thought about it," Vivian admitted. "No one around here makes it look like much fun."

"Well, I do." Florence stood abruptly, shoving the bottle of moonshine and the bandages back into her basket and gathering the bloody ones to toss into the laundry pail. "But I'm twenty-six years old and stuck here. So it looks like you're as close as I'm going to get, unless I want to end up like Mrs. Thomas."

"You might still meet a fella," said Vivian awkwardly, unsure how to respond. When the nuns set them up with jobs and sent them out into the world to scrounge for themselves, Florence had always seemed to accept that was all they could expect out of life. As much as Vivian knew she wanted more for herself, it had never occurred to her to wonder if her quiet, uncomplaining sister felt the same. "You could always come out dancing with me."

The look Florence gave her was withering. "And fall in love with a nice young man who already has a wife at home?"

"They're not all like that," Vivian protested.

"I don't see you finding anyone to marry."

"That's because I'm not looking," Vivian said. "If you want something different, Flo, you have to make it happen."

"Working six days a week for the pittance Miss Ethel pays doesn't leave much room for something different. Right now it's all I can manage to keep track of you and not lose my job." Florence reached out and laid a gentle hand on Vivian's cheek, just for a moment. Vivian stilled, surprised by the touch, and Florence sighed as she let her hand fall away. "Speaking of Miss Ethel, you can't do any sewing with that hand, can you?"

Vivian glanced down at her bandaged palm, a slow feeling of panic beginning to spread through her chest. She had been so distracted by the raid and getting bailed out, knowing all the while that if she managed to get home there was Florence to face, that she hadn't thought ahead to what would happen when she went to work that morning. "Oh no."

Florence shook her head. "I didn't think so. And you look a mess, you know."

"That's so kind of you to say," Vivian snapped, the panicked feeling spreading to her stomach.

"I'm not the one who got thrown in jail, so don't blame me for your bad choices." Florence sighed. "Stay home today and get some rest. I'll tell Miss Ethel that you had to help at church or something, she'll be more likely to excuse that than if I say you're sick."

"Breaking the eighth commandment?" Vivian murmured, unable to resist the taunt.

Florence, in the middle of gathering up a lunch for herself, gave her a look that was distinctly unamused. "Would you prefer I tell her you spent the night in jail?"

"No." Vivian sighed. "I am sorry, Florence."

"I'm sure you are."

"I am, really. And I'm not going out again tonight," said Vivian, shuddering. "Living through one raid was enough for me."

"I'll believe that when I see it," Florence said softly.

"Really, Flo. This time even I need a break."

Florence nodded. "I'm glad, then. And . . ." She hesitated. "It'll be nice to spend some time together. I'll be home for dinner. Try to stay out of trouble until then."

———•———

Vivian was startled out of sleep by the sound of knocking, a friendly, oddly rhythmic rapping that didn't sound like any of their neighbors. Still half-asleep and too groggy to care what she looked like, she pulled Florence's wrapper around herself and hurried to the front door.

Danny's hand was half-raised to knock a second time when she swung the door open, and he smiled at her as he lowered it. "Hey there, sleeping beauty. Made up for last night yet?"

"What time is it?" Vivian asked, rubbing her eyes and squinting toward one of the hall windows, where the bright sun was nearly blinding.

"Little after four o'clock. Glad to see you got home safe. Is Leo in there?"

Vivian rolled her eyes at him. "Absolutely not. Haven't seen him since we all said good-bye this morning. And I certainly never told him where I live," she said, eyeing him in surprise. Before that morning, she and Danny had never seen each other outside the Nightingale. "I don't think I ever told you where I live, either."

Danny shrugged, then crossed his arms over his chest as he leaned against the doorjamb. "Hux knows things."

Vivian's eyes narrowed. "Is she the reason you're here?"

"Well, the immediate reason I'm here is that you don't have a telephone," Danny said, smirking at her impatient expression. "But . . . yes, Hux sent me."

"Why?"

His brows lifted. "You can't guess?"

Vivian grimaced. "Did she tell you about our conversation this morning?" she asked.

He didn't answer the question, instead holding out a small brown-paper parcel. "She wanted me to give you this."

Vivian hesitated, but her curiosity won out before she could talk herself out of it. There was a note tucked into the string.

Vivian, it read, *Thought you might need another pair of these, since it looked like yours got ruined last night, and I know they're hard to come by on a dressmaker's wages. You're always welcome at the Nightingale— but our talk from this morning isn't done.*

It was unsigned. Vivian hesitated, but her curiosity got the better of her before she could talk herself out of it, and she pulled open the package. Inside was a beautiful pair of silk stockings—far nicer than the ones that had been wrecked by the raid and her night in jail. They were so smooth against her fingers that she had to resist the urge to bring them up to rub against her cheek. Instead, she looked up at Danny.

"Do you know what she's going to want?" she asked, her attempt at sounding worldly and offhand undermined by the way her voice caught in her throat.

"Just to talk, far as I know. She said you weren't done chatting about her favor."

"And these?" Vivian held up the stockings, too disoriented by the gift to be embarrassed about showing them to him.

He whistled. "Pretty-looking things. Guess she thought she might need to sweeten you up a little first."

Vivian wasn't cold, but she crossed her arms over her torso as if she could ward off the sudden feeling of vulnerability. Danny frowned.

"You're not scared of her, are you? Hux ain't bad people."

"So you're saying she's good people?" Vivian asked skeptically.

That made him laugh. "I wouldn't go that far. We're none of us angels, kitten, you know that." He tapped her nose. "Not even you. But it won't be that bad. Hux's favors get done because people end up wanting to do them."

Vivian laughed shortly. "I believe it. That woman is persuasive." There was no getting out of it. Honor Huxley had bailed her out, no questions asked. Vivian owed her. "When should I come by?"

"A little before opening tonight. Say eight o'clock? Someone will be there to let you in."

"All right," she agreed, hoping he wouldn't guess that she suddenly felt like her heart was speeding up. "See you then?"

"See you then." He winked and tipped his hat, which made her smile in spite of her racing heart, and took the stairs two at a time on his way down, the sound of his cheerful whistling drifting behind him.

Vivian closed the door. If Honor was expecting her at the club, it was probably best not to go back to sleep. If she moved quickly, she could have dinner set and be gone before Florence got home. Dropping the dressing gown carelessly to the floor, Vivian picked up the clean dress that Florence had folded neatly in the laundry basket and tugged it over her head. The kettle on the stove was still half-full of water, enough to make at least a cup of coffee. She set it to boil and, flexing her injured hand and wincing with each movement, glanced out the room's single window.

She was just in time to see Danny emerge from the front door, his hat shading his face from view but his jaunty walk unmistakable. Vivian shook her head, smiling to herself, as she leaned her head against the window and waited for the kettle.

That was when she noticed two hulking figures in dark suits, hats pulled low over their eyes, slide out from an alley and head in the direction Danny had gone. There was something about the way they moved—carefully, heavily, staying close to the buildings—that set the back of her neck prickling. When Danny turned the corner, they sped up after him.

Vivian's stomach tightened with sudden fear. She knew bully boys and bruisers when she saw them. Danny could take care of himself, she was sure—but they were two to one, and he didn't know they were coming.

Vivian wavered, then cursed loudly and turned off the stove. Grabbing Florence's house slippers from their place by the front door, she shoved them on and dashed out into the hall, nearly tripping over her own feet as she pelted down the stairs.

"Vivian, girl, why are you home?" she heard a querulous voice ask as she reached the bottom level, but she didn't stop to answer, shoving open the building door and stumbling out.

For a moment she was disoriented, blinking in the too-bright sun as she tried to remember which way Danny had been going. The cobbler's shop across the street helped her get her bearings—he had disappeared down the alley just to the left. Vivian ran after him.

They had a head start, but she was the only one running. The alley opened up into another that was little more than a trash-filled gap between buildings; hearing voices up ahead, Vivian checked herself at the corner and peeked around.

The two toughs had Danny backed up against a wall of trash bins and teetering storage crates. He was silent, his body tense while he watched them—one man was talking while the other moved slowly to one side.

"See, pal, I don't think that's the honest truth you're telling us," the chatty one said, shaking his head as if he were disappointed. He was the smaller of the two, with a weaselly face and a cruel smile. "We think your bitch of a boss knows more than she's letting on. You'll be better off telling us what she knows, or next time you'll end up with worse than paying customers in the lockup. Ain't that right, Eddie?"

Eddie, a hulking avalanche of a man, grunted in agreement, still circling. Danny had half turned his body, trying to keep an eye on both men at once.

"But if you tell us what you know, maybe we'll go easy, eh? Maybe we'll just break one arm instead of both of them if, say, you could tell us who he was talking to before he ended up clipped in your alley."

"You're off your rocker if you think I've got anything to say to you," Danny said, his cheerful tone at odds with the tense scene. "It's a shame someone offed your man, since whoever's bossing you now clearly ain't got the brains of a baby."

The weaselly one shrugged. "Have it your way, fella. Eddie?"

Eddie grunted again and charged.

Vivian stared frantically around her alley corner, trying to find something—anything—that would let her help. There was a splintered crate thrown against one wall, and she caught up one of the longer pieces before turning back to the fight. But the scene that met her eyes was terrifying and hypnotic, and for the moment she stayed where she was, shocked into stillness once more.

Danny moved like a spring uncoiling. He dodged out of the way, grabbing a trash can lid with one hand and using the momentum of his turn to bash Eddie over the head with it. Knocked off balance, the bully boy went careening into a stack of crates, bellowing with rage as they splintered around him.

The chatty fellow sighed as he shrugged off his jacket and tossed it over a crate. "Guess we're doing this, then. Don't say I didn't warn you."

He hurled himself toward Danny, moving with more skill than Eddie had, but Danny met him confidently. The grace that served the bartender so well on the dance floor kept him light on his feet. He dodged out of the way, one fist blocking the blows aimed toward his face as he jabbed with the other. He caught the chatty bully boy across the cheek. The man stumbled, spitting out blood as he braced himself against a wall.

By then Eddie had struggled to his feet. Danny turned to meet him just as the bruiser slammed into him, catching him around the waist. The two of them stumbled backward together. Eddie bellowed as Danny slammed his elbows and fists repeatedly against the larger man's neck and face. There was no elegance in his movements now, just brutal focus and desperation. Eddie couldn't block the vicious blows without letting go, and he unwisely hung on. Vivian watched, breathless with fear. Danny continued to hammer the other man, twisting to keep the bruiser's bulk between him and the weaselly man, who was trying to rejoin the fight.

Danny's elbow caught Eddie in one eye, and the hulking man let out a choked sound. He finally let go and stumbled to his knees, clutching his battered face. Blood streamed from his nose and stained the front of his white shirt.

As Danny pulled away, he kicked out, his foot connecting with the side of Eddie's head. The other man toppled over, unconscious.

The smaller man ignored his friend, dodging past him to catch Danny with one shoulder and slam him against the alley wall. Danny's head connected with a sickening *thunk*, and Vivian heard her friend gasp with pain as he dropped to his knees. A moment later, though, he was moving again, slamming his body upward. His head plowed into the bully boy's stomach. The other man grunted and kicked. His foot caught Danny's thigh and made him stumble once more. They broke apart, both breathing heavily. For all Danny's quick reflexes, one arm was hanging limply, and he turned to keep that side away from his opponent.

The weaselly man noticed too, and he circled along with Danny. An ugly smile crept over his face. "Not looking so dandy anymore, eh, fella? Maybe you feel like more of a chat now?"

"Not a chance," Danny spat, and charged before the other man was expecting it.

He caught the tough with his good shoulder, sending the other man stumbling back several feet until he was only steps away from the alley where Vivian was still hiding. She saw her opening.

Wild with fear and adrenaline, Vivian darted out, swinging the splintered board.

As it shattered over his head, the man let out a strangled gurgle. His eyes rolled back in his head as he dropped to the ground.

Vivian swallowed and dropped the board, wiping her suddenly nerveless fingers against her dress as she looked up.

Danny was leaning against the alley wall again, taking deep breaths, but he still managed to smile at her. "Where did you come from, kitten?"

Vivian had to try twice before her dry throat could make a sound. "Saw them following you out the window."

"And what the hell have you got on your feet?"

Vivian frowned at the nonsensical question, then glanced down, remembering for the first time since she ran out the door that she was still wearing her sister's house slippers. Even though her footwear was the last thing either of them should have been worried about, she found herself blushing. "I needed to get out the door quickly. Is he . . ." She glanced down at the weaselly man's motionless body. "Is he dead?"

Danny started to bend down, then hesitated, clearly thinking better of getting too close. Narrowing his eyes, he delivered a sharp kick to the man's crotch. When nothing happened, he bent down and put two fingers to the man's neck, then tipped one ear toward his mouth.

"Not dead," he said, staggering to his feet. Vivian caught his good arm to help haul him up, and he nodded his thanks. "Solidly out, though. Good job."

Vivian shuddered. "I didn't know that would work," she confessed.

"Well, lucky you, then," Danny said with a short laugh. "And lucky me. Let's get out of here before they wake up."

"Do you know them?" Vivian asked as she followed Danny out of the alley, trying to stick close enough to his side that she could help him if he stumbled.

"Not personally." Danny sighed, wincing as he rotated his injured shoulder. "Hell, that's going to hurt for a while. No, nothing about that was personal."

"What are you going to do?" Vivian couldn't help whispering.

"Do?" Danny shrugged, the movement lopsided as he only used one arm. "Watch you go inside and head to work. Hux'll want to know what happened, and I've got inventory to check."

Vivian frowned, looking around in confusion as she realized that he had walked her home without her realizing it. "But . . . they just tried to kill you!"

"Nah." He shook his head, stopping just in front of her building's door. "They tried to make me talk. If they wanted to kill me they would've just shot me. And since I didn't have anything to say to them, that'll be the end of it for now."

"Danny, that wasn't nothing, so don't try to act like it was."

"It was nothing for you to worry about," he said gently. "I'm glad you were there, believe me, but that's how these things go. Hux and I will deal with the rest of it."

Vivian caught his arm. "You swear you're okay?"

"Right as rain. And now I know who to call on if I'm ever in a pinch."

"And should I still come to the Nightingale tonight?"

"Unless you want to owe Hux a favor forever," he said, grinning, though the expression was half a wince. He rotated his shoulder again, grimacing. "I'll have a drink waiting for you when you're done talking to her. My treat, with thanks." He nudged her with his good arm. "Now get back inside before anyone sees those shoes."

TWELVE

Vivian tried not to think about her sister as she knocked on the door of the Nightingale. She had cleaned the stove, done the laundry, and gone to the market. She had left dinner for the Thomas children in a basket at their door, and left Florence's dinner warming between two plates in the oven. She had even left an apple turnover from Mr. Hoffmann's bakery next to a note saying where she had gone, a peace offering to compensate for the guilt she felt at breaking her promise so quickly.

But Honor's favor and Danny's fight were hanging over her; there was no chance of her staying home. So Vivian tamped down her guilt, pulled on her new silk stockings, and slicked on an extra coat of lipstick. She was terrified of what she planned to tell Honor that night, and she hoped that if she looked her best, she'd be confident enough to go through with it.

She made it out just before seven, when Florence would be getting home.

Silence opened the door in response to her knock and looked her up and down without a hint of recognition, though she knew that to be any good at his job he would have to remember her from earlier.

"I'll dance 'til last call."

He grunted and swung the door open. Vivian made her way down the long hallway to the second doorway, where heavy velvet curtains muffled the sound from downstairs. Vivian took a deep breath and pushed through them.

She was met by the bright sound of music. Vivian paused at the top of the stairs. It didn't take more than a moment for her to spot Honor, who was leaning against the bar, surveying her club.

She spotted Vivian quickly too, though she didn't say anything until they were standing next to each other. They eyed each other for a wary moment, Honor's face giving nothing away and Vivian hoping she was equally impassive, before Honor jerked her chin toward a table in the corner. "Come have a drink with me, pet."

Vivian thought of refusing, just to show that she couldn't be pushed around or manipulated. But Honor was collecting two glasses of champagne from Danny, and there was no reason to let that go to waste.

She swallowed half of hers as soon as they were seated, the bubbles striking her throat and making her cough. Before Honor could do more than raise her eyebrows in surprise, before Vivian could lose her nerve, she set the glass down and said in a rush, "I was there when Danny got jumped today."

"He told me. I'm glad you could help him out, but I'm mad as hell that you put yourself in danger like that."

"You want to put me in danger," Vivian pointed out, stung and flattered at the same time.

"I'm asking you to find out a little information and share it with me. That's different than charging into the middle of a fight."

"I like Danny," Vivian said quietly, glancing over at the bar. "He's been good to me since the first night Bea brought me to the Nightingale. And God knows she's the best friend I have." Her voice caught a little, and she had to swallow abruptly to find it again. Imagining Bea cornered in an alley like Danny made her feel sick. "If not knowing what happened to that man, and why, means that everyone who works here is at risk, that the Nightingale is at risk . . ." Vivian shook her head. "Coming to the Nightingale gets me through the day. It's all I have right now that isn't working and arguing with my sister and wondering if we'll have enough money for heat when winter rolls around. I don't know what I'd do without this place."

Honor listened quietly, her head tilted to one side, all her flirting glances gone for the moment. "Does that mean you want to help me out after all?"

"God no, I don't want to." Vivian shuddered as she remembered the awful sound the board had made as it connected with the bruiser's head. "But Danny could have been killed today. Bea could be next. Hell, *I* could be next if someone found out I saw the dead fella in that alley. So I'll do it anyway."

If she hadn't been paying such close attention, Vivian would have missed the small breath of relief that Honor released. But the club owner's face gave nothing away as she smiled. "I'm glad to hear it."

"Well, that makes one of us," Vivian muttered. She settled back against the chair, one foot jiggling anxiously as she wondered what she had gotten herself into. It had taken less than forty-eight hours for Honor to go from *Forget you saw anything* to *Find out what Leo Green knows.*

What exactly had made her change her mind so quickly?

The Nightingale's owner was playing things close to the chest right now. That was fine. If Vivian was unearthing one set of secrets, she could find out Honor's while she was at it.

Vivian took another drink. "So I see what I can learn, and after that we're square?"

Honor raised her glass. "After that we're square."

Vivian hesitated, then clinked the rim of her own glass against Honor's in agreement.

They finished their drinks in silence as Honor turned to glance around the club, a look of pride on her face. The band was already playing, the drinks were starting to flow, and couples were starting to jostle for spots on the dance floor.

"You're not the only one who feels that way about it, you know," Honor said, just loud enough for Vivian to hear her over the sound of the music. "I'll do whatever it takes to keep my doors open, because a lot of folks here wouldn't know where else to go if the next raid shut us down."

Vivian knew it was true; faces of all colors ended up on the dance floor, and Honor wasn't the only woman who danced with other women. Sometimes there were two men in each other's arms, and if anyone batted an eyelash at it, they also knew to keep their mouths shut, that night and any days after.

"The Nightingale's good at keeping secrets," Honor said. "But," she added, glancing at Vivian out of the corner of her eye, "that doesn't mean I don't know what they are."

"Except for who killed Willard Wilson."

For a moment Honor looked annoyed by the reminder, then she laughed and shook her head as she stood up. "Oh, Vivian, I hope that smart mouth of yours never gets you in too much trouble." She leaned over the table, and Vivian froze as she felt Honor's fingertip gently brush her lower lip. "Because I enjoy it far, far too much for you to ever change." She stood up, leaving Vivian no chance to respond as she added, "Your Mr. Green is watching you." Honor nodded toward the bar, where Leo was just accepting a drink from the blond bartender while staring directly at Vivian and Honor. "Ready to ask him for a dance?"

Two could play at that game, Vivian decided, standing as well. "Well, sure, it's no hardship. He's a swell dancer. Strong hands, moves a treat."

Honor's pause was so brief that Vivian would have missed the moment of utter stillness if she hadn't been looking for it. But then the other woman nodded, lips pursing as if she were laughing at herself. "All right, pet. Go put that smart mouth of yours to use and see what you can find out for me."

"Fine," said Vivian, giving her head a little toss to settle her hair into place. "I'll give it a week and see what I can turn up. But I'm drinking for free while I do it."

Honor rolled her eyes, a petulant gesture so at odds with her normal coolness that Vivian had to hold in a snort of laughter. "I'll let the bartenders know," Honor said. "And you let me know what you learn."

Vivian gave a casual salute, not looking back as she sauntered off, though she heard Honor heave an exasperated sigh as she turned away to do the early-evening rounds. Reaching the bar, Vivian slid onto the stool next to where Leo was standing, meeting his narrow-eyed evaluation with her own pert smile before turning to Danny.

"You owe me a drink, Mr. Chin. And none of the cheap stuff, thanks very much. I'm drinking the good booze for free the rest of the week."

"Oh really?" Danny's expression was skeptical, and she saw him glance past her with his eyebrows raised. Vivian didn't have to follow his line of sight to know that he was checking in with Honor, but whatever signal he received made him shrug and pull out a glass. "Gonna tell me why?" he asked as he began pouring.

"You mean to say there's something your Hux didn't tell you?" Vivian asked, delighted, as she curled her fingers around the quickly mixed cocktail.

Danny didn't let go of the glass. "Careful, kitten," he said. "Never assume someone doesn't know the answer just because they're asking the question. They might know it better than you."

His tone made Vivian remember the brutal, efficient way he had fought in the alley. That made her think of another alley, blood slowly covering the ground beneath the dead man—*Wilson,* she heard Honor's voice murmur in her mind. She shivered, wondering what, exactly, she had just agreed to get mixed up in.

But she laughed anyway as she tugged her drink away, and this time

Danny didn't resist. "Well, then, if you know, there shouldn't be any problem, right?" she asked, giving her bob a toss as she swiveled around in her chair and met Leo's eyes over the rim of her glass. "Mr. Green. Fancy meeting you here again."

"Miss . . ." He trailed off, looking adorably confused for a moment as he remembered that he didn't know her whole name. "Vivian." The way his voice curled around it would have made her spine tingle pleasantly if she hadn't been wondering whether he really did know something about the dead man in the alley. "I'll have you know I came here on purpose looking for you."

"Should I be flattered or alarmed?"

"Flattered," Leo said, grinning, though the effect was spoiled when Danny said "alarmed" at the same moment. Leo glared at his friend. "Fat lot of help you are."

"Just making sure Vivian knows to watch out for you, you slick bastard," Danny said pleasantly, before turning to a man in an expensive suit who had sauntered up to the bar. "The usual, sir? Right away."

Vivian frowned into her glass as Danny turned away. His earlier comment had made her assume he knew what favor Honor had asked her for. But if that was the case, would he still be acting so friendly with Leo?

Or maybe the suspicions were all Honor's, and Danny didn't think his childhood friend had anything to do with Wilson's death. Which one of them was more likely to be right?

"So, why are you drinking for free?" Leo asked, sipping his own whiskey as he leaned one elbow against the bar. He looked relaxed, but Vivian could see his eyes narrowing as he watched her face.

If she was going to find out what Leo was up to in New York, she needed to convince him to let down his guard. That meant she had to pick up right where they had left off the night before. Vivian took a deep breath and smiled. "Well, I could tell you, but then I wouldn't have the fun of watching you get all squirmy with jealousy," she said, pleased when a slow flush crept up from his shirt collar.

"What makes you think I'm squirming or jealous?"

"You came here on purpose looking for me," she repeated, feeling reckless. She had gone head-to-head with Honor twice that day and come out, if not ahead in their game, at least not behind. She was, somehow, part of the search for a killer. Leo Green was just one more challenge. She could feel her chest warm with alcohol and her cheeks heating with excitement.

"Does it have anything to do with that favor you were going to owe her for bailing you out?" Leo asked, his eyes never leaving hers as he sipped his drink.

"Maybe it does."

Leo's hat was resting on the bar; his fingers moved restlessly on the brim, absently spinning it around as he watched her. "What did she ask you to do?"

It was hard to believe, with those warm brown eyes fixed on her, that he could have anything to do with a murder in a back alley. But even without Honor's favor, she would have been wary of trusting the smooth-talking man from Chicago. Vivian drained her glass abruptly, set it down with a clink, and held out her hand. "Come dance with me."

The band was playing a lively quickstep, and Leo glanced toward the dance floor. But his eyes narrowed as he turned back. "You didn't answer my question."

"And I won't until you dance with me," she said playfully. "Unless you can't keep up with this one?"

He tossed back his own drink and caught up her hand. "I know you're baiting me, but I'm going to prove you wrong anyway."

"You just want to dance with me," Vivian taunted as he led her toward the dance floor.

"Yes," he agreed, pulling her close—too close, really, for a quickstep, their fingers twining around each other as they raised their hands. "Now let's see if *you* can keep up."

His palm was warm against her back, and Vivian could feel the spark of it all the way down her spine. But a moment later, the buzzy heat faded, leaving her cold with wariness. Honor was right. Leo hadn't appeared at the Nightingale until the night after Willard Wilson was found dead behind the club. It could have meant nothing. He hadn't paid any attention when Bea had mentioned the dead man that morning, after all. But it was a coincidence. It might be something more.

"Why did you pick the Nightingale to come to?" she asked. The question came out more bluntly than she had intended. But there was no way to take it back, so she planted her weight for a moment to prevent him from leading off, waiting for an answer.

He stared down at her, his cheeks flushed with the heat of the dance floor, even though they weren't moving yet. "I told you—I wanted to see you again."

"I meant before that. Why'd you come here last night?"

"I needed somewhere to get a drink," he laughed. "And I heard a rumor that Danny was working here. Did you change your mind about that dance?"

"No, of course not." Vivian shook her head, then raised her eyebrows in challenge. "Let's see how fast those Chicago feet move."

After that, they needed all their breath for dancing, for matching the slide of the trombone and the *rat-a-tat* of the drums. Vivian wasn't sure whether she believed him yet. He seemed honest, but there were plenty of bootleggers who could lie to God himself and get away with it. But the music got under her skin too quickly for her to stay as wary as she knew she should. And Leo could *dance,* she remembered with a rush of pleasure. It was hard to think grim thoughts as they flew across the dance floor, his lead so easy to follow, and so quick to adapt to whatever she did, that it felt as if he had been holding her in his arms every night for years. Vivian was breathless and laughing by the time the music finally flourished to a stop.

Leo grinned down at her without dropping his arms, though all around them couples were breaking apart and re-forming as the next song began. "How did my Chicago feet do?"

Vivian shrugged, pretending to play it cool though she knew her delight was written all across her face. "Good enough, I guess."

He laughed. "Well, you dance like a dream, sweetheart, and if you keep pretending you don't like me, I might just have to kiss you to make you admit it."

Vivian bit her lower lip in a useless effort to stop her smile from spreading. "You'll kiss me when I say you can, and not a moment before," she said, her voice suddenly husky.

Leo's grip on her tightened before he abruptly let go, laughing ruefully as he ran his fingers through his hair. "You know exactly how to get under a fella's skin, don't you?" he asked, shaking his head. A moment later, though, he had to grab her arm and pull her quickly out of the way of a dancing couple. "Come on, let's go bother Danny for another drink."

The bar was crowded, and Leo gestured for her to wait while he pushed his way forward to get their drinks. Vivian was glad to have him step away for a moment. Getting too flustered over a little flirtation was never a good idea, especially not when she knew better than to trust the fellow flirting with her. Fanning her flushed cheeks, she looked around for something to distract her equally heated thoughts.

Her attention was caught by the couple embracing just a couple feet down the bar, a girl with dark hair tumbled across her face, her companion leaning over her shoulder from behind as he wrapped his arms around her waist. He was at least a foot taller than she was, and he had to bend his blond head a long way down so he could nibble on her bare neck and whisper something in her ear.

Vivian couldn't stop her eyebrows from climbing. She never batted an eye at the couples getting frisky in dark corners, but it was rare to see two people necking right out in the open. Shaking her head over folks who couldn't hold their liquor, she was about to turn back when the couple unwound from each other, the girl pushing away with a laugh. Vivian's eyebrows climbed even higher as she realized who the girl was.

"Get me a drink and we'll see," Mags said, brushing her hair back into place with a flick of her wrist. "Something classy, got it? I don't do cheap."

The man, who was definitely not Roy, waggled his eyebrows at her before he turned to push his way through the crowd to the bar. Vivian hadn't quite managed to wipe the surprise from her face before Mags turned and caught sight of her.

"Well hello, shellshock!" she exclaimed, her nose wrinkling up with delight as she smiled. "I see you made it out of the slammer all right. Lord, that was quite the show, wasn't it? I almost didn't come out tonight."

"Guessing you didn't get in trouble with your father, then?" Vivian asked, trying not to sound too pointed. It wasn't Mags's fault that she knew people who could help her out, any more than it was her fault she had money. But it was still hard not to resent her for it.

"He was too busy boozing it up with his Long Island buddies to even notice I'd been out," Mags said, rolling her eyes. "Mother and Dad laid in plenty of provisions before Prohibition. So they've got no cause to fuss at me for going out, don't you think?"

"And what do they think of your new fella?" Vivian asked, tilting her head toward the bar where the handsy man's blond head stuck out above the crowd.

"What?" Mags followed her gaze and shrugged. "Oh gosh no, he's not someone I'd ever take home to the folks. Honestly," she lowered her voice, grinning widely, "I can't even remember his name. I just needed someone to dance with me and buy me a drink, and I do like them tall."

"What about Roy?" Vivian tried to keep her voice casual. Maybe he had missed seeing the man slumped in the shadows—the door had been closed, and it was dark out there. But maybe he hadn't. A shiver chased its way across Vivian's shoulders, but that didn't stop her from adding, "I thought the two of you were pretty friendly."

"I thought we were too. But I caught him in a corner chatting up some mousy girl a couple nights ago," Mags said, her red lips pursing into a pout. "He thinks just because Dad likes him I'll let him get away with anything. But we're done unless he comes crawling on hands and knees. And even then, he'll have to talk pretty sweet to get me back."

Her pout transformed into a smile as her new fellow came back, drinks in hand, and offered one to her. "Thanks, honey," she said, giving him her attention only briefly before turning back to Vivian. "But who needs him, right? I'm all set for the night. And it looks like you are too," she added, her voice dropping to a purr as she glanced over Vivian's shoulder. "Golly, someone's found herself a looker."

Vivian turned to see where Mags was staring and discovered Leo had reappeared behind her, the hat he had reclaimed from the bar tucked under one arm and a drink in each hand.

"Danny mixed it, so no blaming me if he chose wrong," he said, handing one glass to Vivian.

"Well, don't you know how to find a fun time, honey," Mags laughed, looking Leo up and down. Vivian was tickled to see his neck turn red with embarrassment.

"Hey now," the blond giant protested, pulling Mags's attention back to him. She laughed and let him lead her away, raising her glass to Vivian in a toast.

"Who was that?" Leo asked, clearing his throat and still looking red around the ears.

"Just a friend," Vivian said. "A friend who apparently thinks you look like a good time."

"She's not wrong," he said, grinning briefly before taking a long drink. "Well, if you won't tell me who your friend is, are you going to answer my other question?"

"Question?" Vivian asked vaguely, their earlier conversation driven from her mind as she thought about Mags's absent fellow. Which was more likely, that the charmer smiling at her had something to do with Wilson's death? Or that the surly Roy, who had been there the night Wilson died and had apparently been acting oddly enough to fall out with Mags just a few hours later, was involved? If she wanted to pay back Honor's favor and keep the Nightingale safe, which direction should she really be looking?

The Nightingale wasn't the right place to think it over. The band was in full swing, and bodies crowded the dance floor. Mags and her fellow were tucked into one corner, her body wrapped around his. Bea was nowhere in sight, though Vivian was sure her friend was supposed to be working that night, and Danny was shouting to his fellow bartender, though the sound of his voice was lost in the noise of the dance hall.

"It's hot as hell in here," she sighed, snagging Leo's hat from under his arm and using it to fan herself. "What question am I supposed to be answering?"

"What favor Honor Huxley asked you to do," he said, leaning closer so she could hear him over the sound of the trumpet.

"Nothing really," she lied. "She claimed it was out of the goodness of her heart, but I think that just means she'll call it in down the line."

Leo frowned. "That sounds risky."

"Not if I stay on her good side." Vivian hesitated, then pressed recklessly forward, deciding that surprise was a reasonable tactic to try. "Hey, you know a fellow named Wilson?" she asked, stepping close so she could be heard above the music. "Willard Wilson?"

She watched him carefully as she asked, looking for any flicker of guilt or knowledge. But Leo's face gave nothing away. "Don't think so. Why, he owe you money?"

"That would be swell," Vivian said, not really answering. "Maybe I could pay Honor back and be done with the whole thing. Oh well."

Leo, still frowning, started to respond, but whatever he might have said was drowned out as the trumpet player stood for a solo. In spite of the heat, Vivian shivered as she looked toward the band. For a moment, the trumpet took her back to that night—the sound of the music, the cool night air, the stench of trash and death in the alley. And Wilson, slumped on the ground in his expensive suit.

Vivian stared down at her hands, still holding Leo's hat, which had fallen still as she thought. His expensive suit and . . .

She glanced up to find Leo still watching her, his eyes concerned. "What is it?" he asked.

Vivian reached out and settled the hat back on his head, tilting it at a jaunty angle while he eyed her in puzzled amusement. "Nothing." She felt one corner of her lips inching up in a satisfied smirk. "Just had an idea, is all." Her smile grew as she heard the brass start to swing their way into a Charleston beat. "Come on. I want another dance."

THIRTEEN

"So, let me see if I've got this right," Bea said, glancing sideways to watch Vivian's face as they made their way down the sidewalk. "You want to . . . investigate the man's hat?"

Vivian caught her own hat just before the wind yanked it off her head, then winced as the motion pulled on her aching palm. With her hand still injured, she had begged off work at Miss Ethel's shop one more day.

"Though if you're not back tomorrow, Miss Kelly, there are plenty of girls who would be happy to take your place," the dressmaker had said coldly.

Avoiding Florence's worried glance, Vivian had left the shop and set out toward Seventh Avenue. The streets along the way were crowded with shop assistants and laborers heading out for the day. Heaped trash spilled out of alleys, the smell competing with the aromas rising from family-run restaurants and breakfast joints. Crowded tenement buildings stretched toward the glaring sky; on the street level below, shopkeepers set out bundles of fabric, piles of cheese, shoes, books, and anything else a person might want to purchase.

It had been easy to find Howard's on Seventh, its front display filled with bespoke hats whose prices she didn't want to imagine. Through the window she had seen two Black shopgirls behind the counter, their hair pinned severely back and their faces turned silently toward the floor as they wrapped an order for a customer.

The customer was chatting with a fourth person, a man in an impeccable suit who Vivian guessed was the owner. He gestured broadly as the two men laughed together, then pulled two cigars from the inside pocket of his jacket and offered them to the customer. The second man took an appreciative sniff before tucking them away.

The whole place oozed masculine energy and wealth, and Vivian knew there was no way she could waltz through the front door and start asking questions.

No, she needed to head around back. And she would do better if she could convince Bea to help.

"That's the idea," Vivian replied. "A name is a start but not much to go on by itself. I saw the name of his tailor on his hat that night, so I want to see what I can find out about him there."

"You're just trying to prove your new fella had nothing to do with this mess," Bea said.

"I'm trying to find out anything I can," Vivian countered, not wanting to admit that her friend might have a point. Judging by the skeptical sniff she received in response, though, Bea wasn't fooled. Vivian sighed. "Sure, Leo's fun, all right? And he's a swell dancer. I'd rather not find out that he's mixed up in . . ." She hesitated, lowering her voice. "Something like this."

The stores were just beginning to close for the evening as the two girls hurried along Seventh Avenue, Vivian trying to ignore her guilt as she thought of the note she had once again left for her sister. But they didn't have long before Bea needed to be at the Nightingale, and the best time to catch one of the shopgirls from Howard's was right after closing.

"And if he is?" Bea asked.

"Then I tell Honor. But she asked me to keep my ears open, not just stick close to Leo. Finding out something about the dead man seems like a good place to start, right? How can I know who might have been involved, or where to start looking at all, if I don't know anything about him?"

"So you want to just stroll up and say . . ." Bea glanced at the traffic and, spotting an opening, dashed across the street. Vivian followed, ignoring the shouts that were hurled after her. "And say what?" Bea continued as they fell in step together once more. "'Do you know anything about this fellow, he was shot dead in an alley, I'm trying to figure out who did it'?"

"Well, if you think that'll work . . ." Vivian snorted at the glare she received. "No, of course not. I'm not trying to figure out who did it. All Honor asked me to do was fish for information."

"It's a hell of a favor to ask."

"It is," Vivian agreed. "You don't have to come."

"Sure I do," Bea said, slanting an exasperated glance at her friend. "They might not tell me much, but they definitely wouldn't tell you anything if you showed up all by your Irish self."

"I'm grateful, you know," Vivian said quietly.

"I know." Bea sighed. "It seemed exciting when I was just listening for gossip. But this . . . it's real, Viv."

"Well, let's pretend it's still just exciting," Vivian said, trying to put her own worries aside. "And no one has to know we had anything to do with it, right? It's just ahead, by the way." Vivian gestured toward the building a few storefronts down the street.

"I still can't believe you touched the dead guy's hat," Bea muttered.

"It was probably the cleanest thing in that alley."

The owner was just locking the front door, the stylish hat he wore an advertisement for his business, as they turned the corner. Walking briskly to avoid drawing attention, they went past him without looking up and turned into the alley behind the row of stores.

The two shopgirls were seated on overturned trash cans, smoking in the quickly fading light and trading jokes and complaints before they headed home for the night. They nodded in a friendly fashion as Bea approached, but fell silent when they saw Vivian behind her.

The younger one, who looked no more than sixteen, was dressed somberly, her legs crossed and one foot jiggling uneasily as she glanced at her companion. The older one was almost as stylishly dressed as Bea, her flannel coat carefully folded up around her waist so no dust or dirt would mar the powder-blue outside. She looked them up and down warily, frowning as her gaze lingered on Vivian.

"Need help with something?" she asked at last, grinding out the stub of her cigarette against the top of the trash can, then opening her purse to dig for another. Bea offered one of her own, which the girl took, though her wary eyes never left Vivian as she lit it.

Vivian nodded, glancing at Bea, who smiled. "My friend has a question she needs some help answering. Got a minute before you head home?"

"A question about hats?" the younger one asked, her voice surprisingly deep for such a small body. "That's all we know about."

"About someone who buys them," Vivian said. "Willard Wilson? I know he shopped at your store at least once."

The older girl blew out another stream of smoke. "We might have seen him come in a time or two. Why?"

"Do you know anything about him?" Vivian asked. She hesitated, seeing their shuttered expressions. "A friend of mine . . ."

"Had a run-in with him? Wants to marry him? Is thinking about becoming his fancy lady?" the younger girl asked, her husky voice sharp and accusatory. "Tell her he's a nasty piece of work and to stay away."

"Shut your mouth, Doris," the older girl said, her pleasant smile an unsettling contrast to her sharp tone. "Don't talk like that. Don't even think like it. Mr. Wilson's a society fellow. You'll get both of us in trouble."

"Not with him," Vivian said quietly, feeling dazed by the exchange.

She could have guessed Wilson was a society fellow from the sharp cut of his suit, but the mix of anger and fear rolling off the girl's words caught her off guard. She exchanged a quick glance with Bea, whose eyes were wide with worry. "He's dead."

"Dead?" The older shopgirl dropped her hand as she stared at them, not seeming to notice the cigarette that fell from her fingers. "You're serious?"

"Yes," said Bea quietly.

"How?" Doris demanded.

"Doris," the older one snapped. "Don't get mixed up in what ain't your business." She stood abruptly, gathering her things and gesturing for her companion to do the same. "If he's dead, then good riddance. And don't come asking us questions anymore. Come on, Doris, your brother'll be wondering where you got to."

"Thanks for your help," Bea said quietly as the two shopgirls moved to leave.

They both shot her quick glances, the older one accusing, as if she thought Bea was being sarcastic; Doris wide-eyed and worried.

"We won't say anything to anyone about you talking to us," Vivian added.

The older one gave her another hard stare, then nodded without saying anything and turned away, Doris scampering to gather her things and hurry after her.

The sun was low enough now that there wasn't much light left in the alley, but it was enough for Vivian to see Bea's wide-eyed worry. "Don't say it," she warned.

"You shouldn't get mixed up in it, Viv," Bea said anyway, the fingers of one hand tapping staccato agitation against her thigh.

"Well, then, be a doll and go tell Honor that for me," Vivian snapped. "I've got a twenty-five-dollar favor to pay off."

"You could say no," Bea pointed out. "You did once."

Vivian threw her a skeptical look. "And if the Nightingale shuts down?"

"There are other spots for dancing in this city." Bea shivered and pulled her coat more tightly around her to ward off the chill of the shadowed alley.

"Not like the Nightingale," Vivian said, her voice cracking a little in a surge of uncomfortable emotion. "And anyway, you work there."

"So?"

"So unless you want to keep waiting for the police to bust in, Honor needs something to satisfy whoever's so upset about Wilson's death. If I can find something out, things'll settle down, and you and everyone else can work in peace."

"Just looking out for me?" Bea's expression softened. "That's good of you, Viv. But there's another reason you're not admitting, you know."

Vivian bristled. "Oh? And what's that?"

"You want to impress Honor."

Vivian rolled her eyes, trying to ignore the way her crossed arms tensed. "If I wanted to impress her, I'd have said yes the first time she asked."

"You want her to think you're smart and worth something. You want *you* to think you're smart and worth something." Bea's quiet voice was sharp as a surgeon's lancet, and Vivian flinched without meaning to. "You've always got something to prove." Seeing the pained expression on her friend's face, Bea sighed. "Just . . . figure out who he was, find out whether that Leo fella had anything to do with him, and leave it at that, okay? You don't need to get mixed up with why someone wanted him dead."

"Sounds like someone wanted him dead because he was a bastard," Vivian said, glancing pointedly in the direction the two shopgirls had gone.

That made Bea snort. "Plenty of bastards out there, and no one's in a hurry to kill them off. There's more to it than that. Come on, I have to get to work. And Honor has something in her office that'll help you out."

t took some persuading, but eventually Danny agreed to unlock the office for Vivian while the staff got set up for the evening. "Just be out of here by nine, okay? Hux has a couple meetings tonight, and I don't need her chewing my head off when she gets in for them."

"Where is she now?" Vivian asked as Bea lugged over a basket of newspapers.

Danny raised an eyebrow. "If you don't know, I don't tell. Hux doesn't like me gossiping about her day."

"And how will she feel about you opening up her office?" Vivian asked, taking the basket from Bea's hands and letting out a small *oof* of surprise at its weight.

"Keep talking and I'll kick you back out," he threatened cheerfully, and Vivian closed her mouth on the rest of her questions. "Out by nine, and lock the door when you leave. Oh, and don't touch anything else. Believe me, Hux'll know."

Vivian didn't doubt it. As Danny and Bea left, shutting the door behind them, she took one long, curious look at the imposing wood desk and the secrets it contained before settling on the floor with her stack of newspapers.

They were society sheets, gossip columns printed about the glamorous lives of New York's wealthy families and famous faces, which Bea told her Honor read regularly. It made sense. Most people who were rich in New York had some connection to bootleg alcohol, either selling it or drinking it, and knowing a thing or two about their personal lives would give Honor an advantage whenever she had to deal with them. It would also let her spot any society darlings who stepped into her club, even if they went to the trouble of keeping their heads down.

Vivian, however, was interested in only one man, and after flipping through five papers she found him splashed across the sixth. She stared at Wilson's smiling black-and-white face for long, eerie minutes before she glanced at the rest of the article and realized it was an obituary.

Startled, she flipped back to the front page of the paper to check the date and discovered it was only a day old. Honor must have just picked it up—but what on earth could have been printed about a man who was shot in a back alley? Vivian propped the paper up on her knees and leaned back against the desk to read.

Willard Wilson was the sort of man whose business seemed to consist of knowing lots of people and appearing at lots of parties, and the list of his business associates' names read like an advertisement for New York royalty. There was nothing written about his people or where he came from—"a New York family" was all the paper said—but he had lately married. And his wife, by the looks of things, was determined to keep whatever seediness had led to his death out of the public eye. In the obituary, his cause of death was listed as a heart ailment. Below the obituary there was a photo of Wilson and his new bride on their wedding day and a short, gossipy article on the couple. Without realizing it, Vivian sat forward as she kept reading.

Hattie Wilson had become that smiling bride less than a year before, and she was from an old family that had made a fortune in canned food and was probably still making a fortune in imports of the bottled variety. Her own people were dead, and her younger sister, Myrtle, had lived with the Wilsons until very recently.

> We expect that Miss Myrtle, the article ran, who only one month ago left New York for an exclusive school upstate, will return in time for her brother-in-law's funeral. We can only hope that she will bring the sisterly comfort that Mrs. Wilson will need during this trying time— and, perhaps, for several months yet to come.

Vivian let the paper drop and leaned back against the desk, frowning. What could Wilson, from all appearances a society guy with prestigious business partners and a perfect blushing bride, have to do with a back-alley meeting? How was he involved with the two toughs who had cornered Danny?

The sound of the doorknob turning momentarily drove every thought of Willard Wilson from her mind, and Vivian stared at it, too surprised to even think of moving. But instead of coming face-to-face with an irate Honor Huxley, she found herself staring at Leo, who paused on the threshold, eyebrows raised, before he laughed and pulled the door shut behind him.

"You look like you're about to beat me over the head with that and do a runner," he said, nodding at the paper that she had half raised without realizing it. "What's got you so jumpy, sweetheart? Worried Ms. Huxley was about to find you?"

"What are you doing here?" Vivian demanded, trying to slow her breathing to a more normal pace as she dropped the paper so the picture of Wilson was facing down.

"Trying to find you, of course."

"How'd you know where I was?"

"Danny told me." Leo glanced around the otherwise empty office, his eyebrows rising once more as he strolled toward her. "What exactly are you doing in here? Going through Ms. Huxley's things?"

"Of course not," Vivian said quickly as he sat down against the desk, his shoulder pressed against hers. The weight and warmth of it would have been pleasant if she weren't so nervous. "Just reading the paper. Got too hot out there, you know. But I'd be up for a twirl on the dance floor if you want."

"Sounds swell," Leo said, and before she could stop him he plucked the paper out of her hand. He was about to toss it into the basket with the others when he glanced down at the page with the obituary.

Vivian held her breath. He hadn't seemed interested in the dead man before. But if his face gave anything away when he saw the picture of Wilson . . .

"Can't resist the society gossip?" he teased, glancing up, his expression still as open and friendly as ever.

Relief washed over Vivian, though she tried not to show it. "I work for a dressmaker," she said, thinking quickly. "I like to keep up with the clothes."

"Makes sense," Leo said. "Though an obituary's maybe a morbid way to . . ." He trailed off. "Wilson? Why is that name familiar?"

"Is it?" Vivian asked, trying to sound casual as she watched his face, though her heart was racing.

"Yeah." Leo gave her a puzzled look. "Because that's the fellow you asked me about last night. Isn't it?"

Vivian tried to think of an answer, but her mind came up blank.

"You wanted to know if I knew a dead guy?" Leo frowned. "Who was he?"

Vivian stared at him, trying desperately to think of something to say. But then she realized how unconcerned he looked—confused, yes, but not angry or wary. Not even tense. None of the emotions she would have expected if he'd actually had anything to do with Wilson's death.

"Far as I heard, some bootlegger who showed up here on the wrong night," she said at last. "I thought maybe all you types knew each other."

Leo looked back at the picture, frowning in thought, and Vivian couldn't help feeling reassured by how seriously he was considering it. Her heart gave a little leap of relief as he shook his head once more. "I never saw his face before. And if I ever met him, he definitely wasn't using that name."

"Do guys like you often use fake names?" Vivian asked, trying not to look too interested in the answer. "How do I know Leo Green is your real one, then?"

He raised a brow. "I could take you to meet my dad if you want," he suggested. "Or you could just ask Danny."

Vivian laughed, the knot of tension in her chest beginning to loosen.

Honor had asked her to keep an eye on Leo, yes, to find out if there was any reason more than just coincidence that he had appeared at the Nightingale the night after Willard Wilson's murder. But she had admitted she didn't know if there was anything behind her suspicions. Leo was fun and charming and a great dancer, and his smile gave her a delicious, fluttery feeling. And given how unconcerned he seemed about Wilson, Vivian was inclined to believe him when he said he hadn't known the man.

That didn't mean she was off the hook for Honor's favor. But it might mean that she could just enjoy Leo's company without worrying about ulterior motives.

She smiled at him, feeling relieved. "Well, I hope you're more careful than that Wilson fella was about where you spend your nights."

"I think they're mostly going to be spent here for a while." His smile grew sheepish. "You can probably guess why."

"You expect me to believe you keep coming back here just to see me?" she said, rolling her eyes and trying to sound unimpressed.

"Is that so hard to believe?" Leo asked, leaning forward a little.

Vivian leaned toward him too, and for a moment she saw his gaze drop toward her lips before it jumped back up to meet hers. "Not a bit hard to believe," Vivian said, smiling at his surprised expression. Their faces were only inches apart, and she dropped her voice until it was barely above a whisper. "I'm *very* likable."

"Far as I can tell, your Ms. Huxley thinks so," Leo said quietly. Vivian was about to pull away, but he put a careful hand over hers. "I can't really blame her for that," he murmured. "And I think you must like her a bit too. But here's the thing, Vivian." He leaned forward again, until Vivian was sure he was going to kiss her, then stopped, so close she could almost feel his lips moving. "I think you're starting to enjoy spending time with me too. And you know what happens when you give a fella reason to hope?"

Vivian bit her lip. "What?"

"He hopes." Leo sat back slowly, smiling. "And he asks you to leave these boring gossip papers and come dance with him."

The sudden chill where the heat of his body had been made Vivian long to go after him. But if he was playing games, she could too. She pursed her lips, pretending to consider his offer. "All right. Since you *are* a swell dancer."

"I'm pretty darn handsome too," he said, winking.

Vivian laughed at the naked confidence, but she didn't argue with the statement as she glanced at the clock on the wall. "Time for us to get out of here, anyway, if we don't want Honor to catch us poking around her things."

"Hey, you're the one doing the poking," Leo protested. "I'm just keeping you company."

"I'd tell her it was your idea," Vivian said, unable to resist teasing him.

He pretended to look hurt. "You'd do such a terrible thing?"

Vivian shrugged. "Maybe I'm a terrible girl."

"Terribly pretty," Leo said, grinning up at her as he leaned over to let his head loll against her shoulder.

Vivian pushed him away, ignoring his yelp as he lost his balance and toppled to the floor. She began shuffling the papers into a stack to tuck them back into their basket.

"I hope you don't think you can get all—" she began, then fell silent as one of the photos of Willard and Hattie Wilson caught her eye.

"Get all . . ." Leo prompted, but Vivian wasn't listening.

Eagerly, she grabbed several more issues that had mentioned the Wilsons, flipping through the pages for photos. This time around, she ignored the faces, staring instead at the dresses that Hattie was wearing.

She recognized them. Some of them she had even done the beading on herself.

They were all dresses made in Miss Ethel's shop.

If Hattie Wilson bought her clothes from Miss Ethel, then odds were she had placed another order in the last two days. A woman whose husband had just died needed new clothes. And Miss Ethel always had dresses delivered directly to her customers' homes.

"Is something wrong?"

Vivian glanced up, startled, then quickly shoved the papers back into the basket. For a moment, she had forgotten that he was still there. "Just fine," she said, picking up the basket and returning it to its spot behind Honor's desk. "Had an idea, is all. I'll talk to my boss about it tomorrow."

"Tell me more about being a dressmaker," he said, holding out his hand.

Vivian didn't object as he led her from the office, though she remembered to turn the lock before she left so that the door latched behind them. "It's not that interesting. I spend my whole day hunched over fancy clothes for rich people." She glanced sideways at him as they went down the stairs. "What do you do?"

"Used to do illegal things in Chicago," he said, laughing at her surprised expression. "What, did you expect me to lie about that? You already guessed, so there's no point pretending."

"And now?"

"I actually came back to New York to work for my uncle. My dad's retired out on Long Island, and he's thrilled to have me here again."

"Is your uncle a bootlegger too?" Vivian asked, worry creeping over her again.

But Leo shook his head. "Far from it," he said. "Takes some getting used to, I can tell you that. But I'm glad to be back in the city." His face softened. "I missed my dad while I was in Chicago."

The quiet, easy way that he said it, as if he took for granted both having a father and the feeling of missing each other, sent a spike of envy through Vivian's chest. To cover up the feeling—it wasn't Leo's fault he had family who wanted him around and she didn't—she laughed. "You're a big softie."

He winked at her as they reached the end of the hall. "Don't tell anyone."

The surge of heat and noise as they walked into the dance hall put a stop to any further conversation. The trumpet was wailing, the band leader practically dancing on the stand, and the floor was a whirl of limbs and laughter.

Honor watched it all from her place by the bar, hands in the pockets of her trousers and her eyes glowing with satisfaction as she surveyed her club. She caught Vivian's eye for a moment, then dropped her gaze to where Leo still held her hand. Vivian met her eyes defiantly, and a corner of Honor's mouth lifted in a half smile before she gestured them toward the dance floor.

Leo had caught the silent exchange, and as he pulled Vivian toward him, one arm going around her back, he murmured, "I hope you're not just using me to make her jealous."

For a moment, Vivian felt a surge of guilt. But even if he was being honest about what brought him back to New York, she could guess that he was keeping other secrets. So what if she had a few of her own, too?

"I think Honor's got enough on her mind without worrying about who I'm dancing with," she said as Leo settled her still-bandaged left hand carefully on his shoulder. It didn't hurt too badly at the moment, but she appreciated his care. "If I'm using you for anything, it's those talented feet of yours. I love finding a fella who can keep up."

He laughed. "Then I guess I'd better not disappoint you."

He didn't. Vivian still wasn't sure whether trusting him was a good idea, but there was no reason not to enjoy the time they did have together. It was easier to relax into his arms now that she was starting to believe that he had nothing to do with Wilson's death. And they danced as if they had been made to go together. Vivian was so caught up that she didn't notice Bea trying to catch her eye until the music flourished to an end.

It took some finagling to detach herself from Leo, but he was enough of a gentleman that when she pointed out girls who looked like they would appreciate a partner, he couldn't ignore them. Once he was gone, Vivian was able to make her way over to the corner of the room, where Bea was gathering glasses off a table that had recently emptied out. Dropping into one of the chairs, Vivian reached down to loosen the ribbons on her dancing shoes and wiggle her toes. "What is it?"

"I asked around with the other girls who work here, real careful of course, to see if any of them knew him," Bea said, keeping her voice down as she continued to work.

Vivian sat up straighter. *Wilson?* she mouthed. Bea nodded, and Vivian bit her lip. "Any takers?"

"He wasn't a regular here, but we knew that. Eliza thought he might'a been in here once or twice before. At least it sounds like the same person. Couldn't exactly show them a photo. But then . . ." Bea gestured with her chin. "I think I heard one of them mention his name."

Vivian turned slowly, glancing over the entire room so that the men at the table Bea indicated wouldn't realize she was looking at them. There were four or five of them—she glanced away too quickly to be sure—all cheerful and loud and young. "Do you know which one it was?" she asked, keeping her voice low.

Bea shook her head, straightening and lifting her tray. "I was just walking past. I think they were making a toast."

Vivian nodded, considering. If Leo was off the list, that meant she needed to find someone else to go on it. "Well, if one of them knew him, odds are the rest of them knew him too. Guess I'll go ask Jimmy for a dance and see what I can get out of him."

Bea paused, brows rising. "You know one of them?"

Vivian nodded, already reaching down to retie her ribbons. "Pretty Jimmy Allen, the one with the sandy hair. He's here a lot. We've danced before. And he loves to gossip."

"You get around, don't you?"

Vivian glanced up and shrugged. "I like knowing folks. Wish me luck, will you?"

"Don't get yourself killed." Bea said it like a joke, but they both knew it wasn't, not anymore.

Vivian took a deep breath and sauntered over to the table of laughing boys. "Hey, Jimmy."

They all looked over at her, and Jimmy Allen beamed. "Vivian, pretty girl, it's been an age! Want to have a drink with me and the fellas?" His friends bellowed their approval and gestured for Vivian to sit. But Jimmy grinned as the band struck up a friendly, bouncy foxtrot. "Never mind, I know you'd rather dance than drink. Let's go shake a leg."

Vivian took the hand he held out, then glanced over her shoulder at the remaining men, who were grumbling about men who kept pretty girls to themselves. "Feel free to buy me a drink later," she suggested as Jimmy led her onto the floor.

Jimmy laughed as they settled into the dance, glancing briefly at the bandaged hand she settled on his shoulder. "You okay there?" he asked.

"Raid souvenir," Vivian said, raising her brows and smiling mysteriously, as if the night had been an adventure and not a terrifying ordeal.

"Oh, you're a jailbird now, are you?" he asked, holding her in a light and easy lead. "Gonna get too tough for a nice boy like me."

"Nothing wrong with nice boys," Vivian said, her voice friendly while her mind cast around for a way to introduce Wilson into the conversation without it being too obvious. "You missed it, then? I haven't seen you around in a while."

"Been out of the city for a little bit. You know how it is when the family needs a getaway."

"Oh sure," Vivian lied. "We missed you, though. All your pals have two left feet compared to you."

"Those clodhoppers?" Jimmy grinned, glancing over his shoulder at the table he had just left behind. "They're here for Ms. Huxley's excellent booze. I'm here for the excuse to hold pretty girls in my arms."

He winked, and Vivian laughed. Jimmy was one of the few men she'd danced with who had never made a pass at her, so his teasing didn't bother her at all. But there was an opening there in his words, and she decided to take it, even if it felt a little forced.

Mentally crossing her fingers for luck, she said, "I met a fella the other night who I think was a friend of yours. He seemed like he was here to get his arms around a girl, too."

"What was his name?"

"Not sure," Vivian said, warming up to her lie. "Um . . . William? Wilson? Not sure whether he was giving me his first, last, or fake, but he said he knew you."

"Tall fella, light hair, crooked nose?"

"Sounds like him. Seemed like he could be a decent enough dancer, but I haven't seen him around anymore to find out." Vivian fought the nervous urge to hold her breath.

Jimmy shook his head. "And you won't see him around again, I'm afraid."

"Did he get kicked out? He did seem a little handsy," Vivian said, shaking her head. "Ms. Huxley isn't a fan of handsy."

"Actually . . ." Jimmy hesitated. "He croaked."

Vivian stumbled, skipping a step on purpose and letting her eyes go wide with surprise. "Oh hell, I'm sorry. He *was* a friend of yours, then?"

"Wilson was his name. And yeah, I guess you could say he was a friend. Dined in the same circles, if you know what I mean. But he liked places to gamble mostly." Jimmy shook his head, looking sad and admiring at the same time. "Liked to play high because he knew he'd never have to pay. Wilson could wiggle out of anything, he knew that many people. Going to be a less interesting world without him."

"Surprised I met him, then," Vivian said, hesitating. She wasn't sure how much prodding she could do without seeming too interested. "Not much in the way of gambling here."

"Oh, he'd go anywhere he could find a good time," Jimmy said, smiling a little. "Like any of us. We were actually just toasting him a little while ago, me and the boys."

"He was a good friend, then?" Vivian said, patting Jimmy's shoulder. His casual regret made her think that he wasn't too broken up about Wilson's death, even if he had liked the man. And he didn't seem to know there was anything suspicious about how that death had happened.

Jimmy shrugged. "He was a fun friend."

"Well, I'm sorry I called him handsy, then," Vivian said. She liked Jimmy, and she didn't want to upset him. "Hope you weren't offended."

"Oh, sweetheart, I'm not offended or surprised. Wilson didn't have much of what you'd call a type, but he did like pretty girls with dark hair," Jimmy said, laughing as he ran a finger under the edge of Vivian's bob. She pretended to laugh along, but underneath her stomach turned over. She didn't want to hear that she might have been the dead man's preferred kind of girl. "In fact, I bet if he was here, then he was following a particular girl. Poor Wilson wasn't used to hearing no, but she wasn't interested in making herself available."

Vivian could feel her pulse hammering at her neck and wrists. "Poor fella," she said, pretending a sympathetic pout. "She hangs out here, you say?"

"Sure, she does." Jimmy gestured with his chin as they turned around the corner of the dance floor.

Vivian followed his gaze to where a familiar, glamorous brunette was laughing in the arms of her partner. Her stomach turned over again. "Mags knew your friend?"

Jimmy laughed. "She also knew his wife, which is why she wouldn't give him the time of day. She finds her way around, does Mags." He winked at Vivian, a broad grin spreading across his pretty face. "But none of us tell her dad that. I think you should let a girl have some fun, right? And the rest of the fellas who know her are hoping to be the lucky one when she's finally old enough to get married. They won't get her riled up if they don't have to."

Vivian wondered why it had taken her so long to realize that Mags was a society girl. One look at her dresses should have given it away. But if Mags was part of that glamorous world, why hadn't Vivian seen her name or photo in any of the society pages?

"You all right there, Viv?"

Jimmy's puzzled tone pulled her wandering thoughts back in, and Vivian turned quickly back to her own partner. As the implication of his last few words sank in, she gave him a questioning look. "But you're not one of those fellas hoping to marry her, are you, Jimmy?"

He smiled as if it didn't matter, unable to shrug while they were still dancing. "I'm not the marrying type. And I've got an older brother, so I can get away with avoiding it."

There was a softness to the statement, a careful admission that was there if you were paying attention. She glanced over at his friends, still drinking raucously at their own table, and gave Jimmy a gentle smile as she met his eyes again. "Not everyone is," she said quietly, squeezing his shoulder with her fingertips so the gesture wouldn't pull the cut on her palm. "I'm only halfway to being the marrying type myself."

He smiled back, then laughed, breaking the moment. "Well, Mags certainly is. She'd keep every fellow in New York on a string if she could. Wilson was determined to catch her eye. Poor fellow ran out of time, though."

"Guess he was the sort who didn't take no for an answer?"

"Who takes no for an answer?" Jimmy said, rolling his eyes. "He'd have brought her around eventually."

"What if she didn't want to be brought around?" Vivian said quietly.

Jimmy laughed again as the music flourished to a stop, not noticing the seriousness of her question. "Every girl wants to be brought around. You just have to know what to say." He winked. "Thanks for the dance, Viv. You look swell tonight."

"You too, Jimmy," she said. She watched him saunter back to his friends and accept a glass of booze. She thought of the two shopgirls at Howard's on Seventh, remembered the cold warning in their voices, and shivered.

FOURTEEN

"This is most disappointing, Vivian."

Every inch of Miss Ethel, from her crossed arms to her pursed lips, was tight with disapproval. One foot tapped while she looked Vivian up and down, as though she had discovered something unpleasant crawling across her shop floor. Behind her, the other girls moved as silently as possible to avoid drawing her attention.

Vivian could see Florence, already settled at her worktable and tense with anxiety, her brows drawn together with anger that she would never risk acting on.

"I'm real disappointed too, ma'am. I know how lucky I am to have this job," Vivian said.

She had checked the ledger of deliveries as soon as she arrived, stealing two seconds while Miss Ethel's back was turned. If she was going to find out anything about Willard Wilson, she needed to be the one making those deliveries.

Vivian knew the best way to get what she wanted was to show Miss Ethel exactly what *she* wanted: a girl who was humble and eager to please. She dropped both her voice and her expression, biting her lip as she met her employer's eyes. "But I just don't think I can sew anything today."

Miss Ethel sighed, casting her eyes heavenward. "Unwrap it, if you please. I'll be the judge of whether you can work today or not."

Vivian's jaw tightened, but she caught the warning shake of Florence's head in time. Her sister was right. Rent was due in ten days, and she couldn't afford to say no. And if she wanted Miss Ethel to agree to a change of duties, she had to play along, no matter how humiliated she felt. "Yes, ma'am," she said, fumbling with one hand to untie the bandage.

Out of the corner of her eye, she saw Florence half rise to come help before another seamstress pulled her back down. Vivian ignored her sister, not wanting to direct Miss Ethel's disapproval anywhere but toward herself. After a moment, she was able to unwrap her hand and hold it up for inspection.

Miss Ethel grabbed Vivian's wrist with two pinching fingers, turning the hand left and right in a careful inspection. The angry red swelling hadn't gone away completely, and it cut an ugly swath across Vivian's palm, starting just below her thumb.

Without warning, Miss Ethel grabbed Vivian's thumb and bent it forward, and Vivian yelped and tried to pull away as pain shot through her whole hand and up her wrist. Blood welled out of one end of the cut, squeezed out by the abrupt motion. Miss Ethel made a noise of distaste, dropping her hands immediately and pulling out her handkerchief to wipe them off.

Vivian blinked back tears, her jaw clenched tightly against pain and fury as she wrapped the bandage around her palm again.

"Very well, no sewing today," the shop owner said, not even a bit apologetic as she turned back to the counter that divided the seamstresses from the shop. Some stores tucked their workers away in the back room, but Miss Ethel wanted every customer to see that clothes in her establishment were sewn with painstaking care by girls who were grateful to have the work.

"But that doesn't mean I can't work," Vivian said quickly. It was hard to keep the nervousness out of her voice, but she figured that would be okay. Everyone would think she was worried about keeping her job. "I'm sure you have important customers expecting deliveries. Maybe I could handle those today?"

Miss Ethel paused. Vivian held her breath, trying not to look too eager. "That is a very good idea," Miss Ethel said finally, and Vivian sagged with relief. "You taking them will save me the cost of a courier."

As she spoke, she stacked five flat dress boxes, each two feet long, on the counter, their destinations inked on top in her rigid handwriting.

Vivian eyed the small tower. "May I take a cab, ma'am?"

Miss Ethel raised her eyebrows. "If you can pay for it, certainly," she said. "If any need alterations, pin them at the lady's home. Your sister can sew them at home tonight."

"Yes, ma'am." Vivian waited until her employer's back was turned, then pulled the boxes toward her and checked the addresses. At the very bottom of the pile was the one she had been hoping for.

Mrs. Willard Wilson (Henrietta)
925 Fifth Avenue
(mourning gowns, 3, check hem and shoulders for fit)

"Is something the matter, Vivian?" Miss Ethel snapped.

Vivian jumped. "No, ma'am," she said quickly. She stacked the boxes so the one for Mrs. Wilson was on the bottom, giddy with excitement that her gamble had paid off. "Thank you for your understanding."

The shop owner sniffed. "I hope I am always a model of Christian virtue to you girls, who have so little of that sort of example," she said, casting an eye over her workers, all of them bent over their sewing to avoid meeting her gaze. "Now hurry along."

"Yes, ma'am," Vivian said, her mind already jumping ahead to the mansion on Fifth Avenue where Willard Wilson's widow was waiting for her.

M rs. Wilson is attending to some household affairs, but she should be at leisure to see you in fifteen minutes or so," the housekeeper said as she led Vivian upstairs. "As you are delivering her mourning clothes, I assume there is no need to explain the situation?" She glanced over her shoulder as she spoke, her beady gaze skewering Vivian.

She didn't want to seem like the sort of girl who was intimidated when surrounded by so much suffocating opulence. But she also knew there were moments when it was better to play along with what was expected—especially if she wanted to find out anything. Vivian nodded and tried to look suitably cowed. "I understand it was Mr. Wilson who passed away. I'm sorry for Mrs. Wilson's loss."

"It has been a difficult time for her, certainly," the housekeeper said, resuming her climb while Vivian hurried to keep up. "I trust you will be quiet and respectful, and not pry into Mrs. Wilson's personal business."

"Wouldn't dream of prying," Vivian said, eyes wide as she was ushered into an upstairs parlor. She drew as much bubbly excitement into her voice as she could manage as she exclaimed, "Lord almighty, I hope the will don't say she has to move out in a hurry. I wouldn't ever want to leave here."

The room was a stark contrast to the chill grandeur of the rest of the house. Two of the four walls were lined with bookshelves, and one was entirely made up of windows overlooking the bright leaves of Central Park. In front of one window, a writing desk was set to catch the best light, and the rest of the room was furnished with deep sofas and chairs. Around the windows, velvet curtains dyed a stunning sky blue puddled to the floor. It was a room made for leisure and luxury, and Vivian stared at it with hungry awe.

The housekeeper smiled at her admiration. "Fortunately, Mrs. Wilson inherits the house outright after the death of her husband and need not move at all—a great comfort to her in such a terrible time, you can be sure." Crossing the room, the housekeeper straightened a full-length mirror that stood in one corner, then pulled out a handkerchief to rub a spot that smudged its surface. "This room was furnished specifically for her and Miss Myrtle."

"That's her sister, right?" Vivian played the role of a gossip column–loving shopgirl, though her admiration of the sitting room was genuine. "I read in the paper that she'll be coming back to keep her sister company." She glanced over just in time to catch the housekeeper's reflection in the mirror and was surprised to see the woman frown—not at her, but as if she were in the middle of an unpleasant thought.

A moment later, though, the expression was smoothed away and the housekeeper turned back to her. "Yes. Miss Myrtle will be returning from school shortly."

"I imagine she'll be needing a dress or two as well, then," said Vivian, setting the box down on one of the sofas and carefully unwrapping its contents. "Which we'll be happy to do. I'll need to come back a second time, anyway, once the final alterations are done."

The housekeeper nodded. "I will let Mrs. Wilson know you are here. And don't touch anything while you wait," she added before departing, her footfalls muffled instantly in the plush hallway carpeting.

Vivian's fingers itched to explore, to examine every book and crystal knickknack and priceless piece of art. But it wasn't worth the risk. She finished laying out the dresses and waited, standing with her hands clasped and toes tapping.

After five minutes, she decided it wouldn't do any harm to simply walk around the room. The paintings that adorned the walls were beautiful, even if she didn't know a thing about who painted them or what they showed. She let her gaze linger over the shelves of books— she wasn't much of a reader, but she thought that given a chance she could enjoy the activity.

After she had explored the entire room with her eyes and feet—and the clock on the writing desk said twenty more minutes had passed—Vivian gave up and settled into the comfortable sofa. Everything in the room was decorated with perfect taste, but there were no personal touches anywhere. Even the desk was pristine, with every scrap of paper tucked away, and only a small crystal clock, a case for a fountain pen, and a single book left out.

Standing and stepping closer, Vivian discovered that the book was actually an album, open to the image of a family picnic. There were three people in it—a woman, a man, and a girl—captured lounging in the sun. The woman was just looking up from her book to glance at the other two. Even though her hat shaded most of her face, Vivian recognized Hattie Wilson from the newspapers. Next to her sat the girl, scowling at the camera, and there was enough of a resemblance between them that Vivian guessed she was the younger sister, Myrtle. On Myrtle's other side was Willard Wilson, one arm slung over his new sister's shoulder, gazing at his wife and laughing.

Vivian stared at the three figures. The young bride and the grumpy girl felt easy enough to label and tuck away. But the Wilson the photo captured seemed so different from the man she had been expecting—the bootlegger, the bastard, the one involved in something shady—that she stared at his face for a long time.

The tinkling chime of the desk clock made her jump guiltily, as if someone might have come in and found her prying. Glancing down, she saw that it was after one o'clock. Thirty minutes had passed, and there was still no sign of Mrs. Wilson.

Hoping to find a servant who could tell her how much longer she'd be waiting, Vivian peered out the door. The house was oppressively silent, but after a moment she heard faint voices from downstairs.

She took a few steps toward the sound, then froze at the top of the staircase, not sure what to do, as the voices spiked in anger and two people who were definitely not servants appeared.

The first person who stalked into view was a woman in a long silk robe, masses of glistening brown hair tumbled around her shoulders.

The man following her snapped a sharp "Don't!" as he grabbed her arm, pulling her back around to face him.

They glared at each other, too preoccupied to look around the hall, and in that moment Vivian was able to see their faces clearly. She recognized Hattie Wilson, the china-doll prettiness of her photos more striking in person. And to her surprise—surprise that kept her frozen in place, even though she knew she would catch hell if they saw her—she recognized the man as well. It was Roy, whom she had last seen the night Willard Wilson was murdered.

"My husband just died, you idiot, you cannot be here," Hattie Wilson hissed as she pushed out of Roy's arms. "How do you think it's going to look?"

"My God, you can be such a hypocrite," Roy said, grabbing her arm once more. Both of them spoke in angry, urgent whispers that barely carried up the stairs to where Vivian strained to hear. "Anyone can guess you're relieved that he's gone."

"My God, you can be such an idiot," Hattie countered, starting to sound more exhausted than angry. "You cannot say things like that where someone might overhear."

"Who's going to hear?" Roy pulled her into his arms once more, his voice dropping as he brushed the hair out of her face. "We're in your house."

"I told you not to touch me," Hattie snapped, shaking off his embrace. "I have a husband to bury, and my sister is coming home, and—"

"And you need someone to take care of you," Roy said, smiling his Coca-Cola ad smile as he reached for her again. "Let me take care of you, Hattie."

"And you still don't understand, Roy. I can take care of myself just fine. In fact—"

Hattie had started to turn away from him as she spoke. Vivian whirled away from the couple, so quickly she almost lost her balance, and peered down one of the upstairs hallways as if she were looking for something, praying they wouldn't guess she had been able to hear them.

"Are you the dressmaker?"

Hattie's voice carried much more clearly than her whispers had, and Vivian turned around, surprised to find the young widow already walking toward the staircase and leaving Roy behind. If she hadn't been watching them, Vivian would have never guessed they had been arguing, or that Hattie had been in his arms mere moments before.

"Yes, ma'am," she said, eyes fixed on Hattie. She could feel Roy watching her, but he had only ever seen her dolled up and in the dim light of the Nightingale. Hopefully he wouldn't recognize the girl from the dance hall as the dressmaker visiting the Fifth Avenue mansion. "I wasn't sure if you were still able to see me today, so I was looking for someone—"

"I'm ready now," Hattie said. "Mr. Carlton, you can show yourself out." Already halfway up the stairs, she barely even bothered to look over her shoulder as she said it.

Out of the corner of her eye, Vivian could see Roy stiffen and start forward. "A moment please, Mrs. Wilson," he called out, and Vivian could practically hear him clenching his jaw as he spoke. "Just a moment of your time. It's important."

Hattie Wilson paused at the top of the stairs, one hand tightening on the bannister. For barely a second, her face lit with irritation. And then her features settled as if she had wiped them clean, a bland, polite, unfeeling mask. "I'll be right with you, Mr. Carlton." The expression was more than just a lack of distress. She looked as though she had no feelings at all, as if she were indeed the pretty, lifeless doll that she had appeared in the newspaper photographs.

Vivian held back a shudder, wondering what could teach a woman to bury herself so deep that she disappeared entirely.

"Wait in the sitting room," Hattie Wilson said to her. "I'll be with you in a moment."

Vivian did as she was told, her mind racing. That interaction had been plain enough. Mags's fellow Roy—Roy Carlton, Vivian thought, filing the name away—knew Hattie Wilson on more than friendly terms, either from before her marriage or during.

It could have been nothing more than wishful thinking on his part, love or lust from a distance that he felt free to act on with Wilson gone. Hattie, for her part, was clearly ready to be done with Roy. Or at least she didn't want him coming by and starting gossip. But for some reason she hadn't insisted on sending him away at that last moment.

Vivian didn't have time to start guessing why. Whatever Roy had wanted to say, it hadn't taken long, and Hattie followed her into the room only a minute later. She wasn't bothering with her company face, not for a shopgirl, so her weariness was visible as she paused at the threshold, then sighed and yanked the door shut behind her.

"Thank you for waiting, Miss . . ."

"Kelly, ma'am. Vivian Kelly. And it was no trouble."

"My housekeeper tells me you need to do additional fitting?"

"Yes, ma'am," Vivian said, lifting the first day dress. "I'll just check the shoulders and pin the length where you want it."

Hattie sighed. "Very well." She took the dress from Vivian and crossed to the mirror, dropping her wrapper to puddle on the floor behind her.

Vivian didn't bother averting her eyes any more than Hattie tried to hide her silk undergarments and stockings while she shimmied the garment over her head. While she was working, bodies might as well have been dress forms. She retrieved a packet of pins from inside the box and knelt in front of the mirror.

"I assume you will finish them before you leave today?" Hattie asked as she settled into stillness. Only her fingers fluttered a little as she held them out from her body.

"I'm afraid I can't be the one to sew them." Vivian held up her bandaged hand in explanation. "But we'll have them back to you as quick as can be." She hesitated, keeping her eyes fixed on the pins as she added, "I know it's not a situation that lends to waiting much. I'm terribly sorry for your loss, Mrs. Wilson."

Hattie's hands clenched for a moment, then relaxed, and she nodded. "Thank you."

"Hope you don't mind me saying so," Vivian said. "But he seemed like quite the gentleman." Vivian held her breath, keeping her eyes on the hem she was pinning. Plenty of women got chatty with their dressmakers, same as they would with a servant—as if not being part of the same social circle meant they would never have a chance to repeat the gossip to anyone. If she was lucky, Hattie Wilson would be that type.

Out of the corner of her eye, Vivian saw Hattie grow very still before she glanced down. "Did you ever meet him?"

"Oh no, not personally," Vivian said quickly, eyes wide, still playing the part she had with the housekeeper. "I saw your pictures in the paper, though. The columns love to write about you."

Mrs. Wilson made a sound that might have been a laugh if it hadn't sounded so bitter. "They did, that's for certain. I'm sure they have plenty to say now, though I haven't read any of it."

"All real sad stuff, and real respectable. They didn't say what happened, though, him going so young," Vivian said. She held her breath, waiting to see what response her lie would provoke. For a moment, she thought Hattie wasn't going to answer. Vivian didn't dare look up.

"A heart ailment," Hattie said at last, her voice cold. "This one's fine."

Vivian stood and helped her slide off the gown without disturbing the pins. "You must miss him terribly," she said, folding the dress and setting it aside.

"I must," Hattie agreed, her voice blank of any emotion as she turned back to the mirror.

Vivian didn't press. She didn't need to. Any mourning Hattie Wilson felt for her husband clearly was limited to social symbols only. What had caused the romance to fade so quickly? Or had she known, even when she married him, what sort of man he was?

And if she knew he was a bastard with a wandering eye, did that mean she also knew what he'd been up to that got him killed?

Vivian checked the fit on the second dress—it wouldn't need alterations—in silence. When she was finishing the third and final gown, she decided it was safe to risk another comment.

"Will your sister need mourning dresses as well? Your housekeeper couldn't say when she'd be back from school."

She had thought bringing up someone other than Wilson would get Hattie talking, but she could tell instantly that she had misjudged. Hattie didn't move, but every inch of her expression shut down as if she had slammed a door. And then an instant later, so quickly Vivian thought she might have imagined it, the stoniness was gone, replaced by indifference. "I can't say," Hattie said briskly. "Take this one off, please."

"Girls change so much at school," Vivian said agreeably as she eased the day dress over her customer's head and bent down to retrieve the wrapper—silk, she could tell, even before she touched it—from where it lay on the floor. "Here you are, Mrs. Wilson. You just let me know about your sister. Meantime, we'll get these back to you quick as can be."

Hattie nodded, her expression faraway as she slid her arms into the sleeves and belted the sash with quick, sharp movements. Abruptly, she shook her head and reached into the wrapper's pocket. "For your trouble today," she said, holding out a quarter. "You may go."

———

Vivian heaved a sigh of relief as the door to the Wilson mansion closed behind her, the spring air making her feel suddenly lightheaded. There was something oppressive about that house, something ugly that all its luxury and grandeur couldn't hide. Even the chilly beauty of the little sitting room had left her uneasy. And Hattie Wilson . . . Vivian shivered as she pulled her coat closed and headed downtown.

She walked briskly along, head ducked against the wind and the box with Hattie's dresses tucked under one arm. There was no point in going back to the dress shop, and she had a twenty-five-cent tip in her pocket and worn-out feet. Feeling guilty, Vivian turned her steps toward the closest subway line. The New York Municipal was just a few blocks away, and it would take her half of the way home.

The ticket cost five cents, and using her feet would have cost nothing. But Vivian was too tired to care, and her arms and hand ached from carrying dress boxes all day, and anyway that still made twenty cents left over. Tucking herself into a corner seat, she stared unseeing at the swaying, jerking car.

She had seen women trapped in miserable lives. In spite of the tight rein she kept on herself, Hattie Wilson had all the fluttering determination of someone who had just been set free and planned to stay that way. Roy Carlton might have other plans—and how far might he have gone in pursuit of those plans?—but Hattie Wilson had clearly made up her mind.

But there had been something odd—not when she talked about her husband, that anger was reasonable enough. It had been there when the conversation turned to her sister. It was the same oddness that Vivian had noticed in the housekeeper's expression when she caught it reflected in the mirror.

Something about Miss Myrtle wasn't right. But for the life of her, Vivian couldn't guess what it might be. For a moment the wild thought crossed her mind that perhaps Myrtle had killed her brother-in-law. But that made no sense. She had been at a school upstate where, if the papers were to be trusted, Willard Wilson provided for her complete financial support. And in the photograph that Vivian had seen, Wilson had looked every inch the indulgent older brother.

No, there was something else about Myrtle that was setting the household on edge . . .

Vivian glanced up, jerked out of her reverie as the car pulled up to a platform and she scrambled to her feet. She had been so distracted she'd missed her stop.

She had to hurry to make it off the train, and once she was on the platform she was caught up in the buffeting crowd, trying to protect the dress box as she made her way up to the street. She was a few blocks south of home, but she hadn't missed it by too much. Grumbling to herself, Vivian set off, cutting across streets and between crowded buildings to take the most direct route there, her mind still back on Fifth Avenue.

She was still several blocks away when the rain began to fall, a fitful, grimy drizzle that spattered the pavement while sullen clouds rumbled overhead.

"Damn it," Vivian muttered, wiping rain out of her eyes as she glared up at the sky.

Around her, the few stragglers that were still out dashed for whatever cover they could reach. Vivian clutched the dress box against her chest, weighing her options. She was only a few blocks from home; as long as the rain didn't get too heavy, she could make it before the dresses were in danger of being ruined. She shrugged out of her coat and wrapped it around the box. Rain dripped from the edge of her hat down the back of her neck, but it wasn't pouring. She'd be home before she was soaked.

Vivian clutched the awkward bundle against her chest and picked up speed, sticking close to the edge of buildings to take advantage of the occasional awning. She dodged around puddles and piles of soggy trash as the streets and sidewalks around her grew empty.

When she heard the quick jog of footsteps behind her, Vivian barely noticed, assuming they belonged to someone else trying to get out of the weather. If she had looked up, she might have seen the man crossing the empty street directly toward her. But her head was ducked down to avoid the worst of the drizzle, so Vivian was unprepared for the sudden weight that crashed into her, knocking her off balance and herding her into a deserted alley.

Vivian stumbled, trying to catch her balance, not realizing that it was anything more than an accident at first. "Watch where you're—" she began angrily, then froze.

She recognized the hulking man that now blocked her path back to the street. Clutching the dress box to her chest, Vivian spun around, looking for another way out. The other side of the alley was cut off by a second familiar figure.

"Now, girlie, no need to be rude." The thin, chatty man gave her an oily smile, and Vivian could hear his beefy friend—Eddie, she remembered wildly—settling into place behind her. "We're just hoping for a little chat."

"I don't chat with men I don't know," she snapped, trying to look unafraid. "So excuse me, but I'm off."

Under the brim of the smaller man's hat, Vivian could see the ugly bruise that spread across his temple and down his jaw, a souvenir from the board she had bashed him with when the two bully boys jumped Danny. But they hadn't seen her that day, had they?

A heavy hand settled on her shoulder. She flinched away, but hulking Eddie's grip tightened. There was no way she could shake him off until he let her go. She settled for lifting her chin and glaring at the other man, who seemed to be in charge, just as before.

"Now, there's no reason we can't be friendly, is there?" the weaselly man said, shaking his head and still smiling.

"Tell your *friend* to take his hands off me, then," Vivian snapped.

"Sure, sure." He sauntered forward until he was right in front of her. "Eddie, don't manhandle the girl, there's a good fellow."

Behind her, Eddie chuckled, then dropped his hand. But he didn't move, and now she was pinned between them even more securely than she had been before. In spite of the cold rain, Vivian felt sweat prickle along her arms and torso. She wondered if they could see the wild, fearful beat of the pulse at her neck.

"What do you want?" she snapped.

"Tell me what you want with Hattie Wilson."

It wasn't the question she had expected, and Vivian didn't have to fake her surprise. "What?"

"Why did you go see Mrs. Wilson today? And be honest. Eddie here hates it when people lie."

Vivian couldn't stop her eyes from darting to Eddie's menacing bulk before they snapped back to the man in front of her. She swallowed. "I—I work for a dressmaker?" she managed at last, hating the way it sounded like a question. She swallowed again and tried to sound more firm. "Mrs. Wilson ordered dresses, and I was there to fit them. That was it."

The chatty man shook his head. "Lie better, little dressmaker."

"It's not a lie," Vivian said, her voice shaking. "What do you think is in this box?"

"See, I think it is, girlie. Because our boss knows that you spend your time at a place called the Nightingale. That place had an awful lot of significance to poor departed Mr. Wilson. And you just happen to visit his widow?"

"Look, I don't know who you are, or who Mr. Wilson—"

"And then there you are, and our boss finds out you were eavesdropping—"

"And I don't know who your boss is either!"

"Don't interrupt," the chatty man snapped, and this time Eddie's bulky hands shot out to knock the dress box from her hands and shove her against the alley wall.

Vivian gasped in pain as a broken edge of brick caught her head, just under her ear. For a wild moment, all she could think was that the dresses would be ruined and she'd have to pay for them out of her wages. Then the scrawny man's face was suddenly in front of hers.

She could smell the cigarette smoke on his breath and see the water dripping off the brim of his hat. She tried not to move even as the rain sent shivers chasing down her arms and back. She tried not to look at the yellowing bruise on his temple, terrified he would somehow guess she was the one who had left it there.

"That's unfortunate, because now our boss knows who you are, Vivian Kelly. So if you're a smart girl, you'll start talking. Because we've got our eyes on the Nightingale, and people who poke their noses into—"

"Hey!"

The shout cut through the alley. The weaselly man hesitated, cursing under his breath, then stepped back. He motioned to Eddie to follow, and a moment later the two of them had disappeared down the other end of the alley.

FIFTEEN

Y ou okay?"
  The concerned voice made Vivian jump, and she turned so
  quickly that she stumbled, tripping over the bundle of her coat
that lay crumpled on the ground.

"Careful!"

Hands caught at Vivian's arm, hauling her upright, and she muttered
a thank-you even as she winced at the way the motion jarred her aching head. She glanced once more toward the end of the alley, checking
that the two men really were gone, before turning to see who she was
thanking.

The girl watching her, guarded but concerned, had dark hair and
tired eyes. She was probably only a little older than Vivian, though grim
lines were already beginning to etch their way into her forehead. And
she was very familiar.

"How do I know you?" Vivian was unable to place the memory.

The girl let go now that Vivian could stand on her own once more.
She had dropped an umbrella to help Vivian up, and now she hoisted it

above her head once more. "You sure you do?" she asked. "I just thought you could use a hand. I saw them grab you and haul you back here. Hope your coat's not ruined."

"My coat—" Vivian glanced down, then let out a frustrated breath as she remembered what she had been carrying. "Damn," she muttered, hauling the dress box from under the coat to examine the damage. It was soaked, but the cardboard hadn't started to fall apart, so the dresses inside weren't yet ruined. She wrapped her coat around it once more.

The girl was watching her. "Something pretty in there, I'm guessing?"

"Pretty, expensive, and not mine," Vivian said. "My boss'll lose it if they get ruined."

"You're shaking."

Vivian glanced down at where her hands were clutching the box so hard they trembled. "I'm fine," she insisted. She didn't want to think about how afraid she had been. "Just wet, is all. Thanks for your help."

The girl grimaced in sympathy. She hesitated a moment, then suggested, "I live pretty close by. Why don't you come inside and get a little dry before you head off? I'm Sadie," she added. "Sadie Monaldo."

Vivian's memory had just clicked into place. "I thought I knew you," she said. "I've seen you at—" She hesitated, then said carefully, "Honor's place. I'm Vivian Kelly."

Sadie had been staring at the other end of the alley where the two men had disappeared, her eyes narrowed and a hard look on her face. But at the mention of Honor's place, she turned back, giving Vivian a sharp look. After a moment, she relaxed. "Been there a time or two," she agreed. She eyed Vivian thoughtfully, then nodded. "I ruined your lipstick?"

"That was me."

"Thought so." Sadie glanced after the two men once more, then sighed. "Come inside," she said again. "You probably need to sit down after a run-in like that."

Vivian shivered, suddenly feeling every soaking inch of the dress that was plastered to her body, though the rain had never managed to grow beyond a heavy drizzle. "Yeah, thanks. That'd be grand."

———————

A s soon as they were inside Sadie's home, she handed Vivian a blanket and pointed toward the bedroom. Vivian obeyed gratefully.

A few minutes later she was stripped down to her step-in and stockings, wrapped in the blanket, and curled in a kitchen chair, clutching a mug of bitter coffee whose warmth was almost painful against her cold hands. Vivian's dress, along with the two for Hattie Wilson, were draped over the drying rack that hung above the stove, steam rising off them in eager curls.

The apartment was cold everywhere except in front of the stove. In spite of the colorful hooked rug on the floor and several cheerful, cheap prints hanging on the wall, there was a heavy feeling in the room. Sadie herself seemed weighed down, staring at nothing as she dropped into the chair next to Vivian with a quiet sigh, her own mug of coffee in one hand while the other rubbed briefly at the small of her back. A box of matches and a package of cheap cigarettes were already sitting on the table; Vivian shook her head when they were held out to her. The two of them sat, sipping their coffee in silence, for more than five minutes before Vivian cleared her throat.

"Guess I was lucky you were passing by."

Sadie nodded, brows drawn together as she stared at the cigarette between her fingers. "I hope I'd do the same for any girl I saw being grabbed like that. But especially when it's George doing the grabbing."

"George—that's the chatty, weaselly one?" Vivian asked. "You know him?"

"Chatty." Sadie snorted. "That's Bruiser George, all right. Loves to hear himself talk. He and that giant of his have worked around here before. They aren't nice fellas."

"Seemed like you scared them off all right."

"More like they didn't want to cause a scene. They're supposed to keep a low profile in their line of work."

"What line of work is that?" Vivian asked, leaning forward. "They came at me out of nowhere, I don't even know why."

Sadie eyed her, brows raised. "Making folks scared, of course. Whoever they're working for wants you fearful." She dragged a tin plate across the table toward her and stubbed out the cigarette with a sharp gesture.

The sudden movement made Vivian flinch, her mind too stuck back in that alley for her to relax. Feeling on edge, she started to stand.

"Your dresses aren't dry yet," Sadie pointed out.

"Thanks, but I should probably head off anyway. I'd hate for anyone to come home and find me sitting here in nothing but my drawers."

Sadie shrugged, not looking at Vivian as she pulled another cheap cigarette out of the package. Her fingers trembled a little as she lit it and said, "No one else to come home. It's just me here."

Vivian frowned. Even from where she stood, she could clearly see a full set of dishes balanced on the shelf above the stove, women's shoes in two different sizes by the front door, and a large, ratty pair of men's slippers by a rocking chair. In the center of the table, a chipped trinket dish held a woman's brooch and a man's watch—old, pretty things, the sort that were passed down through families.

Vivian hesitated. "There isn't . . . you live alone?"

Sadie nodded. "These days, it's just me," she said, looking up in time to catch Vivian's puzzled glance at the watch. Sadie picked it up, her fingers tightening around it briefly, fiddling with the chain. "My father died a couple months ago."

The bottom dropped out of Vivian's stomach. "I'm so sorry, I didn't realize . . ."

"It's okay," Sadie said quickly. "I just haven't quite been able to change things around here. It used to be him and me and my sister. Now . . ." She dropped the watch back onto the plate with a clatter. "Now it's just me."

"I'm so sorry," Vivian said again. The words felt painfully inadequate, but she couldn't think of anything else that wouldn't sound worse. "I didn't mean . . ."

"I know," Sadie said quietly. "It's why I started going out, nights. It's too strange being here alone. Too quiet."

"How'd you find your way to the Nightingale, then?" Vivian asked, taking another sip of coffee to cover her embarrassment. "Danny—he's the bartender there, I don't know if you—anyway, he said that was your first time there."

Sadie shrugged. "People talk."

"Rough night for your first one out," Vivian said, blowing out a slow breath, her eyes fastened on her hands as she turned her coffee cup in slow circles. It could have been just a coincidence that Sadie's first time visiting the Nightingale was also the night Willard Wilson was killed. But after finding Roy getting cozy with Wilson's widow, she was starting to agree with Honor: coincidences made her uncomfortable. Especially when two bruisers cornered her so soon after running into the handsome Mr. Carlton again, mentioning a boss at Hattie Wilson's who had recognized her. She watched Sadie out of the corner of her eyes as she continued, "I don't know if you heard, but that was the night that a guy got shot out back."

"Yeah, I heard about that," Sadie said. "And then the cops showed up . . ." She stubbed out her second cigarette before it was more than halfway gone. "Haven't been back since, to be honest. Place is a little too hot for me right now."

"I get that," Vivian said, nodding even as she continued to watch the other woman. "You got snagged in that police raid, didn't you? Me too. It was no picnic, though it looked like you got out of there faster than me."

"I had a friend to help me out," Sadie said quietly, lighting a third cigarette, though she didn't even bother to smoke this one, just watched as it slowly burned down, chunks of ash dropping sadly into the dented tin plate. "Shame, really. Nightingale seemed like a nice place."

"It is," Vivian said, ducking her chin with embarrassment when she realized how earnest she sounded. She fiddled with the handle of her coffee mug, the crumbs on the table. Anything to keep her restless hands busy. "Feels more like home to me than anyplace I've actually lived, even with all the rough stuff going on right now. You should find your way back there someday."

"Well, who knows." As Sadie looked up, her expression was almost a smile, pleased and a little surprised, as if she had forgotten what it was like to have someone care whether or not they saw her. "Maybe I'll be back once they figure out who killed Wilson and things quiet down."

Vivian's fingers grew still, and she hesitated, not breathing for a moment before she glanced up to meet Sadie's eyes. "Did you know him, then?"

Sadie also stilled, and the two women stared at each other for a long, tense moment before Sadie laughed shortly and took a drink of her coffee.

"God, that's nasty cold," she said, grimacing. "Yeah, I knew who he was. I recognized him in the club that night." Taking in Vivian's wide-eyed look of surprise, she added, "My pop worked for him from time to time. That's how I know who George and Eddie are, actually. They used to work for him too. Can't say I was sorry when I heard he was dead."

"I've heard that from a few other people, too," Vivian said, unsure how much she should say.

"You should believe it, then."

Sadie was clearly telling something like the truth—the disgust in her voice was real. But she also admitted to knowing the dead man, to seeing him the very night he died.

Vivian hesitated again; then, before she could talk herself out of it, asked, "What sort of work did your father do for him?"

"I don't want to talk about my father," Sadie said quietly, only barely meeting Vivian's eyes before she looked away.

"Look, you said he worked with those men, right? And now they're trying to get me running scared—"

"My father wasn't anything like Bruiser George," Sadie snapped.

"I didn't mean that he was, I'm just trying to figure out—"

"I think it's time you were going." Sadie stood, her chair nearly toppling back with the motion before she caught it. Her voice was sharp as a door slamming shut and just as final. "I'm on nights at the factory this week, I have to get ready for work."

"I'm sorry," Vivian said, standing as well, the blanket still clutched awkwardly around her shoulders. "I really appreciate you helping me out down there. I wasn't trying to—"

"I know. I know, it's all right." Sadie pressed the heels of her hands against her eyes, then looked up. Her weak smile that was worse than no expression at all was back as she went to untie the rope that lowered the drying rack. "But I don't know anything else about them. And I really do need to get ready for work, okay?"

"Sure," Vivian said, gathering up her clothes, which were now warm and damp instead of cold and wet. Shrugging out of the blanket—if there was no one else living there, she didn't much feel the need for modesty—she dressed quickly, ignoring the damp that still squelched in her shoes, while Sadie gathered the dresses back into a parcel.

Neither of them spoke again until Sadie was showing her to the door. Vivian paused on the threshold, a hand over the doorjamb to stop the other girl from closing it. "I meant it, you know. I hope you find your way back there. Dancing helps, I think, when things are hard."

In reply, Sadie shrugged, one corner of her mouth lifting in that bitter almost-smile again. "See you around, Vivian Kelly."

"See you around."

—·—

And she said her dad had died just a couple months ago, and—get this—she knew his name, because they *worked* together."

"She knew her father's name?" Bea asked. "Why is that surprising?"

143

"Not her father's name, Wilson's name, and that those two men worked for him. She knew who he was—she even admitted she saw him at the club the night he died. Which means—" Vivian turned toward her friend.

"I told you to hold still," Bea said, gripping the top of Vivian's head to turn it gently back around. "There are still a few pieces to pull out."

Bea's building was close by, and Vivian had gone straight there after leaving Sadie's misery-heavy home, knowing that since Bea worked nights she'd be around during the day. Mrs. Henry had answered the door, and her visible shock made Vivian realize what she must look like: her clothes still wet, her hair wild around her head, and—she discovered when Mrs. Henry looked her over—a patch of blood drying on her collar from an ugly abrasion behind one ear.

The motherly concern that poured out of Mrs. Henry made the fear from the alley come rushing back, and Vivian allowed herself to be led, shaking, to the kitchen table. There, Bea ordered her to sit and began cleaning her off, pulling fragments of brick from the tiny cuts and sponging away the muck and blood with a surprisingly gentle touch.

"I also told you not to get involved," Bea continued, laying down the cloth she had been using and calling out, "Mama, we got any bandages?"

"There's a tin of those Band-Aids in the kitchen drawer," Mrs. Henry replied from one of the back rooms.

"I'm not going to be involved anymore," Vivian said, shivering. "I've got something to tell Honor now, and that should be enough."

Bea looked up from rummaging through the drawer just long enough to give her friend a skeptical look. "You think this Sadie girl had something to do with Wilson?" she asked before returning to her search.

"I think Roy—" Vivian shivered again and had to take a deep breath before she was calm enough to continue. "He's clearly got a thing for Wilson's wife. If he recognized me from the Nightingale, and he's the reason those two toughs came after me, he might have had something to do with Wilson. But Sadie said her dad worked with Wilson, and she didn't want to talk about it. That means he was definitely not on the up and up," Vivian said as Bea came back to the table, tilting her head to one side so that Bea could fix one of the sticky bandages over the deepest part of the cut below her ear. Wincing at the pressure, she continued, "So if it wasn't Roy who did it, maybe working with Wilson got Mr. Monaldo killed. And Sadie wanted to get revenge."

"You think her dad got offed by a mobster?" Bea leaned forward, sounding intrigued in spite of herself.

"Or shot in a police raid, maybe," Vivian said, leaning forward as well and dropping her voice. "And Sadie's broken up about it, since he was the last family she had after her sister died. So, knowing her father worked for Wilson and that he's to blame, she goes after him."

Bea didn't look quite convinced, but she nodded thoughtfully. "Well, even if she wasn't the one who killed him—because that seems like a hell of a conclusion to jump to, Viv—she still might know something that could help Honor, since her dad worked for him and all."

"Either way, I tell Honor, she shakes Sadie down for whatever information she's got, and I'm in the clear from here on out," Vivian said, blowing out a relieved breath as she sat back. She tilted her head toward Bea. "Does it look awful?"

"Your hair mostly covers it, but I wouldn't go out with it on or anything," Bea said. "I'm sorry it happened to you, Viv, but maybe it's a lucky break anyway. You might not have found out about this Monaldo fella otherwise."

"Monaldo?" asked Mrs. Henry as she came back into the room, juggling two baskets of laundry. Bea leaped up to help her. "You two talking about that poor family?"

The girls shared a puzzled glance before Bea asked, "You know something about them?"

"Lord, girl, everyone's been talking about them. The Italian neighborhood's only a few blocks away." Mrs. Henry sighed as she dropped her basket of laundry in front of the kitchen stove, groaned as she straightened up, and began lowering the drying rack.

"What are they saying?" Vivian asked as she went to help.

Mrs. Henry was still a beautiful woman, though years of worry had left permanent lines around her forehead and mouth. Her eyes were puffy with fatigue, but they were always sharp. Now, they were wide with surprise. "Girl, if you had paid attention at your church lately, you'd already know. The younger sister disappeared, not sure when, and her only fifteen years old. Family wouldn't say what happened."

Vivian nodded. There were plenty of reasons a girl could go missing. Maybe she wanted to run off with a man her family didn't approve of, or maybe she got picked up by the police and ended up in a reformatory. Families usually tried to hush it up when that happened. Dead or missing, it usually amounted to the same thing in the end: no one was likely to hear from her again.

"But the father . . ." Mrs. Henry shook her head sadly. "He killed himself two months ago. Put a pistol in his mouth, and his poor daughter found him dead in the washtub."

Vivian froze, her grip on the pulley rope going slack for a moment before she caught it. A sick knot twisted in her stomach, and for a moment she thought she might start crying. "Oh God," she whispered, glancing at Bea. "No wonder she didn't want to talk about it."

Bea's face was stony, a careful mask that Vivian knew her friend used to hide any strong emotions that threatened to throw her off balance. She glanced at her mother. "Viv and I will handle the laundry. You look like you need a lie-down."

Mrs. Henry gave them a suspicious look. "What are you girls mixed up in?"

"Nothing, Mama," Bea said. "I just need to talk to Viv about work, and you know you never like hearing about that."

Mrs. Henry didn't look convinced, but she nodded. "You leave that poor Monaldo girl alone. She's had enough tragedy to last a lifetime, she doesn't need you bothering her none."

"'Course not, Mrs. Henry," Vivian said quietly, tying the laundry rack off so she and Bea could start hanging clothes to dry over the stove.

More than just Sadie's reluctance to talk about her father made sense now. Her grim behavior, her anger, the feeling of misery that filled her home . . . Vivian blinked back tears. "Thanks again for patching me up."

Mrs. Henry looked unhappy at the reminder of her battered condition, but she didn't argue. With a last sigh, she picked up the mending basket and left the room.

As soon as she was gone, Bea lowered her voice. "What're you going to do now?"

Vivian didn't answer, and for several minutes they worked silently side by side. She couldn't say anything to Honor about Sadie now—not without hating herself for it. And if Mr. Monaldo had taken his own life, all of her wild speculation about Wilson getting him killed and Sadie seeking revenge was just that. Sadie had no reason to want Wilson dead. Just more sadness than one person should have to bear.

But Roy, now. He had been at the Nightingale the night Wilson died, had been mere feet from the man's body. Maybe it was nothing. But he had been at the house on Fifth Avenue, and it wasn't so he could tell Mrs. Wilson how sorry he was that her husband had kicked off. And then, when he realized that Vivian had overheard him, had he told someone who she was? Someone who wanted to find out what she knew about the night Wilson died?

Or was he the new boss, the one who knew she danced at the Nightingale, who sent George and Eddie after her to find out why she was poking around Hattie Wilson, to keep her from telling his lady love that he might have been involved in her husband's death?

She shuddered, her sympathy for Sadie Monaldo swamped in the wave of remembered fear, and she rubbed her fingers lightly against the bandage behind her ear. She had been lucky. If the two toughs who jumped Danny came after her with plans to do more than talk, there was no chance she'd be able to fight them off the way he had. And as much as she wanted to keep her friends safe, as much as she wanted to help . . .

At last she sighed. "I'm out, Bea. I have to be. If that girl hadn't shouted when she did—"

"Don't say it," Bea snapped, not looking at her, her shoulders tense with unhappiness. "I don't even want to think about it."

"I'll tell Honor about that Roy fella, and that's got to be enough, right? She asked me to find out what I could, and I did. I'm not getting myself jumped in an alley again. I'm out."

Bea nodded. "Good. Pass me the clothespins, will you?" As she took them, she gave Vivian's fingers a brief, telling squeeze. "She doesn't want you in danger any more than I do, you know. She'll understand."

Vivian nodded, hoping Bea was right.

SIXTEEN

"Jesus, Mary, and Joseph, what happened to you?"

Florence's voice snapped like a whip as soon as she walked in the door to find Vivian hunched over the kitchen table, the top buttons of her sweater undone and her hair tied up as she gingerly peeled the bandages off her neck with her good hand.

Even though she was nearly certain that her sister was worried, not angry, Vivian stiffened. The same concern that had felt so comforting from Bea and her mother felt stifling from Florence, and Vivian jerked the scarf out of her hair, letting the bob swing down in a dark curtain to cover the injury.

"Tripped," she said, shrugging. "Slipped in the rain." She gestured at the washtub, where Hattie Wilson's dresses were soaking in water that was getting muddier by the minute. "Made a mess of everything. Like I do every time, right?"

Florence looked as if she wanted to say something more. But instead she just sighed, closing her eyes and giving her temples a rub that made Vivian squirm with guilt. She hated worrying her sister. And she hated having to care that Florence was always worried.

"Do we have anything around for dinner?" Florence asked, dropping into a chair, her chin slumping into one hand. "Anything that doesn't need cooking?"

Relieved that there wouldn't be any more questions, Vivian shook her head, then let the motion continue, stretching out her neck and shoulders. "I can make soup or something. My day hasn't been as busy as yours."

Florence dropped her head further forward until her whole face rested in her hands. "Lucky you. Miss Ethel was a right cow today," she mumbled.

"Flo!" Vivian stared at her soft-spoken sister in surprise. "What'd she do?"

Florence sighed. "Nothing, I guess. Just being her lovely self. I wish I could find a new job. But the only thing I know how to do is sew."

Vivian bit her lip, wishing she had something more comforting to say. Awkwardly, she laid a hand on Florence's shoulder. "We could try to find you a fella," she said, attempting to sound cheerful. "You said you wanted to get married, after all."

Florence looked up long enough to roll her eyes. "Real funny, Vivian. No one wants—" She broke off abruptly as a sharp knock echoed through the small room. "Is someone at the door?"

"Maybe it's a husband," Vivian joked, and they shared a tired snicker as she went to answer the door.

Her laughter choked off when she opened the door and found Leo smiling at her. "Hey there, sweetheart," he said softly, looking genuinely pleased to see her. "I hoped I'd find you home."

"Who is it?" Florence asked, and the curiosity in her voice made Vivian blush.

"No one," she answered abruptly, stepping outside and pulling the door shut behind her before realizing what an awkward thing it was to do. That made her blush spread even more, and she could barely bring herself to look at Leo.

"Hiding me away, are you?" he asked, and she could hear the laughter in his voice.

That made her look up, scowling in embarrassment. "What are you doing here?"

"Looking for you, of course. Thought I'd stop by and see if you want to go to the movies. They've got some swell choices playing at the Capitol this week."

"I meant, what are you doing at my house? How did you know I live here?"

"Pestered Danny into telling me," he said, still smiling. "Couldn't wait any longer to see you, Vivian Kelly."

He smiled with pride at having found out her last name, boyish and flirtatious and taunting, and Vivian wasn't sure whether she wanted to wipe the smirk off his face or kiss him right there in the hallway. She settled for rolling her eyes.

"Well, congratulations on being so clever. But I can't go out tonight. My sister's beat from work, so I'm running out to get us some dinner. And I've got to be up early tomorrow. Maybe another time."

She started to turn away, but he caught her hand. Gentle as the touch was, the suddenness of it made her remember being shoved into that alley. She flinched away before she realized what she was doing.

But Leo felt the motion, small as it was, and he dropped her hand immediately. "You okay?" he asked, his brows drawing together in concern.

"People keep asking me that," Vivian snapped, clenching her hands into fists to keep from wrapping them around herself. Taking a deep breath, she found a smile and shook her head. "Your uncle might not care if you're at work on time, but Flo and I can't afford to oversleep and get fired. So good night, Leo."

She was about to turn away when the sudden, quiet coldness of his voice dragged her to a halt. "Who did that, Vivian?"

"What?"

He reached out, the gentleness of his movement at odds with the fury on his face as he brushed a single finger against the side of her collarbone. "Who did that?"

Vivian glanced down, just barely able to see where he was pointing. She hadn't buttoned her sweater back up before coming into the hall, and the collar had slipped to one side, revealing dark bruises speckled across the edge of her shoulder. They looked like fingerprints, and Vivian closed her eyes briefly, remembering her terror as Eddie grabbed her and shoved her against the alley wall.

For a moment, she was relieved. Part of her had still wondered if Leo had been lying about working for his uncle, if maybe he was involved with Wilson's business and whoever had taken over after his death. But if he didn't know about George and Eddie, or the way someone's—Roy's?—suspicions had fallen on her, then maybe he really wasn't involved at all.

That didn't mean she wanted to tell him what had happened, though. Instead, she shrugged off his hand and pulled her sweater back up, buttoning it as carelessly as possible. "No idea where that came from. What makes you think it was a person?"

"We both know it was," Leo said. He didn't try to touch her again, but his voice was icy enough to make her take a step back. "And if I didn't know it, your face just now would have told me. Tell me who it was. I'll make sure he never bothers you again."

"Is that supposed to be comforting? 'Some guy beat the stuffing out of you, but I can be just as nasty, so you don't need to worry about anything'?" Vivian laughed, though nothing about what she had just said was even a little funny. "You don't think I see enough of that around here? I thought you were supposed to be a nice fella."

"I never said I was nice. But I would never hurt you, you know that."

"I *don't* know that," Vivian snapped, wrapping her arms around herself, shoulders hunching toward her ears. She was shaking in spite of the tight grip she was trying to keep on herself. "I don't know a damn thing about you."

"Vivian." The earnestness was back in his expression as he reached slowly forward. When she didn't move, he took her hand—the uninjured one—and rubbed her cold fingers gently between his palms. "I would never hurt you. And no, I wouldn't say I'm a nice fella. I left a hell of a past behind me in Chicago. But I'll never be the sort of man who lays a hand on a woman. I won't do anything you don't want me to do, but tell me what happened."

The comforting friction from his palms was slowly easing the tension out of her muscles, especially because he didn't once try to touch anything other than her hand. Relaxing just a little, Vivian sighed. "Remember how I said Honor hadn't called in her favor yet? That wasn't really true." Quietly, glancing around to make sure none of her neighbors were in the hall to overhear, she told him about Honor's favor, about wiggling her way into making a delivery to Hattie Wilson to find out what she could about her husband's death, about the two bruisers cornering her in the rainy alley. She tried to make it sound like none of it mattered, that she was tough and unbothered, but she couldn't keep the shivers from her voice or her body.

"Why, Vivian?" Leo murmured, his hands never stopping their comforting motion, though his eyes were snapping with anger. "Why the hell would you get involved with something like that? For twenty-five dollars? Hell, I'll give you the money to pay her back, and I won't ask for anything in return."

"It's not just the money," Vivian sighed. There was an ache in her forehead, right between her eyebrows, and she rubbed it wearily. "The raid was because of him. Everyone who goes to the Nightingale—everyone who works there—they all might be in danger."

She pulled her hand away from his. "After I tell Honor what I've found out about Roy, it's not going to be any of my business anymore. That's twenty-five dollars of information, as far as I'm concerned."

"Especially seeing what it got you," Leo said. His hands moved, as if he wanted to take her by the shoulders and look her over once more, but he restrained himself. "You need to see a doctor about it?"

Vivian shook her head. "For a few bruises? I'm fine, thanks. And I'm supposed to be getting dinner for my sister, so it's time for you to clear off."

Leo looked like he wanted to protest, but he settled for sighing and nodding. "If you say so, Viv. But you can call me anytime if you need help. My number—"

"We don't have a telephone," she interrupted.

"Is Circle 2441. Just remember it, okay?"

"Sure." He was right, she did feel a little better. Not good—she wouldn't feel right again until she'd talked to Honor and made it clear she was done poking around into Willard Wilson's murder. But the fear and panic faded more each time she told someone what had happened. And Leo's concern—once he offered it on her terms and not his—had thawed some of the chill that she was holding on to.

So when he started to turn away, Vivian stopped him with a hand on one arm, just as he had stopped her a few moments before. Before she could second-guess herself, she stood on her toes and pressed a quick kiss against his mouth. And when he didn't move, didn't try to hold or grab her, she did it again. The feel of his lips sent a wave of comforting warmth down her spine, and she lingered just long enough that he could start to kiss her back before she pulled away.

He looked both pleased and wary when she met his eyes again. "Is that a yes to seeing a film sometime?" he asked. "Maybe tomorrow night?"

"Not tomorrow. Night after that. Maybe," she said, taking his hat out of his hands and settling it back on his head for him. She was unable to resist running her hand down his jaw. The prickle of stubble made her fingertips tingle. "Thanks for listening."

"Anytime," he said quietly. He hesitated, looking like he wanted to say something more. But he settled for "I'm looking forward to our date."

W ho was that?" Florence asked as Vivian came back inside, not looking up from the dresses she was rolling dry between two threadbare towels.

Vivian shrugged, even though her sister wasn't watching. "Fella I know."

She could see Florence's shoulders tense, and waited for the inevitable questions, the suspicions and warnings. But to her surprise they didn't come. "I think the mud came out," Florence said instead, straightening as she gestured to the gowns.

Vivian sighed. "Thank God. I'm sorry to make more work for you, Flo."

"I'm just glad Miss Ethel let you keep your job. Lord knows we can't afford to lose one," Florence said as they draped the dresses over the backs of kitchen chairs to finish drying. "And it looks like the pins all stayed in place, in spite of your fall, so I should be able to get them finished up pretty quick."

"Well, for now, why don't you take a bit of a breather?" Vivian suggested, grabbing one of the damp towels and the small soap bag they kept hanging by the sink. "I'm going to go wash up and fix my hair, and then I'll run out to get us some groceries."

The washroom at the end of the hall was shared between all the tenants on the floor, and Vivian had to wait for Mrs. Gonzales and her three-year-old twins to finish before she could get in. She washed her face, neck, and hands once it was her turn, checking over her injuries again and making sure they were as inconsequential as she wanted them to be. Her neck was still scraped up, and the bruises below her collarbone meant she'd have to be careful about what she wore for a few days. But overall, she could push her various aches to the back of her mind.

When she returned to the apartment, she was already planning what groceries they could afford and how she could turn them into a meal that might last a few days. She was brought up short, however, when she saw a large paper bag sitting on the table, Florence looking between it and her with raised eyebrows.

"What's that?" Vivian asked, frowning in confusion.

"You tell me," her sister replied. "I told him I wasn't opening it until you got back and said whether it was a good idea or not."

"Told who?" Vivian asked, taking the bag when Florence held it out to her.

Inside were half a dozen paper boxes from the automat: roast beef sandwiches dripping with gravy, baked apples with cream, ham and peas, baked beans, potato salad, and a slice of blueberry pie that was big enough for four people. Two bottles of soda water were nestled at the very bottom. Vivian unwrapped them all and laid them on the table, the puzzled expression never leaving her face until Florence pointed to the note scribbled on the bag in pencil.

I know you can take care of yourself.
But this time, how about I take care of dinner.
Leo

Vivian glanced at her sister. "I hope you're not about to spout some nonsense about accepting gifts from men. Because I'm probably hungry enough to eat all of this myself."

Florence scrunched up her face, then glanced at the food and shrugged. "Pass me a sandwich," she said, pulling out a chair and joining Vivian at the table. "Tonight, I really can't bring myself to care."

They ate in silence, but somehow, the luxury of it cracked the ice that was usually frozen between them. They never went too hungry, but they never bought as much as they wanted just because something looked good. Having more than enough food spread on the table between them made them both relax in a way that Vivian hadn't realized a single meal could do.

They smiled at each other as they passed the boxes back and forth and ate their fill.

A knot of guilt was forming in Vivian's stomach by the end, though. She got to indulge when she went out, usually on someone else's dime. Florence never had any of that. Even though Vivian told herself it was because Florence never allowed herself to go after it, the end result was that her life had fun and excitement and luxury. Her sister's was always just bleak.

"Here," she said at last. Trying to escape her uncomfortable thoughts, she slid the pie box across the table. "You deserve it. You're the one who was stuck under Miss Ethel's eye all day."

"I don't think I could, I'm so stuffed," Florence said, though the last words were muffled by a giant yawn. "I just want to go curl up in bed. You eat it."

"It's too much for one person," Vivian protested. She tried to push the box into Florence's hands, but her sister shook her head, yawning again.

Which was how, three minutes later, they ended up curled on Florence's bed, side by side, a blanket pulled over their laps while both of them nibbled at the plate of dessert balanced on Florence's knees.

It should have felt strange and surprising to Vivian—they had never been the type of girls to whisper and share confidences in bed with each other. In the orphan home, they were in different dormitories because of the gap in their ages. And by the time they left, the friction between them was firmly established, Florence grimly following the plan laid out for her, Vivian eager to see what life would be like with no rules or walls hemming her in.

But something was tickling a memory in the back of her mind. Vivian frowned at her sister. "Have we ever done this before?" she asked.

Florence stilled, a fork halfway to her mouth. "You don't remember?"

"Remember what?"

Her hand shaking a little, Florence set down her fork. Vivian was shocked to see tears along the edge of her sister's lashes before she blinked them away.

"The first few years we were in the home, until you were about six,

I'd save my dessert and come visit you every night after lights out. We'd eat it together, and I'd tell stories until you fell asleep." Florence glanced at Vivian out of the corner of her eye before looking away again. "You usually wanted to hear about our mother."

Vivian stared at her sister, her hands shaking. She *could* remember now, just barely, just a vague sense of another warm body pressed against her under a skimpy blanket, of small, strong arms circling around her neck, of a girl's voice whispering in her ear as she fell asleep. It was almost impossible to fit those memories into the picture she had of her sister, of the distance that had always been between them. How could she have forgotten?

"Why did you stop?" she asked. "Did you . . ." Another memory drifted at the edge of the first, of loneliness, a feeling of being left behind when those nightly visits stopped. She swallowed, and when she spoke, the words came out in a whisper. "Did I make you angry?"

"No, of course not!" Florence looked stricken. "You do remember, then?"

"Only a little, now that you mentioned it. I remember . . . I didn't know why you stopped coming." Vivian struggled to force a deep breath past the knot in her chest. She had always been convinced that she was a bother to Florence, a weight dragging her sister's life down. Maybe she had been then, too. "Did you get in trouble with the nuns for breaking curfew?"

"No." Florence shook her head. "They weren't cruel, Vivian. You remember that, don't you? And they knew family was important. I stopped because . . ." She looked down at her lap, where her fingers were twisted around each other anxiously. "Sometimes I would tell you stories about our mother. You didn't remember her at all, you were so little when she died. But I remembered, and the stories helped me not to forget. But sometimes . . ." Florence's cheeks were pink with emotion, and her hands were shaking. "Sometimes, instead of telling you about her, I'd tell you about how our father would learn where we were and come for us. Or how, when we left the home, I'd marry someone rich and he'd help us find our family." She smiled faintly, though her eyes were still wet. "You said once that I could get married, but you wanted to be in films. So I'd tell you stories about how you'd be a famous dancer in Hollywood one day."

Vivian listened, frozen in place and barely able to feel herself breathing. She could hardly believe Florence had ever dared to imagine so much for them.

Florence's smile had softened. "Maybe that's why you ended up loving dancing so much. But . . ."

Her expression darkened, and her shoulders hunched a little, as if she wanted to protect herself from the memory. "Sister Agnes took me aside and said she was worried about you, about us. She said that if I wasn't careful, you'd end up believing and wanting impossible things. And she explained, very clearly, what we could expect when we left the home. They'd make sure we were trained for a trade and could find work. But life would be hard. We'd be poor. We didn't have any family to come for us. And we'd only have ourselves to depend on, because the odds of anyone wanting to marry . . ." She broke off, her voice shaking. "Anyway, my stories were going to do more harm than good. She meant well, and she was right. So I stopped."

Vivian could feel tears pressing behind her eyes, though whether she wanted to cry for herself or for little Florence, taking on that burden at all of nine years old, she wasn't sure. "She wasn't right."

"She was," Florence said quietly. "Everything she said was true." She glanced up, her mouth trembling as she met Vivian's eyes. "Including the fact that we'd have each other to depend on."

Vivian wanted to argue. She wanted to rage at Florence for giving up on her—on both of them—all those years ago. She wanted to storm out of their dank apartment and throw herself into a wild dance to burn off the emotion that was trembling through her limbs. She wanted to burrow under the covers and cry until she was asleep.

Instead, she moved the pie plate to the rickety nightstand, then drew the covers up over both of them, snuggling down until she was curled against her sister's shoulder. "Tell me a story about our mother, Flo."

She couldn't see her sister's face, but she could feel the exhale that shook Florence's wiry body. "She loved to sing, all the time. She said music was good for any growing thing, including this ugly, dead flower she brought home one day. It was in a blue pot . . ."

SEVENTEEN

Vivian held her breath and her shoes as she tiptoed toward the door.

She had pretended to fall asleep next to Florence, who had drifted off in the middle of her story, worn out from the long day and emotional evening. It had taken over an hour of breathing quietly—struggling against the fatigue in her bones and eyes that wanted her to stay right where she was—before Vivian thought she could risk moving. Florence hadn't stirred as she crept out of the bedroom, gathering her shoes and spangles as she went.

The floorboards in the main room were creaky in the midnight quiet. But Vivian had done this before, and she changed silently, making it to the front door without anything giving her away. The door itself was the biggest danger, crackling like a gunshot no matter how fast or slow she swung it open. Wincing, she grabbed her coat from the nail where it hung and pressed on until she was in the hallway, two walls between her and her hopefully unsuspecting sister.

Vivian didn't linger, shrugging her coat on quickly so that any neighbors who caught sight of her wouldn't see what she was wearing. She padded down the four flights of stairs in her stocking feet. At the front of the building, she paused to slip on her shoes, tying the ribbons in quick, nervous knots. A glance in a window showed just enough reflection that she could settle a spangled headband over her bob and pin it in place, and then she was off, dodging through the darkened streets and between pools of lamplight, jumping at shadows. All around her were the sounds of the other New York City coming alive.

Heading all the way to the Nightingale on foot, alone in the dark, was too much for her that night. Vivian counted the change in her purse—she still had most of Hattie Wilson's tip left over, enough to hail a cab. She gave the driver directions to a corner three blocks south of the Nightingale's back-alley entrance.

Biting her lip, flinching at the sound of a man laughing one street over, Vivian hurried through the shadows. Silence the doorman recognized her face and gestured her inside.

When the second door swung open and a blast of heat and music greeted her, her shoulders relaxed. Vivian took her first deep breath since she had crept from her bed. The music was pulling her toward the dance floor, but she was on a mission. Making quick eye contact with Danny, and getting his nod of approval, she dropped her coat and purse behind the bar, squared her shoulders, and went in search of Honor.

———•———

Vivian couldn't keep her feet still as she talked, moving restlessly from one end of Honor's office to the other. She described what she had learned about Willard Wilson in jittery detail and why she was sure Leo had nothing to do with it.

"He's had enough chances to give away something about Wilson, but it doesn't seem to mean anything to him, and I believe him. He says he's back in New York working for his uncle."

Honor didn't say anything, just stood silently, rigid and slumped at the same time, her hands braced as she leaned over her desk, watching Vivian's restless progress around the room.

When Vivian described the way she had been cornered after seeing Roy with Mrs. Wilson, Honor dropped into her chair, her head resting briefly in her hands. The gesture stunned Vivian into silence.

A moment later, though, Honor lifted her head, brushed a pale curl back into place, and smiled. "God, you are such a brilliant girl, I could kiss you," she said, her voice so warm with approval that it almost made Vivian forget the most important thing she had come to say.

She nearly smiled back before she remembered why she was there and scowled instead, crossing her arms belligerently as she finally sat in the chair across the desk from Honor. "Well, that sounds nice enough, but I think there are more important things to consider. Like the fact that doing your favor has landed me in a whole mess of trouble."

Honor's smile faded a little, and she acknowledged the point with a reluctant nod. "But," she added, "it does leave you an easy way to get back into Wilson's house and see what else you can uncover. Folks like that are always running their mouths off in front of servants and delivery girls. They'll think you haven't got more brains than a table. You can use that."

"No." Vivian thought about sugar-coating her answer and discovered she didn't want to. "No," she repeated, more firmly.

"Just until you find out a little more about Mr. Carlton," Honor said, the warmth back in her voice as she leaned forward. Her eyes were wide and pleading, but her mouth smiled as if it were barely holding back its secrets. "Ever since you mentioned him to me that night, I've had him in the back of my mind. I just need to know whether he actually had a reason to want his boss dead, aside from just having a sweet tooth for his wife—which plenty of men do, without it ever driving them to murder. You have to take the dresses back anyway, right? It's a perfect chance to find out what you can."

"Forget it," Vivian snapped. "I'm done. I found out what I could, and

I nearly got my head cracked open in an alley for my trouble. I think that makes us more than square."

"Vivian . . ." Honor sighed. "The idea of you in danger kills me, it really does. But it also sounds like you would have had your run-in even if you weren't trying to fish for information, if Mr. Carlton is that jumpy about someone seeing him with Mrs. Wilson. And I'm glad to know about him . . . but I need help." She leaned forward, taking Vivian's hand between both of hers, her forehead creased with worry. "The message came through loud and clear the other night. Someone is unhappy about Wilson's death here, and I need to be able to give them something to show I wasn't involved. And you've got to go back to see Hattie Wilson anyway, right? So why not keep your ears open for me then, too?"

"Because I'm scared." It was hard to say out loud. Vivian wanted to seem fearless in the face of the city's underground dangers, the way Honor herself always did. But she couldn't pretend, not this time.

"Vivian." Honor's grip tightened, and her eyes closed for a moment as if she were in pain. "I wouldn't ask if it weren't so very, very important." She hesitated, then stood abruptly, and paced away before coming back. Leaning over her desk, she frowned in thought, drumming her fingers on the wood for several moments before glancing at Vivian out of the corner of her eye. "What if I can make it worth your while?"

Vivian tensed, hesitating, then asked, "What do you mean?"

"I mean that I hear things. You remember asking about my files?"

Vivian nodded, suddenly unsure where her conversation was going.

"Every upstanding citizen has a dirty secret," Honor said softly. Taking a tube of lipstick from her desk, she crossed to the wall with the mirror and studied her reflection, then slowly slid the paint over her lips, her eyes meeting Vivian's in the mirror. "And I know one in particular that you could put to good use."

Vivian let out a breath, her eyes fixed on the reflection of Honor's lips. "About who?"

"About your delightful employer, Miss Ethel Marie Barnes."

Vivian couldn't help it—she laughed. "What in God's name could you possibly have on that monster?"

"Something that could make life a whole lot more pleasant for you and your sister," Honor said, turning away from the mirror.

Vivian's hands trembled. She wanted to be done, to be safe, more than anything. But after what she had learned that night, she also ached to do something for her sister, to bridge the gulf that had been growing between them since they were children. If Honor did know something about Miss Ethel, it could give Florence room to breathe, to maybe even hope for something more out of her life.

If, of course, Vivian had the courage to use the information she was handed.

"What do you say, pet? For me?" Honor asked. "It's a fair trade, I promise." Seeing Vivian still hesitate, she took a deep breath and said, her voice heavy with reluctance, "If you're worried about staying safe, you could ask your Mr. Green to look out for you. Since it seems like he's on the up and up, at least as far as this is concerned, he might not be too bad to keep around. Danny says he's quite the fighter when he needs to be."

"You want me to get even cozier with him?"

Honor scowled, the expression an endearing contrast to her usual cool beauty. "I don't want you to get hurt. And if he can keep you safe . . ." She sighed, leaning back against the wall, her arms crossed. "Or if he can at least put your mind at ease, then I'd rather you keep him around." Meeting Vivian's eyes, she added, her honey-dark voice dropping even lower, "But no, I won't like seeing you with him at all."

Vivian had thought she was growing used to Honor's games. But this was something different. There was a vulnerability in Honor's voice that was not usually there, an honest admission of the potential that always hovered between them.

For a moment, Vivian couldn't stop herself from imagining where that might lead, what might happen if they actually grew to trust each other, if the heat between them had the chance to turn into something real. The thought left her aching with hope.

But where could that hope lead? Vivian danced at the edges of the nighttime world, but Honor lived there. It was a world where each of them could be herself—but the daylight world would never truly offer them that chance, not if they wanted to be together.

And what would she tell Florence?

Honor was still watching her, regretful understanding in her eyes. "Even if I'd rather keep you for myself, pet, I'm not the sort of person who makes promises."

"Did I ask you for promises?" Vivian said, flustered and stung even though she wasn't sure she had any right to be.

Honor smiled. "One of these days you'll figure out what you want. And then, yes, I think you'll be the sort of girl who needs a promise to go along with it."

"If you want to persuade me to help you out, that's the wrong way to go about it."

"I'm trying to be honest." Honor shrugged. "And I'm offering you a trade in return for your help. Take your Mr. Green with you, find out something I can use to prove I had nothing to do with Wilson's death. Help me keep the Nightingale open for the people who need it." Quietly, she added, "People like us."

Vivian stood abruptly, torn between loyalty and longing and fear. She knew what Honor meant—knew what the Nightingale meant. But she had been so scared in that alley. She was still scared. "I'm not ready to say yes."

Honor nodded, her face thoughtful as she straightened and crossed to the door of the office. She pulled the key from her pocket, ready to lock the door behind them; it dangled from her fingers like a dare as she met Vivian's eyes. "Think quickly, then. I need an answer by the end of the night."

EIGHTEEN

The Nightingale was in full, raucous swing when they returned to the dance hall. Honor didn't say anything, just gave Vivian a quickly blown kiss before she strode into her domain.

Vivian stayed where she was, her breath coming quickly as she glanced around the beautiful chaos.

The young Black man in the striped suit was new, but he had persuaded Miss Rose—the best dancer at the Nightingale, streaks of silver running through her curly bob though there wasn't a single line on her perfectly made-up face—to join him on the dance floor. The two of them moved like silk and honey, like poetry, like jazz.

The band was warbling through the end of "My Melancholy Baby." As soon as the last notes faded, Vivian knew the trumpet would swing the tempo back up for "Charleston Charlie," the band leader's favorite. He always played those two songs one after the other. The saxophone would be a beat behind, but he would catch up a bar and a half later. He always did.

The two baby vamps at the corner table, the ones who had arrived separately but been inseparable since, would giggle their way onto the dance floor. Bangles flashing, they would kick their heels toward the air, with eyes only for the dance and each other.

Danny was calling for the other bartender—another new one, sandy-haired, with a thousand-dollar smile and a face you could forget in an instant—to run downstairs for more gin. And when the music was done, Bea would be on her break, free for a talk and a drink and an eye roll when she saw Vivian on the dance floor once more.

A fellow from the bar caught her eye, then abandoned his drink to make his way over. Leaning close, his breath warming her ear, he whispered, "Catch a few bars with me, sweetheart? You'll be the prettiest girl on the floor."

Vivian met Honor's eyes across the floor and nodded her answer. To her surprise, in spite of how persuasive she had been only minutes before, the club owner hesitated. But at last Honor nodded back, her expression a war of gratitude and worry and half a dozen other messy emotions. A moment later her face was smooth again. She turned back to the business of glad-handing the influential patrons who, though they would never give their real names or admit what their lives were like in daylight hours, kept her club in business.

Vivian cut her eyes at the man who was still waiting for her answer, smiling and determined and defiant as she took his hand and let him lead her to the floor.

This was where she belonged. She wasn't going to let anything happen to it.

NINETEEN

After another full day of delivering dresses—this time in waves that had her zigzagging across the Upper East Side until she thought her feet were going to fall off—Vivian met her sister at the back of the shop.

The look in Florence's tired eyes worried her. It was inching beyond exhaustion and into defeat.

"What happened, Flo?" she asked.

"Nothing," Florence said, sighing. "Nothing more than just . . . everything. Miss Ethel being awful. My head hurts. Probably just from beading all day. I'll be fine." She glanced sideways at her sister as they walked. "Where are you heading?"

"Home with you, of course," Vivian said, trying to sound cheerful as she took the lunch basket that Florence had slung over one arm. "I'll cook tonight. And I'll clean up too, so you can go to bed early." She hesitated, then added, "I'm worried about you."

"I'm not the one courting trouble every night."

"I can still worry," Vivian said quietly.

Florence shrugged, and they made the rest of the trek home in silence.

After dinner, Vivian sent her sister to bed and washed up, then fetched a bucket of water from the washroom and brought it into the bedroom. She could feel Florence's eyes on her as she gently scrubbed both her dancing dresses. When she hung them up to dry before crawling into bed, she finally glanced over and met her sister's eyes.

"Yeah?"

Florence opened her mouth to say something, then closed it and looked down at the blanket that was drawn over her lap. "I guess you're really not going anywhere tonight, then?" she asked at last.

"Nope, I'm in for the night," Vivian said, her tone as pleasant as she could manage. "I have to be up for mass in the morning."

Florence groaned. "Really? You get up to God knows what every night of the week, but you'll still go to church tomorrow?"

Vivian scowled. "I always go to Sunday service, you know that. You can skip and sleep in."

"And feel guilty all week that you made it and I didn't?" Florence rolled her eyes heavenward. "Of all the things the nuns drilled into us, somehow that was what stuck with you."

"That was what stuck with me," Vivian agreed. It was an argument they had nearly every week, and the one time she felt like she beat Florence at being good. She didn't care if anyone else thought it was a contradiction; she could like dancing and want to go to mass if both suited her. "Good night."

But even after Florence turned down the lamp, Vivian stared at the ceiling, her mind wide awake. Any lingering doubts she had that taking Honor's deal was the right call had faded as she spent the evening watching her sister's bleak, exhausted face.

She couldn't be the sort of girl Florence wanted her to be. But she could take every chance she found to make her sister's life better. She owed her that much.

She was going to keep her head down, just for one more day, to let anyone who might be watching think she had been scared off.

After that, she'd do what Honor asked. Because whether Florence knew it or not, it was for her own good. And if it helped the Nightingale survive, that was good for Vivian too.

———·—·———

Vivian wasn't sure the next evening whether Leo had taken her "maybe the day after" seriously. But the still-warm meal he had delivered less than an hour later made her think he had been paying attention. So after dinner, instead of kicking off her shoes and falling onto her bed with a long sigh as her sister did, Vivian began primping for a night out.

Florence lifted her head from her pillow. "Heading out?" Her voice was too tired to be disapproving.

Vivian didn't turn from the mirror where she was applying her lipstick. "Yup."

"Didn't know your kind of places were open this early."

"I have a date tonight." Vivian dipped her comb in the morning's leftover wash water and set about smoothing down the flyaways in her bob, trying to pretend she wasn't watching her sister's face in the mirror. There was no point in looking for approval from Florence, and as Vivian settled a hat at a jaunty angle so that it sloped over one eye, she reminded herself stubbornly that it didn't matter anyway.

"Oh." For a moment, Florence looked almost excited. Then her face fell. "Vivian . . . you didn't agree . . . the dinner that man brought us . . ."

"Oh, for God's sake." Vivian turned to glare at her sister. "No, I didn't whore myself out for dinner, if that's the question you're asking. Is it so hard to believe there are people who like me and maybe want to do something kind every once in a while?"

Florence's face was red with embarrassment. "I have a hard time believing that people who . . . that the type of folks you meet when you go out would describe themselves as kind."

Vivian snorted. "Just because you don't think a girl like me is worth anything doesn't mean everyone feels the same way."

"It's not me," Florence protested. "The entire world thinks girls like us aren't worth anything."

"Maybe, but you don't have to go believing them."

"And you don't have to go out of your way to prove them right," Florence snapped, her cheeks bright with anger.

Vivian closed her eyes. So much for building a bridge. Apparently one night of confidences wasn't enough to break a habit of distance and disapproval that had built up over years.

"We're just going to a film and maybe out for a bite afterwards," she said. "Nothing sinister, nothing illegal. So you can quit your worrying and your mothering, okay? I deserve a little fun. You do too, if you'd ever let yourself have it." She hesitated, then suggested, "Maybe we could go out to a film together, one of these nights?"

"We don't have the money for it, you know that," Florence said. "You let your fellas take you out all you want if they're paying, but I'm not wasting what we have." She dropped her head back onto the bed, and her voice was so muffled by the bedclothes that Vivian could barely hear her last words. "I'm too tired to go have fun."

Stung by the rejection, Vivian held back her own sharp answer. "Don't wait up then," she replied at last, just barely managing not to slam the door behind her.

Her stomach churned with anger and guilt in equal measures. She hated that everyone who looked at her would assume she was the sort of girl who needed to get frisky to convince a man to do nice things for her. Or a woman, she thought with bleak humor, imagining Honor's red lips.

She wanted to go back and apologize. She wanted Florence to see things her way as much as she wished she could stop making her sister worry. Or maybe she wanted to tell Florence just what she was doing on Honor's behalf, to point out that someone, at least, thought she was smart enough to accomplish something dangerous and important. Instead, she stomped down the stairs, her steps only slowing when she reached the front of the building and discovered Leo just arriving.

He grinned, his surprise so sweet that for a moment she forgot to be angry and smiled back. "Were you that excited to see me, then?" he asked.

Vivian pursed her lips. "More like I had a fight with my sister and needed to get out. I wasn't actually sure you were coming, to be honest."

"What?" He looked affronted. "We had a date, I'll remind you. You said the day after tomorrow—which meant tonight—*and* you gave me quite the kiss. That's an agreement if I ever saw one."

"It was a normal, average kiss," Vivian protested.

Leo smiled, his voice dropping. "I have a feeling I'll never call kissing you average, Vivian Kelly," he murmured.

Vivian rolled her eyes. "God, you've got a sappy line," she said to hide her pleasure. "Where are we going tonight?"

"Have you seen that new film, *Beau Brummel*?" Leo asked, holding out his hand. After a moment's hesitation, she took it, shaking her head. "Me neither. I don't know a thing about it, but I hear it's a good time. Interested?"

"Sounds good to me," Vivian said, the last of her anger falling away as they turned south. "Lead the way."

———

The film had been entertaining, and Leo—along with half the other moviegoers—had a flask hidden in his jacket pocket that they shared giggling sips of in the dark theater while the ushers overlooked them with knowing but unconcerned eyes. It was simple, being in the dark and letting herself get swept up in the story.

And when the final credits swooped over the screen and Leo leaned close to whisper in her ear, "Want to come home with me for a drink?" that was simple too. Vivian only hesitated a moment before she smiled.

"Sure," she whispered back, her mouth hovering just above his ear, where she could breathe in the scent of his cologne. She thought of her sister's disapproval. She thought of Honor saying that she wasn't the sort to make promises. "Why not?"

———•———

Vivian smothered a giggle as she clung, monkey-like, to Leo's back. He tried to turn his head enough to glare at her but couldn't manage more than an exaggerated squint, which made her giggle even more, bursts of snorted laughter sneaking out of her tightly clamped lips.

"Quiet," he hissed, though he was laughing too, trying to walk steadily up the stairs with her on his back. If his landlady was listening from her apartment, which was right next to the front door—"She hears *everything*," he had said solemnly as they made their way to his building—she would think there was only one person entering the building.

At least that was the hope. Vivian wondered what would happen if the eagle-eared woman poked her head out and discovered one of her tenants sneaking up to his room with a lady friend on his back. The thought sent her into another fit of silent laughter, leaving her shaking so hard that Leo stumbled on the last step before he reached the landing.

"You are an impossible girl," he whispered as they started on the second flight of stairs. "How do you ever manage to get out without your sister noticing?"

Vivian tipped her head so her mouth was as close to his ear as possible. "Florence doesn't make me laugh the way you do," she murmured.

"Under the circumstances, I'm not sure that's a compliment," Leo muttered, nearly losing his footing again as she held back another burst of laughter.

When they reached the third flight of stairs, he decided they were far enough away from the landlady's door that they could both walk. Vivian held her shoes by the ribbons as they crept up to his door, and Leo grinned broadly at her as he unlocked it and they tumbled inside.

"Nice to have you visit," he said, catching her around the waist and pulling her in for a kiss as he kicked the door shut.

He tasted like wintergreen and whiskey, and the evening stubble on his cheeks made her skin prickle. When his hands crept around her waist, she slipped her hands under the front of his coat with a murmur, greedy for the heat of his body. She let herself forget her worries and fears, just for a few moments, before she at last lifted her head and looked around.

Leo's home was newer and nicer than hers, or at least fixed up more recently, with electric lights and an icebox by the stove. It was only one room, and there was a cozy, sagging sofa set at the foot of the bed so that it faced the kitchen table. A tall wardrobe with double doors loomed over one side of the bed, looking like it hadn't been moved in the last fifty years and would probably stay there for the next fifty; the opposite wall was lined with books stacked two and three feet high. Prints were tacked to the walls, and a quilt that was clearly handmade by someone was folded neatly over the foot of the bed.

Vivian glanced at Leo and was surprised by the shy grin on his face. "What do you think?" he asked. "It's small, I know, but . . ."

"It looks like a happy place to live," she said.

"A happy place to live," he repeated, sounding pleased. "I guess that's what I wanted. It's the first time I've ever bothered to have a home since I moved out of my folks' place."

"You didn't have a home in Chicago?" Vivian asked in surprise, dropping her shoes carelessly on the floor, though she kept her coat on as she went to snuggle into the sofa.

"I had a place I slept," he said, shrugging, before going to turn up the gas on the radiator. "Not quite the same thing."

"No," Vivian agreed, tucking her feet under her. "Did you know anyone interesting in Chicago? Any good stories to tell?"

He shook his head, his expression serious as he crossed to the wardrobe to hang up his coat. "I'd rather make sure you like me a little more before I start telling Chicago stories."

"Oh?" Vivian leaned forward, the buzz of the drink they had shared in the theater still making her feel reckless. "Were your pals there so rough you're afraid you'll scare me off?"

"Given the way you tore into me the other day?" Leo paused to give her a pointed look.

Vivian looked away. Maybe she hadn't been fair to him when he came by, but she had been so shaken up. And for all Florence thought drinking and dancing was a one-way ticket to a life of crime, Vivian hadn't been faced with any of the seedier parts of New York's underground world. Not until she stumbled on Willard Wilson's body.

She had good reason to feel jumpy these days. But she liked Leo— liked his big hands and the way his hair fell over his forehead and how he looked at her like she was the only person in the room. She wanted him to like her too.

"I'm sorry about that," she said.

To her surprise, he shook his head. "You don't need to be," he said. "You were scared. It's not a bad thing to be wary of strange men."

"So you're saying I should be wary of you?"

"You should be wary of everyone you meet at a place like the Nightingale, Viv," he said, pushing his unruly hair out of his eyes. "It's not your job to trust me right away, it's my job to show that you can. Which I have, right?"

"You're pretty sure of yourself," Vivian said, getting comfortable on the couch as she unbuttoned her coat.

"You're here, aren't you?" He grinned before turning back to the wardrobe to retrieve a couple bottles of booze.

"That's not much of a hiding place," Vivian pointed out.

"They're hidden from my landlady, not the police," Leo said, tossing one in the air with a flourish before catching it again. Vivian rolled her eyes, and he laughed as he crossed to the kitchen to retrieve two glasses. "It takes considerably less effort to fool her than the coppers."

"You know much about hiding things from the police, then?"

He paused in the middle of uncapping the bottles, though he didn't turn around. "A thing or two," he said at last.

"What sort of work did you do there?"

He turned back toward her, the drinks only half mixed, leaning against the counter with his arms crossed. "The not-always-legal kind."

"And now? What do you do for your uncle?"

"Well, I'm still no upstanding officer of the law," he said with a smile. "But I'm not worried about them banging down my door anymore."

Vivian snorted. "They're not all that upstanding since Prohibition."

"Ain't that the truth." He turned back to finish making their drinks. "Why do you want to know about Chicago, Viv?"

She wished she could see more than his back as she answered. "I want to know who you are," she said quietly. She had noticed—though she let it go for now— that he hadn't actually told her what kind of work he was doing for his uncle.

"I can't say I know much about you either," he pointed out.

Vivian nodded, even though he couldn't see her. Not knowing what to say—and not sure that he actually wanted an answer—she turned to look around the room again, and as she did the stack of newspapers at the other end of the sofa caught her eye. The top one was folded open, and Wilson's now-familiar face smiled out at her from beneath a jauntily tilted fedora. She leaned forward to grab the paper from the pile. As soon as she had moved it, she discovered that the one below it was also open to an article in the society pages about Wilson—and the one below that was about Hattie and her sister.

Vivian spread them out, then looked up to find Leo watching her, unmoving, a drink in each hand as though he had turned around and been surprised into forgetting what he was doing.

"Were you reading about Wilson?" she asked.

He shrugged awkwardly, clearly trying not to spill the drinks. "Forgot I left those out," he said. Gesturing with one elbow, he added, "Why don't you move them out of the way so I can sit? Just push them on the floor, it's fine."

Instead, Vivian gathered the papers into her lap so she could continue glancing through them. There were paragraphs in each one—relating to Wilson, his business, and his wife—that had been carefully circled in pencil. She narrowed her eyes. "What were you looking for?"

"Nothing really," Leo said quickly. He handed her one of the drinks, then sighed as she set it on the floor so she could continue reading. "Actually, I was looking for something to help you."

"Help me?" Vivian stared at him in surprise. "But you didn't think I should be involved at all."

"Well, I was worried about you, so I figured I'd help you solve your mystery as quickly as possible." He shrugged. "But you told Honor you're done, right? So we can think about something else." He took a drink, then set his glass down and reached out to tug the stack of papers from her hands.

Vivian didn't let go. "I'm not done, actually."

He frowned. "With the papers?"

"With Wilson." Vivian found herself speaking gently, as though she were afraid of upsetting him by admitting the truth—though he had no reason to be upset. Nothing she did, least of all her agreement with Honor, was any of his business.

And even though she told herself that she didn't regret her choice at all, she still stumbled over her words as she added, "I talked with Honor. And she asked—and I agreed—and she was right, you know, I have to go back anyway to take Mrs. Wilson her dresses . . ." She trailed off. Leo had gone very still as she spoke. Both of them still gripped the stack of papers, as though it were the object of a tug-of-war between them, though neither had moved. "Anyway, I'm just going to keep my ears open. You know. See if I can learn anything more."

Leo let go of the papers at last, picked up his glass, and drained half of it in one gulp. He didn't move, but she could sense him pulling away from her. Just when she was wondering why the idea of her continuing to look into Wilson could upset him so much, he said, "I guess you've got your reasons for helping her out. Reasons that—" He glanced at her out of the corner of his eye, then looked away quickly. "Reasons I probably can't compete with."

Vivian sighed. She liked Leo, but she didn't want to explain herself. Not her complicated feelings toward Honor, and definitely not her desperate attachment to the little back-alley speakeasy, one that would never make it into a society paper's nightlife column but was the only place where she felt like herself. She chose her next words carefully. "I'm here, aren't I?"

He considered that. "So you're saying you're not . . . close to Honor Huxley?"

"I'm saying I'm helping her out with something she needs and in exchange . . ." Vivian hesitated, not sure she wanted to explain all her worries to him, especially the ones about Florence. "In exchange, she's promised to share a little information that I need. And since she was right, I do have to go back to the Wilson place anyway . . ." Vivian realized she was repeating herself and trailed off with a shrug. "No reason not to see what I can find out."

"That wasn't a no," Leo pointed out, his expression unreadable.

"That's true," Vivian agreed. "But it also wasn't a yes. And like I said . . . I'm here, aren't I?"

"Well then . . ." Leo slid closer, and Vivian thought he was going to kiss her again. Instead, he tucked himself against her shoulder and gestured at the papers. "Let's see what we can find."

"What?" She stared at him, confused.

"I said I wanted to help you wrap this up quickly. Still true. I don't think it's a good thing for you to be caught in the middle of. So let's talk over what you know, and see what's in here, and maybe we'll figure something out." He smiled at her surprise. "Haven't you ever heard the saying two heads are better than one?"

"Sure," Vivian said, unable to keep the skepticism from her voice. "But when you invited me over here, I didn't think it was because you wanted to talk about some dead guy."

He laughed and leaned in to kiss her. The papers slid from Vivian's hands with a soft rush of sound, and she could have sworn she was melting as Leo's hands traveled down her spine.

"About that dead guy?" he asked when he finally pulled away, his voice husky.

"It's not like I've learned anything more than I last told you," Vivian said, feeling breathless herself. "About going to the Wilson place."

"Right." Leo nodded. "And that bastard who sent those thugs after you, Roy something—"

"Carlton," Vivian broke in. "But I don't know for sure he was . . ." She trailed off at the look in Leo's eye. "It was probably him, he was the only one who could have recognized me."

"Roy Carlton," Leo repeated, nodding. "Well, that's something. We should see if he's mentioned anywhere," he added, gesturing at the papers now scattered across the floor and sofa.

"That's a good idea," Vivian said, bending down to gather them up. "Honor pointed out that just because you're sweet on your boss's wife doesn't mean you have the nerve to do anything about it. So there needs to be some reason . . ." Her eyes were fixed on the paper in her hand. "Some reason . . ."

She lost the train of her sentence as she read the gossipy little column. It was just a couple inches on the society page, but the way it described Hattie Wilson jumped out at her.

Mrs. Willard Wilson was not in attendance, despite having been on the organizing committee for the gala event. A little bird whispered that perhaps she is suffering from that well-known complaint that so often afflicts young, newly wedded ladies . . . though of course any such speculation would be considered most crass by This Writer.

"Some reason?" Leo prompted at last when she didn't continue.

Vivian jumped a little at the sound of his voice. "Some reason Roy would decide to bump him off," she finished slowly, thinking of another article she had read about Mrs. Wilson—and the way it had pointedly mentioned that she would need her sister for the next few months. "Some reason like maybe Hattie Wilson was pregnant, and maybe the baby was his."

"What?" Leo snatched the paper out of her hands. "It says that in there?"

"No, of course not." Vivian rolled her eyes. "The way rich folks can talk around plain facts they don't want to come out and say makes my head hurt. But maybe she was—" Vivian broke off. It suddenly occurred to her that they were sitting nearly on top of each other, that maybe she didn't want to be discussing pregnancy—even someone else's—when she was sitting practically in the lap of a man she had just met a week before. Clearing her throat sharply, she changed the subject. "Anyway, whatever happened, someone's gone to a lot of trouble to hush it up. Do you remember the obituary? It said he died of a heart ailment."

"Well, it wasn't wrong. Getting shot in the heart's a pretty severe ailment," Leo joked. When he saw her wince, though, he smiled ruefully. "Too rough for you? Sorry."

"It's fine," Vivian said quickly. The memory of finding Wilson's body in that alley was always at the front of her mind these days, but she still preferred not to think about it too closely. "But really, what would it take to do that? Get a false cause of death printed?"

"Depends on how careful they're being," Leo said thoughtfully. "If the family gave the obituary directly to the paper, they could claim whatever they wanted. But if they wanted to cover their tracks, they'd have to bribe the coroner and any police involved to fill out a false report and death certificate. That doesn't come cheap."

"Well, his widow definitely has money," Vivian pointed out. "Far as I could tell, she's the only family he had around, so she'd be the one to have done it."

"And if she wanted to protect her reputation, she'd have a good reason to hide that her husband was shot in some shady back alley," Leo agreed. "Happens more than you might think."

"So that means she'd have to know at least something about what happened," Vivian said. Caught up in her thoughts, she swung her feet onto Leo's lap, relaxing back against the arm of the couch without really realizing it. "But here's what gets me. How does a fella like this—high society, right, and damn well connected from the looks of things—how does he end up shot behind a place like the Nightingale? And what could that have to do with a bunch of bruisers trying to send a message by beating a bartender senseless?"

"Well, one of two things," Leo said, one of his hands curling around her foot and sliding over her stocking-clad ankle. "One, he was in the wrong place at the wrong time. Also happens more than you might think. Or two, plenty of fancy fellows make their money in dirty ways."

His hand was still making its slow way up her leg, and Vivian shivered. "You trying to distract me?"

"You want me to stop?"

She didn't, but she wasn't going to admit it out loud. "No wonder Danny warned me about you," she said instead.

His hand started traveling back down, raising goose bumps on her skin. "He's one to talk." A sudden frown creased his forehead, and he cleared his throat. "Were you and he ever—"

"No," Vivian said, resisting the urge to laugh at his obvious discomfort. "Actually, before our jailbird morning, I'd never seen him outside the Nightingale."

"You and Bea were friendly before though, right?" His hands resumed their slow journey up her other leg.

"Oh yes," Vivian said, smiling. "We moved to the neighborhood around the same time. Me and Flo from the orphan home—" She broke off, realizing she'd never before told him where she had come from. But his hands didn't falter, and there was no judgment on his face, so she continued. "And the Henrys from Baltimore. Apparently they were pretty fancy folks there. Her father was a Pullman porter, once upon a time."

"Was?" Leo asked. "What happened to him?"

"Influenza," Vivian said shortly, suddenly regretting the way the conversation had gone. "He made it home from the war in one piece, then he died the next year. Her family never recovered. Now all Bea cares about is sending the little ones to school so they can make something of themselves. And Mrs. Henry . . ." Vivian smiled in spite of herself. "Mrs. Henry cares about taking care of everyone she meets, no matter who they happen to be."

"She took care of you, I'm guessing?"

Vivian shook her head. "My sister," she said. "Right after we moved to the neighborhood, Florence got real sick. We were on our own for the first time, and none of the neighbors would come near us. That was just after the influenza was finally gone from the city. Everyone was still so scared of it coming back." Vivian swallowed, remembering too clearly the visceral fear of watching her sister get paler and weaker and having no idea what to do—and no money to do it with, even if she had known. "But Mrs. Henry heard. She came to help, and Flo got better." She was silent for a moment, then shook herself abruptly, glancing up at him with a flirtatious smile. "Sorry, didn't mean to get so serious. What were we talking about?"

"Murder," Leo said dryly. "So definitely not serious at all."

Vivian laughed. "Well, you sure know how to show a girl a cheerful good time."

Leo pulled the papers from her hands and tossed them to the floor, sliding closer until his lips tickled her ear. "Then how about we talk about something more fun?"

Vivian bit her lip, smiling as his mouth moved slowly down her neck. "What did you have in mind?"

TWENTY

The room swam into focus slowly, and for several long moments Vivian was too distracted by the fuzzy taste of her tongue to remember where she was. The dawn light was creeping a sideways path across the floor just below her eyes, and she was snuggled under a blanket with something warm pressed up against her back. Comfortable, well aware that if she woke up completely she'd be nursing a vicious hangover, Vivian would have closed her eyes once more if she hadn't felt the warm thing at her back take a deep breath and roll ever so slightly away.

"Oh hell," Vivian breathed, the words barely making a sound as she remembered where she was. If it was dawn, that meant . . . that meant she had fallen asleep at Leo's place.

They both had, apparently, slumped in a tangled pile of limbs on the tiny sofa. At some point Leo must have pulled a blanket over them. The bootlegged bottles—both empty now—lay on their sides, rolling a little on the uneven floor, as if they had been too drunk to remain upright.

"Oh hell," Vivian said again, even more soundlessly this time.

Florence was going to kill her.

Leo had rolled enough away that she could stand; still half-asleep, Vivian hauled herself upright without waking him. Her bag, shoes, coat, and stockings were jumbled together in a pile just a few steps away; she pulled on her coat and stuffed the stockings in its pockets rather than wasting time putting them back on.

The papers they had been looking at were still scattered across the floor. Vivian hesitated, checking the clock sitting by the stove. Six in the morning. She could afford to take a few more minutes. She gathered up as many as she could carry, shuffling them into a pile as quietly as possible, then paused to smile down at Leo. He frowned a little in his sleep, two grumpy lines creasing the skin between his eyebrows. She thought about bending down to kiss them away, seeing them fade as he blinked awake to find her leaning over him.

But he was just as likely to be the sort who woke up swinging if he was startled. And anyway, she needed to hurry home. Her sister would have noticed she didn't come back last night—again—so there was no telling what kind of fight was waiting for her. Giving Leo's sleeping frown one last smile, Vivian tucked the papers under her arm, picked up her shoes and bag, and tiptoed out.

She didn't put the shoes on until she had successfully crept past the landlady's door and made it to the nearly empty street, the city just getting on with the business of waking up for the week.

But in spite of her good mood and the quiet morning hour, she still glanced over her shoulder, watching for someone following her or hands that might reach out to grab her. Shivering a little, Vivian weighed her options and the change in her purse, then went to catch the nearest streetcar.

—·—

Vivian had done a lot of successful sneaking in and out of buildings in the last few days. This time, it was the newspapers that gave her away.

She was standing with her weight on her toes as she eased the door of her home shut behind her, trying to creep in as silently as possible. But as the latch clicked, the papers shifted, escaping from under her elbow and rushing toward the floor even as she jumped to catch them.

The soft crinkle and swoosh of their fall might not have been a problem, but the clatter of the chair she collided with was.

Vivian saw it falling too late. She stumbled forward, trying to catch it, and ended up tumbling down with it.

She was still on the floor when Florence burst out of the bedroom, an old Smith & Wesson in her hand and pointed straight at Vivian.

The sisters both froze, staring at each other.

Florence moved first, lowering the gun and bursting into angry tears. "Where were you?"

"What the hell are you doing with that?" Vivian countered, stumbling to her feet and hauling the fallen chair with her. She had to resist the urge to put it between her and her sister. Instead, she clung to it with white knuckles. "Do you even have any idea how to use it?"

As suddenly as they had come, Florence's tears were gone, replaced with blazing fury. "I'm not an idiot, thank you. Where were you last night? And what were you thinking, sneaking in like a criminal?"

"You have a gun?" Vivian was sure she needed to be apologizing for something, but she couldn't make it happen. Florence was upset, and angry, and all that was probably justified. But Vivian's mind couldn't move past the sight of her sister, modest nightgown buttoned up to her neck and her hair in a long braid down her back, with a gun in her hand. "Jesus, Mary, and Joseph, Flo, since when do you have a gun? And how did I not know?"

"I bought it as soon as you started going out to those jazz clubs," Florence said, her voice shaking even as she gathered herself into something that resembled calm. "I wanted to be ready in case men started following you home, or strangers turned up here asking for money or favors or the good Lord alone knows what else."

"Why do you keep thinking I'll get mixed up in something criminal?" Vivian demanded, hurt.

"You *are* mixed up in something criminal," Florence snapped, her calm facade fraying. "That's what those places are, Vivian, *they're illegal*. It's only a matter of time before that follows you home."

"I'm not mixed up in anything, Flo," Vivian said, but her mind went to Wilson's dead body as she said it, and she knew that she didn't sound convincing. Trying not to think of how easily Honor had convinced her to keep going—it was for Florence, after all, she reminded herself angrily—she shook her head emphatically. "I'm not."

"And what about that?" Florence demanded, gesturing at the bandage still wrapped around Vivian's hand. She was still holding the gun, though, and both sisters winced as the barrel swung up once more. Looking a little ill, Florence set it down abruptly on the table. But she clearly would not be deterred. "What happened to your hand?"

"That was just an accident. A glass that broke," Vivian insisted.

"Really? An accident that just happened the same night you *went to jail*?" Florence snorted with disbelief, crossing her arms. It didn't look belligerent—if anything, she looked as though she were desperate to hold herself together. But the guilt that swamped Vivian was quickly brushed aside as her sister demanded, "Well, then, where were you last night?"

Vivian ground her teeth, all too aware of the stockings in her pockets. "I told you, I had a date."

"All night? Vivian, what are you involved with?"

"For God's sake, Flo, a man! I'm involved with a man. That's what a date is." Defensive, she gestured at the gun on the table. "And I know full well we don't have the money to buy something like that on the up and up, so don't go playing high and mighty with me, thanks. You're growing a little too shady yourself to be throwing the first stone here."

Florence hissed in a breath, and the sisters glared at each other without speaking until Vivian was sure she could hear the angry thumps of her own heart. At last, Florence put her chin in the air and sighed.

"Since I'm up, I guess I might as well make breakfast. I assume you need something to eat after whatever bootleg poison you were drinking last night?"

As far as olive branches went, it was a weak one, and Vivian wasn't ready to accept it. "I was drinking the good stuff last night, thanks."

She could see Florence stiffen, but her sister only nodded. "You're going back to bed?"

"No, I need to see if the washroom is free so I can clean up before work. You probably need to do the same." Vivian glanced at the pistol that still gleamed angrily on the table. "And get rid of that. We *don't* need it."

She received only a glare in return as Florence snatched up the gun and stalked into the bedroom, slamming the door behind her.

———

finished the dresses for Mrs. Wilson last night. You're welcome, by the way," Florence said when she emerged five minutes later. "Don't forget to bring them to the shop."

Vivian was sitting at the table with her head slumped into her arms, contemplating the effort it would take to make coffee. She looked up in surprise to find Florence fully dressed and shoving her arms into her coat. "It's too early to head to work," she pointed out.

Florence gave her an impatient look. "I need to clear my head. All these secrets are making it ache. I was up all night worrying."

"I told you not to wait up," Vivian muttered, defensive but not meeting her sister's eyes.

"Guess I'll have to remember that next time."

As the door shut behind her sister, Vivian dropped her head once more, sighing loudly. Florence was right, of course—she was keeping secrets. But it was all for Florence's sake, so didn't that make it right? Or at least as close to right as she was going to get these days, so there was no point feeling so guilty.

A gentle tap on the door made her jump a little, wondering for a moment if her sister had come back to say . . . what, exactly? Florence wasn't going to apologize. She never apologized.

"Viv?" The door opened a few inches and Bea's head poked around, looking concerned. "You okay?"

"Hi there," Vivian said, attempting to smile, but the sympathetic expression on Bea's face told her she didn't need to bother. "Guessing you ran into Florence?"

Bea nodded, closing the door behind her as she came inside. "On the stairs. She . . ." Bea hesitated, finally settling on "She didn't seem very happy with you."

"She's never happy with me," Vivian said sullenly, then sighed. "It's worse today. I've got a little time before I have to be at work. Need some breakfast?"

"Sure," Bea said.

"I'll pull something together," Vivian said, standing with a small groan. "Just give me a moment to get dressed."

"That's not dressed?" Bea frowned at the coat Vivian was still wearing.

"I wore this last night," Vivian admitted. "And I don't have any stockings on."

Bea raised her brows, trying and failing to keep the wicked smile off her face. "Sugar, I hope you're planning on sharing that story."

———————

Ll right, spill the beans," Bea said, blowing a cloud of steam off her coffee as Vivian set two bowls of hot Wheatena between them. Each was splashed with the last of a can of condensed milk and topped indulgently with canned peaches, which Vivian hoped would help fill up a stomach that was still protesting too much to drink and not enough sleep the night before. "What did you get up to that sent you home with no stockings and Florence out in such a huff?"

Vivian cradled her own cup of coffee between cold hands, flexing her stiff left palm against its heat. The cut was better but still far from healed. She wouldn't be able to get out of sewing much longer, though, injury or no. She pushed the thought aside and leaned forward.

"Leo Green took me out on a date last night," she said, speaking quietly even though no one was there to overhear. "Out to the movies, and then he asked me if I wanted to come back to his place." Bea's eyebrows shot up and she bit her lip to keep from interrupting. "I didn't make it home until this morning. Flo was not thrilled."

Vivian thought about mentioning the gun her sister had somehow acquired, but before she could decide whether or not to say anything, Bea was already pressing for more details.

"So you and he . . ."

"Definitely not," Vivian said, rolling her eyes. "I know what happens to women in this neighborhood. Once they start having babies they don't stop. Not something I'm interested in just yet, thanks."

"But you did spend the night at his place?"

"Yes, I did. We both fell asleep, actually, after we . . ." Vivian trailed off, blushing.

"Got a little bit frisky, but only a little bit?" Bea suggested, her grin turning into a cackle of laughter when she saw her friend's blush grow. But then her expression turned serious. "Your sister's never going to get on board with you going out, you know."

"I know," Vivian sighed, stirring her cereal absently and scowling into the bowl. "Wish she'd take a hint from your mother and stop worrying."

Bea shrugged. "Mama doesn't like it, you know. But she can't argue with a paycheck. Wish I could do more than waitress. But I'd rather work somewhere like the Nightingale than as a maid in some snooty house. For the most part, no one gives you any trouble there. Honor's good about making sure no one pinches her girls."

"If you could pick any work, what would it be?" Vivian asked, curious.

Bea sighed, the longing in her eyes so intense it was uncomfortable to see. "Be a singer. I'd be swell up on stage. I've got a great voice, you know."

"I know."

"But . . ." She sighed again. "You don't get work like that without connections. And if there was one thing we lost when Daddy died, it was connections." She fell silent, stabbing at her food with bitter intensity.

Vivian didn't say anything, not wanting to intrude on whatever messy emotions Bea was wrestling back down. But the comment about connections reminded her of Wilson, and after a minute she pulled a sheet of newspaper from where she had folded it into her coat pocket.

"Take a look at this," she said. To distract her friend, she unfolded the piece of paper and pointed to the column she had noticed the night before. "What do you make of that?"

Bea frowned. "Why are you still reading about the Wilsons?"

Vivian winced. She had forgotten that Bea still didn't know what she had decided. As she explained, Vivian could feel her friend's worry and disapproval radiating at her from across the table.

But Bea only sighed. "I hope you know what you're doing," she said, gesturing at the paper. "Which part of it am I supposed to be looking at?"

"The bit about Mrs. Wilson not turning up." Vivian leaned forward so they were both hunched over the article. "Am I reading it wrong, or does the writer think she's pregnant?"

Bea scanned it again and nodded. "Looks like it to me. It's pretty vague, but that's always the way these things are written, right? Lots of snide little hints and guesses."

"So maybe she was early days when it was written." Vivian nodded. "When I saw her, she didn't look like she was knocked up. But the way dresses are draping this year, sometimes there's no telling for months. So she'd be less than halfway along, but maybe not by much."

"Is that important?" Bea asked.

"Maybe." Vivian frowned, thinking of Roy Carlton. If he and Hattie Wilson were having an affair . . . and if she had ended up carrying his baby . . . Vivian whistled softly. "That would definitely be something to kill over."

"What?"

"Nothing." Vivian shook her head. "Just something to tell Honor tonight."

"Whoever wrote this also thought their marriage had gone sour," Bea added.

"What makes you say that?" Vivian asked, leaning forward once more.

"That line." Bea pointed and read softly, "'This was the third such event in the last two weeks that Mr. Wilson attended alone—such a surprise for a couple who was so inseparable during their courtship.'" Bea snorted. "Wonder how fast they started hating each other."

"People've been saying he was quite the bastard," Vivian said. "Seems like no one was surprised he got bumped off."

Bea laughed dryly and, after scooping up the last of her breakfast, stood to gather her bowl and mug. As she did, her foot caught on the bag she had carried in and left sitting by her chair, sending her stumbling and the bag toppling over.

"Careful!" Vivian said, half standing and catching her friend's arm. As soon as Bea was steady again, Vivian bent to gather up the things that had spilled from the bag. She was surprised to find that one was a brand-new book, *Harlem Shadows,* its cover still so pristine that Vivian felt bad for touching it. A moment later, she was even more surprised when Bea snatched it from her hands and shoved it abruptly back into the bag.

"Poetry?" Vivian asked.

"I like poetry," Bea said defensively.

"I know that. What I don't know is why you're hiding it."

Bea hesitated, still clutching the bag against her chest. "Because I didn't buy it for myself."

"Well, I know you didn't steal it, so how could . . ." Vivian's eyes narrowed. "Who's the fella, Bea?"

"Who says there's . . ." Bea trailed off in the face of Vivian's skeptical expression, then sank back into her chair with a sigh. "Abraham. His name is Abraham. You remember that cabdriver from the other night? The other morning, I mean? After I bailed you out?"

"You did see him again?" Vivian asked, incredulous. "And you didn't tell me?"

Bea gave her an exasperated look. "You've been a bit busy sticking your nose in dangerous places." Vivian winced, knowing her friend was right, as Bea continued. "Anyway, he remembered where he dropped us off, and he came looking for me. We got to talking, and poetry came up. The next day, he showed up again, and he brought me this." She pulled the book out again, laying it on the table between them. "Don't tell my mother. She'd skin me alive if she knew I was taking presents from strangers."

"You gonna see him again?" Vivian asked carefully. She'd never seen Bea so defensive before, though she couldn't tell whether it was over the book or the fellow who gave it to her.

"No. Yes. I don't know." Bea glanced down at the book, then back at Vivian. "I should give it back."

"Do you want to?"

"No," Bea said, her words coming out quick and defensive once more. "I give every penny I earn to my family. I never spend any of it. I'm certainly not buying poetry for myself. A fella thought I deserved something nice for once. That's not so unreasonable, is it?"

"Of course not," said Vivian gently. "Of course you deserve something nice. You know I'm not judging you for it. We can forget I said anything at all, if you want."

Bea sighed again. "There's no way out, is there?" she asked quietly, chin resting in her hands as she stared at nothing. "Not a legal one, anyway. Not for folks like us."

Vivian didn't answer.

V ivian Kelly."

The steely anger in the voice left Vivian as motionless as if she'd been frozen and equally chilled. Unable to make her legs move any further, she clutched the coat she had been about to hang up so tightly she was worried she might rip it. She turned slowly, not showing any of her anger or fear, to face her employer. "Yes, Miss Ethel?"

"Vivian." The shop owner's face was nearly purple with rage. "I am shocked beyond words."

The room was silent, all the other seamstresses hovering over their work, not moving and barely breathing as they tried not to draw any attention to themselves. Everyone knew what it meant when Miss Ethel Marie Barnes spoke in that tone of voice.

"I am sure you know what I am referring to."

Vivian opened her eyes wide, looking as innocent as possible. "I can't say that I do—"

"A man, Vivian. I am talking about the young man who came into my store looking for you, not fifteen minutes ago. Who announced where any customers might hear him that he wanted to speak to one of my seamstresses!" Miss Ethel trembled with outrage. "Do you have any idea how that makes me look? How it makes every girl who works here look?"

Vivian took a deep breath. It had to have been Leo, and if he had been there at that moment, she could have killed him for it. "Beg pardon, but were there actually any customers in the store? Because—"

"That is not the point." The shop owner looked angry enough to spit. But a moment later, her fury was under control, masked with an expression of concern. "Vivian, you do not seem to appreciate the danger that I am trying to protect you, all of you"—her glance took in the rest of the shop girls, huddled over their sewing machines or counters—"from. How will such things make you appear? How will they make your fellow workers appear? You already toe the line of respectability."

Her glance took in Vivian's bobbed hair, the careful patching around the hem of the coat she still held, which only the eye of a trained seamstress would be able to spot. "Such loose associations do you no favors."

Vivian caught her breath, her hands clenching into fists underneath the coat, where her employer could not see them. They couldn't afford for her to lose her job, but she didn't have any way to stop what was about to happen. Honor's favor hadn't come in time.

"No, Vivian, I am afraid I cannot allow you to endanger the reputation of every young woman who works under my care."

The regret in her employer's voice made every muscle in Vivian's body tense with fury. It would have been so much easier if Miss Ethel had looked smug, if the condescending wrongness of her words was reflected in her expression. But she sincerely believed every word she was saying.

"For their good, as well as your own—"

"Excuse me, but the young man who was asking after Vivian is our cousin."

Vivian's eyes snapped toward her sister, and she could feel the silent, anxious rush of air as more than half a dozen young women drew in a collective breath. Florence's head was just barely raised above her sewing machine, her shoulders straight but her chin ducked down, looking as deferential as she possibly could. Her face was painfully pale, and the red flags of color standing out on her cheekbones could have been caused by so many different emotions that Vivian didn't want to guess how her sister was feeling at that moment.

Miss Ethel blinked several times, her momentum derailed by the simple lie. "Your cousin."

"Yes, ma'am."

"I wasn't aware you had any cousins."

Florence's wide-eyed, polite sincerity didn't waver. "We do," she said simply.

Vivian held her breath, not daring to move or even glance at her sister. She could feel the weight of stillness from every girl in the shop.

"Well." Miss Ethel cleared her throat, the fingers of one hand drumming against her thigh. "Well. Well then." She cleared her throat a second time, then raised her voice. "Is there a reason everyone has stopped working?"

The sudden burst of movement was almost painful, a moment of whiplash that made Vivian's head spin as girls went back to sewing, sorting beads, cutting material, stocking shelves.

Miss Ethel glanced down at Vivian's still bandaged hand and pursed her lips. "There are more deliveries today. See that you don't dawdle while completing them."

"Yes, ma'am." Vivian nodded.

She glanced down at the small stack of boxes that the shop owner thrust into her hands. *Mrs. Willard Wilson,* the top one declared, and the address sent a jolt of determined energy through her. She thought of Honor's promise, silently willing the rigid muscles along her spine to relax.

There was a way out. There had to be.

TWENTY-ONE

The housekeeper recognized Vivian this time and escorted her immediately to the small parlor to wait for Mrs. Wilson. "She'll be glad to have her new clothes finished, poor thing. A woman needs comfort in such a time, but of course it's impossible to see anyone if she's not dressed properly."

Vivian nodded, murmuring something polite and deferential as she unwrapped the clothes and laid them out. In the bottom of the box were drawings for three more dresses, with notes scribbled by Miss Ethel. "Will you tell Mrs. Wilson I also have the new designs for her to approve?"

"I will," the housekeeper said. "But it may be a moment before she has time for you. Please refrain from wandering around."

"Of course," Vivian agreed, with absolutely no intention of keeping her promise.

She needed to wait until the coast was clear, though, so she gave the housekeeper five minutes, timed by the relentless tick of the crystal desk clock. But at four minutes, a girl burst into the room.

She came through the second door, the one that led away from the main staircase, her hair down and wild around her shoulders, her feet bare and a heavy dressing robe belted around her waist. It trailed behind her as she stalked toward the desk. She was halfway there before she saw Vivian and stuttered to a halt.

They stared at each other. The girl looked her up and down and sighed, her lip curling. "God, of course this would happen, now everything's in the papers. Unless you can prove it's his, you won't get anything."

"What?"

"So you might as well leave and save us all an embarrassing scene."

Vivian planted her feet, polite in the face of the girl's belligerent stare. "If Mrs. Wilson doesn't like the dresses, that's no embarrassment to me. I'm just delivering them."

"What?" The girl stared blankly before it occurred to her to glance around. When she saw the clothes plainly laid out, a flush swept from her collarbone to her cheeks. "You're the dressmaker."

"Delivery girl today," Vivian said. Perfectly willing to take advantage of the girl's confusion, she added, "Have you had many women showing up with Mr. Wilson's babies, then?"

"What? No, of course not." The girl's blush intensified, and her eyes widened, making her look even more untamed and childish. "I didn't mean . . . You mustn't say anything to . . ." She gulped. "Please don't tell anyone I said that. Hattie made it clear we can't afford to offend anyone right now, and I don't want to make things worse than they already are."

There were plenty of questions to ask in response to that, of course, but Vivian didn't press yet. Instead, she dropped her voice to something gentler, as if she were soothing one of Mrs. Thomas's many skittish children. It was hard to see the perfectly dressed, sullen girl from the photograph in the disheveled, emotional hellion now in front of her, but she was there.

"You must be the younger sister, then. Miss Myrtle?" When the girl nodded, Vivian smiled, helpful and unthreatening. "Do you need mourning clothes as well? We could rush an order for you."

"I've got no interest in *that*." Myrtle scowled. She was younger than her sister, not more than fifteen at most. With childish bluntness, she tossed back her mane of curls and declared, "I won't be mourning him, thanks."

Crossing to the desk as she spoke, she surprised Vivian by lifting the seat of the chair and pulling out a packet of cigarettes and a silver lighter. She opened the window, oblivious to the breeze that swept in and made Vivian shiver, then lit one cigarette and put the rest back in their hiding place. She took a long drag and blew a careful stream of smoke outside. "I don't know why Hattie's bothering to pretend she does. It's a hell of a sham, all of it."

Myrtle fell silent. Her whole body trembled, and it seemed like it wasn't just from the cold air. Everything about the girl was brittle. Vivian had seen enough women hold themselves together by sheer force of will—women who stared at the awfulness of their lives before shrugging and going on with the business of surviving—to recognize the vulnerability that Myrtle's defiance attempted to hide.

Vivian had no idea what a girl like that could know about needing to survive. But she recognized that kind of carelessness and matched it as she said, "It's good for those of us making the mourning clothes, at least."

Myrtle snorted. "There's that, anyway. How appropriate. 'Gotta keep the wheels of business turning,' Willard always said." Taking another long drag, she eyed Vivian. "Should have known better than to assume . . . well. Should have known." Vivian thought it was an apology until the girl added, almost too quietly to be heard, "Too old for his taste, anyway."

Vivian hesitated, wondering if it was meant as an insult and unsure how to respond, while Myrtle turned away to blow another smoky breath out the window. The moment of stillness left her silhouetted against the light. There was something odd about her, something that caught Vivian's attention. But before she could figure out what it was, the door to the sitting room swung open.

Both of them jumped. Myrtle gasped, a flick of her wrist sending her cigarette arcing out the window as they turned to see who had entered.

Hattie Wilson eyed the scene with wary stillness, then smiled gently at her sister. "Close the window, please. You'll catch a chill." She didn't mention the lingering smell of smoke.

Myrtle obeyed, then took the hand that Hattie held out to her. "I just wanted some fresh air," she said, her voice trembling. Neither sister looked at Vivian.

"Of course you did, dear, but we agreed you should stay in your rooms," Hattie said, pulling her sister close. "It's really for the best right now."

"Yeah," Myrtle agreed, leaning her head against her sister's shoulder.

They stood that way for a moment before Hattie kissed Myrtle's forehead and gave her a gentle push toward the door. "I had some new books delivered. Why don't you go take a look while I finish up here?"

After Myrtle left, Mrs. Wilson's polite mask was firmly in place as she turned her attention to the gowns. But her wariness and the sideways glances she sent Vivian's way made it clear that, for some reason, Hattie didn't like that the delivery girl had been talking to her sister. One hand rose to rub her temples, the other rested for a moment on her belly.

"Must be a relief to have family around during such a difficult time, ma'am," Vivian said, polite and efficient as she presented the sketches for Mrs. Wilson to examine. "These are the new designs Miss Ethel sent for your approval."

Hattie gave them a cursory glance, flipping through the pages with her lips pursed. They had just finished discussing a few changes to the designs, and how soon the new clothes would be needed, when a brisk knock heralded the return of the housekeeper.

"Begging your pardon, Mrs. Wilson, but there's a man just arrived to see you. He says it's about Mr. Wilson's business concerns?"

Hattie Wilson sighed, then nodded, her expression resigned. "No escaping that. Is he in the study?" As the housekeeper nodded, Hattie glanced at the dresses that were still waiting. "Leave these, please. I'll try them on and have my girl take care of any final adjustments. Tell Miss Ethel to send me the bill anytime."

Once she was gone, Vivian gathered up the loose drawings and the remaining boxes she had to deliver, leaving her small handbag on the sofa but out of sight. The housekeeper led the way briskly out of the room. Vivian could hear the sound of Mrs. Wilson's voice and a man answering from down the hall, but the housekeeper was already heading downstairs. Vivian craned her neck, but though the study door was open, she couldn't see inside.

She waited until they were nearly at the side entrance before exclaiming over her forgotten bag. The housekeeper sighed with impatience. But instead of allowing Vivian to go back, she stopped a maid who was passing with a mournful array of lilies. "Fetch this girl's handbag from the ladies' parlor, and be quick about it."

Vivian hid a disappointed scowl as she waited, while the foot-tapping housekeeper sent dark glances at her bobbed hair. The maid was quick, as instructed. Within a few minutes Vivian was hustled out the tradesmen's entrance, the door shut firmly behind her.

Her first plan thwarted, she paused for a moment, pretending to shuffle her boxes into a more comfortable position as she thought rapidly. There was a chestnut seller on the edge of the park, just across the street. That would do.

Vivian purchased a bag of nuts and, deflecting the flirtation of the vendor, settled on a nearby bench.

She ate as slowly as possible while she pretended to watch the passersby, all the while keeping an eye on the front door of the Wilsons' house. At one point two maids left through the lower door, and she worried that she would be recognized. But they went in the other direction without looking around.

Vivian had to wait nearly half an hour before the front door finally opened and a man came down the steps, tucking a handful of papers inside his coat. Vivian frowned as she watched him. His hat was tilted down, and he turned up the collar of his coat as he set off, blocking her view of his face even further. She didn't think it was Roy. But there was still something familiar about the way he moved.

She crumpled the paper chestnut bag, tossing it in a nearby bin and gathering her things while the man headed toward Madison Avenue. She waited until he was halfway down the block before following, sticking to her side of the street. He didn't look around as he walked, and Vivian trailed him to a crowded streetcar stop before she could get close without catching his attention.

The streetcar rumbled to a halt, and passengers swarmed on and off, the man among them. Vivian hung back, letting the crowd hide her. When he turned just enough for her to see his face as he stepped up, Vivian spun away quickly before he had a chance to notice her.

Her mind raced as she allowed herself to be swept along by the departing crowd.

What business could Leo have to discuss with Wilson's widow?

TWENTY-TWO

Vivian made her way back to Fifth Avenue, where her last delivery address was located, in a daze.

Leo had been insistent that he didn't know Wilson, that he had nothing to do with the dead man. So there had to be a good reason for him to be visiting the man's house.

Maybe he had been sent on an errand related to whatever business his uncle did. Maybe he was still trying to help her out—to find out something that she could take to Honor to finally wrap up the whole shady business. Maybe . . .

Maybe maybe maybe. Vivian shivered as she walked. Maybe Leo Green was just a damn good liar. Maybe she shouldn't have anything to do with him again. *I wouldn't say I'm a nice fella.* He had admitted as much.

But she had learned to rely on her instincts in the world of the Nightingale, and her instincts had said she could trust him. Didn't that count for something?

Her thoughts were still crawling in circles when she finally found the right address and gave her name absently at the servants' door. "I've got a dress delivery for Mrs. Crawford?"

The maid who had answered the door frowned. "I don't think she's expecting any—"

"They're probably for Miss Crawford," someone called from inside, and a flustered-looking housekeeper bustled up. "She's in the gold sitting room right now, run up and tell her the delivery's here."

As the maid hurried off, the housekeeper smiled, and the genuine kindness of her expression was so surprising after the coldness of the Wilsons' staff that it shook Vivian out of her distraction. "Sorry, lovey, we're all a mess today. The mister and missus have a party tonight, which is probably why Miss Margaret ordered a new frock. You can leave your coat and bag down here, and I'll show you up."

Vivian followed the housekeeper upstairs, gaping at the beauty and wealth on display all around her once they left the servants' domain. Paintings covered the walls, every frame gilded, while old books and older china crowded every shelf. Vases made of actual crystal overflowed with flowers and ferns at regular intervals along the halls. Vivian, after a quick glance to make sure the housekeeper wasn't looking, couldn't help burying her nose in a tumble of roses and breathing deeply. It was the most extravagant and beautiful place any of her deliveries had yet taken her.

"Miss Margaret?" The housekeeper stuck her head around an open door; from the glimpse of gleaming upholstery and knickknacks that Vivian caught, the gold sitting room was well named. "The dressmaker is here with your new gown for tonight."

A perky voice answered from out of sight, the words muffled, and the housekeeper gestured Vivian inside. "Be sure to return to the servants' entrance when you leave, young lady, rather than using the front door." She smiled again to take the sting out of her words. Catching sight of something over Vivian's shoulder, she called out, "Sarah, the Wedgewood vases need to be put *away* tonight, remember how many were broken during the last party!" before hurrying off.

Vivian, bolstered by the friendliness, was smiling as she entered. And then both her smile and her feet froze as she stared at a familiar face.

"Good God, what are you doing here?" Mags demanded, looking equally shocked.

She was dressed in a stylish, demure afternoon dress and didn't have a bit of makeup on, the curly hair that was tucked into a false bob at night now braided and drawn over one shoulder. Lounging in the corner of a sofa with a book in her lap, she looked far younger than she ever did at the Nightingale—seventeen years old, if that, Vivian thought, unable to stop herself from staring.

Mags stared back, both of them silently sizing the other up and trying to decide how to behave. In a jazz club, they could be equals. But here, as Margaret Crawford, society darling and heiress to a clearly not-so-small fortune, and Vivian Kelly, working-class delivery girl, neither of them knew what to do.

Vivian recovered first. She had done enough deliveries to know the script. "Miss Crawford. Miss Ethel sends her compliments. Do you want to see the gowns or try them on?"

Clearly Mags didn't know her half of the expected exchange, though, because she stayed frozen. "I didn't know you worked for a dressmaker," she said, hesitating.

Vivian winced, wondering how she would look Mags in the eyes the next time they came face-to-face in the Nightingale. "Yes, miss. I usually do the sewing, but it's deliveries for me today." She began opening the box to lay out the dress inside, a flouncy green silk number that her fingers itched to stroke. "Should I call a maid to help you with trying them on?"

Mags tossed her book aside and swung her legs around abruptly. "God, no, never mind the dresses, I tried them on when they were fitted. Remind me of your name—Vivian, right?"

"Yes, Miss Crawford."

The girl hesitated again, then shook her head, suddenly making up her mind. "Mags," she said firmly, then laughed. "What a hoot this is.

Worlds crashing into each other. Thank God Mother had one of her heads today or she'd have seen something was up for sure!" Taking in Vivian's stiff posture, she gestured toward the other end of the sofa. "Sit down, why don't you? This really is too funny."

Bounding up, looking even younger, she stuck her head out the door and called loudly, "Anyone around? Oh, Charlie, there you are. Be a pal and bring two soda waters, will you? No," she laughed. "You don't need to mix anything in, there'll be plenty of that at the party tonight. Unless you want some hooch?" she asked, glancing behind her. Vivian, not sure what was happening, shook her head. Mags turned back to the hall. "Just the soda waters!"

Turning back, she grinned at Vivian before flinging herself across the sofa once more. "Sit down, will you? I'll get a crick in my neck if I have to look at you like that."

Vivian hesitated, then perched on the edge of the sofa.

"This really is too funny," Mags said again, looking more like she meant it this time. "And too perfect. I'm sure you hear absolutely everything when you visit places like this, and I love a good goss. Who else buys from you?"

The entry of Charlie with the soda waters saved Vivian from answering immediately. While he popped the tops off two bottles and handed one to Mags—he hesitated, his confusion clear, before handing the second to Vivian—her mind worked rapidly. Why shouldn't she sit and talk for a few minutes, after all? Mags clearly lived in the Wilsons' social circle, and who knew what she might be able to reveal about them? Vivian took a quick swig of her soda water and coughed as the bubbles went up her nose. If Mags wanted to gossip—well, all right then. That sounded like a grand idea.

"I only just started doing deliveries. Can't sew with my hand like this," she said, gesturing to the bandage. Leaning forward and lowering her voice—Mags leaned forward too—she added, "But I had to deliver mourning clothes today."

"Ohh, who for?" Mags whispered.

"A Mrs. Wilson?" Vivian took another drink, watching Mags over the edge of the bottle. "Do you know her?"

"Hattie? God, what is that house like?" Mags's eyes were wide as she sipped her own drink. "I've never been inside, but I've heard it's the coldest place you can imagine. That's what she gets, I guess, for marrying him."

"Mr. Wilson?" Vivian asked, mirroring Mags's posture and widening her own eyes to encourage the girl to keep going.

"He seemed like a peach before the wedding, and everyone thought they were just the bee's knees together, you know," Mags said eagerly. "Hattie's a bit older than me, but I watched the whole thing happen, though I'm not strictly out yet. Hell of a cautionary tale. Just a few months after the wedding, suddenly she and Willard were never seen together. And I mean *never.*"

"Any idea why?" Vivian thought of Pretty Jimmy's hints that Wilson had an eye for Mags.

"Well, of course everyone thought he had an affair or something when he was courting her, and she found out after the wedding." Mags dropped her voice even lower. "I never heard that he was seen with anyone, though he could get awful friendly. I even thought he might have been trying to make a pass at me once or twice, at one of Mother and Dad's parties. Don't know what he was thinking, old fella like him." She rolled her eyes to show just how ancient a man in his thirties was. "Even if he did have an affair, it was too late to do anything about it. Hattie's not the type to risk her position with something as ugly as a divorce."

"She seemed very proper," Vivian agreed, though she wasn't sure that was actually true. Mrs. Wilson had seemed careful and calculating and polite, but there had been an edge of ruthlessness there. "Her sister was another story, of course."

"Myrtle? You met her?" Mags's voice rose, then dropped again as she glanced at the door. "What did you think of her?"

"Wild. And unhappy," Vivian said honestly.

The girl nodded, her curiosity plain. "No one's ever seen much of her. She was too young to be out before the wedding. And they haven't got parents anymore, you know, so she was living with Hattie and Willard afterward. I guess she wanted to escape whatever nastiness was going on there, because she left for boarding school right after things got so chilly between them."

Vivian took another drink to hide her thoughtful expression. Something about Myrtle had put both her sister and the housekeeper on edge, something more than a girl's normal wildness or surliness. But the family was hiding it well, if even an eager gossip like Mags had no inkling anything was amiss.

Maybe Hattie's courtship with Wilson had left her without enough time to keep an eye on her sister. Maybe Myrtle had been rebellious in the face of her sister's marriage—

"What is it?" Mags said eagerly. "Did Myrtle say something to you? About why her sister and Willard fell out?"

"Oh, no. No, nothing like that." Vivian tried to think of an excuse for her silence and said the first thing that popped into her head. "I saw your fella Roy there. Talking with Mrs. Wilson."

Mags's expression grew sour. "He's not my fella anymore, that's for sure. Real cute to know he's still sniffing around Hattie." She rolled her eyes as she leaned back. "Hope he enjoys jumping as soon as she snaps her fingers, in spite of everything she did."

"What did she do?"

"Turned down his proposal," said Mags, her mouth twisting in jealousy that was less hidden than she probably realized. "And then accepted Willard's less than a week later. Hattie was always going to want the man who keeps his hands clean, not the one who does the ugly work behind the money."

"Did Roy work with Mr. Wilson, then?" Vivian couldn't help the shocked laugh that bubbled up. Mags was so good at her gossip that Vivian could almost forget what she was trying to do with their conversation—almost, but not quite. "God, that's awkward for him."

Mags couldn't keep her petulant expression going, and she ended up giggling too. "It must have been, don't you think? Roy's family doesn't have as much money as they pretend to, and he didn't like people knowing he worked for his cash instead of living on daddy's dime. Luckily Willard's business was the sort where Roy could get paid off the books."

Vivian raised her eyebrows. "Guessing Mr. Wilson was in the drugstore business?"

"Something like, though I don't think he owned any himself," Mags said. "It wasn't even a secret; everyone knew Willard was involved in running liquor. Well, who isn't these days, one way or another? But it was foul, let me tell you. Nasty bathtub gin from Chicago and who knows what else. Dad would never buy from him."

"Do you think it got him killed?" Vivian asked, widening her eyes as if the thought had only just occurred to her and watching Mags's reaction closely. She wondered how far she could push before Mags got suspicious.

But the other girl just shrugged. "I heard his heart gave out, of all things. And it seems like Hattie's not wasting any time moving on. She can be a nasty piece of work."

Vivian thought of Hattie Wilson's careful politeness to even the servants and delivery girls, of her gentleness toward her unhappy sister. It didn't seem to her like a fair accusation. But she didn't say anything as Mags continued.

"Though that's a real pickle for her, him dying before the baby arrives. Or maybe not." Mags shrugged again, starting to look a little bored. "Willard wouldn't have been any good as a father."

"I had heard the baby might not have been . . ." Vivian hesitated. She hadn't heard, of course, but she suspected. And maybe Mags knew something. "She seemed pretty friendly with Roy for a woman whose husband just died."

Mags's jaw tightened for a moment. "Well, if that's the way things were, then I'm glad to be shot of him." She snorted. "It would be just like Hattie to manage everything so neatly." The ugly look passed over her face once more, bitter and hurt and jealous. "Though I'll tell you, Hattie's a smart girl. She didn't care about Roy enough to choose him over Willard, and now she's a rich widow. Why would she give that up, even with a little monster on the way? Roy's a fool if he thinks he'll be sailing back into her life now, even with Willard out of the picture." She looked pleased. "Poor stupid bastard."

TWENTY-THREE

H ow late will you be out tonight?"

Florence didn't look up from her magazine—three months out of date and one she had read five times already—as she asked the question.

It was the first she had spoken to Vivian since her lie to Miss Ethel that morning. They had left the dressmaker, come home to make dinner, and washed up, all without Florence saying a single word. Vivian had wanted to thank her sister, but Florence's silences were like the border to a foreign country. She was afraid to cross, even with a white flag in hand.

"Not too late," Vivian said. She wanted to be relieved that it was a simple question instead of a fight, but she couldn't be. She watched her sister warily, waiting for some sign of how much more Florence could bear.

Florence nodded, still not looking up. She would have looked like she didn't care at all if it hadn't been for the small tears spiderwebbing out from where her fingers clutched the magazine pages too tightly. "Home before dawn then?"

"Absolutely." Vivian hesitated. "Flo—"

"It doesn't matter." Florence's words dropped like icicles, dangerous and brittle, shattering on impact. "Just don't forget we have work tomorrow."

"I'm trying to help us," Vivian blurted out. "We're stuck, Flo, we're going in circles and there's no way out or up or through, not honestly. And if I can just—"

"Find a man?" Florence asked. She turned a page, smoothing out the creases and rips.

"Not a man," Vivian snapped. She took a deep breath, remembering the white flag. Florence was all she had. They had spent years cultivating the distance between them, but they couldn't lose each other. "There are people who know . . ."

"Know what?" Florence snorted. "Dark secrets that can help us, if we know the right place to use them?"

"Yes," said Vivian, helpless, close to begging. She said again, "I'm trying to help us."

Florence shook her head. "There's no need, Vivian. You found your escape, and that's . . . that's fine. If it makes it all bearable for you, that's fine. I'll stay here in the real world."

"I'm not leaving you, Flo."

A shrug. "You left me the first night you put on dancing shoes. You picked a world where I can't follow. Even if I wanted to." She glanced up at last, her expression bleak. "Just make sure it's worth it. Before you can't get out, make sure it's worth it."

"Plenty of people in this city go out dancing or have a drink and a smoke from time to time," Vivian protested, though she wondered whether she was trying to convince Florence or herself.

She wanted to help her sister, but she had agreed to Honor's favor long before that. Was it because of the money she owed or because she didn't want to say no when Honor smiled at her? Did she love the Nightingale because she felt at home there or because she couldn't stop fighting against the narrow prison of the life she had been born into?

Florence shook her head, her eyes on her magazine once more. "Those aren't what worry me, Vivian. And you know it."

There was nothing to say, so Vivian didn't try. She thought of the gun, wondered where it had come from and whether it was still there. One of these days, Florence would bend so far that she ended up breaking. Vivian wondered how much of the blame would fall on the world they lived in and how much of it would fall on her.

TWENTY-FOUR

I t was too early for the speakeasy to be open when Vivian arrived at
the Nightingale, but this time Silence only gave her a quick once-over
before he sighed and stood aside.

"Evening, fella," Vivian said jauntily. She took a deep breath as she
stepped inside, the air alive with the memory of smoke and Shalimar
and wild joy. She pushed Florence to the back of her mind. "Honor
around yet?"

Silence shrugged, and Vivian shrugged in reply, mimicking his stoic
scowl until it almost cracked into a smile. "Bandstand," he grunted at last.

Vivian savored the victory as she blew him a kiss and went in.

Honor was arguing with the band leader over the set list, while
Danny and several other employees ferried liquor from the cellar in
preparation for the night. Vivian smiled, remembering Mr. Lawrence's
approving assessment of the Nightingale's bar, as she went to a nearby
table and waited for Honor to notice her.

It didn't take long.

"I'm not objecting to a waltz," Honor was saying. "I know we need something slower after the quickstep unless we want everyone to drop dead before midnight. I'm just not sold on this one. It's too dreary. I'm running a jazz club, not a funeral parlor."

"Folks seem to like it, and you're not the one out there on the floor," the band leader countered. "Why not try dancing to it and see what you think?"

Honor sighed. "I suppose that's fair. What do you say, Vivian?" she asked without turning around. "Care for a waltz?"

Vivian jumped at the sound of her name. She hesitated, then, as Honor glanced over her shoulder, nodded. "Sure thing. Though I warn you, I'm not a girl who loves a waltz, so I'm not going to be the best judge."

"Perfect. We need an unbiased opinion here." Honor held out her hand. "Hope you don't mind me leading?"

Vivian shook her head, not trusting her voice to push any words past the knot of excitement in her chest. Honor had asked her to dance more than once, but this was the first time she had said yes. As the first melancholy notes filled the dance hall, she took Honor's hand and allowed herself to be drawn close.

Like all the best leads, Honor barely used her hands or arms to direct the dance. Instead, she moved them with her whole body. Vivian followed without needing to think about it, their path tracing a slow, beautiful sweep around the dance floor. Honor wore perfume, she discovered, a heady mix of vanilla and spice that hovered around her wrists and collarbone.

She had thought it would be awkward, dancing together for the first time and her unable to hide her thoughts in the darkness of a crowded dance floor. She knew that the entire band and every employee currently hovering around the bar was watching. But when Honor smiled, it wasn't her normal sultry, taunting expression. Instead, she looked happy, relaxed in a way that she usually couldn't be. Vivian found herself relaxing too.

"You like to waltz," she said. It wasn't a question. No one could move with that kind of easy joy unless they loved it.

Honor nodded. "It's my favorite dance," she agreed. Then, pursing her lips in self-mockery, "Don't tell anyone I'm a sappy romantic."

"Your secrets are safe with me."

She had meant it to be teasing, and the serious look that she received in response caught her off guard.

"Are they?" Honor murmured. "I sure hope so." Changing the subject abruptly, she asked, "How are things with your Mr. Green?"

"You want to talk about Leo while I'm dancing with you?" Vivian asked, flustered enough to lose her footing for a full count of the music before Honor got them back into the rhythm. "He's not my Mr. Green."

"Whatever you say," Honor said, an edge of laughter undercutting her placating tone. "I never mind a little competition, you know. But if you like we can talk about something else. Have you learned anything interesting since we last talked?"

Vivian snorted. "Too much. Seems like he ran around on his wife, made passes at everyone from debutantes to shopgirls, gambled, ran bad liquor, got other people to run his ugly errands, and—" Vivian broke off, stumbling to a halt in Honor's arms as two men on the stairs caught her eye. "And I think those are his errand boys."

Honor turned sharply, putting herself between Vivian and the front door in a single smooth movement and motioning the band into silence.

Vivian peered over Honor's shoulder, then whispered urgently, "Those are the two who attacked Danny. And who . . ." She swallowed. "Who cornered me. The big one's called Eddie, the other one is Bruiser George."

"Good to know. Now head to the back of the room, please," Honor said, her voice perfectly even as she stepped forward. "I've got this handled."

Vivian shrank back, eyes fixed on the two toughs sauntering down the stairs. Honor didn't flinch as she planted her feet wide, blocking their way forward.

"Fellas. I'd tell you we're not open yet, but I suspect you know that.

So I'll just say that if my doorman isn't still in one piece, you won't be for much longer either."

Bruiser George and his hulking friend stopped, both clearly expecting fear and taken aback when it didn't materialize. "He might have a bit of a headache," the smaller man said. "But you shouldn't need to hire a new one."

"Glad to hear it." Honor crossed her arms.

Vivian caught her breath, her knees trembling as she wondered whether she needed to get the hell out of there.

"Say what you were sent to say then, and get out," Honor continued. "I've got a business to run here."

The chatty George smiled, slick as oil. "That's maybe not the smartest thing to say right now, Miz Huxley. You've had a couple warnings already. And this business you're so proud of . . . well, you're just one woman." He glanced at Eddie, who cracked his knuckles and scowled. "I'd really advise you to tread a little more carefully. You don't want to make any enemies."

Honor waited a beat. "Was that all of it, then? Seems a waste to send you boys down here just for that nonsense. You should talk to your boss about making better use of your talents."

An ugly look crossed Bruiser George's face as he stepped forward. "Listen here, you f—"

"Ah-ah, careful." Honor raised one finger. Vivian couldn't see her face, but something about Honor's expression must have scared George, because he stopped in his tracks. "You might want to rethink whatever it is you're about to call me."

She tipped her head to one side; the men looked where she indicated and blanched. Vivian, whose attention had been glued to the simmering drama playing out in front of her, glanced around the room for the first time. Her eyes grew wide. The musicians had put aside their instruments and come down from the bandstand, while the bartenders and Honor's silent bruisers had drifted in from the back hall and stood only a few steps away.

Danny was only a pace behind Vivian, and he put a quick, reassuring hand on her arm as he stepped past and took up his post behind Honor's shoulder. The two toughs eyed him warily, clearly remembering their last encounter. Honor didn't look around, but judging by her posture she knew Danny was there, knew all of them were there, standing loyally at her back. Vivian felt dizzy with fear and adrenaline. Like the rest of them, she would have rushed forward the moment Honor gave the word.

"Was there anything else you needed to say?" Honor asked, soft and dangerous.

Eddie cracked his knuckles again, looking uneasily at his partner, as if resigned to the inevitable need to go down swinging. The smaller man glanced around the room once more before turning to glare at Honor. "Smart girl, having so many men around," he taunted.

There was a shift of weight around the room, and a low, angry murmur from the Nightingale employees, but Honor laughed. "You want to settle this just you and me? Fine, I'll tell my muscle to back off if you'll do the same."

"We're here to deliver a message, not fight," George snapped. "And if you know what's good for you, you'll give us the name of Mr. Wilson's killer."

"Can't give you what I don't have," Honor said. "And anyway, I read in the paper that he died of a heart ailment." She glanced at Danny. "Ain't that right?"

"Sure is," he replied, his entire body coiled and ready to fight.

"So if that's all, gentlemen, my boys here will show you out." Honor gestured behind her, and Vivian jumped as the two bruisers brushed past her to go stand by their boss. "Be gentle, fellas," Honor added. "We wouldn't want word to get out that we're looking for a fight."

A quiet chuckle went around the room, but Vivian couldn't bring herself to join in. Even once the two errand boys had been escorted out of the club, she couldn't relax. Instead, she shifted from foot to foot, full of jittery energy that had nowhere to go, as the musicians went calmly back to rehearsing and Danny conferred with Honor in low voices.

"We'll talk about hiring a few more man-sized deterrents," Honor agreed as they both turned away from the door. "Benny and Saul will check on Silence and—" Honor broke off as she caught sight of Vivian's tense figure still hovering behind her. "Oh, pet, I'm sorry you were here for that," she said, her voice soothing. She reached out to gently rub her hands up and down Vivian's arms; Vivian was surprised how warm they felt against the chill of her skin. "Go wait in my office while you calm down, it should be unlocked. Danny, bring the girl some bubbles, will you? You know she loves them."

"Sure thing, boss." He glanced at Vivian. "You need me to walk you back there?"

Their concern was embarrassing enough to help her pull herself together. "Don't worry, I don't need to go anywhere. I'm peachy, really."

Honor shook her head. "Do it for me. Please. I'll feel better if we can talk for a few minutes once I get this all sorted out." She smiled gently. "You can tell me how you liked the waltz."

She was lying, of course—Vivian caught the worried glance Honor and Danny exchanged. But it was enough to let her save face, so she nodded. "See you in a bit, then." She added, with an effort at her usual sauciness, "Don't forget my bubbles, Danny boy."

Dancing had given Vivian smooth feet and tight control over her movement. She would let herself shake, she decided, when she was safely in Honor's office with the door closed against watchful eyes.

She sauntered across the dance floor without letting her trembling knees give her away. The band leader caught her eye as she left and gave her a quick wink, and the brief moment of camaraderie bolstered her as she walked down the empty hall and up the stairs. Behind her, the music rose once again, a clamoring warm-up that almost drowned out the shouts of the staff as they hurried to finish setting up for the night.

That feeling of comfort lasted until the door to Honor's office clicked shut behind her. She let herself sag back against the wood, closing her eyes briefly as she gulped in a breath and wondered if her heartbeat was going to slow down anytime soon.

She opened her eyes when a strange *whooshing* noise echoed through the room. There was a jumbled mess of papers on Honor's desk, and a pile of them had toppled over and slid down to the floor.

That didn't seem like Honor, to leave her papers out with her office door unlocked. Frowning, Vivian walked across the room, already stretching out her hands to pick them up.

The sharp movement in the corner made her draw up short. Heart leaping, Vivian spun around. She wasn't alone in the room.

"What the hell are you doing here?" Roy Carlton growled.

TWENTY-FIVE

They stared at each other, Vivian hovering near the desk, Roy casting worried glances toward the door, neither sure what to do next. Vivian thought about calling for help, but it had been so loud downstairs. There was a good chance no one would hear her.

No, if Roy was sneaking around Honor's office looking for something, the best thing she could do would be to keep him busy, keep him talking, until Danny arrived with the champagne. He'd know what to do next.

Vivian took a deliberate step back, putting herself between Roy and the door. She squared her shoulders and tried to look like her knees weren't still shaking. "I don't think you're supposed to be in here, Mr. Carlton."

He flinched at the sound of his own name. "*You* weren't supposed to be in here," he muttered, his eyes darting around the room before locking on her once more. "No one was."

"You're with those boys out front, then?" Vivian asked carefully. "They were supposed to distract Honor and the rest of the staff while you were in here." She glanced at the scrambled piles of paper. "What were you trying to find?"

Roy's gaze had started to wander around the room, but that made it snap back to her. His eyes narrowed, and the fury in them made Vivian take an involuntary step backward.

"D'you know what she has in there?" he snarled, taking a step toward her. "Go on, ask her next time. You'd do the same, to find out what dirt she has on you. On everyone who comes here." He took another step forward. "Get away from the door."

If he wanted to hurt her, she told herself, he would have done it already. Danny would be there soon. She just had to hold out a few minutes more. "Not until you answer my question."

Roy's face twisted, and he moved forward suddenly, grabbing her by both arms and yanking her toward him. "Or maybe you already know." He shoved her away from the door, back toward the desk. But instead of running, he turned to follow her. "You're here, aren't you? You've been following me."

Vivian caught herself on one of the chairs by the desk, dragging it between them as he stalked toward her. "I'm not—"

"You've been following me," he repeated, sounding desperate now. "What do you know?" Another step forward. He yanked the chair from her hands and shoved it aside. The backs of Vivian's hips were pressed against the edge of the desk. She could see the sweat standing out on his forehead, could see his hands shaking. "What do you *know*?"

Where was Danny? Vivian could still hear the music and shouts from downstairs. Now that Roy was between her and the door, she had to keep him talking or he would make a break for it. His eyes were wide and panicked, and men who were scared and angry were dangerous.

But maybe this one could be manipulated.

"Trying to see what she had on Wilson, then?" Vivian suggested, her fear making her defiant even though she knew she should have been cautious. She needed to placate him, to convince him that she was no threat at all. But her mouth kept talking, as if it knew exactly what to say to goad him. "Or maybe one of his rivals?" Her gaze flicked up and down, looking him over with scorn. "Still running his ugly errands, even after he's dead. Don't you want to be better than that?"

She regretted the taunt as soon as it was said, waiting for him to slap her or lunge at her. But it landed just as she hoped. Roy shook his head, his hair flopping limply into his eyes. "No. No. You're just like her. You all think I'm just . . ." His tongue fumbled around the words. Glaring as if it were her fault, he suddenly grabbed her arm and hauled her forward, until they were only inches apart. "I'm *not*. Hattie doesn't know I came here, but I'll show her—I'll show *everyone*—I'm no one's errand boy anymore. I'm as good as Willard was—I can do what he did even *better* than he did—"

Vivian held as still as possible, though his grip was bruising her arm, while he stumbled through his protests, desperate to prove himself to anyone who looked down on him.

"Were you hoping that with Willard out of the way, Hattie would admit the baby was yours?"

He stared at her, his face blank with panic. "The baby?"

"He was a right bastard, as far as I've heard," Vivian said, lowering her voice. "It probably seemed like a swell idea, didn't it? Your boss out of the way, you get his wife and your baby back, move up in the pecking order—"

"You don't know what you're *talking* about," he insisted, looking desperate.

"Poor Roy. All it took was one little bullet. But now your new boss wants to know who did it, and you've got a hell of a secret to keep."

He was shaking his head. "Hattie and I . . ." His eyes suddenly narrowed, sharp with anger. "I didn't kill him."

"Can't even admit it?" Vivian taunted. "What a big man."

She had finally pushed him too far. The back of his free hand struck her cheekbone like an explosion, sending her head snapping back. "You keep your filthy mouth shut. I didn't do nothing. *Nothing.*" He shook her fiercely, and Vivian stumbled, her head spinning from the blow. "You even think of saying trash like that to Hattie—"

He shifted forward, and Vivian yanked her knee up.

Her aim was off, and instead of falling to the floor in howling pain, he stumbled, cursing.

Vivian shoved the chair at him as he lunged toward her. She darted past, trying to reach the door as she drew breath to scream.

He recovered too quickly. He grabbed her around the waist, cutting off her cry and throwing her to the ground. Even as she tried to stand, he grabbed one arm and hauled her upright. "You'll keep your trash mouth shut—"

"Vivian?" The cheerful voice from outside interrupted him, and they both turned in stupid shock as the door opened. "Danny sent me with the—"

Leo stood on the threshold, the door swinging shut behind him as he stared at the two of them. Vivian had a moment to see that he held a bottle of champagne in one hand and two coupes in the other before the sound of shattering glass filled the air. Leo dropped the glasses and swung the champagne bottle.

Roy pushed Vivian aside to duck out of the way; the bottle glanced off the side of his head, shattering as it struck the wall. Leo didn't hesitate, thrusting what was left of the bottle toward Roy's face while the other man stumbled backward. Vivian scrambled out of the way. She was too transfixed by the fury on Leo's face to think of calling for help.

Roy wasn't a fighter. Looking panicked, he retreated from Leo once more, grabbing Vivian. He might have tried to put her between himself and the jagged remains of the bottle, but he didn't have the chance as Leo tossed it aside.

Vivian heard the sound of shattering glass as if from a long way away. Her eyes were fixed on Leo, trying to understand how he suddenly had a gun in his hand.

He pointed it at Roy. "On the floor." The gun was steady, the look in his eyes so cold she felt as though she were staring at a stranger.

She wondered for a split second what it would be like to see some-one die in front of her.

Roy's grip tightened on her arm, a moment of indecision before he shoved her toward Leo. It was only a few feet, but she was between him and the gun, and it was enough. Roy ran past while Leo, acting on reflex, caught Vivian with his free arm.

Roy kicked the door closed behind him while Vivian and Leo were still catching their breath. Even though Vivian pulled away and yanked the door open moments later, he was already gone. Darting down the stairs, she was just in time to see the door to the alley swing-ing closed.

The deep, panicked breaths she was gulping caught up with her a moment later. She doubled over in a fit of gasping coughs until Leo got her back inside the office and urged her into one of the chairs, their feet crunching over broken glass.

He tucked the gun into the back of his waistband as he did, and she flinched away as he crouched in front of her.

"Viv?" he asked. The coldness was gone from his eyes as he looked her over. Whatever he saw made him draw in a sharp breath, and he reached out to brush a hand against her throat, though he dropped it when she pulled away. "Talk to me, Viv. Are you okay? Can you breathe?"

She caught her breath through sheer force of will, just long enough to pull away from his hands and stand. "You should have gone after him."

"He's long gone." Leo's voice was still gentle, as if he were trying to calm a scared animal. She still flinched again as he stepped toward her. "I'll get Danny to send someone after him as soon as I make sure you're all right. You should sit down, sweetheart."

"I'm not your sweetheart," Vivian snapped, trembling. She could feel the fear building into a knot of tears that she refused to let out.

"Viv, it's okay, he's gone. We're going to—"

"No." In the silence that hung between then, she could hear the pud-dle of champagne fizzing against the broken glass. "What the hell are you doing here anyway?"

Leo frowned. "Danny had to finish getting the bar set up. He said you were in here waiting for a drink and asked me to bring it to you."

The hurt and fear were bubbling up, sharp as the champagne and far more bitter. She couldn't keep them inside. "And did Danny also ask you to show up where I work?"

"What? What does that have to do—"

"I almost got sacked this morning because of you."

"You snuck out without a word. I wanted to make sure you were okay." Leo stared at her, his expression growing wary. Vivian glared back defiantly, but he must have seen behind that. His voice grew soothing again. "Viv, I think you're mostly upset about what just happened. And you have every right to be," he added quickly, seeing the quick flare of fury across her face. "I'm sorry about showing up at your work, but you have to know I'd help out if I got you in trouble. You don't need to worry, about Roy or anything else."

"I don't need anyone to take care of me." Her breathing was too fast, her heart was too fast, but she couldn't think of a reason, much less a way, to calm down. "Especially not someone as shady as you."

"Viv, that's not fair—"

"How many people have you killed?"

"What?"

Vivian reached out to yank his coat aside, gesturing at the handle of the revolver sticking out of his waistband. "You were more than ready to shoot him just now."

Leo jerked away from her. "He *attacked* you—"

"How many people have you killed?" she repeated.

He was glaring as fiercely as she was now, and his anger fueled her own. It felt right and good, because if she wasn't furious—if he tried one more time to be sympathetic—she was going to break down in the middle of Honor's office. And Vivian hadn't cried where anyone else could see since she was six years old.

"None," Leo snapped. He took a deep breath, and Vivian was

dismayed to see him drag his emotions under control. "I may be a shady bastard but I haven't—"

"Sure, I believe you," she interrupted, uninterested in whatever reasonable-sounding excuse he might offer. "You've never killed anyone, you just happen to carry around a gun. Just like you didn't have anything to do with Wilson, you just happened to visit his widow earlier today."

Leo's head snapped back as if she had struck him. "I don't know who said that—"

"I saw you." Vivian's eyes were as hard as her voice, and she crossed her arms against the urge to soften either of them. Leo's expression had gone utterly blank, giving nothing away, and she refused to meet him halfway. "I saw you leaving the house today, after a *business associate*"— her voice dripped with sarcasm—"of Mr. Wilson's came to call on his widow."

"You just think I offed the man? Even after I told you I never met him?" When Vivian didn't say anything, Leo's expression darkened into a scowl. "Yeah, sure, I was there. You want to know why? I wanted to help you—anything to get you out of this mess before you get hurt."

"And you want me to believe you?" Vivian gripped the back of the chair, glad it was between them, a barrier against the trust that she wished she could give him and couldn't. "Fine, then. Tell me why you came back to New York."

"I told you—"

"Not who you work for. What you do," she snapped.

For a long moment, Leo didn't say anything. Then he shook his head. "No."

Vivian stared at him. She hadn't thought he'd answer, but she'd expected a glib runaround, not an outright refusal. "No?"

"No." He crossed his arms. "Why do you need to know so bad? Everyone in this club is involved in something illegal—so are you, just by being here. That doesn't seem to bother you. So why are you so hung up on how I make my dough?"

"There's a hell of a difference between serving liquor and killing someone," Vivian pointed out, her hands clenched so tightly she knew if she looked down the knuckles would be white.

"Sure is, but I told you I haven't done that." Leo took a deep breath, and his voice was soothing as he reached for her again. "So why won't you trust me?"

"Of course I don't trust you, Leo, I don't know you!" Vivian snapped, pulling away from his hands. They were gentle now, and she wanted to be held until she stopped shaking. But all she could see when she looked at them was the jagged edge of that bottle swinging toward another man's face. "You just appeared in my life a few days ago."

"That didn't seem to bother you last night."

Her hand flashed out before she realized what she was doing; he caught her wrist right before she slapped his face. The two of them stared at each other. Vivian could see a muscle twitching in his jaw.

"It was a statement of fact," he said at last, letting go of her wrist, though neither of them moved apart. "Not a judgment and certainly not a complaint. But hell if I'm going to stand here and keep defending myself to you."

His movements were jerky as he yanked a small bundle of papers from the inside pocket of his coat and threw it on the floor between them. "Those were in the top drawer of Wilson's desk. Do whatever you want with them." His jaw twitched again, as if he wanted to say something else, but instead he turned on his heel and stormed out.

The sudden burst of cheerful music as he opened the door was so jarring that Vivian couldn't quite understand what had just happened. By the time she thought to wonder if she should stop him, the door was already swinging shut, and she was left alone.

She shivered and rubbed her arms, trying to soothe away the goose bumps that had appeared. Leaving the papers where they had fallen, she started hunting around for something to clean up the glass and champagne.

Honor found her awkwardly sweeping up with a handful of newspaper. "What the hell happened here? Danny said Mr. Green was keeping you company—"

"He left," Vivian said stiffly, bending back to the mess.

"Never mind that, Vivian, someone else will clean it up." Honor gripped her shoulders, raising Vivian up gently and taking the newspaper from her hands. "Why are you shaking?"

Honor was right—the beaded fringe along the edge of Vivian's dress was trembling, and she noticed with surprise that her hands were too. She let herself be tucked into one of the comfortable leather chairs while Honor poured them each a finger of amber liquor. Vivian took a sip, grateful for the fiery warmth, before she told Honor what had happened.

Honor listened silently, then drained her own glass in a single gulp. "I'm so sorry," she said, meeting Vivian's eyes. "Are you—"

She reached out, but Vivian pulled away sharply. "I'm fine," she said quickly, tossing back her own drink. She couldn't bear to let anyone else see her fall apart that night.

"I never meant to put you in danger," Honor said softly.

"Well, I ended up there anyway. Twice," Vivian said, her voice cold. The look of pain on Honor's face made her feel grimly satisfied. If she had to be hurt, at least she wasn't the only one. "Even after I told you I wanted out."

She had wanted out, but she had let herself be persuaded back in, knowing it wasn't safe. Honor's doing, or her own? Vivian put down her glass and stood abruptly. Wrapping her arms around herself, she sighed. "My own damn fault, I guess."

"It was my fault too," the club owner said. "I promise, you're done now. That's the end of it."

Setting her glass down, she reached out again. This time, Vivian didn't pull away. Taking her hand, Honor drew her in close, one arm going around her back and the other hand resting against her cheek. For a moment, Vivian held herself stiffly, unsure she wanted to be comforted. Then she sighed, relaxing as Honor's lips brushed hers, gently, far more gently than she would have expected. Honor's hands moved soothingly over her back, and when she pulled away she didn't let go, just let Vivian's head rest against her shoulder for several still moments.

When she straightened at last, Honor smiled, pressing one more kiss against her lips before stepping away.

"You okay?" she asked.

Vivian tried to wrap her head around what had just happened. She couldn't tell from Honor's face what the kiss had meant to her, whether it changed anything between them or was just one more in the series of careful moves that the Nightingale's owner was always taking. But those moments had been what Vivian needed to pull herself together. Pushing aside the fear and uncertainty—she would deal with it later—she nodded. She even managed to smile.

"Really, it was nothing. Some drunk throws a temper tantrum in our building once a week, at least. What I want to know is what he was getting into." She gestured at the papers still scattered over Honor's desk, hoping to distract them both. "Any chance he found something in your files?"

"I'll make sure someone asks him in the next twenty-four hours," Honor said, her voice grim. She was back to business as usual, and Vivian was glad she hadn't made a big deal about the kiss—glad and hurt and confused. "My boys'll know where to find him, and I'm sure a few people out there will be glad to learn everything you just told me. If that baby's his . . ."

"And he had something to prove to Mrs. Wilson, and to whoever the new boss is now that Wilson's out of the picture," Vivian added.

Honor nodded. "Hell of a chip to carry on your shoulder. But people get stupid in this business." She gathered the papers together, giving the edges a sharp tap against the desk to sift them into a tidy stack.

"Do you really have something in there on everyone who comes to the club?"

Honor looked up, surprised. "Not everyone, no. Just anyone who comes back enough times."

"What sort of something?"

Honor looked bemused. "Where they live, what I can find out about their work or family. Anything that can be used as leverage against them." She leaned her palms against the top of the desk. "It's hard to be a woman alone in this business, especially a woman like me"—she smiled a little as her eyes dropped briefly to Vivian's lips—"so I like to have insurance. I rarely have to use the information, but it's nice to have."

Vivian hesitated, but she asked the question anyway. She needed to know. "Do you have anything about Leo Green?"

She got a wary look in response, and it seemed like Honor wouldn't answer. But at last she shrugged. "Not much, sorry. Where he lives, he's got a father, he's friends with Danny . . . though I don't know if either of them could be used against each other." She leaned forward, brows rising and her voice growing a little mocking. "Is there anything *you* could tell me about him?"

"No," Vivian said quickly, looking away and wishing she hadn't asked. Talking about Leo with Honor was a bad idea. To change the subject, she said abruptly, "I want to see what you have about me."

Honor didn't move, and her eyes didn't leave Vivian's. "Why?"

Vivian didn't look away. "I'm curious."

At last the other woman shrugged and began sifting through the stack of papers. She didn't look long; the sheet she wanted was right on top. Coming around the desk, she perched on the edge and held the paper out. "Suit yourself."

Vivian only hesitated a moment before she took it. The notes were handwritten, and the mention of where she worked reminded her that Honor owed her a piece of information about her employer— something she was more than ready to collect. But the part that caught her eye was further down the page. *Leverage: sister (Florence), Beatrice Henry, HH.*

Vivian glanced up, her mouth dry. She already knew the answer, but she had to ask. "Who's HH?"

Honor reached out to take the paper back, but instead of letting go, Vivian allowed herself to be pulled gently forward. Honor met her eyes. "Me."

"You can't be used against me," Vivian protested.

"Are you sure about that?" Honor's hand slid from the paper and traveled slowly up Vivian's bare arm. "I'm not above using myself as a weapon. Are you?"

There were only a few inches separating them. Vivian took a deliberate step back. "I'm sure you're not," she said, feeling cold again as she looked away.

Her gaze fell on the papers that Leo had left, still scattered across the floor, and she bent to pick them up. "Leo took these from Wilson's study for me," she said. "He said they were on top, so they were probably the last things Wilson was going through before he went out that night. Though I guess they're not important anymore, if your boys are going to find Roy soon."

"What do they say?"

Vivian flipped through them, frowning. "It looks like . . . notes about properties he owned? A few of them, actually. The Fifth Avenue house, a place on the North Shore, and . . . That's odd."

"What?"

"It's for a building on Baxter Street." Vivian looked up, confused. "Why would someone like Wilson have property in the Chinese neighborhood?"

"Let me see it." Honor took the paper, staring at it for long enough that Vivian grew concerned. She was on the verge of asking what was wrong when Honor shrugged, handing it back. "Maybe he was a sleazy landlord as well as a sleazy bootlegger. You're right—it's probably not important anymore." The club owner's voice was all business as she walked back around her desk.

Vivian folded the papers absently over each other, not sure what to do now. She cleared her throat, her fingers worrying at the edges before she found her calm again and managed to smile. "I should . . . I suppose I'll take off."

Honor had begun tidying the mess of her desk once more, but she glanced up and nodded. "Go get a drink. And have a dance. You'll feel better afterward." She gestured broadly, her arm sweeping across the whole office as she shook her head. "I have to go through things here and make sure Mr. Carlton didn't get into anything else. And Vivian?"

Vivian, her hand on the door, turned back, waiting.

"I'll find him," Honor said quietly.

Vivian shrugged, her defensive walls firmly back in place. "Sure. See you around, I guess."

That made Honor smile. "Count on it, pet. I'm looking forward to our next waltz."

TWENTY-SIX

When she got back to the main room, the band was swinging their way through "Sister Kate" and the dance floor was full. Vivian glanced around, hoping to find Bea on a break, but it was a busy night. All the waitresses were running their feet off. Instead, she squeezed her way between shoulders until she found an open stool at the bar.

Danny caught her eye when she scooted her way up, and gave her a quick smile. There was an edge of concern to it, though—maybe her poker face wasn't as good as she thought. He flipped a towel over his shoulder and poured the last of a champagne bottle into a glass as he came to where Vivian was waiting.

"Since you didn't get any of the bottle I sent," he said quietly, sliding it across the bar to her. "You okay?"

She scowled. "How do you know?"

"Leo told me what happened. He's gone now," Danny added as she swung around.

Vivian turned back, wishing she hadn't been so obvious. "I don't care," she said too quickly. Leo deserved everything she said to him, hadn't he? He had lied to her. But Honor was the one who had put her in danger. And she had agreed to it. Vivian gulped down a mouthful of champagne, coughing as the bubbles struck the back of her throat. "Anyway, I'm fine."

"You will be," Danny agreed. "Carlton won't bother you again. Hux'll take care of it."

"Wish I were better at taking care of myself," Vivian said. Scowling into her glass, she added, "Wish I knew how to throw a punch like you."

Danny chuckled. "Thinking of that alley brawl? I had to learn how to fight young." He raised his eyes, taking in the men filling the club with a cynical smile. "Too many people think it's okay to use a Chinese fella as a punching bag. Some need a lot of discouraging."

"Your dad taught you, then?" Vivian took a slower sip of her drink this time.

Danny shook his head. "Leo did, back when we were kids. We lived on opposite sides of Bowery, and I jumped into a fight with him and some other Hester Street boys when I was ten. I'd've got the stuffing kicked out of me, but Leo said he'd teach me how to punch first so it was a fair fight, and then we could get back to it."

The mention of Leo made Vivian scowl again. She wondered if he had mentioned his friend's name on purpose, just to see how she would react. She wondered what he thought of how she had. "Danny . . . what do you know about him?"

"About Leo?" The bartender shrugged. "Not much, these days."

"Is he a good person?" she asked quietly, running a finger along the edge of her glass.

He shrugged again. "Are any of us good people here, Viv?"

"You are."

"I'm nice," Danny said, shaking his head. "That's not the same thing. I know what it takes for Hux to stay in business."

Vivian tried not to shiver. She was getting an idea of what it took for

Honor to stay in business, too, and finally realizing how much Danny's devil-may-care attitude might hide.

The Nightingale had given her glamor and fun and music that she could lose herself in. She had danced in and out, carefree and careless, without asking what it took for that world to exist.

"And I'd help her out with anything she asked me. So no." Danny smiled. Instead of his usual flirtatious grin, his expression was a little sad. "I'm not that good either. You probably shouldn't spend as much time with me as you do," he added, playful again. "You're too sweet for us here."

"I'm not that sweet," Vivian protested. "And I'm not that good."

Danny studied her. "You are when it counts, Viv. I hope you don't lose that." He turned away from her as another customer approached the bar. "What's your poison, kitten?"

The newcomer was Mags, transformed once again from innocent society girl to daring baby vamp, her hair pinned up into a faux bob and held back with a sparkling headband that, Vivian now realized, might be real diamonds. "Bubbles and gin, please. Vivian, you promised to introduce us for real."

Her expression was so pouty that it made Vivian shake her head and smile in spite of herself. "Mags, Danny, you two should know each other better. Danny's a peach, and Mags is a hell of a doll. You should ask her for a dance when you're on a break."

"I might do that," Danny said. "For now, sadly, I'm on the clock." He winked as he slid a glass across the counter and into the girl's carefully manicured hands.

Mags sipped her drink and sighed. "Golly, that's good."

"I'll have one of the same, please."

Vivian jumped as someone slid into the seat next to her, and she found herself staring at a familiar face.

"Vivian, right?" the other woman asked.

"Sadie," Vivian said, surprised. "You made it back after all."

"Do I look that different all dolled up?" Sadie asked, handing over a crumpled bill as Danny slid a drink across the bar to her. "You almost didn't recognize me."

"You look pretty," Vivian said honestly. It was true. Besides being dressed for a night out, Sadie looked more relaxed, some of her brittle grief smoothed away by the heat and noise.

Sadie laughed a little. "Thanks. I decided you were right. Dancing's good for the soul, so I could probably use more of it." She smiled over the rim of her glass at Danny. "And a little glass of something doesn't hurt."

"Looks like the pickings are slim for dancing tonight," Mags interjected, sighing. "It's early yet, though, so maybe there's still hope?"

Danny laughed. "I'm sure a looker like you will have the gents falling all over themselves."

"If only they danced as well as I like." Mags rolled her eyes at Vivian. "Ever since I tossed Roy over, it's hard to find a fella who can keep up. Oh, but there's Laurie!" She put her glass down and hopped up, already waving as she scampered off.

Danny shot Vivian a quick glance at the mention of Roy's name, and her hands tightened on the stem of her glass. Her mind wanted to go back to those moments facing him down, but she turned instead to the best distraction at hand. *Dancing's good for the soul,* she had told Sadie. Maybe, if she followed her own advice, she could pretend the world of the Nightingale was nothing more than a fun escape for a little while longer.

She swallowed the last of her drink in one gulp and, as the band launched into a new song, turned to Sadie. "Want to dance?" she asked, holding out her hand.

Sadie's eyes widened. "Do you lead?"

"Sure do," Vivian said, her heart pounding recklessly. "What do you say? No reason to waste a perfectly good dance just because all the menfolk have two left feet."

Sadie hesitated a moment longer, then laughed. "Why not?" she said, taking Vivian's hand. The warmth of her palm made Vivian realize just how cold her own fingers were. "Show me what you can do."

Vivian could feel Danny's eyes on them, but she kept her gaze on Sadie as she smiled. "Let's find out," she said, hopping off the bar stool and leading them toward the dance floor.

There was a lot of night still ahead, and she didn't want to waste it being scared. After that, she could decide which world she wanted to belong to.

TWENTY-SEVEN

After last call, when the patrons had stumbled into the early-morning dark and the staff were sweeping up under the glare of the electric lights, Danny put Vivian and Bea in a cab together.

Vivian had been waiting at a corner table, her dancing shoes kicked off and her feet tucked under her, until Bea was off work. Bea had spent the rest of her shift watching Vivian nervously, looking more concerned every time Vivian said that she was fine. Vivian tried to point out that they could walk home as usual, but Danny was insistent.

"Humor me," he said, dry but firm, over Vivian's protests as he handed the driver a folded wad of bills. "It's safer tonight."

"He's right, Viv," Bea pointed out as she untied the ribbons on her shoes and leaned back with a tired sigh. "And anyway, I bet that's Honor's money paying for our ride."

Vivian scowled. She had planned to tell Bea what had happened herself and was frustrated that either Danny or Honor had beaten her to it. But they were right. And she wasn't stubborn enough to walk through the dark streets of Manhattan when Roy and his friends might be lurking out there, waiting to have another chat with her.

"There's a girl," Danny said when she finally nodded. "See you two later."

They were quiet for the first half of the drive. Vivian leaned her forehead against the glass of the window, catching glimpses of the tops of the buildings. She thought Bea might have fallen asleep until her friend asked quietly, "Do you want to talk about it?"

Vivian glanced over. Bea's eyes were still closed, her head tipped back against the seat. There were creases around the corners of her eyes, tight spidery lines of fatigue and concern. Bea had enough to worry about without adding to the list.

"No need," Vivian said, her voice light as a shrug. "And anyway, I'm off the hook for good now. Things'll be calmer."

"That's good," Bea said, yawning.

Vivian had been thinking about asking Bea to keep her company that night. Then Bea yawned again, reaching up to rub a tight spot in one shoulder. Vivian told the driver to take them to her friend's building first.

"I almost forgot, this is from Honor," Bea said, handing Vivian a sealed envelope just before she slid out the door.

"What is it?"

"No idea." Bea shrugged. "Love letter?"

"Aren't you funny." Vivian rolled her eyes and shoved the letter into her evening bag, deciding she would wait until morning to read it. "Go get some sleep."

She watched until her friend disappeared inside. It was only a few blocks to her own building from there; she started to slide out the door before the cabdriver stopped her.

"The Chinese fella already overpaid the fare," he pointed out. So she let him drive her home as well.

The street was reassuringly empty as the cab pulled away, no dark figures lurking in the shadows that puddled around the streetlights or padded the gaps between buildings. Vivian could have imagined herself alone in the world as she climbed the stairs.

The illusion was broken on the third floor. Mrs. Thomas was leaning against the wall, a cigarette between her rough fingers and one rickety window open to let in what passed for fresh air.

"What are you doing up?" Vivian asked. She should have continued on without speaking. But she never ran into anyone when she returned from her nighttime outings.

Mrs. Thomas took a slow drag, her expression unreadable. "Grandbaby's teething," she said, tilting her chin to blow a stream of smoke out into the night. She looked Vivian up and down, and even in the dim light the curl of her lip was obvious. "No rest for the wicked, I see."

Vivian's stomach knotted with embarrassment. "Oh?" she said, pretending she didn't understand.

"Careful, girl. You'll end up like your poor whore of a mother one of these days."

The words were like a slap, and Vivian sucked in a pained breath. Normally she was the one who could withstand Mrs. Thomas's barbs. But her defenses had been worn down by fear and exhaustion and the feeling of her world shifting precariously under her feet. "You don't know anything about my mother. Or me."

Mrs. Thomas laughed bitterly. "You expect me to believe it's that sister of yours who's the wayward one? Men don't come looking for a nun like her."

"There's no—" Vivian broke off. Leo. She could have killed him. He knew what it had meant when he showed up at her work. And now he hadn't just come to her home, he was asking the neighbors about her . . .

A sudden chill snaked its way down her spine. What if it hadn't been Leo? What if the man looking for her had been one of Roy's bruisers? What if he had found Florence?

"Who was it?" she demanded. One hand clenched the banister so tightly that the spindly rails trembled. "Did he give a name? What did he look like? Is Florence—"

The look Mrs. Thomas gave her was pitying. "Not my job to keep track of your men if you can't do it yourself. I thought you were a smarter girl than that."

"It's not—"

Mrs. Thomas had already tossed the stub of her cigarette out the window and slammed the sash down. "We could use some milk in the morning," she said by way of answer. "Unless you're too high and mighty to help out a neighbor anymore."

Vivian wanted to smack the woman. But the weariness bruising the sallow skin under Mrs. Thomas's eyes kept her in check. She might be bitter and angry, but she would have said if anything had happened to Florence. Vivian bit the inside of her cheek and took a deep breath. "Anything else you need?" she asked when she could speak calmly again. Debts were a burden, but that didn't mean she could stop paying them.

"What do I always need? Fewer mouths and more money." Mrs. Thomas shrugged, already heading for her door. "Take my advice. Get what you can from your fella and kick him to the curb quick, or you'll end up like me before you know it."

Vivian climbed the stairs slowly. She wouldn't end up like Mrs. Thomas. And if the letter in her bag had what Honor promised, she was going to make sure Florence never did either.

All of a sudden, she couldn't wait until morning to read it. The front room was dark when she unlocked the door and let herself in: the building wasn't wired for electricity, and Florence always put out the lamp when she went to bed. But there was usually a light left in the hall washroom.

Toeing off her shoes so she wouldn't make too much noise, Vivian tiptoed to the bedroom door and pressed her ear against it, waiting until she heard the sound of a sleepy sigh. Whoever had come by, he hadn't bothered her sister. Reassured, Vivian fumbled in the dark for the lamp and slipped out to go light it.

As she made her way down the hall, Vivian heard a door behind her creak open and shut again quietly; she grimaced as she lit her lamp at the washroom light, wishing she had changed her clothes before wandering around. Any neighbor who saw her now would make the same assumption Mrs. Thomas had.

But there was no help for that. Lamp in hand, Vivian hurried back down the hall to her own home. Slipping quietly in, she closed the door behind her and placed the light on the table, looking around for where she had dropped her purse.

The soft click of a lock behind her echoed through the silent room.

Vivian spun around, her eyes fixed on the man standing between her and the door.

TWENTY-EIGHT

He wavered a little as he stepped toward her. The reek of cheap gin filled her nose, and he stumbled, unsteady on his feet, but his narrow-eyed gaze didn't waver. Vivian gulped, then tried to smile, wondering if she could distract him long enough to do . . . something. Anything.

Mrs. Thomas's contempt made horrible sense now. There hadn't been a man asking about her. There had been one waiting for her to get home. She remembered the sound of the door quietly opening and closing behind her when she went to the washroom. He had snuck in while she was lighting the lamp.

Her eyes locked on her key dangling from Roy's hand, her purse at his feet. She wondered if he knew she had a sister sleeping in the next room, or if he would leave once he had dealt with her. She wanted to put the table between them, but a drunk man was like an angry dog. It wasn't smart to make any sudden moves.

"Hey there, Roy," she said, her voice so hoarse she could barely get the words out. "Fancy running into you again so soon."

Roy paused just a few steps away from her and laughed. For a moment Vivian felt her shoulders relax. Yes, he had locked them in the room together, but if she screamed for help, some neighbor would wake up and batter down the door. Maybe she could handle him this time. Maybe it was just a misunderstanding.

Then he took a step forward and smiled, the expression twisted and triumphant. Whatever hesitation or insecurities he had felt back in Honor's study were gone, pickled in gin and replaced with ugly fury. Vivian was sharply aware of the extra foot of height and God alone knew how many pounds of weight that he had on her. "What do you know?" he asked. "Saw me and Hattie together, talkin' about Willard and a baby . . . Think you should tell me just what you mean by all that."

The words slurred together, and Vivian frowned as she figured out what he had asked. That moment was all it took for him to snap. His face darkened with anger. "Tell me what you *know*," he yelled, lunging at her.

Vivian stumbled backward, trying to get away, but her stockinged foot caught on one of the chairs. She tripped just as he grabbed her. Her fall dragged them both down, the crash echoing through the silent room.

Her head hit the ground with a sharp crack. A wave of nausea rolled through her belly. All she could see was a burst of painful light. His weight pinned her down, driving the breath from her lungs before she could scream for help.

Before her vision could clear, before she could pull any air into her shocked lungs, she felt his hands close around her throat.

"Tell me what you know!" The slurred demand beat against her ears.

She scrabbled at his wrists with her nails, trying to drag them away, gasping for air. She kicked out as best she could. He cursed loudly, and the pressure around her throat eased. She nearly sobbed in relief.

A moment later, all the air rushed out of her in a hoarse scream as he dragged her upright, the force of it pulling her feet from the ground. One hand tightened around her throat. She could feel the other twisting in the front of her dress, heard the fragile fabric rip as he shoved her back down on top of the table.

She would have screamed again, but the breath was gone from her body once more. Both of his hands were back around her throat, his words a drunken jumble she couldn't have understood if he hadn't been repeating himself over and over.

"What did you mean, huh? You leave her alone, you hear me? Tell me what you *know*."

Vivian clawed at his face, trying to reach his eyes. He screamed in pain. But the pressure from his hands didn't let up. Bright darkness was starting to sparkle around the edges of her vision. She heard yelling from outside her door, someone hammering on it and calling out, but it sounded a long way away.

"What do you know? Tell me what you *know*. Tell me—"

The sharp crack of a gunshot echoed through the tiny room.

The hands around Vivian's throat spasmed, then fell away as Roy stumbled backward, his eyes wide with confusion. He and Vivian stared at the dark stain spreading across one of his shoulders, both of them suddenly, painfully silent. Their eyes met. He stumbled forward, one hand reaching out as if begging for help.

A second gunshot burst through the air, and this time Vivian screamed. She saw him stagger back from the force of it, saw the ruin it made of his chest. His mouth worked silently for a moment before his eyes went blank. He slumped to the ground, as if someone had cut the strings that held him upright.

For a moment, Vivian was too stunned to move. Her throat spasmed gratefully as she sucked in huge gulps of air. She slid off the edge of the table and used it to haul herself upright.

She knew what she would see when she turned around. But that didn't make the sight of Florence, the hand that held the gun still raised as if she had forgotten how to move, any easier to bear.

"Oh God, Flo," Vivian breathed, barely able to force the words out of her bruised throat.

"Vivi," Florence whispered, her face frozen in horror. "What are we going to do?"

TWENTY-NINE

There wasn't time for them to think before the door burst open, forced off its hinges by the full weight of a neighbor's body slamming against it.

Her head still spinning from hitting the floor and the table, her breath coming in sharp, coughing gasps, Vivian couldn't keep up with what was happening. There were too many people all of a sudden, too many faces peering through the door. Someone was trying to get past her to reach Florence. Vivian stumbled to her feet and shoved them aside, placing her body protectively in front of her sister.

"Dammit, girl, I'm trying to help!" Mrs. Thomas's sharp voice broke through the haze. "I just need her to put the gun down—"

"The police arrived!" someone called from the hall.

Mrs. Thomas swore violently. "Who the hell called them?"

There was a chorus of confused voices. Vivian heard heavy boots tramping up the stairs as if from a long way away.

"Florence," she coughed. "Flo, you need to get out of here—I'll tell them it was me, I'll tell them he attacked me—"

But Florence had backed herself against the wall and was clutching the gun to her chest, her face utterly blank. "He was going to kill you," she whispered. "And I killed him. God forgive me, what have I done?"

"Flo, please," Vivian begged, throwing off Mrs. Thomas's restraining hands to grab her sister's shoulders. There were raised voices in the hall, the police trying to force their way through the angry neighbors. The noise made her head ring, and black spots still danced around the edges of her vision. "You can't stay here like this, they'll arrest you. *Please.*"

Florence pressed more tightly back against the wall. "God forgive me," she whispered, trembling all over.

"Get the gun from her," Mrs. Thomas hissed. "She's going to fire it again in that state, and we can't have—Vivian, hurry—"

"Flo, please—"

"God forgive me."

"Stand aside, everyone. Now." The deep voice sliced through the confusion. The coldness of it made Vivian shiver. "Out of the way or everyone's getting arrested tonight."

"You can't do that!" one voice protested.

"I'm the law," the policeman said, his voice rising even louder. "I'll do what I like. Are you getting out of my way or do I have to move you myself?"

There were too many people, too much noise. Mrs. Thomas was still saying something. She grabbed Vivian's arm and shook her, and the sudden spike of pain that shot through her head and back made Vivian want to sob. The gasp it wrenched out of her made her start coughing again. The people were parting and she could see the boots of the police coming toward her. She pulled away from Mrs. Thomas's frantic hands and put herself squarely in front of her sister.

"It was self-defense, sir, you have to believe me," Mrs. Thomas was saying. "I've known these girls their whole lives, good girls, never make any trouble, and that man comes bursting in here tonight, I've never seen him before—"

A stern face swam into Vivian's vision, with a blue hat shadowing his eyes in a way that made her flinch away. Someone was reaching past her, trying to get to Florence, who was still whispering *God forgive me* and shaking. Vivian knocked the hands away and wrapped her arms around her sister, feeling the cold barrel of the gun between them. She wondered if it was still loaded. She wondered if it would go off, and which of them it would kill if it did.

"You can't take her," Vivian whispered, faces fading in and out of her vision as she swayed on her feet. She couldn't tell if it was her own trembling or Florence's that made her feel as though she was about to break apart. "You can't take her, you can't . . ."

"Viv, it's okay."

The gentle, familiar voice broke through her dizzy thoughts, scattering them like light reflected through a bottle of champagne.

"It's okay, sweetheart, you're in shock. Both of you are. No one's taking Florence anywhere." Gentle hands slid between them, easing the gun away from the two sisters. "Open your eyes. Let me see that you're okay."

Vivian hadn't realized her eyes were closed. She blinked at the familiar face so close to hers. "Leo?" she croaked. "What are you doing here?"

"Trying to make up for my terrible timing," he said. His voice was still gentle, but she could hear the weight of regret in it. "I didn't get a tail on him in time, Viv. I'm so sorry." He held out his hands. "Can you stand up?"

They were on the floor. How had they gotten there? Vivian let herself be helped to her feet, Leo's arm strong around her waist to keep her from falling. Most of the neighbors had been cleared away, but a few curious faces still peered in from the hall. The room was a mess. One policeman was clearing two broken chairs out of the way while another settled a white sheet over Roy's body, still crumpled on the floor.

Vivian stared at the still figure, her mouth flooding with the taste of bile. "Florence . . ." she whispered. Then, "Florence!"

She spun around, but the sudden movement made her lose her balance, and Leo had to catch her to keep her from falling. A policeman and Mrs. Thomas were easing Florence to her feet. "Leo, they can't take her, it was my fault, I promise, I won't let them—"

"It's okay." Leo wrapped his arms around her and pulled her against his chest, the pressure of his body easing the shock and fear. His tight grip felt like the only thing that could keep her from flying into a million pieces. "No one is taking Florence anywhere." He raised his voice, speaking to the policeman who had just scooped the limp Florence into his arms. "Put her to bed, and make sure Herman called for a doctor. And a nurse—she's in shock and shouldn't be left alone."

The policeman didn't move.

"You remember who the commissioner put in charge tonight, I hope," Leo said quietly.

The other man's face tightened, then he sighed. "Yes, sir," the policeman said, nodding as he turned toward the bedroom. "For tonight."

In spite of the warm body holding her, that *sir* made Vivian feel suddenly cold.

"You'll stay with her until the nurse arrives?" Leo asked, glancing at Mrs. Thomas.

The woman looked like she wanted to argue, but she glanced around the crime scene of a room. Swallowing her questions, she nodded and followed the policeman.

"Leo, what's going on?" Vivian whispered, pulling away from him.

She could feel his reluctance as he let her go, but he didn't try to stop her. "I'm so sorry," he said again, and she thought he might be about to cry. "I should have gotten here faster. I should have had a tail put on him right away. One of the men spotted him by accident and followed him here before calling it in. If I'd gotten here sooner . . ." He trailed off, looking sick. "I'm sorry I didn't stop him in time."

"Coroner and doctor are here, Mr. Green," another policeman said.

Leo cleared his throat. "Send them in," he said, his voice suddenly

251

brisk. A moment later, two men in rumpled suits who looked as if they had dressed while half-asleep entered. One went straight to the sheet-covered body, his movements impersonal and efficient as he pulled it back and began his examination.

Vivian turned away quickly, the movement making her wobble on her feet. The other man caught her arm. "Steady there, girlie," he said. "You should be sitting down."

He eased her into a chair, his eyes narrowing. Vivian flinched away from his stern expression, but his voice was gentle when he spoke again. "Seems like our dead fellow was quite a brute," he said, and the sympathy made Vivian's eyes fill with tears.

"Seems like," she whispered.

The doctor's hands were gentle, too. He cupped them against her cheeks and tilted her head from side to side while he inspected her bruises, checked her pulse, and wiggled her fingers and toes. He asked her to bend forward while he pressed his fingers along her spine, eliciting winces and gasps of pain. Finally, he pulled a flat pocket light from his vest, holding her chin still when she would have flinched away from the bright light and instructing her to follow it side to side with her eyes.

The examination only took a few minutes, but Vivian could feel Leo's anxious eyes on her the whole time. And last the doctor stood, looking satisfied. "You're battered and bruised, young lady, and your voice may take a few days to recover. But I don't see anything worse than that."

Pulling a small bottle from his pocket, he shook out two white tablets and held them out to her. Leo's hand shot out and grabbed his wrist. The doctor looked startled before he chuckled and eased Leo's fingers away. "Just aspirin, lad. She's going to ache for a few days after a beating like that. But you're young and healthy, girlie," he added. "You'll be okay."

She nodded, silently accepting the aspirin and the glass of water another policeman offered her, swallowing them obediently. She ignored the strange men surrounding her and kept her eyes fixed on Leo, though she didn't speak.

He met her gaze for a moment, then turned to the doctor again. "The sister is in the bedroom, the one who . . ." He cleared his throat. "Who fired the shot. Did he get his hands on her?" he asked, turning to Vivian.

She shook her head. "Just me," she whispered. "Florence was asleep. She heard him and . . ." Vivian trailed off, unable to say it.

Leo nodded. "Physically, she should be okay then," he said to the doctor. "But I'd still like you to look at her."

The doctor nodded and took his bag with him to examine Florence. Vivian half started to her feet before she remembered that Mrs. Thomas was in there and would make sure there was no funny business. Sinking back down, she gathered her courage and finally glanced to where the coroner was finishing his examination.

She caught a glimpse of Roy's face, the bloody mess of his chest, before the coroner tugged the sheet back into place and stood. "Time of death between three and four o'clock in the morning," he said calmly, dusting his hands off. "Two gunshot wounds, one to the shoulder and one to the center of the chest, both at relatively close range. I assume the scratches on his face were your doing?" he asked, glancing at Vivian with the bland curiosity of someone who faced death every day. She swallowed and nodded. "Smart girl. Always go for the eyes and the balls." He turned back to Leo. "If we're done here, we can take him to the morgue now."

Vivian couldn't look away as the two policemen lifted the body onto a stretcher. As they maneuvered their way out the door, she started shaking again, and couldn't stop until Leo wrapped his arms around her.

"It's over, Viv," he murmured. "It's all over now."

She pulled away from him as soon as she had herself under control, standing and putting the chair between them. "You're a cop, then?" She winced at the pain in her throat.

"No." He shook his head. "My uncle is the commissioner. My father's Jewish, and my mother got herself disowned for marrying him, so I'm not officially part of the family. But sometimes my uncle likes having someone he trusts who can work outside the law, here and in Chicago. And he pays well, even if he is an ass. I was back in town, so he put me on investigating Wilson's death from the other side of things." He smiled, the expression sad and wary and hopeful all at once. His eyes never left hers. "I'm also a hell of a supplier. I knew just about every bootlegger in Chicago before I left."

Vivian was still trying to decide what to say to that when the doctor came back, along with the policeman who had carried Florence. "She's in shock, but nothing a little rest shouldn't set to rights," he said, easing the bedroom door shut. "I've given her a sedative, and the neighbor woman will stay until the nurse arrives. You'll want to make sure she eats when she wakes up," he added, glancing at Vivian. "The nurse can stay for a few days to help out."

"We can't afford a nurse," Vivian said, a familiar knot of worry tightening in her chest.

"It'll be taken care of," Leo said. Vivian sent him a sharp look, but he ignored it. "Thanks, Doctor. You can see yourself out?"

The doctor jerked his chin toward Vivian. "She needs her rest as well."

"We have to go to the station first," Leo said. Seeing Vivian's sudden fear, he added, "Florence's name will be kept out of the report, and so will yours if I can manage it. You just need to make a statement about Carlton. Whatever you overheard him saying to Mrs. Wilson, what he said to you tonight, what happened when he got here, that sort of thing. The whole business can be officially ended. Then I'll bring you right back here."

It wasn't a request. One of the policemen had retrieved her bag and key from where Roy had let them fall and set them on the table. Vivian picked them up, ignoring the blood that spotted one corner of the bag, and nodded. "Lead the way, Mr. Green."

—•—

Vivian cupped her hands gratefully around the mug of coffee the butler had handed her. She didn't drink any, but she was greedy for its warmth. Someone had draped a coat over her shoulders before she was ushered into the police car—she had fought down her panic when the door closed behind her, grateful for Leo's presence in the seat next to her even if she wouldn't look at him—but she was still shivering.

They hadn't gone to the police station. Instead, Leo had taken her to the back door of a beautiful residence on the Upper East Side, where a stone-faced butler showed them into the study. A moment later, an older man with a luxurious mustache and a beautiful brocade dressing gown had entered.

"Commissioner," Leo had greeted him, polite and distant.

Vivian had swallowed, unable to say anything.

Leo's uncle had eyed them with impassive curiosity before ordering the butler to prepare coffee for the young lady and gesturing them into the two chairs that stood before his desk. Taking his own seat opposite them, he had looked her up and down, his eyebrows rising as he took in the tattered mess of her evening clothes and the bruises around her throat. He didn't miss Leo hovering protectively behind her chair, either, but both his expression and voice were neutral when he finally spoke. "Start from the beginning."

Vivian didn't do that—there was no way she was telling this man she had been the one to find Wilson's body in that alley—but she did say she knew where he had died. Leo didn't correct her, and the commissioner didn't show any reaction to the admission that she visited a dance hall, so she kept going. Delivering Hattie Wilson's dresses, the whispered conversation she overheard from the top of the stairs, the men who cornered her on her way home. The gossip about Hattie's pregnancy and her affair with Roy Carlton, the two toughs who showed up at the Nightingale to distract the owner and staff while Roy rifled through the office for more information. His near admission that the baby was his, that he was hoping Hattie would come back to him now her husband was out of the picture. His appearance in her home that night, his frantic, drunk insistence that she tell him what she knew.

"And then he grabbed me . . ." Her hands and voice both shook, and her words stumbled to a halt. How could she describe what it felt like to have his fingers around her throat, the sight of Florence standing there, her face blank with horror, the gun still in her hand?

"I thought he was going to kill me," she whispered. "And instead, he's the one who died."

She couldn't meet the commissioner's eyes, and she didn't want to look back at Leo. So she took a gulp of the bitter coffee, grateful for its scalding heat, though it made her cough. She was alive. Florence was alive. The Nightingale and everyone in it would be safe. It was over.

"Well." The commissioner steepled his fingers on the desk in front of him. Glancing up from under her lashes, she could see the thoughtful expression on his face. He looked up at Leo, then nodded. "Officially, of course, Mr. Wilson died of a heart ailment, so none of this has anything to do with his death. But I believe it will satisfy the remaining questions of all interested parties." He gave Vivian a serious nod. "Thank you for your information, young lady. And you, Mr. Green." He pulled a fat envelope out of a drawer and slid it across the desk to Leo, who pocketed it with a nod. "I am grateful for your assistance."

There was nothing affectionate between them, nothing that would have told Vivian they were related if Leo hadn't already admitted it. They didn't even look anything alike.

The commissioner stood. "I'm sure you've made the necessary arrangements, Mr. Green. Tell anyone who needs payment to send their bills here. You'll hear from me if anything else arises requiring your talents. Good evening."

And then he was gone once more. He hadn't asked her name once or wanted to know how Roy Carlton had died. Vivian shuddered and put her coffee down on the desk so sharply that it sloshed over the edge.

"Who are the interested parties?" she asked, wanting to know who had been behind all the Nightingale's troubles, who Roy had been so desperate to hide his involvement from.

Leo shrugged. "No idea. But that's that." He held out his hand to help her to her feet. "Come on. I'll take you home."

The sergeant in the police car was still waiting outside the back door. Vivian expected that Leo would send her on her way, but he slid into the back seat with her once more and directed the driver to take them back to her building.

He didn't say anything, but he kept glancing at her as they drove through the night, the darkness broken by the glow of electric lights and brief bursts of laughter and music. The world was carrying on, not knowing and not caring that Roy Carlton had died that night.

Vivian wondered if he had parents or friends who had loved him. She wondered what would have happened to Florence if she had died. She was achingly conscious of Leo, sitting silently only a foot away from her, of the quietly curious presence of the sergeant in the front seat. Something inside her felt like it was shattering, or freezing, or bursting free at last. She stared out the window, craning her neck to catch a glimpse of the starless sky.

They didn't speak the whole ride, didn't speak when the sergeant parked in front of her building and came around to open her door. They didn't say a word when Leo slid out after her and walked her to the door.

But she did meet his eyes at last, and for a moment she wanted to drown in the worry and relief and tenderness there. But when he reached for her, she flinched away. "Don't touch me," she said.

His eyes were pleading. "Please don't be angry, Viv."

"Don't be angry. Don't be angry, you say." Vivian could hear her voice rising hysterically and didn't care. Half of her wanted to punch him right in his puppy dog–sweet face; the other half wanted to throw herself into his arms. "Don't be *angry*? You lied to me, Leo." She laughed bitterly, rolling her eyes up. "And I fell for it. The boy with the sweet smile who dances a mean quickstep and just wants to make sure I stay safe. You were lying the whole time."

"None of that was a lie."

"You were using me."

"I was trying to make sure you were safe." Leo's hands flexed as if he wanted to grab her shoulders, and Vivian tensed to pull away. But instead he ran both hands through his hair, pulling at it in frustration. "What did I say to you that was actually a lie? I told you I was working for my uncle. Can you really blame me for not mentioning what kind of work that was?"

"You told me you didn't know who Wilson was."

"I told you I'd never met him. I told you I'd never heard his name until after he was already dead," Leo pointed out. "Both of which were true. My uncle didn't ask me to help him out until Wilson had already been killed."

"And I'm sure the fact that you remember those very honest statements so well proves how honest they were," Vivian snapped. "Clearly, you didn't have to think about them carefully at all."

She pressed the heels of her hands against her eyes. There was a numb, heavy feeling settling in her chest, chasing away her anger and leaving her deflated and exhausted in its wake. Dropping her hands, she looked back at Leo, whose own defensive anger had faded into concern as he watched her. "Did you feel honest when you said them?" she asked.

His face fell. "No," he said. "I felt like a sleazy bastard. Which is what I am, Vivian, and what I told you I was. Fellas like me aren't the nice, upstanding boys that girls are supposed to spend their time with. You knew that."

Vivian nodded. "I knew that. I just really hoped you weren't lying to me."

"What was I supposed to say?" Taking a step toward her, he reached out a careful hand. When she didn't flinch away, he cupped his palm around her cheek, lowering his forehead until it rested against hers. "I like you, Viv. I've liked you since the first time we danced together."

Her whole body wanted to sway toward him. She couldn't let it. If she leaned on anyone now, she'd fall apart completely. "I liked you too," she whispered. Gently, she stepped away.

Leo's jaw tightened. "And yes, I used you to find out what I needed to know. But I also wanted to make sure you didn't get mixed up in anything more dangerous than you already had. I could have killed Honor Huxley for putting you in the middle of this."

"I'd have ended up in the middle of it anyway. Roy recognized me from the Nightingale. I wasn't safe after that," Vivian said, feeling numb. Was there a point in being angry at anyone? "And Florence—" She broke off. How could she ever face her sister?

"She'll be okay, you know," Leo said, his voice gentle again. "I meant what I said. The whole thing over and no one coming to ask any questions or take her anywhere. I promise."

Vivian nodded. The numb feeling was spreading into her arms and legs and eyes, leaving her too tired to keep arguing. "Thanks for that, anyway," she said. "I could use one more favor."

He moved forward half a step, as if he couldn't help himself. "Anything."

"Tell Honor. Or find Danny and have him tell her. She needs to know it's over."

Leo's face darkened for a moment. He clearly didn't want to think about Honor Huxley just then. But he sighed and nodded anyway. "Will do." He was silent as she turned toward the door. Then, "Vivian."

The naked regret in his voice made her pause, though she didn't turn back around. "Yeah?"

"I'd still really like to take you out again."

She let out a long breath. "I'm not saying never." She glanced over her shoulder. "But you have to give me some time."

He shrugged. "Roy Carlton is dead, and the Wilson mess is wrapped up. I've got a pocket full of cash from my uncle and all the time in the world. Right now, every minute of it is yours."

"You say some awful sweet things, Leo," she sighed, turning back to unlock the building's door. "I just have to figure out whether I can believe them or not."

Out of the corner of her eye, she saw him nod. "If you or your sister need anything . . . If anyone else bothers you . . ."

She nodded. "Yeah. Thanks."

"Good night, Vivian Kelly."

She didn't reply as she went inside. The door swung shut behind her, and she slumped against it, almost too tired to move. But Florence was up there. So Vivian sighed once more and started up the four flights of stairs.

THIRTY

Vivian stared at the dingy light that crept through the window, feeling just as sluggish as it looked, while she waited for the water to boil. There had barely been enough coffee left for two cups last night, but the stream of neighbors had been trickling through since they first saw the light appear under her door, questions in their eyes and food in their hands. A few asked awkwardly about Florence as they handed over their offerings of coffee and pie and beans. Vivian was able to answer truthfully that her sister was still sleeping.

None of them had asked about the man Florence had shot, but that was only a matter of time. Vivian was grateful for their discomfort. She hadn't decided what to say.

Mrs. Thomas had still been there when Vivian returned from the commissioner's home the night before. The two had sat in crackling silence, watching Florence breathe instead of looking at each other, Vivian still in her torn dress, Mrs. Thomas smoking one lumpy cigarette after another and rubbing the small of her back.

"I wouldn't have let him in if I'd known he was violent," Mrs. Thomas said at last, her voice tense with guilt.

"I know."

"You don't need to mourn him. And she shouldn't carry it with her. She did what she had to. The world don't need another man battering its women."

"I know." Vivian took Mrs. Thomas's cigarette without asking, and the woman lit a new one for herself without protesting. "I don't care that he's dead. I care that she had to kill someone because of me."

"Guess she wasn't as much of a nun as I thought."

Vivian almost laughed, but the sound caught in her bruised throat, and she ended up coughing instead. She let the cigarette burn down without smoking it.

Neither of them spoke again. When the nurse arrived, Mrs. Thomas left without wasting time on good-byes. But she was the first one to appear at dawn, a pot of soup in her hands.

The nurse who now sat by Florence's bed accepted the mug of cheap coffee and asked if Vivian would open the curtain pulled across the room's single window. A book rested on her lap, a basket of knitting by her feet. Her face was pinched and plain, and there was nothing sentimental in her manner, but her brisk voice was reassuring. "Still sleeping. She'll be out for hours yet, with that sedative, and in bed for the rest of the day."

Vivian nodded. She was already dressed, a chiffon scarf—the only pretty thing Florence had ever bought for herself—wound around her throat to hide the bruises. "I'll be at work for the morning. There's plenty of food in the main room, and I won't be surprised if more shows up. You can help yourself."

The nurse glanced at the window. "You start your workday early."

Vivian nodded again. She slid one hand into her pocket, her fingers twisting the corner of Honor's letter about Miss Ethel. She had read it first thing that morning. "I need to talk to my boss before my shift begins."

thel Marie Barnes lived in a respectable house, the top two floors of which were let to tenants. Miss Ethel's rooms, according to Honor's letter, were on the top floor, and the dressmaker left for coffee and eggs at the automat every morning at six thirty before catching the streetcar to her shop.

Vivian eyed the elegant windows with their lace curtains and ivy-filled boxes, the quiet street with quiet workers heading out to find breakfast, the nanny just leaving the landlady's apartments with two small children in tow. She ignored the hot anger in her chest as she waited for her employer to emerge, then followed her to the automat.

Miss Ethel got her food and coffee without looking around, pulling out a ladies' magazine to read as she sat down. She didn't get a chance to open it, though, and she jumped as Vivian took the seat across from her.

"Vivian!" she exclaimed, one hand on her heart and her mouth pinched even tighter than usual. "What is the meaning of this intrusion? You nearly gave me a heart attack."

"I think you'll be all right," Vivian said, pleased by the instant irritation that flared across Miss Ethel's face at her casual, almost disrespectful tone. "I thought I'd join you for breakfast."

Miss Ethel sniffed. "Whatever you have to tell me, it can wait until you and your sister arrive at the shop. This sort of behavior is highly inappropriate."

"Well, that's the thing. Florence isn't going to be in to work today. She needs about a week off. And when she comes back, I'm going to expect a few changes."

"This is the last straw." Miss Ethel threw down her napkin, her cheeks splotchy with fury. "I have been more than patient with you. I have lightened your duties when any other employer would have simply fired you. Do you know how lucky you are to work in such a respectable establishment? Do you know how many girls would love to take your place, should I make it available? But you, you flaunt your wayward morals, you abuse my generosity. Well, I'll not have it anymore." Her voice was a low hiss—even in her anger, Miss Ethel was conscious of appearances, and she had no intention of drawing the attention of the other diners. "Either you and your sister will both be at work today—with your heads down, your mouths closed, and your sewing machines busy for your full shift—or you can find other places of employment. If anywhere else will have you."

"All right then, have it your way." Vivian shrugged and stood. She smiled in the face of Miss Ethel's righteous fury. "Tell little Mathilde hello for me when you visit her on Sunday. Sounds like you found a nice, respectable family to take her in." Vivian picked up her handbag and turned toward the door. "How lucky for you."

"Vivian!"

Vivian turned back. Her stomach was knotted with apprehension at what she was doing, but none of her nerves showed on her face. "Yes?"

Miss Ethel's face was pale except for those two red splotches, which had grown even brighter. Her fingers clenched around the edge of the table as she stood, but the tight grip couldn't hide how her hands were trembling. "What did you say?"

Vivian smiled. "Mind if we sit down? I think our talk might not be finished after all."

———————

The servants at the Wilson house recognized her by now, or at least they recognized the box under her arm. Vivian didn't have to state her business before they showed her in, the housekeeper calling a maid to escort "the dressmaker's girl" upstairs.

"She wasn't expecting you yet, but no matter. She said to send you up whenever you arrived, even if her visitors were still here."

This time the maid didn't show Vivian to the pretty ladies' parlor; instead, she knocked timidly on a door further down the hall.

"Come in."

Vivian glanced around curiously as the maid held the door open for her. She had a brief impression of an oppressive and masculine room, its walls lined with books, heavy curtains covering the windows, and an entire shelf of liquor flaunted out in the open. Then her eyes landed on Mrs. Wilson sitting behind the desk. A short, wiry man, his hat held politely at his side, was speaking to her with his back to Vivian.

"We'll take care of the Baxter Street place tomorrow," he was saying. "There won't be any sign that she was ever there—"

"Ah, Miss Kelly. You've returned." Hattie Wilson cut him off. Gesturing for Vivian to come in, she nodded a dismissal to the maid. "Anne, shut the door."

Vivian caught her breath as the man by the desk turned toward her, and the sound of the door closing behind her echoed loudly through the now-silent room.

"Hello there, girlie," Bruiser George said, a leer spreading across his face. Over his shoulder, Vivian could see Mrs. Wilson smiling faintly. "Fancy meeting you here."

Vivian clenched the dress box with both hands to keep them from shaking, wanting to raise it in front of her like a shield. A wave of nausea left her cold and sweating with fear. She had wondered who George and his cronies were working for now that Willard Wilson was dead—the new boss who was threatening her and the Nightingale both. Looking at George's posture in front of Mrs. Wilson's desk—a spot that had clearly once belonged to her husband—she thought she had an answer.

Bruiser George took a step closer to her. "Now, let's see. We've met one time in an alley, one time in a nightclub, and now here. Our acquaintance is getting downright respectable, wouldn't you—"

"That's enough, George," Hattie Wilson said, her voice mild, though her eyes never left Vivian. "I think you've made our point."

Vivian didn't know where to look. She didn't want to take her eyes off Bruiser George, but she was starting to realize that he might not be the most dangerous person in the room.

"Yes, ma'am," George said, his voice polite though the smile he gave Vivian was anything but. "You let me know if me'n the boys can do anything else."

"And I'll expect you to jump when I do." Hattie Wilson's voice wasn't demanding; she even smiled as she said it, but the iron will behind the words was clear.

George nodded deferentially. "Yes, ma'am," he said again, giving her a little bit of a bow. He grinned at Vivian as he walked to the door. "Just business, girlie. No hard feelings, I hope?"

Vivian took a deep breath. She wasn't going to let herself be afraid anymore. "Four times."

He paused. "What was that?" he demanded. Behind him, even Hattie looked puzzled.

"We met four times, not three." Vivian knew she should have kept her mouth shut, but she couldn't let him leave thinking he had won. She was tired of folks looking at her and seeing fear. She lifted her chin and tapped one finger against her temple, the spot where he still had the shadow of a nasty bruise. "How's your head, George?"

It took him raising his hand to his own head to realize what she meant. Then his face darkened. "Why, you little b—"

"I said that's enough." This time Hattie Wilson's voice cracked out like a whip, and her bully boy subsided instantly. "You're done here."

"No hard feelings, I hope?" Vivian couldn't help one last taunt as he reached the door, thrilled to be ending the exchange with something like the upper hand.

He turned back, one hand resting on the doorknob, and glared like he wanted to wring her neck. Then he laughed. "Just business," he agreed. "Maybe we'll meet a fifth time to discuss it."

"Peachy," Vivian said, too quickly, glad her voice didn't crack on the word. She made herself keep smiling as he left, though her expression grew wary as she turned to Mrs. Wilson.

They eyed each other. Vivian wondered how she had missed how far the other woman's hardness, her flinty determination, went. Hattie Wilson might have been a debutante, but she knew something about surviving in a dangerous world.

She was also already moving on, standing up and closing the curtains behind her. "Well, don't stand there looking smug, get the dresses out. You'll need to fit these ones—they were made from my measurements on file."

She was already unbuttoning her day dress with careless immodesty, and Vivian scrambled to catch up with the sudden change of topic. Her hands were shaking as she laid the two dresses out over the lounging sofa that took up one side of the room. Half of her wanted to rush out of the room, far away from the dangerous woman in front of her. The other half, the one that wanted to show she couldn't be scared into submission, kept her feet firmly in place. But it wasn't until she was on her knees pinning the hem that she got up the courage to speak.

"Guess you sent them after me because I asked too many questions that first time?"

"Yes." Hattie Wilson glanced down. "And since you work at the Nightingale."

"I don't work there," Vivian said. "Just dance."

"And you just got curious all of a sudden about the man who died there?" Hattie asked, plainly skeptical.

Vivian bit her lip, wondering for a moment how much to admit. "I was the one who found your husband," she said at last. "In that alley, after Roy shot him."

"What do you know about Roy?" Hattie asked, the iron back in her voice.

Slowly, Vivian sat back on her heels and unwound the scarf from her neck. She didn't look away as Hattie took in the bruises it had been hiding.

"You were the girl he attacked last night. You shot him?"

"Someone else did."

"Well, sorry about that." Hattie shrugged, stepping aside to pull off the dress and toss it over a chair. "That one's fine, hand me the next."

Vivian hid a flare of anger at seeing the beautiful garment flung aside and did as she was told. "Guess you were the commissioner's interested party, then, who was so curious about how Willard Wilson died?"

"He was my husband," Hattie said, tugging the black-and-gray day dress over her head. She shimmied a little to settle it over her hips and shoulders. "And it's bad for business if folks think someone got away with killing him. Never dreamed Roy would have the nerve to shoot anyone, though."

"I saw him coming out of the alley that night," Vivian said quietly. "At first I thought he had been the one to take over, and that's why he was sending George and Eddie after me. Then I realized he just had a secret he needed to hide."

Hattie laughed. "Roy, take over the business? Even if he had the brains for it, I never would have let him. Willard may have been a monster, but he built a nice little empire. I'd have been a fool to let anyone else get their hands on it." She frowned, twitching a little. "Are there still pins in this one? Something's scratching my hip."

Vivian knelt in front of her to check, thinking that Mags had been right. Hattie Wilson was completely cold, at least where anyone but her sister was concerned. Her careful fingers skimmed across Hattie's hips and belly, searching for any stray pins—and that's when she realized that something was wrong.

Vivian let her hands fall, staring at the other woman in astonishment. "You're not pregnant."

Hattie took a step back, her face suddenly pale. "What?"

Vivian's mind raced. There were any number of explanations: that Hattie had lost the baby, that the gossip writers had been mistaken. But Vivian remembered seeing Myrtle during her last visit, that moment when she had been silhouetted against the window. There had been something odd about the girl that caught her eye. Just like there had been something odd about the reactions in the Wilson household whenever she mentioned the younger sister.

Vivian rose slowly to her feet, remembering the deliberate, careful way Hattie had kept touching her belly after she sent Myrtle away. "You never were pregnant. You let that be spread around so you could raise your sister's baby for her."

For a moment Hattie stared at Vivian. Then her brows drew together. "Who told you such a nasty rumor about my sister?" she demanded. But that flash of panic had given her away.

"I know she's expecting the same way I know you aren't," Vivian said. "I've fit hundreds of dresses. I can tell when clothes are hiding something, and when they're not." Her eyes narrowed. "So how did you fool your husband? I might not have known him when he was alive, but I feel pretty safe guessing he wouldn't have agreed to raise another man's child."

"No," Hattie agreed, and the naked anger in her voice sent a chill skating over Vivian's skin. "He wouldn't have."

They stared at each other for a long moment. *Too old to be his type,* Myrtle had said. It hadn't been meant as an insult. Vivian swallowed. "Jesus, Mary, and Joseph. Did you kill him because he—"

"What do you care?" Hattie cut her off.

"I don't," Vivian whispered. "Good riddance."

The flare of emotion in Hattie's eyes made Vivian take a step back, but a moment later it was gone. Hattie turned away, gripping the back of a chair.

"I would have. I absolutely would have, if I could have figured out how to get away with it," she said, her voice low and shaking. "But his men were so loyal—no one wants to cut off the hand that's making them rich. And I couldn't risk going to jail myself. What would have happened to Myrtle then?"

There was an obvious question, and Vivian heard herself asking it, though she knew she should have left it alone. "Do you think she did it?"

"Absolutely not," Hattie said firmly. "She wasn't even here."

Vivian couldn't help rolling her eyes. "You gonna keep telling me she was at boarding school?"

"Of course she wasn't at boarding school," Hattie snapped. "But do you think I'd force her to wait out her pregnancy in the same house as that monster? She was with our great-aunt on Long Island. And—" Hattie drew herself back up. "She has kindly returned to be with her pregnant sister, who's in mourning and won't be out in society until after the baby arrives."

"You think it was Roy, then?" Vivian said, not bothering to hide her disbelief. "That he killed your husband to win you back?"

Hattie stalked to the door. "I think my husband died of a heart ailment. Which was a great shock to us all, because a heart was clearly the one thing he was utterly without. And now, Miss Kelly—" Mrs. Wilson opened the door so sharply it nearly flew out of her hand. There was an unmistakable warning in her eye. "I'll thank you to get out of my house."

THIRTY-ONE

B ut . . ." Bea stared at Vivian across the table, a frown puckering her brows. "If it wasn't that Roy fella's baby, does that mean he didn't kill Wilson after all?"

"That's what I'm wondering," Vivian said.

She had practically been jumping out of her skin with the need to tell someone what she had learned after she left the Fifth Avenue mansion. Going home to Florence was out of the question, and she wasn't ready to face Leo yet. She almost went to find Honor, but she wasn't sure that anyone at the Nightingale would care what had really happened, so long as Hattie and the police commissioner called off the heat. Bea had been the only one she trusted.

First, though, she had to fill in the details of Roy's break-in, their confrontation, Florence with the gun in her hand . . . Vivian's throat closed when she got to that part, and she hurried through her story to talk about Leo instead before jumping forward to her conversation with Hattie and Bruiser George.

Now, she cast a quick glance over her shoulder to make sure neither of Bea's brothers or her sister were around and listening. "And Mrs. Wilson said all his men were loyal. *No one wants to cut off the hand that's making them rich,* she said, and she's right about that for sure. So would someone like Roy, who stayed loyal even after his girl left him for his boss, kill that boss without a real reason? A reason like wanting to raise his own child? I don't think he would've."

"Or maybe he thought it was the way to finally get her back," Bea pointed out. "Get the husband she hated out of the way? It could've worked. You thought it was him just yesterday. Why are you so sure now it wasn't?"

"I thought he attacked me to keep me from running my mouth off about what he did. But maybe he just couldn't figure out what I was talking about when I mentioned the baby, and he was dumb and drunk and—" Vivian shook her head. "I think she did it, Bea. If the sister was on Long Island, it had to be Hattie. Wouldn't you kill any man who hurt your sister?"

"But why would she push the commissioner to find out what happened if she was the one who shot him?" Bea pointed out.

Vivian frowned. "She said it was bad for business, folks thinking someone could just off Wilson and get away with it. So maybe she just had to put on a show, and Roy ended up dead, and she didn't care."

"But . . ." Bea looked suddenly thoughtful. "Hold on a sec."

She went to the wall that served as a kitchen, sorting through the stack of newspapers that every household kept around. The one she pulled out was one of the society papers they had looked through together what felt like a million years ago.

"Here," Bea said, flipping through the pages until she found the column she wanted. Vivian skimmed it, reading about a dinner dance with one Mrs. Willard Wilson in attendance. Bea tapped the date at the top of the page. "That's the day after Wilson was shot, which means she was at a party when her husband was dead in that alley. She couldn't have done it."

"Maybe she hired someone. Or maybe it was her sister, then," Vivian said, pushing her chair back and standing abruptly, unable to stay still. Pacing back and forth across the small patch of open floor, she crossed her arms. "Maybe she wasn't away on Long Island. And Hattie didn't know about it, which was why she wanted the commissioner to—"

"Will you give it a rest?" Bea broke in. "You gotta know when it's time to stick your nose in and when you mind your own business. This is one of the times to mind your own business, so why can't you just let it go?"

"Because it's *my* fault he's dead." Vivian said. She sank into the chair next to her friend, elbows braced on the table while she stared at her hands. "Florence shot him because of me. And we've both got to live with that, so I want to be *certain* . . ." She broke off. "I've been holding on to this for so long. How can I just let it go without knowing?"

Bea's hand settled gently on her shoulder. "He's dead because of himself," she said. "You asked if I'd kill anyone who hurt my sister, and I would, in a heartbeat. That's what Florence did, so stop blaming yourself. Some things aren't worth the heartache of holding on to, and I'm pretty sure Roy Carlton was one of them."

———

Vivian's steps were slow as she arrived home.

The nurse was in the front room, rocking in Florence's chair and knitting, needles clicking softly together. "She's awake," she said in response to Vivian's silent question. "I lent her some of my needles—she's a quick study, your sister—but she said she wanted to be left alone."

"Does she seem . . ." Vivian swallowed, not sure what she wanted to ask or how to say it. "Is she okay?"

"She's quiet," the nurse said. "I couldn't get her to eat much. Physically, she's perfectly well. Her shock has passed. But . . ." She shook her head and stood, gathering her things. "Whatever happened last night, she's not going to forget it in a hurry. But you shouldn't need to worry about leaving her alone or letting her go on with things as she normally would."

"Thank you," said Vivian, not sure what else to say. She watched silently as the nurse gathered up her things and pulled on a sensible blue coat. "I'll go get your needles from Florence if you'll wait a moment."

"She can keep them," the nurse said with a shrug. "She wanted to try to finish the scarf today. Very determined girl."

"She is," Vivian agreed, trying not to remember how Florence looked with a gun in her hand. Determined didn't even begin to cover it. "Thanks again for your help."

"Don't mention it. Anyway, it's my job."

Vivian stared at the door after it closed, then at the door that stood between her and Florence. She paced around the tiny room—nine steps each direction—put on water to boil, turned it off again. She thought about Honor and Leo, about Danny and Bea.

She thought about the bargain she had wrung out of Miss Ethel, and what she would need to do next if she wanted the better life she had promised herself. She stared at the spot on the floor that had been scrubbed clean of Roy's blood only hours before.

She took a deep breath and tapped on the bedroom door. "Flo?" she called quietly. "You awake?"

There was a long pause, and she could hear the iron bed frame squeaking as her sister shifted position. Then, Florence's quiet voice: "Come on in."

Vivian closed the door behind her and stood with her back pressed against it. The two sisters stared at each other without speaking. Then Florence flung herself out of bed and tore across the room. Vivian was yanked into an embrace so crushing it forced all the air from her lungs and brought all the aches and pains in her body rushing back. Everything that she had intended to say scattered out of her mind. She couldn't remember the last time Florence had held her so tightly. She could feel hot tears on her neck, and she wasn't sure which of them was crying.

"Flo, I'm so sorry," she whispered. "I never meant—"

"To hell with that." Florence's voice was muffled, and at first Vivian thought she'd heard wrong. But when Florence lifted her head, Vivian almost took a step back at the blazing heat in her eyes. "I'd do it again," she whispered, her hands cupping her little sister's cheeks. "I'd shoot him again in a heartbeat, Vivi. I'll never let anyone hurt you."

Vivian wasn't sure if the sound she made was a laugh or a sob. "I had no idea you were so fierce," she said, pressing her palms against her sister's hands. "But I'm so sorry, Flo. I can't imagine what you've been going through, thinking about—"

"Don't say it." Florence shook her head sharply. She shivered, fumbling her way back to the bed to sit down and wrap her arms around herself. "I'd do it again, but that doesn't mean I want to think about it. Well, that's not quite true." She glanced up, her jaw set. Vivian wondered if she had ever really known who her sister was before. "I don't want details, but . . . what happened?"

"I saw something I wasn't supposed to," Vivian said, choosing her words carefully as she sat down next to her sister and drew her knees up under her chin. After what happened, Florence deserved at least some of the truth. "Or he thought I did. His name was—"

"Not that," Florence broke in. "I don't want to know his name. What did he think you saw?"

"He thought I saw him kill someone," Vivian said quietly. She would tell Florence the easiest version, she decided. The version she could probably live with. "He shot his boss, a man named Wilson. Fifth Avenue type. The fella last night was trying to find out what I knew."

"So he wasn't a nice man," Florence said quietly.

Vivian snorted. That much she could answer with perfect honesty. "Neither of them were, apparently. There are plenty of men who can enjoy their liquor or make their living on the wrong side of the law and not turn into murderers or woman-beaters," she added, feeling a little defensive. She thought of Leo's gentle insistence that she could trust him. "One of them helped us out last night, you know."

"One of your friends?" Florence asked quietly, pulling the skimpy blanket around her shoulders. "What did he do?"

Vivian stared at her feet, not sure how to explain her complicated feelings toward Leo or exactly what he had done for them last night. "He knew the fella was dangerous," she said at last. "And he also knew some people in the police commissioner's office. When he found out R— found out that man was on his way here, he . . ." She swallowed. What would have happened to Florence if Leo hadn't been there to help? And he had just stood there and let her lay into him. "Leo showed up too late to stop him but took care of things afterward. There won't be any more questions."

Florence let out a shaky breath. "Thank God," she whispered. "The nurse said I didn't have to worry, but I couldn't quite believe it. I've been terrified that someone would come and . . ."

"You're not going anywhere," Vivian said fiercely, gripping her sister's hands. "I would never let that happen."

"Well, except to work," Florence said with a short, bitter laugh. "If I still have a job. I can only imagine what Miss Ethel said when you showed up alone today. She must have been furious."

She hadn't been happy, that was certain.

"Be careful, Vivian," Miss Ethel had warned, her voice soft and laced with venom as they faced each other across the table. "I'm strict with you girls for your own good. I started down a wayward path once, and I've spent the rest of my life clawing my way back to respectability."

"Actually, she was very understanding." Vivian didn't quite meet her sister's eyes. "She's making some changes. You get a raise and Saturdays off. I'm going to stick with deliveries so she doesn't have to hire couriers."

"That doesn't sound like her," Florence said. "Any idea why she'd do us a favor like that?"

"And what you are doing is more than wayward. It is illegal. If you ever want a chance of being part of respectable society—"

Vivian had interrupted her. "I don't much care about being respectable. What I want is freedom."

"No idea," Vivian said to Florence, shrugging. "But I'm sure not going to argue about it."

Florence's eyes never left Vivian's. "I guess I won't ask her why then."

"Probably best not to," Vivian agreed. She was determined to give Florence a better life—and to give herself the freedom she ached for—but she didn't want her sister to know how it had happened. Florence wouldn't approve of blackmail.

They were silent again, until Florence reached out to squeeze her hand. "You don't have to worry, you know. I'll be all right. We'll be all right."

"Oh, Flo." Vivian lay down, her head in her sister's lap. "I'm sorry I didn't grow into the kind of girl you wanted me to be. But I promise, things'll be better for us from now on. I'm going to make them better."

I don't much care about being respectable. What I want is freedom.

"You're here, Vivi, and you're safe," Florence said. Her voice was fierce, but her hands were gentle as she stroked the bobbed curtain of hair away from Vivian's eyes. "That's all I want."

———·———

Vivian waited until her sister fell asleep before retreating to the main room. Everything was still a jumble. Someone had tucked Florence's Smith & Wesson into one of the kitchen cabinets—to hide it from the police?—and she left that uneasily on the counter, not sure what to do with it while she dealt with the rest of the room. Two broken chairs had been pushed into a pile in one corner. Florence's sewing basket was overturned under the table, along with everything Vivian had been carrying when she got home.

As she started cleaning up, she frowned at the papers jumbled on the ground, unsure where they had come from. It took a minute of staring at them before she remembered what they were: the papers Leo had stolen from Wilson's study.

The Fifth Avenue and North Shore places were obvious, but the

Baxter Street one was odd. Vivian stared at the address, then closed her eyes tightly, trying to remember where she had heard someone mention Baxter Street recently.

We'll take care of the Baxter Street place tomorrow. There won't be any sign that she was ever there.

Bruiser George, speaking to Hattie Wilson. Vivian opened her eyes. *She,* he had said. And suddenly, Vivian had an idea of who that *she* might be. Hattie Wilson had insisted that her sister was out on Long Island when her husband was murdered. But if Myrtle had actually been in the city, hidden downtown, away from where anyone would recognize her . . .

Hattie might not believe her sister was capable of murder. But Vivian remembered the wild, desperate look in the girl's eyes. Someone so badly hurt was capable of anything.

Vivian was glad to let Florence think that Roy was a murderer. It would help her deal with what had happened, and the police were convinced of it, anyway. But Vivian needed to know.

THIRTY-TWO

Lurking in the shadow of a nearby awning, Vivian eyed the building on Baxter Street warily.

It was tall and run-down, as if the buildings on either side were the only reason it was still standing. Judging by the washing lines trailing from the windows and the few people going in and out, it was divided into homes inside.

From what she had overheard at the Wilson house, George and Eddie would be there the next day to clear out any remaining traces of Myrtle's presence. If she was going to find anything, it had to be today. Still, she hesitated.

She had been determined to head to Baxter Street on her own, to prove to herself, at least, that she could handle whatever came her way. She didn't want to see Leo or Honor yet, and Bea had made it clear she thought Vivian needed to be done with the Wilsons. She remembered Danny mentioning his parents' restaurant, and vaguely thought it might not be far from Baxter Street. But she wasn't sure exactly where— and she didn't, when it came down to it, know Danny well outside the

Nightingale. He probably had better things to do with his time than watch over a girl who was jumping at shadows.

She didn't want to be that girl, so she hopped on the Broadway line, heading south, alone.

The gun she had tucked in her coat pocket before she left was a reassuring weight against her thigh when she emerged into the sunlight at last. But she still had the eerie sensation that someone was following her. Each time, she would stop, glancing over her shoulder, before deciding that she was imagining things and continue on.

Now, Vivian crossed the street until she was just to the right of the building she was actually interested in. This one had a restaurant on the first floor, and through the windows she could see two groups— one table full of older Chinese men, the other one of laughing white boys visiting downtown for a bit of adventure and cheap dinner after work. Vivian pretended to study the menu in the window, waiting for someone to come out of the building next door. After a few minutes, someone did: a middle-aged man with his hands full of bolts of cloth. He let the door swing carelessly behind him; Vivian was able to catch it before it closed and slip inside.

It took a moment for her eyes to adjust to the dim light; when she did, she jumped. Staring at her, arms crossed, was an old woman, her hair completely white and her face wrinkled like week-old newsprint. A cane dangled from one hand, and she tapped it impatiently against her thigh.

"Um, I . . . sorry," Vivian stammered. "I'm looking for a girl? Or a place where a girl was staying? Probably by herself?"

The old woman was silent for so long that Vivian wondered if she had understood. But at last she jerked her head toward the staircase. "Mr. Willard keeps the top rooms for himself," she said at last in a creaky voice. "But there's no girl now, her sister already took her home."

Vivian caught her breath. Myrtle *had* been there. "Oh, okay. Thanks. I'll just . . . she might have left something behind . . ."

The old woman laughed. "Steal whatever you like, girl. Not my business." Giving Vivian a final look up and down, she shrugged and pushed past, her cane thumping the ground as she headed out the front door.

The cooking smells were different, but otherwise Vivian could have been walking up the stairs to her own home. Most of the building was divided into cramped apartments, families stuffed into too-small spaces. The noise of arguments, laughter, and what sounded like a very frisky romp in the sheets drifted into the stairway.

There was only one door on the sixth floor; apparently Mr. Willard had kept the largest space for himself. And it was open, just a crack, as if someone had left it carelessly unlocked. Vivian was reaching for the handle when she heard voices on the other side of the door.

She froze.

There were two men in there. And she recognized their voices.

"So what're we supposed to do, then, George?" one deep rumble inquired.

"Nothing, I guess," the second voice answered. "Beats me where she got to, but less work for us. Come on."

Vivian glanced frantically around the stairwell as the sound of footsteps drew closer to the door. If she ran, they might hear her and wonder who was trying to get away. But there was nowhere to hide at the top of the stairs. Heart in her throat, she crept down as quietly as she could. At the next floor down she paused, listening.

"Should you lock it?" Eddie asked.

"Nah, not our problem." She could hear George's weaselly chuckle echoing down the stairs. "Mrs. Wilson already sold the whole building. Doesn't want anyone connecting it to her. Just leave the key in the door."

If they were leaving the place open, there was still a chance that she could look around. She just had to make sure they didn't see her on their way down. Vivian spun around, looking for somewhere to hide, when an arm wrapped around her waist, dragging her back from the stairs. She tried to scream, fumbling at her pocket for the gun, but a hand clapped over her mouth.

"It's me," a familiar voice hissed in her ear.

Vivian went limp with relief. As soon as she relaxed, the hand eased away from her mouth, and the arm at her waist shifted. Turning, she found Danny with one finger to his lips, tugging her away from the stairs.

George and Eddie were just behind her, and there was nowhere to hide. Danny backed her up against the wall, shielding her from view with his body and keeping his back toward the stairs. They looked like a young couple stealing a moment together. Between their bodies, Vivian eased the gun from her pocket as she peered around him.

Hattie Wilson's bruisers thumped down the stairs bare seconds later, arguing and chuckling together. They paused for a moment on the landing, and Vivian ducked back behind Danny's shoulder, barely breathing.

"Who's that?" George demanded.

Danny's hands gripped her elbows tightly, tense and ready for a fight.

There was the sound of someone spitting on the floor. "Trash," she heard Eddie say.

"No morals in this part of the city," George agreed.

A moment later their footsteps faded down the stairs.

Vivian and Danny stayed frozen in place until they heard the door slam downstairs. Drawing in identical breaths, they stepped apart.

"What the hell are you doing here?" Danny demanded.

"Me? What the hell are you doing here? And what were you thinking, grabbing me like that?" A thought occurred to her, and she gasped. "Did Honor tell you to follow me?"

"No, I decided to on my own when I looked out the window of my parents' restaurant and saw you wandering around by yourself," Danny said, yanking off his hat to run an agitated hand through his hair. "Don't you know better than that? Especially after you were . . ." He glanced at her face and changed whatever he had been about to say. "It isn't safe for a girl like you to be in this part of town alone at night."

"It's not night yet," Vivian argued.

"It almost is," he sighed. "What were you thinking?"

Vivian sighed too. "Come upstairs and I'll show you. It's probably something Honor will want to know about anyway. She likes to get dirt on people, right?" she added as she led him back toward the stairs. "Well, Hattie Wilson's taking over for her husband. Those two weren't supposed to be here until tomorrow, but if they were careless, there might be some real good dirt on her in that top room."

Danny frowned but didn't say anything as he followed. When they reached the top floor, Vivian took a deep breath and pushed open the door.

It wasn't fancy, but it was the sort of place someone used to a nicer home would still feel comfortable spending time. It was divided into a sitting room and bedroom, both furnished with plush fabrics and the bare minimum of furniture. In the sitting room was a table with two chairs; a separate washroom had a flush toilet and a basin for bathing. Vivian wondered whether any of the homes lower down in the building had such nice plumbing.

In the basin a charred pile of trash still smoldered, books and food and women's clothing.

"Viv," Danny called, and there was a tightness to his voice that made her neck prickle.

She found him in the sitting room, standing in front of the windows. There were long gray curtains hung at each one, stretching from the ceiling to puddle on the floor. But Danny had pulled one of those aside to expose the bars that cut across the window in unforgiving lines.

"Why do you suppose a room on the top floor would have those?" he asked. His shoulders were so tense she could see a muscle jumping at the side of his neck.

Vivian stared at the bars, then went from room to room, jerking the curtains aside. Each window was the same. She glanced around, realizing for the first time that there was no kitchen or old lamps, nowhere with flames or knives or gas.

Danny was in the middle of the sitting room; she went to join him, standing close enough that their shoulders could press against each other. Vivian needed the comfort, and Danny didn't pull away.

"Someone was worried about her killing herself," Vivian said. She didn't intend for the words to come out as a whisper, but she couldn't bring herself to speak at a normal volume.

She could feel Danny's surprise as he turned to look at her. "You know who was here?"

"Honor told you about Roy and Hattie Wilson's baby?" Vivian glanced at him, and he nodded. She let out a shaky breath. "Turns out it wasn't her. The little sister, Myrtle, was the one who got in trouble. Mrs. Wilson pretended she was pregnant and said Myrtle was at boarding school. She told me that Myrtle was actually staying with a relative on Long Island, but now I bet she was really here."

Danny turned, taking in the whole room. "Why would someone worry she would kill herself?"

"It was Wilson's kid," Vivian said bluntly. She thought back to her conversation with Pretty Jimmy, remembering Wilson's interest in Mags, who was barely old enough to be going around in society. She wondered if she was going to be sick. "Apparently he liked to force himself on schoolgirls."

"Jesus."

"Yeah." Something white on the floor near the front door caught Vivian's eye. Bending down, she discovered a pile of lumpy cigarettes, as if they had tumbled from someone's coat pocket or handbag. "Myrtle's a smoker," she said absently, remembering. "She and Hattie both hated Wilson for what he did."

"You don't think Roy killed him," Danny said.

Vivian shook her head. "Hattie couldn't have done it, she was at a party that night. If Myrtle had been on Long Island, she couldn't have either." She glanced around, shivering again. "But it doesn't look like she was on Long Island."

"You going to do anything about that?"

Vivian glanced at Danny, but his face was as expressionless as his voice. She remembered abruptly that he worked for Honor, that he wanted the Nightingale freed from the shadow cast by Wilson's murder as much as anyone. They had all been glad to have Roy Carlton guilty and gone and the whole mess put behind them.

"I don't know," she said. She was still kneeling on the floor, and she absently picked up a couple cigarettes and turned them over in her hand before slipping them into her coat pocket. "I don't think I blame her for it. But Honor should probably know."

She glanced at Danny again. His jaw was clenched, but after a moment he nodded.

"She should know." He smiled grimly. "Hux likes to know everything. Come on." He looked around the room, then reached out a hand to pull Vivian to her feet. "This place gives me the creeps. Let's shake a leg."

Vivian didn't disagree.

———

They heard the commotion while they were still inside, raised voices calling out in a babble of languages. Danny, looking suddenly worried, bounded down the last few steps and out the front door, barely glancing over his shoulder to make sure she was following.

On the sidewalk in front of the building, the old woman who had shown her in was struggling to support a man—himself white-haired but with far fewer wrinkles—while he bent over, gasping and clutching his chest. Unable to understand them, it took Vivian a moment to realize what was going on. But Danny was already there, easing the man from the old woman's grasp and asking a quick stream of questions. The man was having trouble standing; a look from Danny goaded Vivian into action. She got there just in time to help lower him to the ground while the old woman bombarded Danny with instructions.

The man was breathing wheezily, but his color was still good; Vivian held his head in her lap while he took deep, gasping breaths.

"Hey, mister, it's going to be okay," she said quietly, ignoring the hubbub around her as more neighbors appeared. She thought she heard someone talk about a doctor, someone else mention a daughter. Taking his hand gently, she gave it a little squeeze. "I'm sure someone's going to get you a doctor real quick—nothing to worry about at all, right?"

She didn't know if he could understand her, but his breathing was growing calmer. She kept up the flow of words while the people around her decided what to do. But she was unprepared when he opened his eyes at last. They widened, and he raised one shaking hand to her cheek.

"May?" he murmured. "Is that you?"

Vivian froze, staring at the man as another wheezing gasp shook his body and he dropped his hand once more. Before she could think of anything to say, several neighbors were swooping in, lifting the man and carrying him off in a clamor of instructions and suggestions.

"Wait!" Vivian called, stumbling to her feet.

"They're taking him to a doctor," Danny said, catching her arm. "Don't worry, I'm sure he'll be fine. Time to get you home."

"Did you know him?"

"Never seen him before in my life," Danny said, bending down to scoop up his hat from where it had fallen to the ground. As he straightened, he frowned at her. "You okay, Viv?"

"I thought he said . . ." Vivian trailed off, still staring after the man. Could she have misheard him?

"Come on." Danny took her arm. "It's getting late. You've got to get home, and I have to get to work."

Vivian, her thoughts racing with questions, let him lead her away.

THIRTY-THREE

D anny had to go back to his parents' restaurant, but first he walked her to the closest station for the elevated train on Ninth Street.

"Honor'd sack me or shoot me if she found out I let you wander around on your own today," he said dryly when she tried to insist she was fine on her own. He gave her a sideways look. "Have you seen her since . . . ?"

"No," Vivian said quickly, feeling her face and neck heat. She wasn't sure which direction his thoughts were headed, but either way, she didn't want to talk about it. As the train pulled away from the station, she could see Danny's concerned face still watching her from the platform.

When she got to her stop, though, she didn't immediately head home. Instead, her steps carried her past her front door, until she reached the riverfront. There were plenty of people around, workers heading to and from the piers or couples strolling together. But they were all too caught up in their own business to pay any attention to her, and Vivian reached the end of one of the piers without being stopped.

She waited until there was no one around before pulling the gun from her pocket. She would never have been able to fire it herself, and she didn't want Florence to have to again, either. After a moment of hesitation, she let it drop. It hit the water with a splash that startled two nearby seagulls into flight, but no one else seemed to notice.

Vivian turned her steps toward home.

———

Vivian found Florence awake and a pot of soup simmering on the stove.

"Mrs. Thomas dropped it off," Florence explained. She was wrapped in a heavy shawl and an old pair of men's pajamas that she'd had for the last five years, seated at the table with her own bowl of soup in front of her. "I think she's feeling guilty, though I'm not sure what for. I'll take it over all her nasty comments, though."

"She let him in last night," Vivian said, kicking off her shoes. In her head, she could hear every ugly thing Mrs. Thomas had ever said or not said about their mother. "She can feel guilty for as long as she likes, and it won't be too long."

Florence frowned into her bowl, then shrugged. "Well, she can't afford to keep feeding us, so she'll probably get over it soon enough."

"And be back to her normal comments about our mother?" Vivian dropped into the other chair and grabbed her sister's hand. "I met someone who knew her today."

"Vivi, *we* know her."

"Not Mrs. Thomas. I met someone who knew our mother."

Florence froze, a sudden hopeful look in her eyes, before she shook her head. "No, you didn't."

"I did, I'm sure of it." Vivian described the old man collapsing on Baxter Street. "He was hustled off to a doctor pretty quick. But he looked right at me and called me May. He called me *our mother's name*. Mrs. Thomas always says I look like her, aside from my hair. Maybe—"

"Be reasonable. What's the chance anyone in that part of the city knew an Irish girl who got kicked out by her family?"

"Then why would he call me that?" Vivian stood abruptly and paced around the room, too wound up to stay sitting. "If I can find him again, I can ask him. If he knew her, he might know where she came from." Vivian gripped the back of the chair so hard it made her hands ache. "We might find out we have family after all."

"I do have family," Florence said quietly. "I have you."

The comment was so unexpectedly sweet that it made Vivian's train of thought pull up short.

"And even if it's true, how could you possibly find him again?" Florence shook her head. "Why were you there anyway?"

Vivian slowly unclenched her hands from the chair back, not meeting her sister's eyes. "Had a quick errand to run."

Florence bit her lip, then nodded slowly. "Okay. Well, you should eat something first."

"First?"

"Before you go out." Florence looked up, pale but resolute—or maybe just resigned. She was being as understanding as she could, but her expression was still edged with worry. That wasn't going away. "I assume you need to talk to someone about whatever that errand was?"

Vivian pictured Myrtle, staring through the bars that covered her windows, smoking and plotting revenge. *Hux likes to know everything.* And she was beginning to understand why.

There was a lot of power in being the person who knew things—the person who could find the answers to other people's questions.

"For a little while, at least," she said. "I shouldn't be out too late."

If she found enough answers, maybe one day she could piece together who she really was.

But first, she'd start with who really killed Willard Wilson.

289

THIRTY-FOUR

New York was a city of streetlights now, puddles of gold breaking through the shadows, leaving the spaces in between even darker than they used to feel.

Heading out that night, after everything that had happened, was harder than she expected. Vivian hesitated at the door of her building, taking a deep breath as she stepped into the street. Music drifted out from somewhere, voices raised in shouts and arguments, laughter and song.

Maybe there were parts of the city that fell quiet at night, but there was never silence in the New York that Vivian belonged to, the world that came alive at night, where you didn't need to have a mansion on Fifth Avenue to be someone who mattered.

She only had to go a few blocks on foot before she was able to hail a cab, unconcerned for once about the cost. She was going home.

V ivian looked for Honor as soon as she was on the stairs. The whole place was laid out before her: sweaty couples dancing as if their lives depended on it, tables tucked in dark corners, music filling the air like magic. The trumpet was wailing like it could hold the roof up with sound, like it could sweep her onto the dance floor without even trying.

Silence had held the door open for her without waiting for the password. Vivian wasn't sure, but she thought there had been something like respect in his sullen eyes. Maybe he had heard about last night. Maybe there was gossip about her and Honor. Maybe he was finally used to her coming around.

Whatever the reason, when she paused at the top of the stairs, she knew she was where she belonged.

Bea was already working, and she caught Vivian's eye from where she was waiting by the bar for a tray of drinks. When Vivian finally made her way through the press of bodies, Bea was still waiting—the bar was packed that night.

"Everything okay?" Bea asked, her eyes warm with concern.

She was asking about so many things—about Florence, about the police, about whether Vivian was going to keep poking at things that were better left alone.

But Bea couldn't say all that, not in the middle of a crowd when she was supposed to be working. The table closest to the dance floor was hollering for drinks, a group of young men in sharp suits and girls in spangled dresses. Money was flowing at the Nightingale that night.

So was the champagne. Vivian smiled as a glass slid next to her elbow, and she turned just in time to catch a wink from Danny before he went back to the other customers.

Vivian took a sip, bubbles hitting the back of her throat. "It will be," she said, leaning her head next to Bea's so she could be heard over the noise. "I promise, I'm not going to do anything stupid."

"I'm never sure about that," Bea snorted, picking up her tray. "Honor's busy at the moment—I assume that's who you were looking for?" At Vivian's nod, she gestured toward a back corner with her chin. "Wait until she's done if you're looking to stir up trouble," she added over her shoulder as she went on with her work.

Honor was sitting with a woman in a gold dress, both of them with their heads bent close together. Vivian eyed the tableau in surprise, unable to decide what kind of meeting it might be, before turning away. What she had to say would wait until she could have Honor's full attention.

"You okay there, kitten?" Danny was back, watching her from across the bar.

Vivian downed the rest of her champagne. "Thanks for the bubbles. I'm in desperate need of a dance—who do you recommend?"

"You'd be doing us a favor if you got the tallest fella from Bea's table onto the dance floor—he looks like the sort to get rowdy if he's not distracted. Plus, his dancing feet ain't half bad. Or, if you're feeling adventurous, there's the pretty blonde at the other end of the bar."

The blonde was pretty, all right, with a wavy bob and lips painted the same deep red as her dress. Vivian glanced at her out of the corner of her eye, then turned toward the table of well-dressed boys. "I'll ask her for the next one," she said. "The tall one, you said?"

He was happy to jump up from his table and ask her for a dance as soon as she smiled at him, and he was more than able to keep up with the Charleston the band was playing. Vivian stayed on the dance floor—first him, then the blonde from the bar, then Mr. Lawrence surprised her by requesting a waltz. Vivian had a sudden memory of waltzing with him the night Wilson died, but she pushed it aside and accepted with a smile. She kept an eye on Honor the whole time, her feet moving through the rhythm of the dance almost without her.

Just as the waltz finished, the woman in gold stood and held out her hand. The two shook—a business meeting, Vivian decided. Honor held the woman's hand a moment after she would have pulled away, and even in the dim light Vivian could see that her expression was serious. But the woman shook her head, patted Honor's shoulder, and walked away.

Honor remained at the table as the waltz ended, chin in her hand as she gazed at nothing. Vivian thanked Mr. Lawrence and started to cross the dance floor toward her, but as she moved through the press of bodies the woman in gold crossed her path.

It was Sadie Monaldo, and the sight of her made Vivian pause, though she had to dodge out of the way of a dancing couple a moment later. She hadn't realized Sadie and Honor knew each other. Honor noticed everyone that came into her club, of course, but their talk in the corner had seemed personal. Frowning, Vivian changed course, following as Sadie left the dance hall. She had to dodge around several more couples on the way, and by the time she made it to the back hall, Sadie was already heading out the door to the alley.

Stepping outside made Vivian shiver. It felt the same as it had the night Willard Wilson died, the same staccato bursts of light, the same distant noises. She glanced at the corner where Wilson's body had been, though there was no trace now that anything had happened there. She wondered how many other corners of the city had seen death swept so casually away.

"You coming out?"

Sadie's voice cut through her thoughts, making Vivian realize that she was still standing in the doorway. As Bea had done—it wasn't that long ago, was it?—she snagged a brick with her foot and used it to prop the door open before walking to where the other woman leaned against an alley wall, a lit cigarette in one hand as she stared up, the light flickering across her gold spangles, watching the smoke drift slowly away.

"Hey there, Vivian Kelly," Sadie said, smiling grimly. There was no sign now of the shrinking wallflower from her first night at the Nightingale or the heavy-hearted daughter still mourning the loss of her family. "Come out for a smoke?"

She held out a cheap package of cigarettes. They were the same kind she had smoked in angry bursts that day at her kitchen table, the day Vivian had learned from Mrs. Henry that Sadie's father had killed himself shortly after her younger sister disappeared.

Vivian drew in a sharp breath. Her dress had a little pocket sewn into the slit of one seam; she reached in and slowly pulled out the two cigarettes she had brought to show Honor—lumpy, poorly rolled things, she realized now, that a society girl like Myrtle would never touch.

Beats me where she got to, but less work for us, Bruiser George had said.

Hattie Wilson hadn't been the one bringing a sister home from Chinatown.

"I think I already have a couple of yours," Vivian said.

Sadie took a drag from the one in her hand, several emotions flickering across her face in quick succession before she met Vivian's eyes. "Where'd you find those?"

"Someone dropped them in a pretty sad building on Baxter Street."

"Huh." Sadie turned to look up at the sky once more.

Vivian swallowed, her skin prickling all over. "Why'd your father kill himself, Sadie?"

Sadie blew out a stream of smoke. "He'd been skimming. Stupid thing to do, but he was desperate. Aren't we all?" She laughed bitterly. "Wilson probably would've just had him bumped off to send a quick message, but he remembered Dad had two daughters. Turned out Elsie, all of fifteen years old, was just his type. He took her. Dad couldn't handle the guilt."

"Is she okay?"

Sadie looked at her then, her expression fierce with pain before she shrugged it away. "She will be. I hope. If you went to Baxter Street, you saw where he was keeping her." She looked back at the sky. "You can guess what she went through. But she's got a lot of life to get past it. And he's not going to hurt her anymore."

Vivian shivered at the offhand words and the depth of feeling they hid. She glanced again at the corner where Wilson had bled out, a single cigarette burning a hole through his pants as he sat in a puddle of his own filth and blood. There had been cigarettes on the ground then, too, she remembered. As if two people had come outside to smoke and talk before things got out of control. "Did you mean to kill him?"

"I honestly don't know." Sadie shrugged. "I followed him to three different places that night before I finally got him alone here. I told myself I only wanted to find my sister. But maybe I was lying. It doesn't really matter. It's not something I'll ever regret." She glanced at Vivian. "What're you gonna do about it?"

"Does Honor know?" Vivian regretted the question as soon as it came out, and the pitying look in Sadie's eyes made her face heat, though she was pretty sure there wasn't enough light for her blush to be seen. She clenched her hands into fists, feeling sick and angry and confused. "Take care of your sister, Sadie. You're lucky to have her back."

"I am." Sadie took another drag of her cigarette. "Thanks for your help, by the way."

"My help?"

"Yeah." Sadie's smile was somehow both grateful and mocking. "I couldn't have found her without you."

Vivian's chest tightened. Kicking the brick out of the way, she let the door swing shut behind her as she stalked back into the hallway and headed for the dance hall.

She ignored the blond girl smiling at her once more from the bar and the tall man with dark hair who sidled up and tried to coax her onto the floor again. Instead, she went straight for the corner table where Honor was staring into a glass of whiskey.

She looked up when Vivian arrived, her pensive expression sliding into surprise. Then those beautiful red lips turned up slowly at the corners.

"Vivian." The relief in her voice was genuine. "I can't tell you how glad I am to see you. Your sister's okay?"

"Yes." Vivian slid into the seat opposite her and leaned forward. Fifteen feet away, the trumpet wailed, cocooning them in sound. For a moment, it was just the two of them—no one else would be able to hear a word they said. Vivian leaned in close, until there were only inches between them. She could see Honor's lips part, her brows rise in disbelief.

"Did you want something, pet?" she asked, her voice husky.

"I did," Vivian said. She hesitated, her bottom lip catching between her teeth, before she took a deep breath and asked, "How long have you and Sadie Monaldo known each other?"

Up on the bandstand, the cymbals crashed, and a long run on the piano sent the dancers spinning happily across the floor. But in front of her, Honor grew still. After a moment she shook her head, her lips pursing with grim amusement. "Would you like a drink?"

"No. But I would like an answer."

Honor nodded, her face unreadable. "I knew her when she was a girl and I was only a little older, though I can't say we've stayed close. She came to me after her sister was taken. She thought, in my business, I might have information that could help."

"And you knew," Vivian said, her hands clenching the edge of the table. The music hit a downbeat, and she waited for the trumpet to raise its brassy voice before she continued. "As soon as you saw that Wilson was dead, you knew she had done it."

"Yes."

There was nothing like apology or regret in Honor's expression—there was nothing at all, in fact. She watched Vivian's face, impassive, waiting. A wave of fury rose in Vivian's chest.

"Then why ask me to get involved?" she demanded. "If you wanted to help her cover it up, why risk me finding out what happened?"

"Because of your Mr. Green." Honor took another drink, her gaze drifting out to the dance floor. Vivian followed her gaze and saw that

Leo had arrived and was dancing with two baby vamps in bright lip-stick and brighter silk at the same time—though Vivian thought he might be keeping an eye on her also. "He appeared right after Wilson's death. As careful as he was with his questions, I could guess he was interested in what had happened. I hoped you'd find out which side of this he was on. And you did."

Vivian thought about that for a moment. It didn't take long to see. "Leo thought it was a secret, but Danny knew about the uncle."

"And Danny told me. He and I have a hell of a partnership, you know," Honor added, glancing proudly at the bar where Danny leaned on one elbow, chatting with a blushing girl while her friends looked on and giggled. "We're both risking our lives any time we walk out into the real world. But here, we watch each other's backs."

"And I'm guessing Danny told you that Leo seemed to take a shine to me? The morning after the raid?"

"He's a clever one, our Danny boy." Honor lifted her whiskey again and smiled over the edge of the glass. "If I liked men, I'd have snatched him up long ago. Yes, he told me. Mr. Green was so clearly smitten with you, I thought you'd be able to help me keep an eye on him."

"To protect Sadie."

"And the Nightingale. Yes."

"And what about protecting me?" Vivian's voice shook. She knew she should stop talking, that she was giving away too much, but she had to know. "You didn't mind putting me in danger? Taking the risk that I'd find out something important?"

"I didn't expect you to end up at Wilson's home," Honor said. "I didn't think you'd be in so much danger. You didn't know anything about Sadie. I thought, if you were just getting cozy with Mr. Green . . ." She closed her eyes briefly. "I hoped you'd keep him distracted until the trail went cold. But when you started suspecting Roy Carlton, I thought, this could work too. Maybe you'd convince him that someone else did it, and he'd convince his uncle."

It was time for the final trumpet solo, a long, intricate river of improvisation and inspiration. The dancers were swept up in it, moving faster and wilder every moment, and everyone in the dance hall cheered and clapped, egging the trumpet player on.

Vivian couldn't help it: even though it wasn't actually funny, she laughed, head dropping into her hands, then falling back as if looking at the ceiling for inspiration or answers or just someone to laugh along with her. "So you were using me, too."

When she lowered her gaze, Honor was watching her, one elbow propped up on the table and her cheek lying in the cradle of her fingers. "I never hid that I wanted something from you."

"You said you wanted me to find out something about Wilson."

"And did you trust me?"

"No." Vivian crossed her arms, chin tucked as she eyed Honor from beneath lowered brows. The band finished the song with a flourish, and while everyone was applauding loudly, she added, "But I did believe you."

Honor's smile was heavy with possibility and regret. "You shouldn't have done that, pet."

"No." Vivian looked away while the band leader raised his hands. The trumpet began alone, crooning a plaintive rhythm that made her shiver. "You put me in danger. I could have been . . . My sister killed someone because of you."

"I never would have asked if I'd known what would happen," Honor said. "And, if you'll forgive me a moment of real honesty . . ." She tilted her head, her voice growing soft. "I liked having the excuse to spend time with you."

Vivian took a deep breath. "Would you have chosen the Nightingale over me?" she asked, her voice cracking. She was afraid of the answer, but she had to know. "If it came down to it?"

"I don't know." Honor was as tense as Vivian had ever seen her. "Is this when you walk away from here forever?"

"Is that what you want?"

"It would keep you safe."

Vivian wished Honor would tell her to leave or beg her to stay. But in the end, it could only be her choice.

"I'll take that drink now."

Honor's eyes widened in surprise. But a moment later, the vulnerable expression was gone, her cool self-control firmly in place as she looked toward the bar. She must have caught someone's eye, because she raised two fingers and nodded.

The rest of the instruments were slowly joining the trumpet, the tempo of the music rising into something exciting and wild. Soon, it would drown out conversation again.

Honor turned back to Vivian, leaning forward. "You surprised me again, you know. I thought if you were distracting Mr. Green, Sadie and I would have time to find her sister. Sadie was following Wilson's boys around, hoping they'd lead her to where Elsie was being kept." For a moment, her expression smoldered with rage. "Apparently it took over a week before it occurred to them to tell their new boss about her." Honor took a breath, then let it out slowly and gave Vivian a small smile. "Because of you, we got there first. I never thought you'd be the one to learn where she was."

"Leo found it," Vivian said, though she had no idea why she felt the need to be so honest.

"But only for your sake," Honor pointed out, her husky-honey voice curling through the air between them. "So in spite of everything, I was glad that I'd asked you to keep going. I still am. Who knows what would have happened to Elsie otherwise."

The two women stared at each other, and Vivian had the feeling that they were caught out of time. Around them, the club was wild with laughter, light reflected from a hundred thousand spangles, the smell of smoke and booze and sweat making her feel light-headed. Someone arrived with their drinks, but Vivian didn't look away as an anonymous hand slid them onto the table in front of her and Honor nodded whoever it was away.

"Why not just tell me what you wanted?" Vivian picked up her glass and drank far too quickly. Clearing her throat, she met Honor's eyes. "Why feed me a line in the first place?"

"If I had explained why, would you have kept quiet? Or would you have turned her in?"

"Who's to say I plan to keep quiet now?" Vivian said, her voice dropping. "Leo's right over there. He'd believe me if I told him Roy wasn't the murderer. One word from me, and you and Sadie are both in jail before the end of the night. So what am I getting out of it for keeping my mouth shut?"

Honor's brows shot up. "We had a deal, Vivian. I already told you about your delightful boss's illegitimate daughter. You're a smart girl, I assume you can make good use of that."

"But now there's more to consider," Vivian pointed out. One hand was still wrapped around her glass; she clenched the other one in her lap to keep it from trembling. She had felt sick playing this game against Miss Ethel that morning. Playing it against Honor now was terrifying. "You gave me that information in exchange for my help. Now you're also asking me to keep a pretty big secret."

Honor crossed her arms. "Fair enough, pet. What's your price for staying quiet?"

"A job." Vivian put her elbows on the table, propped her chin on her laced fingers, and smiled as if she knew what she was doing. "Miss Ethel and I came to an agreement this morning. I'm going to have a little more free time, and I want a job here, at the Nightingale."

Honor looked surprised, but Vivian thought she was trying not to smile. "Doing what?"

"I'm not asking for anything special, I'd be happy as a waitress. I'd be good at it, too."

"I'm not saying you wouldn't be." Honor propped her own elbows on the table, considering. "But I've got all the staff I need right now."

"You'll need someone to replace Bea."

For the first time, Honor looked genuinely startled. "And where is Beatrice going?"

Vivian took a deep breath. "You're going to give her a job as a singer. Your band could really use one, and she'll be dynamite."

Vivian held her breath while Honor looked thoughtful. "I assume she can sing, or you wouldn't be suggesting it," the club owner said at last.

"She's got pipes like you wouldn't believe," Vivian said, watching the floor where Bea, on a break, was dancing a quickstep with Danny. "And you won't have to ask her twice."

Honor nodded slowly. "All right then. You've got yourself a deal, and you and Beatrice have new jobs." She leaned forward. "If you're sure you want to work for me."

Vivian stood, hoping her trembling hands wouldn't give her away. Honor was smiling, and Vivian wondered for a moment if she hadn't come out quite as far ahead as she had expected. But Honor was always smiling, she reminded herself. "We're square, then?"

"We're square," Honor agreed as she stood. Vivian was about to walk away when Honor caught her arm. She lowered her voice, though there was no chance anyone could overhear them. "Shall I tell you a secret? Since we're finally being honest with each other?"

Vivian nodded, barely breathing.

"I'm happy to hire Beatrice to sing, and I'll be even happier to have you working here. But that's just out of the goodness of my heart." Honor gently pulled Vivian toward her. "Because you know what Wilson was. And I know you don't blame Sadie or me at all for what we did."

"How do you know that?" Vivian said hoarsely.

"Because, pet," Honor whispered. "I know you."

She leaned forward, but before their lips touched, Vivian stepped back, her fingertips resting against Honor's collarbone to stop her from following.

"No," she said quietly.

They stared at each other, neither one moving. Vivian could feel her own heart pounding, feel Honor's heartbeat shivering through her fingertips.

After a moment, Honor nodded and stepped back. "Smart girl," she said, though her voice shook. "This world isn't a pretty place. Better for you if you stick to dancing. And work, since that's what you want." Her expression grew mocking as she added, "If you think you can handle seeing me that much."

Vivian could feel heat pooling at the bottom of her spine, but she said, as calmly as possible, "I can. Can you?"

For a moment, Vivian could see naked regret in Honor's eyes, regret and sorrow and longing. She felt as though she were seeing the real Honor for the first time. Not the suave businesswoman or the smiling flirt, but a woman who had taken a risk and discovered it cost more than she expected, more than she perhaps wanted to lose.

Honor shook her head. "I don't know, pet. You get under my skin."

"Well, that makes two of us," Vivian said honestly. "Guess we'll just have to figure out how to make it work."

"We'll see what happens, won't we?" Honor raised one hand halfway, as if she wanted to reach for Vivian one more time, but drew her fingers back and shook her head, smiling. "I'll see you soon, Vivian."

Vivian watched her wind through the crowd by the bar, parting the people around her through sheer, smooth confidence. Only when Honor had disappeared from the hall did Vivian turn back to the dance floor.

Leo was waiting there, saying a cheerful good-bye to the baby vamps, who had apparently cajoled him into a second dance after their wild Charleston. Whether he had seen her good-bye to Honor or not, he clearly knew Vivian was there, because he turned just as she approached.

"Hey there, Vivian Kelly," he said, sticking his hands in his pockets as he eyed her warily. "Looking for me?"

"I guess so," she said, feeling light-headed with confusion. Something had ended there with Honor. And something else, perhaps, had started. "I've been doing some thinking."

"Oh?" His voice was carefully neutral.

"Thank you for helping my sister," Vivian said, then took a deep breath. "And . . . I'm sorry for a lot of the things I said last night. I wanted to tell you that I understand. Why you didn't tell me the whole truth, I mean. I get it." She was talking too much, and she closed her mouth abruptly, frowning in embarrassment.

"Is that you saying you forgive me? Or that you still need more time before you're ready to see me again? Or . . ." He hesitated. "Or that you get it, but you still want me out of your life?"

"I think the first one."

"Oh." He stared at her, his look of surprise melting into one of delight. "Oh, Viv, that's—" He pulled her close, and for a moment he looked as though he wanted to kiss her. But he just stared at her seriously before saying, "I have to ask. Where exactly do things stand with you and your Ms. Huxley?"

Vivian blushed. "I don't know," she said, looking down.

Leo slid a finger under her chin and lifted it until she met his eyes again. "And where do things stand with us?"

"I don't know that either."

He nodded slowly. His arms dropped even more slowly, but he didn't step back, and Vivian could still feel the heat of his body, could still smell the spicy scent of his cologne. "Well. Let's keep things simple, then." He smiled and took her hand. "Kick up your heels with me?"

"Leo . . ." Vivian planted her feet as he started to turn toward the dance floor. "I need to ask you something."

He frowned at her serious tone. "What happened? Is your sister okay?"

"She's fine. We're both fine. But . . ." She took a deep breath. "What would you say if I told you that Roy Carlton didn't kill Wilson?"

She could see his shoulders tense. "Do you know who did?"

Vivian hesitated. "I found out something about Hattie Wilson. I was fitting a dress for her today, and she's not actually pregnant. I don't think she ever was. So . . . I don't think Roy had a reason to kill Wilson." She bit her lip, watching Leo anxiously.

"Is there more you're not telling me?"

Vivian swallowed and made herself meet his eyes. Somehow, this was harder than facing down Honor—maybe because with Honor they were finally being honest with each other. And she was starting to suspect that Leo, in spite of everything, was a pretty straightforward fellow. She pulled away from him gently. "Yes."

He blew out a breath, running a hand through his hair. "Your sister shot Roy Carlton in your defense. He was going to hurt you, Vivian, maybe even kill you. Nothing can change that." He took her hand again and, feeling it shake, rubbed it between his own. "Officially, he was never accused of Wilson's murder, because officially Wilson wasn't murdered. He died of a heart ailment. And officially, I'm not the police, so I don't much care who killed a rat like him. If they're satisfied to wrap up the case as it stands, I don't have to tell them anything else."

"Do you know something, Leo?" Vivian asked, eyes narrowing.

"I could probably put together a few pieces, since you're telling me there's more to it. Do you want me to?" When Vivian shook her head, he took a deep breath and nodded. "All right then. I trust you. If you're telling me to leave it alone, I will."

"I'm not sure you should trust me."

He grinned. "That makes us even, because I'm not sure you should trust me either."

"Have you ever killed someone?" she asked, expecting him to say no, as he had before. Or at least hoping.

He raised a brow. "Your sister killed someone. Does that make her a monster?"

She swallowed. "That's a yes, then."

He shook his head. "Look around," he said, his gesture taking in the whole club. "None of us would be here if we were upstanding citizens. You don't have to trust me, but you can believe me when I say that I would never intentionally do anything to hurt you. And—"

"And what?"

"And I really love this song." He smiled. "Dance with me, Viv?"

Vivian took a deep breath and closed her eyes. She loved the song that was just beginning. She would love it even more when Bea was up on stage singing. She thought of Florence, safe at home. She thought of the man on Baxter Street, the answers she still wanted to find.

She thought about freedom.

The trumpet wailed, and she smiled.

"Yes," she said, opening her eyes. "Let's dance."

ACKNOWLEDGMENTS

I owe a debt of gratitude to the many people who helped take this story from an idea in my head to the book in your hands.

Nettie Finn is in all ways a dream editor to work with, and I feel so grateful that she saw the potential in this book. I am thankful for her enthusiasm and insight every day (and for her flexibility when I told her I needed to take maternity leave in the middle of revisions).

The team at St. Martin's Press, from copyeditors to publicity experts, worked so hard to polish and promote this book. I can't thank them enough for helping me share Vivian and her world with you.

When I told my agent, Whitney Ross, that I had a Jazz Age story in mind, she immediately told me to go for it. Her encouragement (and much-needed edits) kept me writing when I worried that I needed to scrap the whole thing and start over.

Shannon Mound and Zan Gillies generously read early drafts. Their sharp eyes saw plenty of flaws that I had missed, and their ideas helped me find exactly the right way to fix them.

I am incredibly grateful to my sensitivity readers. Yas McClinton and Dani Moran shared their time and insight with me early on, helping many of the characters come to life with honesty and accuracy. And

D. Ann Williams's words about the final draft were something every writer dreams of hearing.

It would be much harder to get a book written without my husband, Brian. Whether he needs to rearrange his entire work schedule so I can make a deadline or convince me to go to sleep and leave the scene to be fixed tomorrow, he does so with love and humor that I will never take for granted.

My endless gratitude goes to the people who have spent countless hours loving and teaching my children while I worked on this book, especially Mary Ann, Reagan, Maribel, Shauna, Courtney, Lupita, Marilyn, and Makisha.

Neena helped me with on-the-ground research before there was even a book to read. Gemma and Bryan are willing to let me borrow their home office at the drop of a hat, even during the witching hour. Mike gives me a beach house to write in every summer, while Kelsey, Josh, Ross, Becky, Ben, Diana, Beau, and Jen are the kind of supportive friends every writer—and every person—should have in their life. I am thankful for all of them.

And you—if you are reading this, I am beyond thankful for you.

AUTHOR'S NOTE

The Nightingale and the people in it are thoroughly my own invention, but they are based on real places and experiences of New Yorkers in the 1920s.

The Jazz Age—particularly in New York City—looms large in the American imagination as a wild free-for-all with short skirts, lots of gin, and no rules. Prohibition lasted from 1920 to 1933. In theory, it ended the nationwide production, import, transport, and sale of alcoholic beverages. The reality was much more complex. Drugstores, for example, could sell alcohol for "medical reasons"; fans of F. Scott Fitzgerald may remember characters in his books who are in the drugstore business. Any alcohol that was already in private ownership could be legally finished at home, so wealthy families stocked up on "provisions" before Prohibition officially began. Vineyards sold bricks of dehydrated grape juice with explicit instructions about how *not* to turn those grapes into wine.

And there were the speakeasies.

Speakeasies came in many varieties. Some were upscale restaurants that attracted the wealthy and famous. (Lois Long, a wildly popular Jazz Age writer for *The New Yorker,* would stay out all night dancing and drinking at the most upscale places in town, then write about her adventures in a weekly column.) Other speakeasies were back-alley rooms where the poor could pay pennies for a glass of moonshine that might end up killing them.

In between were the speakeasies that weren't too different from today's bars and clubs: places with jazz music, dancing, and drinking. The big difference from today, of course, was that they were illegal.

Luckily for everyone at them, politicians and police were as likely to be involved in bootlegging as anyone else. Many of them made small fortunes from importing and selling; others made a living from the bribes that speakeasy owners and bootleggers paid to stay open and do business. To learn about the (sometimes unbelievable) dynamics of power and business in Prohibition-era New York, I recommend *Last Call: The Rise and Fall of Prohibition* by Daniel Okrent and *Gangsters & Gold Diggers: Old New York, the Jazz Age, and the Birth of Broadway* by Jerome Charyn.

A dance hall like the Nightingale would have fallen in that middle category of speakeasies. And that was a place where a lot of the lines that divided daily life were blurred.

New York in the 1920s was highly segregated, with immigrant groups staking out specific corners of the city and Black families separate from those considered white. (This did not, at the time, always include Irish or Jewish immigrants, especially those who were more recently arrived in the country.) Then as now, the city was also segregated along lines of wealth and class. Eric Homberger's *The Historical Atlas of New York City* is a fantastic reference for following the shifts of these neighborhoods over the decades, as well as seeing a snapshot of daily life in different parts of the city. (And yes, there was indeed a neighborhood where Vivian and Bea could have lived on adjacent blocks.)

High-end speakeasies and jazz clubs, catering mainly to the upper class, often had Black staff and performers but only white customers. Many dance halls, though, saw a variety of faces on their floors.

That didn't mean those distinctions were forgotten, especially once patrons returned to their daytime jobs and lives. But when everyone was already taking part in something illegal and forbidden, crossing lines of race and class became one more exciting, naughty thing to add to the list. "Black and tans" were nightclubs and dance halls, usually in the Black neighborhoods of cities like Chicago, Detroit, and New York City, that were famously integrated. One Black journalist, writing for the *Amsterdam News,* noted that "the night clubs have done more to improve race relations in ten years than the churches, both black and white, have done in ten decades." Newspapers warned middle- and upper-class white parents that daughters who went to jazz clubs would be out dancing with Chinese, Jewish, and Black men—a far bigger shock than the illegal drinking that went on in such places.

There was also a thriving queer subculture in the Jazz Age. Places like the Renaissance Casino in Harlem were famous for "masquerade and civil balls"—drag balls that attracted thousands of attendees across racial and social lines who were gay, lesbian, transgender, straight, bisexual, and more (though not all these labels existed at the time). Gay men and lesbians established enclaves in neighborhoods like Harlem and Greenwich Village. Illustrations from the time show that it was not uncommon for transgender men and women to find a spot on the dance floor, and songs like "Masculine Women, Feminine Men!" and "Let's All Be Fairies" could be heard on the radio. Blues music, in particular, often reflected a fluid attitude toward sexuality in the 1920s and 1930s.

This doesn't mean that it was safe to be openly queer in public. Lesbian, gay, or transgender folks were more likely to be attacked, arrested, rejected by their families, or otherwise persecuted, especially if they were non-white. Queer women, or women who were considered "wayward" or promiscuous, could be locked away in reformatories, especially if they were poor or didn't have families to protect them. But as cultural expectations and gender roles shifted, those changes spilled over into sexual roles as well.

One of the most well-known cultural changes was the role of women. The flapper, with her bobbed hair and short skirts, is probably the most iconic image of the 1920s.

As young women moved into cities, they entered into the liberation of the Jazz Age: drinking, dancing, dating, and working to support themselves. This was, of course, easier for some women than others. Poor women were, and always had been, responsible for helping to support multiple generations of their families, and many of the jobs available to single women only paid enough to cover the bare necessities of living in the city. Women in immigrant communities were often expected to stay with and work for their families, rather than strike out independently.

But many women did find the freedom to live and work on their own. (Most of them still referred to themselves as Miss, though Honor's preferred title of Ms. certainly existed then, rather than being an invention of the 1970s.) Unsurprisingly, these women also joined in the sexual liberation of the 1920s. Courtship was no longer a process overseen by parents; it happened in movie theaters, amusement parks, dance halls, and the back seats of cars. Clothing became less restrictive, costume jewelry became affordable, and makeup became something that even respectable women could wear from time to time. Dating, which was not exclusive the way we often think of it today, became a social necessity for many young women, as men earned more and were able to afford things like eating out and nights at the movie theater. And everything from movies to advertisements for dish detergent traded on sex and sexual liberation.

It's worth noting, though, that this revolution was still supposed to end with a respectable marriage, hopefully one that also came with economic benefits. Wife and mother were still the ideals women were expected to aspire to, once they were done being liberated. I highly recommend *Flapper* by Joshua Zeitz to learn more about the women of the 1920s and the often contradictory roles they were expected to perform.

The Nightingale might be my own invention, but the cultural changes that made places like it possible were real. Would a single speakeasy have accepted people who were rich, poor, Black, Chinese, white, queer, straight, Jewish, and more? It's not impossible. And I like the idea that so many people, looked down on by a society that still loved its hierarchies and rules, could create a place where they could take care of each other.